SING A BLACK GIRL'S SONG

ALSO BY NTOZAKE SHANGE

Plays

for colored girls who have considered suicide/
when the rainbow is enuf
Daddy Says
Spell #7
From Okra to Greens/A Different Kinda Love Story
A Photograph: Lovers-in-Motion (1981)

Novels

Sassafrass, Cypress & Indigo
Betsey Brown
Liliane: Resurrection of the Daughter
Some Sing, Some Cry

Poetry collections

Nappy Edges
Ridin' the Moon in Texas
A Daughter's Geography
Some Men
Wild Beauty: New and Selected Poems

SING A BLACK GIRL'S SONG

THE UNPUBLISHED WORK OF

NTOZAKE SHANGE

EDITED BY IMANI PERRY

W&N
WEIDENFELD & NICOLSON

First published in the United States in 2023 by Legacy Lit
First published in Great Britain in 2025 by Weidenfeld & Nicolson,
an imprint of The Orion Publishing Group Ltd
Carmelite House, 50 Victoria Embankment
London EC4Y 0DZ

An Hachette UK Company

The authorised representative in the EEA is Hachette Ireland,
8 Castlecourt Centre, Dublin 15, D15 XTP3, Ireland
(email: info@hbgi.ie)

1 3 5 7 9 10 8 6 4 2

Versions of "The Dark Room" and "Ellie, Who Is My Mother" have been published in other volumes of the author's work. However, the content in this book is substantially different than previous published versions and has never before been published in this form.

Photographs on pages 1, 21, 81, 95, 105, 343 are courtesy of the Ntozake Shange Revocable Trust Collection of the Barnard College Library and Special Collections. The photograph on page 425 is by Adger Cowans.

A CIP catalogue record for this book is available from the British Library.

ISBN (Mass Market Paperback) 978 1 3996 2580 7
ISBN (Ebook) 978 1 3996 2581 4
ISBN (Audio) 978 1 3996 2582 1

Typeset by Born Group
Printed and bound in Great Britain by Clays Ltd, Elcograf S.p.A.

FSC www.fsc.org
MIX
Paper | Supporting responsible forestry
FSC® C104740

www.weidenfeldandnicolson.co.uk
www.orionbooks.co.uk

For Savannah and Harriet

"I am gonna write poems til i die and when i have gotten outta this body i am gonna hang round in the wind and knock over everybody who got their feet on the ground."

—Ntozake Shange

CONTENTS

FOREWORD

I knew Ntozake Shange before I knew her. As I wrote in my memoir, *Unbound*, I grew up listening to my mother's record of the Broadway production of *for colored girls who have considered suicide/when the rainbow is enuf.* My mother listened to it so much when I was growing up that I had memorized a good deal of the play by the time I was twelve years old. Shange's words gave me language for my own experiences with trauma and with love. My mother was a reader and our home was a Black women's literary paradise, but Shange held a particularly special place in my home and heart.

I was thrilled to finally meet Ntozake Shange when I directed the annual Celebration of Black Writing that was held at the Art Sanctuary in Philadelphia in 2013. Zake didn't put on airs. She was warm and funny. Best of all, she was real. I learned from her that your best writing comes from being authentic, honest, and brave. We laughed for hours and every time I saw her after that, whether on the page, at ceremonies, or in my very own mirror, I felt fully embraced. I was devastated when she passed, but I keep returning to her words and her legacy. We still need her.

This collection is a treasure. I can't believe we have the gift of more work from Zake, even though she left us with so much. These poems, reflections, plays, and stories flesh out more of her art and her life and tackle issues we still deal with today—sexual violence, misogyny, racism, exploitation, and cruelty. And the solutions she provided:

justice, love, community, and sisterhood, which are still available to us as these pages encourage. I hope *Sing a Black Girl's Song* leads to a much-needed Shange revival across the country and world. May we be encouraged and resolved in her memory and honor.

—Tarana Burke

INTRODUCTION

In the spring of 2022, I traveled to New York with my two of my friends, Tarana Burke and Yaba Blay, and Tarana's adult child, Kaia Burke, to see Ntozake Shange's classic play, *for colored girls who have considered suicide/when the rainbow is enuf*, on Broadway, directed by Camille Brown. For our generation and that of our mothers, *for colored girls* is what could be called an urtext, an anchoring work of art that captures twentieth-century Black women's lives. Filing into the theater, we each privately recalled the other times we had seen *for colored girls*, or performed it ourselves. We quietly anticipated Shange's potent passages, repeated them along with the actors, lines like "I found god in myself and I loved her fiercely" and "somebody almost walked off wid alla my stuff..." We cried and laughed and chatted happily afterward, as we had before. The show was a palimpsest, reaching back to 1976, and reaching forward in time to the vexing yet beautiful web of Black women's lives.

Ntozake Shange is singular. Tender, tough, and so very brilliant, Shange ruptured and re-created literary forms, using innovative spelling and grammar to capture the sound and sensibility of Black women's speechways. She insisted on the lushness of Black women's interior lives while never shying away from the brutality of the world in relation to them. A consummate artist, she brought her powerful verse to life with music and dance and innovated the choreopoem as a theatrical form. Transforming the conventions of the Greek chorus,

Shange's plays spoke to collective Black female experience. She offered ample space for individual testimony within community.

Shange was prolific. Shange was the second Black woman to have a play on Broadway (1976), only after Lorraine Hansberry's 1959 play, *A Raisin in the Sun*. Most of her work remains in print today, including *for colored girls*, novels such as *Sassafrass, Cypress & Indigo* and *Betsey Brown*, numerous books of poetry, and children's books. *Sing a Black Girl's Song* now arrives as a distinct addition to Shange's impressive canon. This curated collection of Shange's previously unpublished writing spans roughly forty years. It includes poems from her early years as well as from the last two decades of her life. There are also several plays, including her 2003 *Lavender Lizards & Lilac Landmines: Layla's Dream*, which was produced while she was a scholar in residence at the University of Florida. Shange's personal story also emerges in these pages through several never-before-seen essays about her childhood, her experiences in therapy, and her life as an artist and activist.

Shange was born in 1948 in Trenton, New Jersey, as Paulette Linda Williams to surgeon Paul T. Williams and educator and social worker Eloise Williams. *Sing a Black Girl's Song* opens with Shange's tender recollections of her mother and their social milieu—a sophisticated and erudite Black world, filled with art and aspiration. When she was eight years old, the family moved to St. Louis, Missouri.

When Shange was thirteen years old, her family returned to New Jersey, and she later graduated from Trenton High School. The earliest piece in this collection is a poem published in 1966 while she was a high school student. Even at that young age, she already had a pervasive literary voice. Shange matriculated at Barnard College of Columbia University, where her papers are now collected. During her college years, she briefly married and, after the marriage was dissolved, struggled with depression. The poems in this volume, written in the early 1970s, reveal a woman who was undergoing a transformation, wading through grief toward self-creation. In some writings, she still refers to herself as Paulette Williams, in others she has adopted Ntozake Shange—and often Zake, tosake, tozake, or tz for short—the first name meaning "she who comes with her own things" in Zulu and the surname meaning "walks like a lion."

She graduated from Barnard in 1970. In the midst of the Black Arts Movement into which she came of age, Shange composed poems consistent with the political urgency of that moment, but far more intimate than what many of her peers produced at the time. In the late 1960s and early 1970s, Black Arts Movement artists approached their work with an explicit political Black nationalist sensibility, frequently creating pieces that focused on collective Black liberation rather than the interior individual experience. Their emphasis was on "we" rather than "I." Shange shared much of that sensibility, but she blended critiques of racism, imperialism, slavery, Jim Crow, and economic exploitation with particular attention to emotion and feeling. Love, heartbreak, injustice, desire, self-discovery, devastation, and political awakening all pulse across the pages. Shange also immersed herself in the Nuyorican Poets scene, an early 1970s community of Puerto Rican and other Latine artists. The impact of that experience is evident in her interest in Afro-Latine history and culture and her frequent use of Spanish words and phrases in her work.

Shange earned a master's degree in American Studies from UCLA in 1973. Her academic rigor is apparent in the writing. Diligent attention to historical detail, a passionate interest in the Black diaspora, and keen awareness of literary form reveal how much she was an intellectual artist in addition to one who could be profane, deeply spiritual, and joyfully vulgar. Her consistent celebration of vernacular Black culture as the root of great art instructed everyone in her midst to choose beauty over bullshit and substance over status. She understood herself as someone who was breaking English since it had been used to break Black people, and remaking it as an act of love to all oppressed people. Most of all, these writings reveal Shange as someone who was always writing herself to freedom. Readers will also encounter her extensive knowledge of jazz and dance, and the joy she took in being in community with musicians and dancers, as well as fellow writers. Shange lived fully, a renaissance woman par excellence.

From 1976, when *for colored girls* was first staged, to her death in 2018, Shange was a much celebrated and awarded writer. She raised her daughter, Savannah Shange, now a professor of anthropology and critical ethnic studies, and remained politically and intellectually engaged, writing creatively as well as critically, and participating in theatrical productions of her work in various cities. Shange was a mainstay in artistic communities, treating young artists with warmth and encouragement. I witnessed this firsthand when Shange attended the annual Celebration of Black Writing at the Art Sanctuary in Philadelphia. Shange, though an elder who inspired awe, disarmed everyone with her friendliness. The archive shows this as well. She read the work of many other writers, including those much younger than she was, and she commented thoughtfully on it. Unsurprisingly, she has had a major influence on younger generations of writers. As playwright and inaugural resident of the Ntozake Shange Social Justice Theater Residency at Barnard Erika Dickerson-Despenza wrote, Shange is a "literary mother" with a legacy that must be preserved.

Sing a Black Girl's Song is a testimony to Ntozake Shange's journey. That there is so much of her unpublished work that is of superior quality is stunning. That much of it is autobiographical is breathtaking. She left behind the framework for gorgeous biography. And her self-reflection is, generally speaking, a model for how to do the work of living well. For the many readers who love her writing, it is unquestionably a bounty. It is worth noting, however, that this volume, though extensive, does not include every unpublished work. Rather, it is curated to give a substantive overview of Shange's unpublished work. Where possible, the years in which individual pieces were written are included. Where the exact date isn't available, context clues were used to place it so that readers can read through the book in both a thematic and chronological sequence. Because Shange often wrote by hand I have redacted sentences that include words that were illegible, noted with brackets, as well as incomplete type, noted with ellipses there. Spelling errors and typos were corrected where there was a danger that a reader might mistake the meaning if the error was left intact, but I have maintained many of the small mistakes that allow the reader to experience the rush of ideas and excitement Shange felt as she put words to page, and to acknowledge that many of these were works in progress. I have included footnotes where she mentioned people and contexts that might not be readily understood by contemporary readers, and where knowing whom she spoke of is important to gather meaning. Likewise, I have provided translations for words and phrases in Spanish, and with the specific dialects (Puerto Rican, Cuban, or Mexican) referenced in mind. Shange's Spanish was both vernacular and precise in terms of historical reference.

Before each section, I have written brief introductory notes for historical or social context that illuminate specific entry points to the work. Readers should be prepared that difficult themes and offensive language appear in some of the pieces. The decision to include this material was driven by Shange's courageous effort to reveal the anguish as well as the beauty of Black women's lives. She didn't shy away from the underside, as it were, and to honor her it seemed essential to approach this work with a similar ethos.

By and large, I step back so that Shange might tell her story. In some ways, this collection has the shape of a self-authored bildungsroman. I approached this project as a posthumous editor, simply giving shape to what can be described as a eulogy of her *ownself*, taking us along with her from cradle to grave.

On October 27, 2018, a tweet came from the Ntozake Shange Twitter account. It read "To our extended family and friends, it is with sorrow that we inform you that our loved one, Ntozake Shange, passed away peacefully in her sleep in the early morning of October 27, 2018. Memorial Information / details will follow at a later date. The family of Ntozake Shange." The message sent shock waves through generations who had found sustenance in her art. Immediately a chorus of Shange quotations went up across social media, reminding us that her words live even as her body has departed. Memorials were held in New York and Washington, DC. Articles praised her influence. People of all stripes remembered their encounters with her and her brilliance. But the most mournful and celebratory elegies came from Black women. As playwright Lynn Nottage put it, "Our warrior poet/dramatist has passed away." She died fighting for us. But through her words, she lives. She lives in the actors who don the colors of the rainbow to embody her characters nearly fifty years after they were written, with themes that are no less powerful today than they were then. She lives every time we laugh, reading about how the precocious girl-child Indigo wants a fine china tea party for her fifteen dolls who have begun to menstruate. She lives every time someone cooks her mouthwatering recipe for "Zaki's Feijoada Brazilian Hominy" or "Chicken Fried Steak" for a loved one. Shange famously wrote, in *for colored girls*, "Somebody, anybody, sing a black girls song." Sitting with my friends Tarana and Yaba, watching that classic work brought to the stage again so beautifully, something became abundantly clear: Shange's words resonate as much today as they did a half century ago. Witness here how she answers her own supplication, for herself and for Black girls everywhere. Sing, Zake, sing.

—Imani Perry

EDITOR'S NOTE

The poems, essays, prose, and plays in this book are published in their original form. Except where a change was necessary to avoid errors that altered meaning in the work, Shange's original handwritten notes and the misspellings are how they appear in her archives. The editor aimed to maintain the integrity and urgency of Shange's writing style, and to publish her work as she left it. Footnotes have been added throughout for clarity.

EARLY LIFE

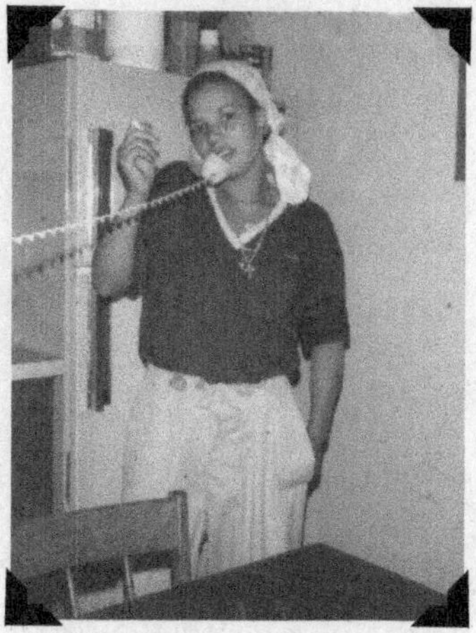

This section includes essays and vignettes in which Shange reflects on her coming-of-age. The pieces are emotional and introspective. They also provide important context for her formation as an artist. These pieces are untitled, with the exception of the first two, both titled "Ellie, Who Is My Mother." The final piece in this section is one of Shange's first published pieces from Trenton High School's literary journal, *The Phoenix*, and demonstrates Shange's extraordinary early talent.

Ellie, Who Is My Mother

> "In the fullness of time, we shall know
> why we are tried and why our love brings us tears
> as well as happiness"
>
> THE TORAH
>
> * *(Her favorite quotation from childhood)* *

There is a memory of the wish-swishing of skirts, the smells of powders and coffee, my father's cologne seeps from her skin and the pillow I nestle my head, my whole body curved again as in the beginning. I am the only one. This is my mother, Eloise, who married Paul who was my father and that's how she became my mother.

Mirrors, small delicate bottles. Dresses with pearls and lace from Paris I knew this. I saw it on the globe that lit up at night like the neon signs across the way, letting me know we were colored in the colored part of town. Yet, the movies and photographs were black and white. Not fitting all the different shapes and odors of folks who came to see my mother. Laughter from the kitchen. Laughter up the stairs Aunt Emma was here, Uncle Jimmy was here with Aunt Margaret. So, were my Grandmothers. My mother had a special greeting for each one, as if there were something in her soul that let her know what touch or hug a body needed. My Grandmother hovered like Billie Burke. I couldn't distinguish my mother from Jean Seberg, Marilyn Monroe, Kim Novak, or Dorothy Dandridge. I remember her eyes glowed as mine widened when Carmen de Lavallade[1] danced.

The lindy hop was not the only vernacular activity my mother mastered. There were collard greens and smothered porkchops.

---

1 Movie stars of the 1950s. Dorothy Dandridge and Carmen de Lavallade, also a distinguished dancer, were African American.

There were the nights when sleep came dragging its heels and my mother had a rhythmic pat that was so soft, yet steady that sleep gave up staying away from me. Let my mother calm my soul so that when my dreams came, I dreamt in color.

I liked to hide in the back of my mother's closet with her dresses and smells. Now I realize many many other little girls did the same. Even my own daughter waltzed about in my robe, wrapping my scent about her like some kind of magic.

Ellie, Who Is My Mother II

Once we all wore the same color blue dresses, my sisters, my mother and I. We were one for a long time. I could not tell long after I should have known better that I was not my mother. I wanted to be my mother. I liked her. I liked that way people liked her. I liked my father. But, I could not be him. I could be her. I could deep-sea fish, play baccarat, sing like Marian Anderson, defend the race. We were a vulnerable people. I could tell from the stories my mother told with her friends when they played inscrutable games of cards for hours. Bridge. What did I know then about mother, this bridge called my back. What do I know now about my mother?

I live with the myth of her, my indisputable legend of her. Executing intricate steps of the cha-cha-cha- in La Habana, dressing us all for The March on Washington, surviving disastrous lover after lover that I chose for myself, since I was not my mother. Since I was not mother, I am still learning to mother myself which Alta and Adrienne told me years ago. But, I couldn't give up the black and white films of Ellie, who is my mother to another time, or other places. I see horizons sometimes and think of what she saw for me. I am guilty of spending days under huge oaks imagining myself as my mother when I became a mother, yet I am not. I really know I am not my mother, but if I were to ever lose my myth of this woman of independent thought and chutzpah during the fifties, who actually demonstrated the meaning of 'each one teach one', I would be less a woman than I am, less a mother than I am becoming. I respect Ellie. Then, sometimes I feel sadly for her because as colorful and colored as we were, our world was defined in black and white. Our world was featured in Ebony, Jet, Sepia. Now when I look at us, Ellie and then, me and my daughter, something is awry. I become uncollected. I never saw my mother, 'uncollected'. She was not one to accept or expect to survive on Blanche's risky kindness of strangers, nor was she 'invisible'. But, I'm saving all my images, all the touch recollections I can sustain because the depth of Ellie's presence in me is ante-deluvian, fierce, and infinite. So unlike what she appears to be, all of which she gave to me.

Ntozake Shange
18 September 1997

The Silk Road

I could say, imagine. I am the ultimate conclusion of the allure of silk, the shimmer and breeze of silks, After all my skin is silken. My grandmother's hands sheer as silk. My mother's cherry-blond hair hard to picture without the capricious play of light, changing her thick mane of a coif moment to moment from golden to cerise, ash blond to emboldened chestnut. These are but a few of the qualities of silk that are my blood, my blood memory, my dreams. Yet without the extraordinary vision of Ferdinand and Isabelle, Cristobal Colon would not have been charged with the mission to find an alternate route to India, thence, China, where silk was born. Colon, Columbus, the adventurer would not have set foot on Santo Domingo in search of the riches of silks and gold, then synonymous in the Old World, never suspecting sugar, tobacco, rice, and cotton would be as gold to silk; that Africans, wrapped in a tight ivory cocoon of bondage, we call slavery, would inhabit these 'Indies', indigo damask demographic, fertile, furtive, hybrid, glistening as silk does when the moon changes phases, as we do under a tropical sun. Silken and foreign to these shores and to the thought, these are the origins of my genealogical essence, my blood trail in the New World, another Silk Road.

Though my earliest recollections of all that is silk, all that swish, soft fondling fabric conveys is perfumed and gliding my eyebrows in the depths of my mother, Ellie's closet. What shrouded my young head, braids and all was the miracle of the night, of conga drums, claves, and castenets, formal dinners, chandeliers of translucent swirls of lights dancing above the heads of very important guests whose crepe, velvet, chiffon, and silk, I'd bask in under the dining table. So like an ocean of unexpected sensation were the skirt hems tickling my shoulders, sometimes I'd forget to gaze at the ankles in silk stockings that left ordinary brown and bronze calves the magic of rose quartz, moonstones, tourmaline, sculpture as secret as the next brush stroke of Sonia Delauney or Raoul Dufy turning silk painting to a landscape abstractly worn by Parisian women adept at becoming art that could walk. While we in the New World far from St. Germain de Pres or Tours, ignorant of the smell and thick layers of medieval Venice, we drew La Habana to us, as if the satin-bodiced and feathered brocatelle of the mulatas at The Tropicana were more than our senses could bear, enough to sate our sense of beauty and illicit treasures. Were not the seeds of white mulberry trees upon which the silkworm dined contraband, smuggled, hidden, dangerous cargo transported by the foolish or fool-hardy headstrong bent on wealth and stature. But we needn't concern ourselves with distant and ancient menace. The flickering of home-style black and white movies after the flan, after the cigars and cognac, bringing lampas skinned brown beauties swinging from trees, swinging their hips was intimidating enough. Surely, there was no one more beautiful than a woman in silk smiling down at me from a gargantuan Cuban cypress tree, while I hid at the foot of the stairs waiting for the exception.

. . .

As I understood with the mind of a child befuddled by the Cold War and immersed in films of WWII, my mother visited a fashion showroom not far from La Place de L'Opera where an impish French model paraded in front of her as she sat, probably in chairs of chine velvet with thickets of exotic plants, peacocks, and bizarre Oriental leitmotifs. As she sat admiring the models, my father, Paul T., who was smooth as silk, decided upon a white silk taffeta strapless sheath embossed with pearls with a flying panel of the same materials, that I now know to be a 'robe a la francaise' on the back, so that my mother's figure was virginal, salacious, and regal at one and the same time. A velvet cape with the same pearled pattern was strewn over her left shoulder as she mysteriously moved down the winding staircase. I was speechless, not because I'd been found out, but because I was sure I was not to see my mother in such a state of ethereal sensuality in my lifetime. I almost believed the glow on her face was a reflection of the moon flirting unabashed in front of my father. My father who was smooth as silk, though not named 'Silk' like so many others of us. His muscular frame interacted with the world as something precious to behold, beyond the possibility of an ordinary anything. This couple slipping into a black Missouri night to hear the raw silk voice of Tina Turner, the velvet cisele intonations of Gloria Lynne or the heightened boucle of Maria Callas were mine. I came from this phenomenon as Toomer said rare as a "November cotton flower".

Ntozake Shange
25 May 1998
Houston, Texas

St. Louis

Above all else St. Louis was a colored town: 'a whiskey black space'. That's not to say there were no white people. It's just to say I had to go out of my neighborhood to find some and then they'd wish I hadn't. This maybe all new for those of you born after 1964, but I grew up in St. Louis in the midst of a struggle for the soul of the country and I'm not talking about Sputnik. There was nothing but struggle surrounding us as colored children in America from 1954 on. But, aside from some political meetings held in my house late into the night, I just knew there were a lot of Negroes in St. Louis, that I lived among them, and that I was one. Race defined my reality and if more people would admit this it'd be a saner world we live in today…

For years my sisters, my brother and I went to Clark School which was luckily at the end of our block and we only had to cross one boulevard to get there. I had a wonderful teacher, Mrs. Smith who always lucked swank and rouged her cheeks just a wee bit too much. From Mrs. Smith I learned about decorum and that colored children must always have it. Mrs. Smith loved Paul Laurence Dunbar, so any time she could that's what we would read aloud. Now the problem presented by Dunbar is that it's written in black English which we were not encouraged to speak at all. Yet there was Mrs. Smith, letting the 'de's and 'dahs' roll off her tongue with a smile. This was also true of my mother who lawled in her Dunbar as if she could she see Malindy right in front of us or Ike just as Dunbar described him. So I grew up in this strange world of contradictions.

Yes, we were Americans and my uncles fought in the wars, but we couldn't try on hats in the store. We could take pride in Hughes and Dunbar, but we mustn't use double negatives if any white people around. Yes we ate 'chitlins' but we mustn't tell anyone one.

Yes we traipsed off to the Veiled Prophet parade like the rest of St. Louis, not realizing we were watching a ritual that grew from white supremacy. The Veiled Prophet himself was clocked in satin and beaded robes. Now I think he should have been carrying a burning cross, but then I was drawn into the beauty of it all with the rest of St. Louis. There's something about childhood that finds joy and excitement almost everywhere. Anyway all these tidbits about growing up in St. Louis will mean nothing to you, if I don't talk about the veneer of elegance that is the city. No matter what kind of house or what neighborhood there were medians and granite sculpture at the end of the blocks. The bricks of the houses hid the crumbilin' insides of many of them or exalted the many mansions. & Oh, the churches and synagogues were just like in the Bible, and our songs, especially "in my Father's house there are many mansions;" which meant to me that there was a colored one for sure.

I stayed at Clark School for two years surrounded as folks like to say among my own kind, happy as I could be. Then one day a woman came to see a few of us. She took us in a little room where we had to repeat number backwards, define words, look at strange images and tell her what they were. It was all very strange. I think maybe ten of us went into this room and were asked to complete logical sequences of objects, ideas, things. This was the first clue that I was being singled out to join the true struggle of my people, but you couldn't have told me then. The lady came back for a meeting with our parents and told them we had high IQ's and belonged in the gifted program which for us was in a far off white working class neighborhood. They didn't tell us we'd end up being the only colored children around, that we'd have to take a trolley and two buses, or that we weren't welcome where we were going.

Going to Dewey School was nothing like what the children in Little Rock endured. There were no crowds or police, but there was a silence my sister and I met that was hurtful and intimidating. My fifth grade teacher Ms. Baldwin tried to Ameliorate the situation, but my classmates insisted that I was Greek or Sicilian. It was inconceivable to them that I was a Negro amongst them. This meant for a lot of tight rope walking. I didn't want to do or say anything that might get me beat up and I still wanted to say 'Yes, I am a Negro'. When a brown-skinned boy arrived the next year, my fate was sealed. Robert Alexander and I were paired off together to projects, to square dances. You name it, if we had to have partners Robert had to be mine. It was as if we were being treated 'separate but equal' in the very place integration was to be buoyed. But we weathered the 'togetherness' as best we could; exchanging as few words as possible. Here is my contradiction. I'd get on my bus to go home with such relief. Home was nothing but colored people and everyday I couldn't get there soon enough. Yet, poor Robert and I couldn't make a go of it in the very white environment we shared everyday.

On Windermere Place where we lived. There was always something going on: double dutch, kick ball, monopoly, or bid whist. We had free reign of the street, since only those who lived on it had the right to drive on it, so we rode our bikes right down the middle of it, or if we felt brave we'd ride up to the parking lot of Harris Teacher's College and ride in circles around the parking lots. This when our parents sent out messages that we were 'missing' and we got in trouble. But this was not my only world, I lived in the world of books as well.

We were lucky that the Cabanne Street Library was within walking distance because I walked it as often as I could. To learn, to feel, in some cases to see. That's where I discovered Susan B. Anthony and Toussaint L'Ouverture. I also read every Nancy Drew there was at the time. I found Carter G. Woodson "100

Facts about the Negro"[1] and DuBois, Countee Cullen, James Weldon Johnson, and Jane Austin and Charlotte Bronte, Wild Bill Hickock and so many more. Then, too, my father brought home a mass of socialist literature like "The Ukraine" with a cover of a White woman surrounded by brilliant roses lauding the success of collective farming. Or he'd he'd have the latest "Science Digest". Or my mother would sneak Books like Baldwin's "Giovanni's Room" or "Mandingo" into the house, but her favorites were Frank Yerby's romance novels like "Foxes of Harrow". She took special delight in Yerby because he'd made it in publishing and in Hollywood never denying he was a Negro as well. I loved books. I slept with them and tried to eat with them at my side, but mother insisted that I take part in dinner table discussion which was really interesting. My parents would facilitate discussions about the race and our individual lives. But, nothing was like finding a quiet place to hunker down with a stack of books, be they poetry or medical journals. I actually wrote a letter to one journal asking for more information about the newest discovery that could prevent pregnancy. I guess they were taken aback by an eleven year old wanting this information and wrote me the sweetest reply explaining that I should speak with my parents. That makes me laugh now, but then I was very serious. I also wrote away to a physicist who was working on the quantum theory who wrote me back too. And I knew for sure they wouldn't have responded if they'd known I was colored. This is how racism warps one's perceptions. I was raised when these perceptions: ours of white people and theirs of us were in violent upheaval and childhood did not last long. **Childhood however, can last forever in many lands and times, if you always keep a book near you. I do and I travel the world from my back porch.**

---

1 J. A. Rodgers (1880–1966) was the author of *100 Facts About the Negro*. But given that Carter G. Woodson (1875–1950) was popularly known as the Father of Black History, this may be a misattribution, or two references in the list.

Coming of Age as a Writer

As a child I was raised on Paul Laurence Dunbar, Langston Hughes, and James Weldon[1] the poets my mother felt comfortable with and held precious. Later she introduced Edna St. Vincent Millay, Robert Hayden, and Sterling Brown. So before the age of five, this was my literary world. I, therefore, never took to what was called children's literature. Simultaneously, my father my father enveloped my world s a sea of black and Latin m.[2] of all kinds. I listened to the early Miles Davis, Hank Mobley, Ellington, Count Basey through to Art Blakey[3]. Somehow the two worlds integrated themselves as one realm of sounds. This has never changed. If it hadn't been for my parents obsessions. I would have had a traditionally classic education. I am saying all this because the dichotomy of learning that racism created for me has never disappeared. I have always had to think very hard about which audience I was addressing and which language I could use. I was smitten with the cadence and characters of black English and the rhythms of the bl.,[4] jazz, and Afro-Cuban improvisations.

I stole *Giovanni's Room* from under my mother's pillow and *The Invisible Man* from my father's bookcase. I scoured St. Louis libraries for biographies of artists and politicians mentioned over the dinner meal. So Toussaint L'Ouverture[5] and Adam Clayton Powell Jr.[6] were

1 James Weldon Johnson

2 music

3 Important jazz musicians

4 blues

5 Toussaint L'Ouverture (1743–1803), was the leader of the Haitian Revolution, which culminated in Haitian independence from France and the emancipation of slaves in 1804.

6 Here Shange may be referring to either Adam Clayton Powell Sr. (1865–1953), the prominent leader of Abyssinian Baptist Church in Harlem, or his son Adam Clayton Powell Jr. (1908–1972), who was a pastor, civil rights activist, and the first African American congressperson from New York.

circulating in my head as one continuous phenomenon. Once I left the all black schools I attended in St. Louis, none of my teachers knew of whom or what I was talking about. This situation remained so throughout my graduate school. Although I applied myself diligently to Greco-Roman classics, French, English and Russian poetry, there was never a space for me to express the realities of my black/Puerto Rican worlds or to bring our language to the page. When I tried, which I did, I was told, 'I was beating' a dead horse'. This comment was specifically directed at a eulogy I had written for Malcolm X. I never challenged my Euro-American education because I was learning something and that was foremost on my mind. Very early on I was introduced to Consciousness –raising groups that drove me to discover/recover women's art, verbal and visual. With a doggedness that still plagues me, I sought out fields of study which were not fields of 'study'.

I have no idea of how I came across LeRoi Jones,[1] Ted Jones, and Richard Wright, but I did. Immediately I found antecedents for whatever I was going to write or see. I wrote my first poem in high school during the Vietnam War. This poem focused on a small girl burning up in napalm while steadfastly holding on to her doll. I did not write again until my senior year at Barnard College, when a young white woman associated with the literary magazine mistook me for thulani davis[2] and asked me to make sure I got my poems in on time. I was a bit miffed about this, so I wrote some poems, focusing on Jimi Hendrix and John Henry which they accepted not realizing they now had two blacks in the table of contents. Shortly after this I saw the Original Last Poets, not the current fraudulent

1 LeRoi Jones, later known as Amiri Baraka (1934–2014), was a well-known African American playwright, critic, and community activist.

2 Thulani Davis (b. 1949) is a distinguished African American playwright, novelist, journalist, and librettist who was close friends with Shange. They attended Barnard College together and Shange saved some of Davis's early work in her personal files.

group, but Felipe Luciano,[1] Gylan Kain, and David Nelson who absolutely rocked my world as poets in performance that was also politically driven. Gylan Kain actually invited me to join the group, but I was pregnant before Roe V. Wade and had other matters to contend with.

Nevertheless, I met poets Pedro Pietri, Etnairis Rivera and Jose-Angel Figueroa who took me under their wing.[2] It was at a fete for Jose Luis Gonzalez, the noted Puerto Rican fiction writer, that I read some poems publically at the behest of Pedro even though they were not in Spanish. That was a pivotal moment in my writing career because that meant that I could rely on my use of language to reach almost any language due to the musicality and rhythms present. Later I would begin to write bilingual poems using my familiarity with French, Spanish, and Portuguese. From that point on I was included in the poetry cadre that warm up audiences for the political speakers of The Young Lord's Party which championed the culture and self-determination of the Puerto Rican people. This is how I learned to hold an audience, since we read at the projects, corners of the South Bronx and Lower East Side where the crowds were not expecting us. When I moved to California, my process remained evolved. I added an acoustic guitar to my 'act' and opened up on Main St. for a play about Angela Davis[3] who was still incarcerated.

When I went to Boston to continue my graduate work, I joined the black Artist's Collective. I was appointed Poetry Curator for our

---

1 Felipe Luciano (b. 1947) is an Afro–Puerto Rican poet and community activist who, in addition to being a member of the Last Poets, a New York–based Black Power–era spoken-word poetry group, was a leading organizer in the Young Lords Party, a Puerto Rican activist organization.

2 These three men were important figures in what was termed the Nuyorican Poetry Movement, which gave birth to the Nuyorican Poetry Café (founded 1972), a long-standing cultural institution in New York City.

3 Angela Davis (b. 1944) is a globally recognized Black feminist intellectual, Marxist organizer, and author.

weekends of cultural activities. I met more black musicians with whom I would work, The M7s-Ra Brothers, David Ware, Scorch, and Bill Saxton.: all of whom have names for themselves. I invited poets from Rhode Island and New York City to come to our space to perform in our space. I had a band, Zaki and the Palm Wine Drinkards[1] which was all percussion as well as a trio with Miles Cockfield (bass) and Gene Mason (horns). We worked very hard for 'the door' in Boston and Cambridge.

Between Boston-New York and San Francisco my skills evolved as a performer, a writer and dancer. I spent equal amounts of time studying dance as I did writing. The readings I put together for my self, after I was a featured poet at the Grant Street Bar and Minerva's, always included music, dance, what they now call, the spoken word. Belonging to the Third World Communications Collective led me to such a depth of cultural reciprocity that my last group in San Francisco was black, Latin, Native and Asian and our band was Martiniquan, the jazz group integrated. This grouping of dancers, musicians, along with Jessica Hagedorn and myself, was known here, as 'for colored girls…' However, our program changed form night to night and space to space. We were gratefully supported by the black dance community. I imagine that the fact that I belonged to Ed Mock's West Coast Dance Works, Halifu Osumare's Company, and Raymond Sawyer's Afro-Asian Dance Company, helped, but these choreographers believed in me as a writer as well.

Once I got to New York on the tails of our groups success at Minnie's Can Do Club, I started dancing with Sun-Ra[2] and the Heliotropic Arkestra and reading once a week at the Old Reliable

1 The band's name was a play on the title of Amos Tutuola's 1952 novel, *The Palm Wine Drinkard*, the first African novel published in English outside of the continent.

2 Sun Ra (1914–1993) was an avant-garde jazz musician and a key figure in Afrofuturism, performing with his "Arkestra," which included both musicians and dancers.

Bar where many Beats had read before me. Subsequently, producers Woody King and Joseph Papp, heard about the shows I was giving and ushered me into a thoroughly foreign landscape which was theatre. Since then I have written four volumes of poetry, five children's books, three, novels, four if we count the one I am currently finishing and a myriad of theatre pieces. I have performed with a galaxy of world renowned black jazz musicians, and danced with Dianne McIntyre's Sounds in Motion and Jawole Za Zollar's Urban Bush Women[1]…

Yet I have never had the opportunity to actually 'study' poetry. That is why I feel compelled to make this application to the New College of California's Graduate Program of Creative Inquiry. I want passionately to be as acutely knowledgeable about form and metre as I am about the last thirty years of what we call \Great Black M. from Coltrane to David Murray. I need/want to know more about poetry. I do not want my work to be attributed to some nat'chel ability of the Negro to sing and dance. I am not Topsy and I can learn.[2]

1 Urban Bush Women, founded in 1984, is a New York–based professional dance company whose work addresses the experiences of Black women.

2 For a more extensive discussion of these dance companies and Shange's work as a dancer, see Ntozake Shange's *Dance We Do* (Beacon Press, 2020).

From—
THE PHOENIX
Trenton High School literary publication
1966 issue (page 27)

They Are Safe for Now

Paulette Williams

There is a tiny child playing amidst trash and squalor.
Her play-pen is the cracked, cluttered pavement that shelters, too,
An old man, his pants infested with lice and dragging on the
Cement as he wanders thru the maze of depression.
But the child plays with her doll,
Oblivious to the despair enshrouding her,
Oblivious to the shattered face of the matted-haired doll.
She is safe for now.

There is a film of young men writhing on army cots,
Buckshot tangled in their limbs.
There are rice fields destroyed,
Fields spawning nutility in brilliant sunlight.
There is a tiny child playing amidst trash and squalor,
Burned huts and butchered bodies.
All around her, victims shrieking, pleading to die.
But the child is playing with her doll,
Oblivious to the horrors,
Oblivious to the shattered face of the matted-haired doll.
She is safe for now.

Those who play with shattered toys as if they were new;
Those who envision verdant glistening spaces instead of dismal ruin;
Those who see war heroes instead of dead soldiers:
They are safe… for now.

EARLY POEMS

This section begins with early poems written soon after Shange's graduation from Barnard College. Her transition from Paulette Williams to Ntozake Shange is apparent in her signatures, and she often placed a copyright sign after her name at the end of her poems. It was a way to claim ownership of her words and demand recognition. However, just as Shange prioritized her own actualization as a young Black woman artist, her work reveals how she was concerned with collective Black liberation. Her use of the lowercase in her signature is a sign of her participation in the radical Black political milieu of the time, one in which the individual was understood to be secondary to the collective, therefore one's name and "I" were written in the lower case but "We" was capitalized. We also see her embrace of Black diasporic cultures with a particular interest in West African Yoruba traditions. Yoruba culture, generally speaking, was the source of many of the African retentions of the descendants of people enslaved in the Americas. In the Black Arts Movement it became one of the traditions overtly maintained. You can see in these poems, Shange describing her own fledgling experience adopting an Afrocentric identity and set of cultural practices in her young adulthood. Over the following decades, Shange would formally explore and embrace multiple continental and diasporic African traditions, and develop Pan-African liberationist politics. Finally, in this period she is beginning to combine the particulars of Black vernacular speech with her experiments in poetic form, structure, and content, planting the seeds of her signature style.

untitled #1

anonymity.
so i'm gonna imagine me some high-toned
swashbuckling niggahs. Who'll stand up free of
charge.
                & leave you un-articulated
                        imaginary
                            suckers,
nothing at all.
i mean, what have you got that i don't
al/ready have?
                to do w/ anything.

paulette williams
march, 1970

untitled #2

a seeds lonely
watermelon seeds looped warm tongues wet
kissed 'n spit out i go inside
sylvania memories solo flights of du-wop du-wah
crocheted scarlet (& whisper love)
Philadelphia neon peeks nakedness tossin sheets
cower under fierce tender flesh losing ground to
which how silken
whiskers damp rub dimly glares
why
come see abt me little blk sambo come see abt me
donchu know the war is ovah
jocko u was talking too fast dools burst
ruby cheeks lips heart stained eyes showered stubby
mudcaked fingers blessed me w/ howdy doody
hey hey
i'm singin from the brooklyn bridge
harlem-rendez-vous harlem-rendez-vous
woncha come see abt me little blk sambo
tower soar fly huge shadow rush rush ebony marvel rush
tornado-sam
apollo funnel wild blk winds funnel of love tornado-sam
whip away grow catch contours nude streetlights sticky pains
windows
undressin to the radiator rag vibrations cry catch tomorrow
catch tomorrow tornado-sam singin on steel suspensions
ovah th bay lookin at stars caught in deep waters
i'm ridin the wind wreckless w/ ya tornado-sam
ebony marvel feel me.

Paulette Williams
5-70

untitled #3

(thula thula

tingle me sleep brown

calves sigh

tingle

me sleep

brown calves

sigh

hands warm

ooooooh be still

breathe twilights mingle

brown sigh

) thula thula

paulette williams
5-70 (revised 10-70)

untitled #4

i am breathin too deep
when i read out loud
i slow to sink into
mere words/ how i
make my livin joshin me
wrestlin from me to/
enclose and fill me
sounds like a common
    they come into me boldly
unveilin what seems/ i am knowin
only hazes waverin of beyond
a sense that is all/
to wait

joinin all/ you pass
thru bus stop visions
as truth beckons/ in the footsteps
of yr song is air hardly
touched, by (leaves/ i follow
not you/ but directions
away from singularity
moments only of an i
lookin for / ever
always must to be an
of/ the eternal

tozake shange

untitled #5

you
can't
always
tell
who's
comin
when
you'll
be asked
to
dance

louder
tomorrows
samba
unheard
to/o
quick
content

paulette williams
6-25-70

brown hands

(for Philip 12-10-70)

strong brown fingers
whimsy
creators of the wet purge
the other worlds

blk music
brownblack musicman brownmusician blkmagicman
yr horn
plays my lips
wraps roun my neck
pulls oooh at red strands in my hair
molten volcanic sounds
ring melodies thru my flesh
(soft-meant kisses in
brown fingers)
rhythms of my
wanted so long
in the small of my back
between my thighs
screeching hoodoo

brown hands

my mouth opens slightly
my tongue clings to itself
waitin
ready
to catch
the music
you spread my legs to

paulette williams
12-10-70

to all interested brothers

i'm thru

being

let down/ stood up
rapped to/ wrapped in
fucked with/ screwed over
cried on/ laughed at

chains gone
i'm free black &
four hundred forty years old.

you better show
me
your best stuff
cause
i'm in a hurry.

P. Williams

the receiving line

a salaam alaikum
wa alaikum salaam

do you see me? can you see me?
don't you see me soul writhing?
wrenched. beneath my gele seething.
my eyes plead.

a salaam alaikum
wa alaikum salaam

i'm crying out to you, brother
can you hear me? the chaos
catapults my limbs against this
ewe fabric. can't you see?

a salaam alaikum
wa alaikum salaam

i'm ndekedehe abidurahman,
solani otieno, or chima, or
maybe paulette.

a salaam alaikum
wa alaikum salaam

if i stood here naked, no name,
uncostumed, unmasked, would you
see me?
if i, my 'meness', was thrown to/ at you,
blatant and whole, could/ would you
see me?

a salaam alaikum
wa alaikum salaam

i'm from lawrenceville, you know.
never saw dar-es-salaam or port
harcourt. i'm exiled presbyte-
rian…i….

a salaam alaikum
wa alaikum salaam

stop. please stop. and see me.
beneath caught in all this. i'm
wander/ wondering. played double
dutch. loved coney island and still
eat pork. stop. please stop. and
find/ found me.

a salaam alaikum
wa alaikum salaam

suffocating, stunt/ stifled. i'll
die here. breathing and buried. But
i'm leaving/ living paulette's
leaving alive. I'll see you, brother,
i'll see you sister, when you get there,
when you get to where i'm going...when
you get to where i'm me.

a salaam alaikum

Paulette Williams

easy rider see what you done done

(for walter vandemeer,[1] dead at twelve)

captain amerika and billy
glistening   machines
                                        7500   hp
redwhite&blue
        easy riders   sightseeing
seeing
        toothless chicanoes and waving sharecroppers

deserts   communes   crazy white whores   and
their own   KIND
their own
        FLESH OF THEIR FLESH.
        BLOOD OF THEIR BLOOD.
        KILLED   THEM.

BLEEDING
BLEEDING FIRE
BLEEDING SCAG

on the way from mardi gras.
they could have lived ______stayed alive
                                                SCAVENGERS
where sand dunes erupt from garbage- asphalt and
                                desert-ed people
communes infest the nearest project and hookers straddle
        every other fire hydrant

with toothless spics and wandering waving niggahs

---

1 Walter Vandermeer was a twelve-year-old child who was found dead of a heroin overdose in a Harlem tenement on December 14, 1970. Vandermeer had been through several placements in the child welfare and juvenile detention systems.

waiting for them   dying for them

DYING

to go glistening to mardi gras
riding
        7500   hp   redwhite&blue
easy riding
        rusty needles.

Paulette Williams

on getting my new self together

well
nde…nde?
oh yeah
ndekedehe___
your
yoruba was
pathetic
today
can't say
nothing but
FUNGA ALAFIA ASAY ASAY *[1]
please
keep your mouth shut
don't know BENI * from BEKO *
gele
tumbles at
sight (all six feet).
Oh shit, uh, oh igbe
when are you gonna
take that hem
down

---

1 Shange is referencing the West African greeting song "Funga Alafia" meaning "peace and goodwill to you." Beginning in the 1970s the song became a mainstay of African dance classes taught in the United States.

flashing your
ankles
straight cross town.
Folks gonna think
oh
they gonna know
you the girl from
right next door.

*funga alafia asay asay-welcome, *how are you, fine, fine**
beni-(behanee)-yes
beko-(beyako)-no

P Williams

for sapphire[1]

yes
i am a BIG LEGGED black woman
thighs like stuffed drumsticks
taut-bow calves
and a walk
all
my own.
a strutting sashay
hinged on my
freefloatingbehind.

PHAT MAMA.

1 Sapphire was a character on the *Amos 'n' Andy* radio show (1928–1960) and the 1950s television program of the same name. The character has been widely derided for feeding stereotypical ideas about Black women. Sapphire was loud, brash, and hostile.

r&b chorale

(for big mama thornton[1])

proto-midnight cowboy
dealing like he was
selling REVELATIONS
asked
/who's at the fillmore/
ike & tina turner
/who the hell is tina turner/
OOH. I'M JUST A
FOOL
YOU KNOW
I'M IN LOVE.
OOH.AAH.AAH.

cheap thrills joplin
over a warm scotch
bourboned
/ tina turner is my idol/
with 14 million ameripigs
merv griffin asked
/ who the hell is tina turner/
UH.UH.
I'LL BUY YOU ANYTHING
YOU WANT ME TO BUY
YOU IF
YOU JUST MAKE LOVE
TO ME
MAKE ME SAY
UHHH.UHHH.

---

1 Willie Mae "Big Mama" Thornton (1926–1984) was a Black rock and roll and R&B pioneer, most famous for her hit song "Hound Dog," which Elvis Presley covered.

charles 'chuck' berry
blackballed for
kidnapping some oldass[1]
white chick* in mo
              while he was exiled
the beatles rolled over beethoven
& the stones ran off with maybelline
leaving charles 'chuck' berry to
big time edsullivan

                                        GO
                                        GO JOHNNY GO
                                        GO
                                        GO GO GO
                                        JOHNNY BE
                                        G   O   O   D.

*(actually teenage indian)

1 Chuck Berry (1926–2017) was another Black rock and roll pioneer, whose hit songs "Roll Over Beethoven," "Maybelline," and "Johnny B. Goode" are all referenced in this poem. In December 1959, he was arrested in St. Louis, Missouri, and charged with violating the Mann Act for transporting a fourteen-year-old girl across state lines for "immoral purposes." The Mann Act, intended to address prostitution rings, was selectively enforced and commonly used to target Black entertainers who had interracial sexual relationships. Though Berry's victim, Janice Norine Escalanti, was popularly described as white, she was Mexican and they had met in Juarez, hence Shange's reference to her as "actually teenage Indian." Berry would serve two years for the crime.

blk folks, it's this thing callt love

sistah say sistah. i ain't digging yo po-e-try.
i ain't diggin it no kinda way. u ain't po/li/ti/cal/
        a non-political-academic-poet is whatchu are
'n we ain't got no time
                no time for that.
ya don' mention bloodshed
                bullets
                blood 'n killin.
naw sistah u ain't inta the truth that we gon' haveta fight 'n
some of us die for the rest.
                sissstah u non-political
'n u wasti time.
                wait up now. wait up.
i ain't gon' talk to my folks bout dyin or blood or bullets
cause we know bout death.
        we die every mornin when we open our eyes, toss flimsy
        blankets offa lumpy bed, leave cold runnin quickie showers
                        (dirty imitations of life).
        we die every time a niggah beats his woman til she
                        can't stand no more. every
        time one of us forgets infants on prickly horse tracks.
naw. naw. i don' haveta talk to my folks bout dyin
                        we know bout death.
i wanna talk bout suns we aint nevah seen
            (cept thru sweat drippin cross our eyes) 'n
evenins withchyo man when ya know he's happy cause u jus' alive.
yeah, i'ma talk bout suns we ain't looked at proper 'n love we
                        ain't felt cause we too busy
                        hustling dead.

yeah. blk folks know bout death
everyday annihilation
cutting us off from each othah
makin blk women bitches 'n n men muthafuckahs
havin invisible hemorrhages 'n no medicaid available.
no don' raise yo voice bout bein non-political.
I heard felipe
u gotta smell the shoe leather before u know
the man's got his feet both feet up yo ass.
i heard Dhoruba
niggahs singin fingerpoppin while the man is getting
ovens ready.
i heard stokely
move ovah or we'll move ovah u.
'n i answered i shouted raised my hand when imamou cried
WILL THE MACHINEGUNNERS PLEASE STEP FORWARD.
i'ma be there. i'm here withchya now but i gotta talk to my folks
bout livin. i gotta talk to 'em bout lovin each othah
so they'll know they precious
that they everything n that our lives are all togethah
cause we all here with each othah.
don' call me non-political jus' cause I want my folks to
undahstand. to undahstand that them
carolinian razors them carolinian (shave 'n a haicut) razzzors
ain't meant for our veins. lye 'n poison lye 'n smack that
ain't for us.
i wantem to feel that blk love holdin on protectin us guidin us
when/evah we lost.
i want my folks to see themselves.
to look, dammit 'n say
all what i got for my sistahs
all what i got for my brothahs
is everything i have.

naw. i ain't gon' talk no bloodshed no bullets 'n killin. i'ma
talk bout blk love that's what the revolution is abt.
revolution ain't bout bloodshed or death.
the revolution is bout our lives. the suns 'n horizons we
gonna see. the folks we gonna havea chance to love.
yeah.
the REVOLUTION is bout
bein torn every time a brothah puts a sistah
on the street highsteppin for smack for a dose 'i
penicillin.
bein wrenched every time a blood decorates his
blk soul w/ hypodermic riffs beneath echoes of
broken days.
bein sick, i tellya, sick when every/any blk child
is cold hungry 'n unloved.
i'ma keep writin keep ona talking bout blk love 'n blk beauty
cause revolutionaries don' grow on trees, my man.
revolutionaries grow from pain 'n hurt from anguish
watchin blk folks our folks die/
revolutionaries grow are made spring up from carin so bad
'n lovin ssoo much.
i'm recruitin.
i'm recruitin me some machine gunners some bombadeers some
riflemen.
every time i cry
blk folk i love u 'n u killin me when u kill yoself.
i'm makin me some revolutionaries every time i say
i love u blk nappy headed bastards i love u.
u wait. u wait 'n
u watch how many pick up the gun
how many lay down they lives 'n
deeeestroy this thing w/ its dumbass foot round our throat.
the revolution ain't comin til we love each othah.

we gon' have to believe
to pray like we ain't nevah prayed
for a blk thing a blk beauty to grab
us tight 'n strangle our resistance
to blk life. pray for a blk love
blk love to set us straight.
'n we won't miss a target.
won't miss cause we love blk folks
tooo much to be makin errors.
yeah. we gon' be soooo careful w/ ourselves/ssooo powerful
(ain't no which way abt it). we got the power 'n
the power is blkness.

when u gonna get them m-14s?
when u gonna get them m-14s?
i tellya i gotta know, blk folks, cause i don' i don'
wanna/can't go nowhere withoutcha. i gotta know cause
i love u i love u, blk folks, i love u.

my man & some boy

(for thulani and redbone)

there's blood on the bathroom floor
next to the rusted spots
where the water leaks
under the sink
there's blood on the floor
just above the place where the
cats piss under the house
three drops
each one
bigger
bloodier
loaded
he wants to tell me
how he's bursting
how he's got/to/let himself
be wanted
how caught how hurt he's been
how he wants to love me
loaded
there's blood on the bathroom floor
he wants me to know
how he's gonna feel
for me & the kids
feel for us cuz we
love/he can't
stand
the pressure
gotta get it off
with some boy

so there's the blood on the bathroom floor
he can touch me now
with his veins swellin
eyes dead-glossy
he can love me now
not feel inadequate cuz i paid last
month's rent
i can feel his dry
hands reachin out to me now
& i wanted that/him to come to me
to get me from my self
to love me
but not with numbness
with some boy massaging his heart
what do i do
when he comes to me
a junkie/lover
a man poisoned/tender
not knowing that
i saw the blood on the bathroom floor
next to the rust
the smells of shit & cat piss

zake 7/14/71
(paulette williams)

a banjo

(for Leon Damas)

i am strange rhythms
life-tones vibrating
my fingertips are music makers

i am song
i sing infants torn from suckling nipples
okra and rice, high-topped sneakers
blond wig-ged ladies prancing
nappy-head women walkin

i am three braids that swell-up by midday

i am dust
my grandfather's soil, rice before we eat
last sacraments for lynched geechees
far off cousins in oklahoma territory
dirt farmers, indian fighters in
blood dusted uniforms

i am that blood
wrenching me from my earth, my soil
leaving me bloody in front of my sisters,
whose scalps somebody close hung round his waist
for luck;
i am the screaming blood of rape, incest's child
i am sorrow's wailing mother

my songs are blood songs

i am little sally walker
shakin to the left, shakin to the right

shakin to the one that ran off the plantation one starry night,
    slept with swamp creatures, went off to san quentin silent
    and bitter, nods death-like on alvarado street, denies me
    from the front seat of a velvet green el cappillero

i am fear
i am warnings of nightriders, tar and syrup
guineas and polaks with chains in little italy
i am a steel pipe, a zip gun, i am cotton
picked in harsh sunlight, a chain gang, a shack,
a sparse garden

i am hoppin-john and greens
i am strange rhythms
i am drums at east village sets
jesus banging on the doors of the apostolic church
i am the sound of clandestine meetings, invocations
of spirits with no names
i am deacon jones and the sunday picnic
i am a red ban-dana
i'm broken bottles and sulphur fumes
i am the james brown
i am throbbing

i'm grits and potted meat

i am dance
ring shouts, sun-ra's shakers, touched by the holy ghost
truckin down 8th ave., i am a harlem record store
twichin all night long, i am creole gumbo, soft-shell
clams and hot sauce
i am blues
i am a banjo picking dawn from outta no where
i am a nightmare, i'm dream

i'm russet, the mississippi delta

i am three tricks a night

i am strange rhythms
a geechee twice removed from Charleston's home
i am a banjar, an african music maker
my strings are yr strings yr

blood my blood songs dances fears loves are
my mourning call
i am corn rolls, geles, and kalimbas
i am yams in butter

i am a family of 16 caught in the projects

i am strange rhythms
i am the sparrow, my song makes the wind move
i ease yr restless sleep, i cause
the lizard's teeth to protect you
from inside torture
i am cairo and cast st louis
i'm four for a dollar

i'm cleaning chitlin's in july

i am a banjo picker passing yr windows and yr doors
yesterday heaped up on my shoulders, tomorrow jumpin from
  my eyes
this moment gyrates thru my fingertips

i am strange rhythms
i cake-walk thru crashin glass in riotous streets
singing my always song of truth
strange rhythms of dirt and laughter

i am sapphire's second cousin

i live only when hear me
i am our secret of curried goat and red rice
i am a high-tailed jig from everywhere
i strike black notes to intimately mingle our blood
i slash the overseer's wrists

my songs are blood songs

zake shange
(paulette williams)
7-16-71

dark phrases

of womanhood/never having been a girl

half-notes
scattered/without rhythm/no tune

distraught laughter/falling...
over a blk girl's shoulder
it's funny, it's hysterical
the melody-less-ness of her dance

cora lee
ached
    for five days
her groins
writhing/never easing
                (don't tell nobody, don't tell a soul)
funny discharge ruined her cotton panties
grannie put her to bed
w/ fever and pain
    the intern cackled something abt
        'do you know what a douche is?'
            (don't tell nobody, don't tell a soul)

a fifteen yr.old
blk girl/wd be woman
sterile.../a population controller...
left st.luke's dancing
cuz she cd make it
w/all
    the heavy dudes
in her hallway/the stairs
                        her loving place/

no new songs
a dance on throw-away bottle tops
dancing on beer cans and shingles
this must be the spook house

linda marie was late, anyhow
so didn't nobody notice/when the red time
didn't show for some/long time months
(it aint never regular when you first start/
& you. you, probably won't have another period
no way/look at you/16, just startin)
linda marie knew better/she cd
she cd do it just as good as any of them
she got that womanhood power now/so what
how late/too late/too late for linda marie
the intern tried to look away
from linda marie's poutin tummy
'it's too late/there's nothing we can do'
the other girls cd'nt look
linda marie's growing parts/nobody wanted
to dance/nobody
knew/danced to anciently new
blk hearts/nobody knew
linda marie after what she did/nobody
nobody knew

another song with no singers
lyrics, no voices, & /interrupted solos
unseen performances
are we ghouls/children of horror/the joke

sandy cd'nt get her
stingy hair /to billow
like so many peacock feathers into a <u>real</u> afro

she cd'nt get /her legs
to look
curvy
piano-stick legs
a flat chest/she cd'nt
be a pretty blk girl
(you know some girls are pretty for ablkgirl)
hahahahaha, sandy was an ugly blk girl

she hid
her face
when she
laughed
hung her
head if
she felt
proud
turned her
back, when
she was abt
to be cared for
sandy was by her/self
an ugly blk girl, when every other blk girl
was queen of universe, cleopatra,
at least, a blk pearl)
one day she just disappeared/
they found the regular number of
bodies in the east river/wd'nt anybody
know sandy's/
just
that's probably where she went/too
funny-looking to take seriously
shit, her hair was juuuuuuusssst long

enough/
        to clap at/

DON'T TELL NOBODY, DON'T TELL A SOUL

are we animals/have we gone crazy/
i can't hear anything/but maddening screams &
            the soft strains of death
you promised me, you promised me...
are you liars?

somebody/anybody
sing a blk girl's song
bring her out/
            to know her self/you

zake
(paulette williams)
7-19-71

i want so much

i do want from you
whatever you have
anything to spare
whether I've space or not
i'll grow to fit/yr needs
i want
what you are be/coming
a spirit of new realities
of the continent and outer space
you are cosmic
giggles and music/
touching you is so
good to me

ntozake shange
1-10-72

untitled #6

i didn't know what
he wd feel like/ seem like
to me, his lips are very full
he's very very brown, scatters
of a beard, but i didn't know
what his chest cd do for me
how his hand fit snugly round
the back of my head, how i cd get
tangled in his legs or want
any one so strange to me
so very much

ntozake 1-29-72

a scarlet woman

a scarlet woman
that's
what
i
am
always lurkin/flirtin
jus lookin round for something i aint done/yet
my hair smells like strawberries/cocanut
my ankles are soft/thin like
my thighs are strong
i'm magic
wheeeeeeeee, an unscheduled appearance
i wear bright colors bangles
things that fall/slowly
whenever i move/smile
yeah.
n my cheeks are perpetually flushed
red/crimson.

those folks they look at me
like i/ was weird
another brazen/hussy
i was seekin the good/i was jus seekin
the good/stuff of bein alive

ntozake

scarlet woman

without make-up or girdles
excuses / no half steppin
i was approachin the world
from my single angle, my one road
__my way to go__ scarlet.

this one wreckless child
w/ a poet's leanings givings
my soul at peace with universal rhythms
i love like so many spirit/s
when i'm needed, my golden
scarlet ways are warm saving
nothing earthly
complex as crystalline skies
a thunderin/lightenin poet-talkin
female/ is a sign of things to come
scarlet
magic
a sassy assed tongue &
wide strung hips
cuz bein scarlet is/ prerequisite for
wife/mother
a gift for the man hot enough to hold.

ntozake shange
2-2-72

on marion brown[1]

a silhouette/another
still silence
a possible echo
sound is defiance
clashing tingling
a rhythm sequence
of undetermined eloquence
a wrench bell cymbal woodblock
pipe scraps worn artifacts
harried life appendages
                    an everyday
is sound sacred/a cry
against voids/a song
in uneasy tauntin silence
movement/horns have no monopoly
a melody wanders thru a chosen space
from/anywhere to truth/refusing
gagged mouths/ our breath in
swayin bodies/sounds
create /decide to live
marion is blowin

tozake shange
2-8-72

---

1 Marion Brown (1931–2010) was an avant-garde jazz alto saxophonist and composer.

untitled #7

i am very afraid
of not bein looked for
maybe no one is searchin
for the likes of me
any/how do i go abt
bein found if he doesn't know
he's s'posed to
look/what i write
notes to midnight's changin spirits
sayin/if you see the one
let him know i'm
real/am available in
multiple dimensions
& was wonderin/
if he minded
my bein so late
to arrive in
myself

tozake shange
2-8-72

bonakele

watchin you laugh w/
bird's chucklin horn runs
a slow tickle thru my ribs
        didnchu know
i travel w/you all days
        in the streets
            yr warmness follows me round corners
        teases me at the bodega
makin me laugh out loud
    in wonder
                yr wisdom slows, my pace /
       catches me
                    forgettin to see
                    forgettin to feel
special everyday faces
      i am bashful/quiet
                            sassy new/in the wind's
taunts
        a half smile
               my fullness makin me to want you
        & you are always there

tozake shange
2-20-72

untitled #8

the old woman
had touched my head_____
the / efon had graced
my palms/
    i shook the stones
and she read to me
the will of the spirit

in the town
where you live /there is
a big river
go there
        tell oshun of his
                gentleness
if in yr countenance
oshun comes to know
this man
        she will be pleased.

tozake shange
(2-20-72)

untitled #9

what i'm
gonna give you
is much
healthy like
rice or soybean butter
clean sheets/swept floors
hand-woven cloth
jute knotted into belts
tempura
broccoli
carrots
buckwheat
sweet potatoes w/ cocanut
& sometimes
my own
geechee macrobiotics
warm hats
inspired patience
a poem/
for yr
every
which way
yr nuance
brings
the me
out of
myself
i
am
devoted
to you

tozake shange
2-20-72

untitled #10

when you see yrself in my words
watch yrself move
across a page
in my voice
are u trying to remember
when
all that
little things wriggling w/ sensation
were so loudly felt &
i was around

don't misunderstand, please
my intensity is not binding

if my heart leaps as you lean toward me
&
i write reams abt the way you pout
saunter down sidewalks
i'm not catchin you
just the essence
a feeling i was/into you enough
to sense the stuff of my life/poem
pulsating in/i mean
it could have been anybody
but it had to be you

tozake shange
2-21-72

what we were abt on a dismal saturday night in the city or catchin up with ourselves all in all

fur coatd
        velvet afghans, silver climbin rabbits
wide brim hats/ angled obliquely
potions shimmy up red n' white straws
it's snowin/a blizzard
storm warnings from richmond to maine
the apple is gnawed away
        ice, quiet, deadness__________what's happenin
is lost cloud strewn is steeples gawkin lonely
in a harlem night
            but small's/small's is swarming
w/ suede boots wrappin darker
thighs/orange glasses   paunchy faces
& jigglin bartenders make inconspicuous
tips thru pannelled wall mirrors
would be apollo stars push tired
jaded sounds into soaked bodies &
it's awright
            love, let's get together
            i'm lovin you whether times are
            good or bad happy or sad
bluish lights tint pock marks
and stray eyelashes/ heavy lids escape in
vinyl smiles / with the grace of a deaf mute hyena

lots of folks had nothin to do
i mean, w/ the snow and all
sides lee morgan got shot last night at slug's
        baby, you make me feel sooo
        brand new/ i want to spend
        my whole life with you
        let's stay together
poorer f******[1] showboat-flashin their
higher behinds toward interested glances
she looks young to be so old w/ 2 ft
of flaxen blk braids & no choices yeah
what stands out abt her is no choices
no choices & it's snowin
we were lookin for something
not in ourselves / brown peopled walls
reluctance balanced in sadness
small's is close to itself
smotherin in turned down possibilities
        & i'm lovin you whether whether
        times are good or bad happy or sad
        baby let's stay together

tozake shange
2-22-72

---

1 In the original, Shange uses a slur for gay men. Although the offensive language was common in the early 1970s, her political commitment to LGBTQ liberation later in life has led us to remove the term without censoring it.

on malcolm x

(for the muora celestial experience)

yr image is common, now
like one again
in a bloodied shirt
a carried coffin
faces blur on stairways/ in the podium
street corners come alive
everyone knows everyone knows
malcolm
everyone knew/
few listened/guffawed in pool parlors
continued to run roughshod over their mothers/some
decided
to
grow
with
you/ be an integral force
something of life
then,
in shattering seconds
you were taken away/given up
we are always taking the lives of our only sons
& now
from dollar twent-five cent posters
you point yr fingers/
at the guilty
wink at us (as if) we knew
the way
of coming into ourselves
yr image is common, now
everyone knows malcolm, yet

magnificence of yr presence
is escaping us is suddenly avoidable a thing
to be essentially denied/life
our holiness
in god's hands
our visions/our dreams
to come back / he taught of life
becoming
men/women
nurtured souls/ anation of blk folks
in motion/ revolving around each other/ a sun
binding us with a common swerve/ a common rhythm
like childbirth at mama's chasing ladybug's up a
tree trunk/ everybody run free___toward growth
our sense of newness/ riding self-determined energies
on the nearest corner our futures stalk mighty
in each of us, malcolm
yr image is common, now
our pulse is steady

tozake shange
(2-9-72)
revised
(2-25-72)

to become a more discerning self

i must live my life w/
more scrutiny a thriftiness
of style should come
into my way of handlin stray
moments/ a concentrated focus
needs a home somewhere in my
visions of this physical place
my here n now
approaches mysteries
allowed solely for higher
realms
how is it that i indiscriminant-
ly jog thru my days
        seizing finite glimpses of
shorn tree limbs in beige night fogs
a sister's hallowed voice askin for a
can of beer/ i must
live my life w/ a lil delicacy
a lighter touch

ntozake shange
2-26-72

sterile eviction

a sterile eviction
at home/ in my room
propped up on
pushed together dressers
legs tossed in the air
like propellers
cuttin in the wind

i remembered the trip to philadelphia/
like grime/ crippled houses leered at
me/ everyone knew i was lookin for him/
the butcher doctor

as i laid there
i cdn't see or move
nothin but the ceiling
i just

he was fat n sordid lookin with
fallin over lips/ $550 this aint
gonna be no easy job

SCREAMED
for daddy or jesus
god/any body
to kill off/those
webbed hands metal drills
& winding things

movin inside me
tearin me up
    & dale didn't know/ he didn't
    know abt me and babies/ how cd
    i tell him such a stupid/feminine
    pre-occupation
for twenty-four hours
catheters rumbled in my
womb/ whenever i looked
grey stallions galloped
straight across my head
i tried i tried
to keep their hooves off
my face/i was bleedin
noises mangled scarlet pains
tramplin everywhere
    then
    i heard them/the butcher man &
    my father move away in silence
    it was late/ it had been very/vvery
    late/ but whoever that was s' posed
    to have been was/finally/very very
        dead

ntozake shange
1-10-72
(revised)
2-26-72

untitled #11

my father always
said that a sense of humor
was absolutely
necessary to stay
alive in this hard hard
world &
i've been laughin ever since i grew
up

ntozake shange
2-28-72

for pedro[1]

i always see you
climbin chartreuse fire escapes
that hang sideways in
colodium skies/ have you
heard the sambas skippin
backwards towards the
moon/they were on their way
to visit me/ but stopped
to see my sister's next
best friend/who just decided
to give natural childbirth
to orange water lilies and
brown-eyed siamese cats

i was missing you the
last time i checked out
the lonely people's star
to the far right hand lane of the
5th Solar Intra-Galaxy
Expressway_you really must
show me how to make mirrors
reverse and disappear into
the crocodile man-holes

1 This likely refers to Pedro Pietri (1944–2004), one of the key figures in the Nuyorican Poetry Movement.

that the human beings left
after they went extinct/ i've
changed my color too/am into

yellow/ misty saturn blue
turned out to be too much
for my buckwheat spirit
and i needed liftin up into
what we used to call
daylight/ when is the next
time we can catch up with
the Universal Music Purification
Choir/ i've been singin tunes the daisies
taught me in my last lifetime/
but nevermind, i'll just
wander around in you til
i find my way out/to
the store

ntozake shange
3-5-72

charlotte 'n philip

i hear you gotta new
somebody to raise
besides yr selves who
is orange and laughs
always garnerin yr
resources so she comes
round out the best of she
maybe knows that
one of you is music
& the other is sight
senses are into her
innately she knows
beauty/ wisdom comes
as she unravels from
you/ & makes her own

ntozake shange
3-6-72

untitled #12

how can i not from myself
keep from lovin him do i
know even how true it is
hearin him call my name
tozake
tozake in a taxi's
rush hour downtown where
i haven't been callin me
from somewhere & he maneuvers
my dreams makin me wake up
blushin and crazy

tozake shange
3-8-72

for me on the lady's birthday

knowin how to
        throw my stuff
    where to pick up
whatever i need
whenever i need it
                laughin
        in
        the one pointed center of
        corniness
& gettin by w/ a one cent loss
                    coyly
                    knockin
some extraneous fool
upside his head
            jus cuz
he
obviously didn't know who
he was messin w/
&
always
        tellin mama (abt)
how i'm really gettin married sometime soon
    to a male person i haven't met (yet)
                        but
                        it's in the air

&

i've gotta/ swing
soft and smooth
like green crepe
in san francisco

stayin
remarkably
naked, touchable

&

easy to handle like
an unexpected
smile from a long
awaited stranger/
one sequin on carmen's gown

tozake shange
4-8-72

oshun's daughter

i come to you in feathered gowns
& answer questions
you cannot ask

i dance cross candlelit skies
singin low like celia cruz
round drums
swayin in spangles
i am the carnival queen
ma rainey swingin low
seekin dawn
wishin you life

oshun's daughter
grows red she grows mute
in the wickedness of the subway
strangles in her own cries
razors in yr face
shots blazin in darkness

won't you share yr breath with me
breathe my ancientness toward yr soul
& swoon
in my heat/

oshun is golden laden
with the scent of wild flowers

she knows the ways of men
can taste the blood in yr fury
carry my anger with you
                    take this burnin up inside me
                    bring us triumphant/ out of this
glistenin with the upside down skulls
arms hangin jagged with buckshot
won't you share yr battles
let me let me free/ my time
                         knows
                           no
                            end
               eternally i am beauty
               birth of new poets/warriors
               ruddy fingered farmers
               makers of gold cloth
               well in my loins/ infinitely
               i am yellow heavens & blue echoes
          won't you listen
won't you listen my song fontella sings
bring it to me/ bring it to me/ bring it to me

shango fought
in a man's frame like you
anxious for/ to make a home
                         a land
                         one child

like shango's bold
        a child of the sun fire
& flowers jewelled round in the soil

build me a home/ somewhere to go

    i am oshun's daughter
      i need a place
      to create
      to make
      beautiful
      yr life
      a place to sigh
      love family
      & dance the dance of the cosmos
      rejoicin
      for the righteous
      have inherited
      the earth

tozake shange
4-24-72

sing her rhythms

caring/struggle/hard times/
but sing her song of life/
she's
been
dead
so
long

closed
in/silence
so long

she doesn't
know the
sound of
her own
voice

her
infinite
beauty

she's
half-notes/scattered/without rhythm/no tune
sing
her sighs/her melody/sing the song of her
possibilities
sing a righteous gospel song/
the making of a melody...
let her be born
....handled warmly.

EARLY VIGNETTES

These four vignettes offer early inklings of how Shange would develop as a prose writer and a novelist. While presumably "Mabel" is a work of nonfiction, it has the vernacular style and tenor of the fictional characters she would create later in life. "Three Weeks Ago, Tuesday," which is fiction, provides an example of the relationship between her reflective writing and her fully imaginative work. "Arlene Francis Show" and "Geoffrey Holder" are personal reflections regarding a radio show appearance of Shange's and a narrative account of a fellow artist that morphs into a diary-like account of her relationship to artists she admires, respectively. As with a number of her other early pieces, it is apparent how much Shange valued the thriving Black art community and how deeply critical she was of racism, classism, and sexism. Some of Shange's language in these pieces is undoubtedly offensive to contemporary readers and yet her early attention to marginalized groups within Black communities—particularly gender-nonconforming people—is nevertheless notable.

Mabel

my new acquaintance, mabel, was frankly insulted. assuring me that she, 'a lady', never spoke to a man accompanied by another woman, she looked at me with how-cd-u eyes, as tho i were giving him away. the ridiculousness of mabel's backwards sisterhood. i could hear queen mother tellin us we don' own no blk men and ellen from women's lib bemoaning women who are dumb enough to be jealous of another one of us…Yet i was sure that mabel was not interested in 'right' sisterhood, so when kain returned i introduced him to lovelyladymabel.

i watched her and could almost feel her long-leg girdle popping. gracious kain accepted mabel's onslaught of compliments like a trouper. when she finished, mabel turned round quickly. her middle-aged date would have accused her of 'tippin', if she spent another second with that 'tv star' and his chick. (for the night, only of course) mabel, it seems, had seen SOUL, the same show i had watched as part of the live audience. i was the only one up there shouting: ooooh kain, read that stuff.

we ran into two female impersonators at small's. one was fine whichever way he decided to go. the other was too much paunch to be attractive he/she.[1] strange thing was that the cute-one had his hair straightened. not permanented or processed, i thought that was rather anachronistic. i still do, anyway, they spoke to us abt the same SOUL show mentioning the blues quality of kain's 'life ain't nothin but a rivah,' chubby went on to talk abt how blk folks had lost so much. the over-blue mascara, sak's lookin eyelashes, and matted

1 It is unclear here whether Shange is speaking about trans or nonbinary people, or simply men performing in drag. This lack of clarity is exacerbated by the relatively thin public discourse about trans life in the 1970s. And while the flippancy of her language is jarring, it is also clear that Shange considered these two people she encountered to be an integral part of her community.

powder, began to gnaw at me as he ran down our losses, and here he was, one more lost blk man in the night.

i hadn't seen kain[1] since ralph metcalf's party back in '68. i had traipsed round the city to see the last poets, but i hadn't spoken to kain in that time tho he gently insisted that 'we' were two years old. when i toppled home that daybreak, i settled my wanton soul with the sleep-bringing feeling that i had just spent the night with 'the last horizon', **a kainesque twilight.**

paulette williams

1 Here she is referring to Gylan Kain, one of the founding members of the Last Poets.

Arlene Francis Show

my little act on the arlene francis show today was inane. the reason for the inanity is that the arlene francis show and world have an intolerant, but innocuous audience that will deal only with the dilute or what is chicly acceptable.

to say 'well, i jus' don' believe' or even distinguish 'white folks' from my folks is to approach crudity, gauche, not air quality, to say to me 'discuss jazz poetry' and add that i'm not to mention leroi jones is telling me to shut-up. how can even any ignorant someone mention blk arts and not serenade imamu amiri baraka.

that is heresy or deliberate deception.

i have no stomach for things of that sort. and have witlessly become ill. hives. nausea. aching and puffed face - - - all of this because i have to communicate with white folks on their terms.

during the interview i said that my readers/listeners wd have to deal with me/my writing on my terms. the point was lost- since white folks assume that all terms are their terms- - their insipid little white terms.

i know why i didn't want to work out here, why i wanted to stay in school. universities cover their disdain for blk folks by attributing our culture to the madness that accompanies every art: to the bizarre in the 'artist'. If i say 'fuck you' they wd say that 'oh my she is using the vernacular, how quaint.' Then with straight-bleached faces they wd say, '& exactly what did you mean bythat"

like i said 'fuck-you-.'

paulette 6-25-70

Geoffrey Holder[1]

geoffrey holder is having this girl named jackie moore do her dissertation on him. she is a taut-featured, cafe-au-lait, but whatever hints of tension exist in her face, they are smooth ones. she wears rather simple clothes, like any student, but her face is a dancer's face. at first, that's what i thought she was. with auburn-brown hair pulled back and an ascetic aura wisping round her, i assumed she was a dancer. then, i checked out her legs. no dancer's vigor or discipline in her calves or thighs. (and i have to admit i was disappointed) she wasn't dancer at all, but a grad student.

watching her fiddle with her cassette tape recorder, i had visions of myself in a year or two. i'll be diligently following somebody, tryin to stay outta the way, but in the fullness of things; catch my 'topic's' idiosyncracies and dismiss the trivia. all the while fighting to maintain (create ?) an ethos/reality of detachment so that i remain unadulterated p-lette and he/she whoeverhe/she is.

my ability to transubstantiate myself into one of my heroes' mystique is quite amazing to me. i'm sure i wandered abt,a 'kainsian' creature, after that short adventure i had with him. my perspective suddenly became a barrage of images: blk satin amazon, nubianll, a blue guerrilla. new york and my life were a melange of kain's words for months.

i still suck my lip and turn a fluorescent scarlet inside whenever i think of how he swiveled j.b.-like on a single foot, looked me over indignantly, whipped his brown-bearded chin thru the tavern air, and pouted, 'fuck-you'. with that he relaxed, performance over,

1 Geoffrey Holder (1930–2014) was a Trinidadian-American principal dancer in the Metropolitan Opera Ballet Company who also worked as a professional actor, singer, and director. He directed and designed costumes for the groundbreaking African American musical *The Wiz* on Broadway, for which he received three Tony Awards. He was also married to dancer/actress Carmen de Lavallade, mentioned earlier.

enjoying the release, the niggah-poet-flippancy, and galloped into the madness…

in one of the bars we invaded that night, he informed me that i was not a 'lady'. kain had no use for 'ladies'. he grooved on women who could hang-out, but hang-out like only us sistahs can. what or how we do that, i don' know. i was just riding, weird enough. this teetotaler chugged about 10-ten drinks in full that morning. i was so gay that i was asked to make love on the mountain of earth that climbs the walls of the black nationalist bazaar next to michaux's. i was asked, in the king's english, to love in the restoration site in the heart of harlem with the last poet. what more could i have asked for in my most sepia-soft fantasy?

well, i asked to be left alone. to enjoy kain, in spite of his sadistic sexuality, required me to stay out from between his legs. i'm sure he would have hurt me somehow. not on purpose, but naturally as the 'ebony marvel' figure he created would be obliged to. if a women knew his poems by heart, and i did.

kain's magnificence stuns me, tho. jackie fleming used to say that plunky's skin was like blk velvet. kain was/is blk velvet. grizzly eyebrows, a piquant van dyke, the glossiest white teeth, and a searing enveloping smile is kain in blaring red bells and gold brocade vest, carrying a satchel (everyone knows is filled w/ the magic of juju). how devastating is a man who lives thru words. we sniggle-giggled together, knowing that neither of us was seduced-tingling to spoken images. we were both in a sense disarmed: no magic language wand to keep us 'turned from loose'. anything said was respected for the chance of it, the ephemerality of what 'we say'.

one night spot that had 4-5 tiny-steps leading down into it was painted what must have been red. kain and i took a table for two on the left side. the place was jammed with day-people out for the night and the two of us were casual tourists. it was early for our folks to be out, only 11:00. kain went for my 3rd tom collins and i began a curious exchange with one of his admirers. the woman behind kain's empty chair stared at me to catch my eye. i nodded. she was a broad brown with a 34th st. discount type wig on. i remember an aqua jersey and a huge necklace wrapping round her buxom self as she asked, 'is he the poet?' i gathered up all my chic and sighed, 'yeah', and suggested that she speak with him.

Three Weeks Ago, Tuesday

Paulette Williams
10-18-70

Lissa caught the doorknob. Jammin the two/three keys in the resistant locks, she pushed against the empty room right into the edge of the marble slab that was the kitchen table. Her short, brown body doubled forward. Her cheeks quivered crimson, but she kept onto the phone. Dialin in time to the throbbin in her side, Lissa sat. Numb and clammy. Lissa sat dialin, getting closer to her man, swayin back 'n forth, in time to the pain.

Her brown eyes drifted back to the blazin stretch in the ocean. That penninsula was like one of her limbs, doused in oil/lit. Lyin in water, saved 'n dyin all at once. She grapped herself, while the ringing phone soared like cascades of brazen flames, easin up her arm. He didn't answer.

The fire returned stagnant, burning just for the hell of it. Lissa twisted her mouth aroun til it fell into her routine libra-pout. Her lower lip pushed sensually toward the cleft in her chin, but held tight enough to ward off possible lovers. She pulled air, joltingly thru her nostrils, mimicking drawin on some good grass or recoverin from a longlong cry. When she finally tucked her legs up to her bosom, she swayed again, back 'n forth, but now, in time to minee 'n moe. Yeah, Daniel, the first guy to look at Lissa's lil bosoms, named them minee 'n moe. Remeberin the warmth of Dan's eyes, relieved the stingin pressure of the aborted phone call. Lissa relaxed, sighin with a deepdown hint that her man would call her, later.

As Lissa realized she was thinking of him, she felt her chest tighten and moisture rise between her legs. She shook herself out of her foetal-rest, and nervously sat, straightup, at the phone. "I've gotta get up 'n go to bed", Lissa shouted to herself in her head, " I've gotta get up. Can't be losin any more sleep behin this fool. Go to bed, Lissa, please go to bed." The copper alarm clock, her precious poems, and raggity ann sauntered away from her reality. Any other night, Lissa'ld set the clock, straighten/caress her poems, and and pat raggity's yarn head, before windin her way thru thru the sheets. But, tonight, she was too hot. The room was too close. Liss' wanted the ocean back, the fire, and the music.

And Lissa sat, whimperin to herself, asking the posters of Imamou and Archie why they didn't come do something for her. Why they didn't just come off the wall and make her shine with sound 'n words. Let the spirits, them juju spirits, coat her skin. Protect her from this rushin fire that kept churnin her flesh.

Somebody came. One of her black magicians slipped from his two-dimensional statue. Led her to Mingus' "Theme for Lester Young". Left her open to Dolphy's soothesome wails.

Open 'n shut. Open 'n shut. Lissa's eyes wrestled with themselves, grappin images of then.

lissa, it's me. morgan. lissa, it's me. i'm in new york. lissa, it's me. i'm in philadelphia. lissa catch the 11:50 train… lissa, it's me. the phones rang. they stopped. she looked at her watch, tryin to be early… lissa, it's me. i don't think i can make it.

Lissa pushed her hand down her side to where she had bumped herself. Her hip bones had begun to peek out again. The baby fat was disappearing. She had bruised herself. As she felt the blk/blue, she let go of a muffled sob, held herself so tightly she felt her nails comin on one another. One sharp jerk and she lay flat on her stomach, imagining she had been stabbed and couldn't move or the dagger'ld kill her. She lay still, sufferin in the past.

lissa, here's your key. morgan nonchalantly handed her an ordinary house key and started walkin out the airport, lissa didn't hold the key. she let it settle in the palm of her hand like a dandelion wish. she followed morgan's thin-awesome figure, never lookin away from him. they took the regular route cross the river into town, sayin little as they shared a joint with their eyes holdin each other. morgan stopped twice for lissa to explore new boutiques in her neighborhood, but she didn't have any money. he stood in the front of the shop with his shoulders in a feigned academic slump, hands in his pockets, and scattered grey hairs ticklin his upper lip, so that he'ld run his tongue roun every so often to put his moustache back inplace. lissa ran to him with a lilac dress. morgan raised one eyebrow as he tilted his head just a little to the left, so she would know he wasn't actually lookin at her. at the house lissa had never seen before, morgan tried to carry her over the threshhold. but there were two doors, lissa was fairly heavy and morgan was tired. she finally got in with one leg in morgan's arms and the other dangling awkwardly from her hip. they were home. a mustard green colonial house divided into apartments, the room narrowed into a kitchen. a latched door led to a city garden. morgan's desk blocked the french window. twin beds, side by side, took half the room. lissa sat on one waitin for morgan to say somethin to her, to catch her up in his arms 'n ravish her, or just lay 'n caress. morgan gazed starkly thru her and fastened himself to an old easy chair to watch the news. lissa felt the three weeks without him pass in front of her on the tv screen… somethin about the local weather forecast…

The alarm was tingling, but all Lissa knew was that a noise was in the way, in the way. She sensed her eyes open and daylight. She hit the bed with her hands in fixed fists, groanin, "There must be more than that. There's gotta be more". Her toes were still twitchin to Dolphy's sax, Lissa had to laugh at herself and curled into ago slowly.

the snows had trapped the town that winter, but lissa and morgan were wrapped/ sweet roun each other, when a man person knocked on their outside door. they stopped/ started. morgan still, movin, in side her, listenin for a name, lissa felt 'n watched him doin everything at once….

Lissa seemed to be peaceful as she slept. Mingus and Dolphy did soft pirouettes on her back. Ishmael's neo-hoodoo was slinkin from her desk thru her quilt and roun her fingertips. The sun was a quiet bright. Liss was catchin up on missed sleep, but she was awake.

wow! the kids were havin a gooood time, but one ninety-beige one was jabberin bout his cashmere coat. lissa was chaperone, so she went to look for it 'n she wasn't at the door when the cops came to turn the party out. she got the message, tho, and began shufflin the dancers to the foyer. a tall fella refused to leave, beboppin with sly in the back of the room. lissa put her hands on her hips 'n strode over, to pause as morgan wisked her under, talkin bout this party they 'ld have for their son one day… let's go to mexico 'n get married, huh, lissa… lissa, sometimes i'm goin to ask you to do things that you don't understand, things that might hurt you, lissa, i need you to do those things…things that might hurt you, lissa, let's go…

The weight of the quilt was annoyin her in this daysleep. Lissa tossed, throwin one thigh over the other. Breathin lethargically, with the newly-felt pasts she had overlooked. She found a warm place under her pillow for her hands. She stretchedout, takin a cursory account of the black phone by the side of the bed. Then, inspite of herself the tremors by the ocean ran across her.

morgan was under the cliff at big sur, in the wet sand, alone. the earth was shakin. he didn't turn around to see if she got over the boulders. the earth was shakin 'n he stood lookin in the ocean. the fires on the other side of the bay shivered closer, but morgan was with the ocean. silence creeped on them and he turned innocently with his hand reachin out for her. she cried with morgan, the ocean, the fires til twilight, when they all mingled incognito…

She couldn't sleep. That was that. Lissa pumped herself out of the bed over to the kitchen. She pummeled the dishrack for the top to the coffee pot. The yellow coffee pot she had always wanted. Now, she had it and couldn't find the top. Lissa vehemently decided to have chicory in her coffee today. Liss was gonna treat herself good 'n right if Morgan wouldn't.

Lissa lit the front burner. Sat still, catchin, Morgan's echoes.

lissa that's silly, you know, to shelve me for some arbitrary reason. to do us in cause you think it's time. lissa, you can't live life like that, touch 'n go. lissa tensed every shred of her body, realizin that morgan was tellin her she couldn't cut him loose. morgan had to go. morgan had to go. morgan had to go. morgan kept drivin down the freeway, kept talkin. lissa i know it's silly cause i've done that. lissa was full, brimmin, and inarticulate.she shut herself up, wantin him to be with her for a while. knowin better. she took his honesty about what he had done as empirical fact. Lissa lookedout the window at the neon signs, 'motel', flashin. morgan sent his hand over her knee sayin, softly/clearly, lissa, i've shelved you any number of times, haven't I ?

The yellow enamel coffe pot was stainin, brown, sputterin. The gas fire was jumpin. Lissa leaped to the stove with a dishrag in her hand complanin about the chicory she had messed up, the last she had. As she wiped the spilled coffee from the burner, Lissa felt her fingers singe. The phone rang. Then, rang again. Lissa leaned over, her fingers on fire. " Hey Lissa, it's me. Morgan".

DARK ROOMS

The following three short essays describe Shange's experience with psychoanalysis. After the success of *for colored girls*, she struggled with bipolar disorder, depression, anxiety, and drug addiction. Her mental health challenges continued for decades, and she was remarkably open about them and diligent in seeking help through psychoanalysis and traditional talk therapy. Characteristically, Shange's complicated emotional landscape is rendered with tenderness and beauty, which is particularly important given our collective recognition of the importance of mental health care. In this, too, Shange was ahead of her time.

The Dark Room

When "For colored girls . . ." was at the height of its controversy/ popularity, I found myself wearing very dark glasses and large hats so that folks wouldn't recognize me. I couldn't ride elevators, up or down. If someone figured out who I was, I calmly stated that I was frequently mistaken for 'her'. I'd had other occasions in my life, when I was the only African-American in a class or banished to the countryside that my family loved so much, when I'd been known to disassociate, to refer to myself in the third person. Then, I was 'Paulette'. Now, Ntozake repeating the pattern of the girl I'd gleefully left behind. This was very troubling. I'd just become who I was and was in the frenzied act of 'disappearing' me. Now, I confess to discovering many, many roads to oblivion, but I rarely recounted these episodes with warmth or a sense of well-being. So, I did what I thought troubled writers did, I went to my producer, Joseph Papp, to seek counsel. To my alarm, Joe recommended against analysis or other therapies, "because, then, my writers can't write anymore'. Well, writing I was, living I was, living I was not, even though I wasn't always a strong supporter of my own perceptions. The ability to write in isolation for hours about anything and enjoy it is a gift, but it is not life. Even, I knew this. I could not hide in a dance studio, either. My presence was unavoidable , yet unbearable.

Off to find a shrink , I went. I was looking for a wizard, some magic, some chant, or breath that might make being me something to look forward to in the morning. I have the capacity to sleep for four days at a time, if I am so inclined. At one point I refused to get up and live my life among the living because my dreamlife was so much more interesting. Wizards I did not find. I did find that finding the right shrink/ analyst is as important a decision as finding a soul-mate. Anyway, to make a long story less long, I've been involved with over seven mental health care workers in the last twenty years. The overwhelming period of time spent with three: one psychiatrist, and two analysts. I lost one analyst to the Emergency Room which he saw as a challenge. Four years of quasi-sane mourning passed before I was able to seek out another with whom I have been working for nearly a decade.

N.Shange

The Angriest Patient

With his help and astounding patience, I have lost my title as "the angriest patient ever encountered during all my years of practice" to become the 1991–93 Heavyweight Poetry champion of 'The World", as you see, a much healthier management of violent proclivities. In all seriousness I've learned to feel what I see. What I've been blessed to conjure in words is no longer two steps removed; my body is not a hindrance to my spirit, but a manifestation of it. I am still crazy, but not so afraid with that part of me. I can even tell jokes to my 'crazy' person and realize that to be one of my saner moments.

I've dressed up as a 'guinea girl", the ones who stole all the basketball players at my school just to prove that I could be one. That was a session to remember. I've felt what I swear to be electricity in my body. I've known the ocean and intense heat. All this actually while on the couch. Talk about terrified. Try being the Atlantic Ocean all by yourself in an eight by twelve room with ancient fertility statues placed like buoys on what I guess I took to be signs of land ahead. I don't know to this day. I've talked in tongues. I've only been able to do some sessions in Spanish, or a mixture of French and Portuguese. I don't know why. I know that is all that would come out. Sometimes, I sleep. Other times, Paulette speaks. Her voice is different from mine as Zaki. Sometimes, I want to knock her out, but since we can only use language as a tool or weapon or doll or whatever I need, I learned at least to talk to her, if I am not wildly gesticulating in some recollection of a dream; legs flying, arms of a flamenco dancer, long Balanchine neck I could never actualize outside my 'dark room' where things, me, memories float out of syllables and become benign or empowering, as they must because they are never without meaning.

Joe, my 'Art-Daddy' as I called him was wrong about one thing, not many, but one. Psychoanalysis has made me a finer writer, a fuller person and a funnier one to be sure. I've found characters I would literally shun to be beauteous. I've been able to take on the persona of someone puzzling to me with no need, not a desperate one, to figure her out. I have/ am plumbing the primordial depths of me, not without trepidation, but with a magic I thought I could pick up somewhere in the night. My analyst's Anthony Molino. He's a poet. He lives in Italy and like a guardian spirit, with me.

Ntozake Shange
10-9-97
Houston, TX

The Couch

Though long before I'd come to know myself as 'Ntozake' or, a writer, I had wanted to be a psychiatrist. This no doubt had something to do with my parents' involvement with hospitals, sick people, poor black people, and me, following along to wards, living rooms, boarding houses, examination rooms, and dark rooms where X-rays were read or where violently mentally disturbed folks were sequestered. My father as a surgeon, excised with delicacy what was malignant, diseased, out of tune with the body, while my mother, as I understood it, assisted individuals or families to get in tune with society as a whole, to make 'living' work for them as opposed to against them without necessarily challenging anything about the world as we know it. Both these approaches left me wanting. What if what was wrong couldn't be seen or couldn't be excised? What if life as some soul knew it wasn't worth living without some violent catharsis? I credited Toussaint L'Ouverture and Dessalines, Tubman and Anthony with what ever legitimacy I had, and they were not the sort who 'fit' in. I'd seen "Snakepit", in all its simplified black and white depiction of living in our world with a pained contorted mind and spirit. I was caught somewhere in between the institution and slavery and the loose cells of The Bastille. Surely, there is some where more peaceful than The ER or the Settlement house. My ultimate answer was the analyst's couch, but before that I had to learn to live with myself madly for a while longer.

I saw things. I was not delusional or schizophrenic, I apparently could reach areas of my unconscious as a child that never left me which turned out to be as much a burden as a blessing. I had visions. I wasn't playing. I was laying on the grass or upside a great tree, listening and seeing historical figures, artists, people I didn't know dancing with me, taking me to salons in Paris or roadhouse in Alabama. I was daydreaming, I imagine, but I never diminished those episodes to anything less than my 'real life.' That's why journalists have such a hard time fact-checking stories on or about me. I will tell them an anecdote which is impossible to chart in any methodology. They ask me did something happen and I'll probably say 'yes' because I remember my dreams, both night and day, as authentically as I experience my daily life. Before I started menstruating, this issue of truth was very much alive. What I believed or felt I could not prove to anybody in a reasoned fashion. That's why I knew instinctively that I should not argue or debate because at, a certain point I, knew my 'truth' was simply mine and not a collectively recognized reality. Yet it could not be a lie because I thought/felt it. The only place I know where anybody else believes this is the psychoanalyst's office. There, it is enough to paraphrase Marie Cardenal to find 'the words to say it'.

That's why I dance. I can't always find the 'words' to say it. I've come to believe there are words as we know them for some things; that the body has a grammar for these constructs which are not beyond articulation, but of another terrain. I'm becoming trans-lingual so that I may speak myself. Maybe I was a passionate gopi girl at Krishna's feet, I don't know, I do know that my body extorts from me what hangs silent in the air. That's why psychopharmocology can only take me so far. I need my body to talk to me. My analyst watches all these gestures of mind and body, listens as closely to my muscle burns or prone attitude turns as my dreams.

Most of my characters have visions and dreams with which some of you are acquainted. Bessie Smith and Billie Holiday visit Sassafrass.[1] Indigo speaks with the spirits of the moon and the Ancestors. Everybody, even, The Magician, in "Spell#7" opens their interior world to the whole of the audience, thought no one else in the scene itself is aware of Allega brushing her hair or Maxine

1 This is in reference to Shange's 1982 novel *Sassafrass, Cypress & Indigo.*

collecting gold chains that bound her in resistations of The Middle Passage. Liliane, actually, has an analyst. No. He's not my analyst, he is Lili's. Sean, the debonair photographer in "A Photograph: Lovers-in-Motion" needed an analyst. I didn't give him one. I let him suffer. He didn't have visions, couldn't talk to spirits, shoot the breeze with his own myths, memory weighed too heavily. An example is simply that my father hadda monkey/ he liked better than me", from the mouth of a grown man who is still that little boy. Did that 'happen' to me? Not in the material world/. But, living with my being i know now that if I 'know' about it, it happened to me, belongs to me now. I was not here during The French Revolution, but I can describe Marat's bath and exude Charlotte Corday's[1] rage and naivete. Just as I named Crack Annie's daughter, Berneatha in honor of Hansberry's Beneatha.[2] There is no doubt in my mind that Walter Lee woulda smoked everything in that house away and pledged the money to Beneatha's African boyfriend to get himself in on some wild Dallas-Chicago-Lagos drug deal. Was I conscious of this? No. Can I discuss all this eccentric personal peculiarity now? Yes. Without heart palpitations? Yes. Without clammy palms? Yes. Without blinking an eye? No. All of this is very precious. I must keep my eye on my self/s. I've learned this on a yearly, hour by hour disciplined manner. It was not easy. I was not happy. I was not always careful. It costs a lot. What do I get in the end? Do I get better? How will I know when I get there? I could get coy. Answer, Beckett knew what detained Godot, but we don't know that. I know I don't know that. Anyway, I have a hard time explicating "le texte'. The characters never die. The stories never end for me. That's why like Rapunzel I go unravel my loose ends with my psychoanalyst. Nothing is wrong. No one else knows. A pin

1 Marie-Anne Charlotte de Corday killed Jacobin leader Jean-Paul Marat during the French Revolution. Though she was a revolutionary she opposed the more radical elements of Marat's writing. Corday was executed by guillotine for her crime.

2 Beneatha Younger is a character in Lorraine Hansberry's play *A Raisin in the Sun*.

could drop, but usually what's falling away is not so piercing, not so singular, only the shreds of living I must make space for somewhere in myself/s who is not only the writer and, therefore cannot continue to find herself whole solely on blank pages.

One of Simon Bolivar's[1] houses was hexagonal, seated on a cliff in such a way that from any point, he could feel/ see land and peoples who would be free. When I lie nestled on the couch in the room of no color and all colors, I am in that house. I am on that cliff. I am one of those people.

Ntozake Shange
© 12.21.97.
Houston, TX

1 Nineteenth-century Venezuelan military and political leader popularly known as the liberator of Latin America

PLAYS

Although Shange's post–*for colored girls* publications were overwhelmingly poetry and fiction, she continued to write plays and experiment with combinations of theater and performance poetry. Included here are five plays of Shange's, the one-act *Mother Courage and Yvette*; *Daddy Says*, which is a tender, grief-soaked conversation between two girls whose mother has died; *Guess What?*; and an excerpt from an incomplete play that takes place at a 1970s Puerto Rican party in New York. The two works that follow are longer: *The Lizard Series* (though untitled, it is described this way in Shange's papers), which follows three generations of a family of musicians who are called to create despite the constraints of a Jim Crow society; and finally *Layla's Dream*, which was performed at the University of Florida in 2003, where Shange served as a faculty member from

2002 to 2006. *Layla's Dream* is a fugue-like performance of the interior experiences of a young Black woman finding herself in the thick of messages from ancestors and spirit guides. Readers should be mindful that, as with her groundbreaking play, *for colored girls*, *Layla's Dream* includes depictions of sexual violence and trauma.

Mother Courage and Yvette

From *Mother Courage*, 1979[1]

YVETTE

Who say I'm sick, ce n'est pas vrai; it's a damned lie.

MOTHER COURAGE

Everybody from here to New Orleans says so.

YVETTE

They are all lying dogs. I'm beside myself. I just don't know what to do now. They all stay away from me like I was a wounded heifer layin too long in the sun; all on account of those lies. Merde. Sacre Dieu, why should I even mend my bonnet?

(she throws the hat down)

That's why I need a little drink in the morning- I never usedta, but now round my eyes those little wrinkles- it don't matter. In the 9th Cavalry every man jack of em knows me. I should have stayed home in Louisiana after my first love jilted me. But pride ain't for the likes of me...if we can't put up with a niggah's shit, we're through, fini, n'est-ce pas?

MOTHER COURAGE

Don't start in with that stuff, and don't commence the tale of your Peter in fronta my virgin daughter.

YVETTE

Non. Perhaps it is time for her to know. It'll save her from the cruelties of love.

---

1 This work was inspired by Bertólt Brecht's 1939 play, *Mother Courage and Her Children*. Whereas Brecht's work was set during the European Thirty Years' War of the seventeenth century, Shange's work focuses on Yvette's memories of a Civil War love affair.

MOTHER COURAGE

Can't nothing save em.

YVETTE

I feel better when I talk abt it. It all began in glorious new orleans/ if I hadnt met him there/ I wdnt be sittin here in texas/ such a bronze tangle…

of a Yankee freedman, he was the Army Cook, can you imagine, but skinny. Katie, keep an eye out for them skinny ones. But I didn't think but how skinny he was or that he had another girl up north, and they all callt him Pete the Pipe, cause he didn't never take that thing out his mouth, even when he was- la la – doin it.

(YVETTE sings the song of fraternization)

i waz just a yng thing
when the union boys came marchin
laid aside the swords & rifles
took my hand wit a fine smile

after fat tuesday's jamboree
low-down music & home made whiskey
the union boys dressed up so right
cdnt anybody make em out that lousiana nite
we ran wit em thru the bayous
neath spanish moss & starlight
toutes les nuits j'etais avec lui (2X)

there were so many northern boys
& mine worked over a blazin fire
I cdnt bare him in the daylight
but with darkness I waz driven by desire
j'etais avec lui toutes les nuits

magnolias reached up toward the sun
when my first sadness lemme know it'd come
the union boys dressed up awright
& marched to the west/ clean outta sight
the conqueror/ the enemy/ my lover
marched on away without me
j'etais avec lue touted les nuits

Well. I went right on after him from Texas to New Mexico territory, but I never found him. Jamais trouve, jamais lui trouvé. That's five years ago awready.

(YVETTE goes behind wagon with an unsteady gait)

MOTHER COURAGE

Yvette, your hat.

YVETTE

Give it to somebody- anybody who wants it.

MOTHER COURAGE

See there/ katie, don't take up wit no soldiers.
love is mighty powerful/ now take heed to what i'm saying…

Daddy Says: A Play

Scene I

(The scene opens with the two girls, LUCIE-MARIE and ANNIE-SHARON, practicing rope tricks and tie-down roping in their bedroom, which is decorated with rodeo and riding paraphernalia. There are lots of portraits of their mother in riding gear and rows of trophy belts that she won covering the walls. There is a large bed, a window and a saddle on a sawhorse. The doorway opens to a stairway which leads to the kitchen which is also a living room. It should be adequate but a little worn)

LUCIE-MARIE: Ain't that the way to do it?

ANNIE-SHARON: Well, I taught you, so you oughtta know whatchu doin' by now…

LUCIE-MARIE: Mama showed you everythin' you think you know/ & every single
thin' you call yo'self teachin' me/ so there…

ANNIE-SHARON: You know I don' like discussin' Mama/ so cut it out, ya hear me.
This bein' the day she died and all…

LUCIE-MARIE: By the time she was yo' age, she was awready a champion
(*pronounced "champeen."*) Whatchu call yo'self, since ya learnt how to walk, talk,
crawl 'n' rope all single-handed like/ a new born heifer or somethin'?

ANNIE-SHARON: I call myself me, okay? 'sides I am a champion.

LUCIE-MARIE: Naw ya ain't. Ya jus' won some first prizes/ bein' a champion means

ya win everythin' there is to win/ more 'n' a few times/ likes season after season & year
after year/ like Mama/ Twanda Rochelle Johnson/ that's my mama's name.

ANNIE-SHARON: Waz yo' mama's name.

LUCIE-MARIE: Yeah. You right abt Mama. (*Shifts mood*) Ya know what Lincoln
Maceo tol' me?

ANNIE-SHARON: Nope.

LUCIE-MARIE: He say that it gets up in there/ and ya getta baby.

ANNIE-SHARON: No lie.

LUCIE-MARIE: But if it's wiggly & squiggly lookin'... like Mavis' li'l boy...

ANNIE-SHARON: Uh humph. All cush and curled up...

LUCIE-MARIE: Well, how could it get up anywhere?

ANNIE-SHARON: Mother Dear say it don't matter how/ it ain't s'posed to git nowhere/
sides where all it gonna go/ or are you fixin' to let me in on that?

LUCIE-MARIE: Up in here somewhere. (*Feeling her tummy.*)

ANNIE-SHARON: Girl, it cain't possibly get all up in there.

LUCIE-MARIE: Yeah it do. (*She gets up & they start to measure the lengths of rope
against the inches from their pelvis' to their navels.*) See heah...Now look at that. (*Sees it's shorter.*)

ANNIE-SHARON: See, it'd have to be this big.

LUCIE-MARIE: That cain't be. Don't nobody want nothin' <u>that</u> big up in there!

ANNIE-SHARON: Well, I don' get how that's gonna happen. We jus' said whatever
Them li'l dicks is they still li'l ol' squiggly wiggly things.

LUCIE-MARIE: Look like covered up snakes. (*Laughing.*)

ANNIE-SHARON: But they's all kinda snakes.

LUCIE-MARIE: Like Diamondbacks, right?

ANNIE-SHARON: Ya leave him outta this, heah. He don't talk to me 'bout stuff like this.

LUCIE-MARIE: But Mama wda tol' us, huh? Whatchu think?

ANNIE-SHARON: Whatchu mean? Don' talk bout Mama. I don' wanna talk bout her.
See you jus' cain't remember the way I do.

LUCIE-MARIE: But Annie-Sharon…

ANNIE-SHARON: I don' wanna talk bout her. (*Goes over to the wall where there are all kinds of prize winning buckles from rodeo races.*) Ya think she rides wit us when we race? (*Takes one belt down & wraps it around herself.*)

LUCIE-MARIE: Ya know Daddy don' like talk like that/ he say "let the dead rest" he say.

ANNIE-SHARON: I know what "he say"/ I don' know what make me think somethin' simpleminded like that.

LUCIE-MARIE: See, it's only Mama could tell us all we need to know/ so we could/ oh be beautiful/ you know like Linda Beauville or Tootsie Woo/ they Mama's do they hair up wit them perms 'n' stuff/ put that no chippin' polish on they nails/ fringes on they rodeo git-ups/ ya know make pies 'n' do for when they entertain/ that's what they Mama's do/ that's what our Mama wd be doin' too/.

ANNIE-SHARON: Well, we ain't got one. (*Throws belt across the room.*)

LUCIE-MARIE: You cain't do that/ Look whatchu did wit Mama's prize. (*Runs to pick up the belt.*)

ANNIE-SHARON: It ain't nothin' but a damned piece of raw hide wit some silver on it/ that ain't yo' Mama, fool/ that a symbol/ that's how she died/ that's how come she died/ broncbustin'/ everybody in the world knows cain't no woman in her right mind be no bronc-buster/ oh no/ but not your growed up Mama/ she gonn show the world what all she could do/ she the virgin mary in a cowboy hat/ cain't no wild thing buck/ she dead/ trampled for her living/ trampled to death like so much hog feed/ tryin' to prove she more powerful than a STALLIONNN/ that's yo' precious Mama/ who's gonna tell ya how to be a woman/ tell you whatchu need to know/ like she could grow nails on a cowgirl's hands/ all you need to know/ that's some dream ya got/.

LUCIE-MARIE: Don'tchu talk like that/ you take all them things back/ heifer. (*Lunges at her sister.*) Mama was wonderful/ don'tchu say no mo' mean things bout my mother.

ANNIE-SHARON: I ain't said nothin' but you ain't got one/ you aint't got no mother more 'n' I do/ she cared mo' bout them damn animals than us.

LUCIE-MARIE: STOP IT! I'm tellin' you/ She was a great bronc-buster…

ANNIE-SHARON: Daddy say bronc-bustin' ain't ladylike.

LUCIE-MARIE: What he know bout it? He a big ol' man.

ANNIE-SHARON: You think she knew somethin' bout it? Huh? (*Fighting over belt intensely*)

LUCIE-MARIE: Don't say nothin' else bout Mommy/ Don't/ don't. (*Starts crying & shoving.*)

TDB: What's that in yo' hands? (*Takes belt & slaps her.*) I tol' you to let what's past be past/ If I said it once I said it ten hundred times/ & today of all days.

ANNIE-SHARON: But Daddy, we was jus' lookin'.

TDB: Ya don' look wit your hands.

LUCIE-MARIE: Daddy, please, just this one time/ tell us somethin' bout Mama.

TDB: She died from bronco-bustin'/ tryin' to be more a man than a man/ that's all/ now put these things back/ & stop all this noise/ of all the damned days to ride.

LUCIE-MARIE: Daddy/ Please listen to me/ Daddy, did you love her? What was she like when she acted like a girl?/ Daddy/ not when she acted like a boy/ what was she like? Daddy, I've gotta know somethin' sides she died/ Daddy, did you think she was pretty?/ you usedta say I looked like her/ Do you think I'm pretty/ Daddy?/ please/please tell me.

ANNIE-SHARON: Leave him alone Lucie/ Leave everybody alone/ ya heah.

TDB: Yeah/ listen to yo' sister/ What's in the past is in the past.

LUCIE-MARIE: But I look like her & I ain't in the past/ Daddy/ Please Daddy/ I wanna be just like her/ & oh I don't know…

ANNIE-SHARON: Lucie/ why are you talkin' all this mess? Cain't you see Daddy ain't up to this/ why you gonna put us through all this heah?

LUCIE-MARIE: You shut up/ I'm talkin' to my father.

ANNIE-SHARON: And he ain't mine too/ I ain't got no mama either/ but you gonna ruin my daddy's life talkin' 'bout how you gonna be jus' like her/ look what she did to Daddy/ he cain't hardly talk 'bout nothin' when somethin' brings her to mind/ you wanna take my Daddy 'way too/ you actual mo' dumb than I though you was.

LUCIE-MARIE: I ain't dumb/ I jus' wanna heah some mo' 'bout Mommy/ I gotta right/ I'm her girl.

ANNIE-SHARON: And whatchu think I am, some kinda she-goat?

TDB: Lucie-Marie/ Annie-Sharon/ Hush all this quarrelin'/ Stop now, I guess/ I ain't been handlin' this like I oughtta. (*Takes two belts from the wall. Wraps one around each child.*) See, yo' mama & me/ Well/ we was jus' kids'/ she was the prettiest li'l ol' thing/ look jus' like you.

LUCIE-MARIE: See/ I tol' ya/ I look jus' like her.

TDB: Most times in the summer/ when the sun wd getta settin'/ wild-like/ all red & orange wit magnolias & cypress reachin' up thru them clouds that be hangin' from the sky like cotton candy 'n' the grass smellin' ripe like/ times like that/ yo' mama 'n' me/ we'd jump on Masaya/ that's that mare Twanda set so much store by/ we'd climb up on Masaya/ & walk her thru them woods past the corral/ walk her real slow/ 'til we cd hear most everythin' there was to hear/ & then she/ Twanda wd sing/ to me/ some ol' somethin' she made up in her head/ jus' sing to me...then alla sudden she'd kick up, & off we went duckin' branches/ jumpin' fences/ damn fool/gal/ 'most run us into the off we went duckin' branches/ jumpin' fences/ damn fool gal/ 'most run us into the swamp/ Lawd, I'll never forget/ fearin' Masaya was fallin' I was fallin'/ Twanda was leanin' here & then thisaway/ & here come the mud up my pants legs & I cdn't tell if yo' mama was under the horse or down in there smotherin' to death in the mud/ good jesus, that woman didn't have no kinda sense/ justa singin'/ & here we goin' right down offa this animal into the center of the earth/ humph/ that was somethin'/ I'm tellin' ya/ her cheekbones come way up like Cherokees/ real high & glowin' brown/ but—but, ain't no way to get 'round it...Both of ya favor her/ from time to time/ always on this day...

ANNIE-SHARON: How Daddy?

TDB: Right there by yo' eyes/ I reckon/ Annie/ but Lucie-Marie's carryin' her mother's mouth...yep/ y'all is Twanda's daughters/ that's for sho'/ Daddy's roughtough ridin' cutiepies/ right?

Guess What?[1]

CHARACTERS

MILAGROS -successful writer, actualized feminist single mother frustrated, trying to juggle career, motherhood and teaching alone.

GABRIEL_ THIRTY SOMETHING BLACK MAN , WELL EDUCATED sophisticated manipulative deceitful

ACT ONE

A well appointed room leading to a terrace where Joy, Suzette, and Liz are dancing all in Halloween costumes . In the room on the bed is Milagros playing a game of solitaire while keeping up with the rhythm of a classic Celia Cruz salsa. Around the corner of rear door a handsome black man, GABRIEL. PEEKS IN AT Milagros. he approaches her. He has on a broad brim felt hat and a linen suit. Milagros is in black silk gathered dress with pink organza flowers.

GABRIEL
TU HABLAS INGLES?

MILAGROS
Why wdnt i speak english ?

GABRIEL
Well the whole house is filled with people speaking Spanish

MILAGROS
Why wdnt they , They are Puerto Rican like me .

---

1 This is the first act of an unfinished play. Though not a complete work, it is of interest because it is an example of Shange's interest in the African diaspora in the Hispanophone world that is also evident in several of her novels. Note that Shange's original papers include a full cast list but it has been amended here to include only characters who appear in the act.

GABRIEL
Oh tu puedes hablar conmigo. That is about as far as my Spanish will get me

MILAGROS
Well that's a start

GABRIEL
By the way what is yr name

MILAGROS
Milagros y tu?

GABRIEL
Me llamo GABRIEL, BUENO

MILAGROS
Good. Who are you sposed to be ? I dont recognize any' body i know abt

GABRIEL
Why Elton John. How cd you miss it?

MILAGROS
I DON'T KNOW WHAT HE LOOKS LIKE

GABIREL
Oh my goodness another woman of color who has blacked out America

MILAGROS
it is where i live right now it is not a settled state. i live in boriquen, soy jibarita linda

GABRIEL
NOW YOU LOST ME. I LIKE IT BUT I AM LOST

MILAGROS
(slyly) Maybe a bit bewildered, but not lost. all i said is what you meant to say to me. THAT I AM TOO PRETTY TO BE playing cards all by myself

GABRIEL
But who are you sposed to be,. you never said

MILAGROS
Carmen of course (takes red rose off the bed and puts it between her teeth then removes it) now you get it ?

GABRIEL
You DIDNT have to dress up to be irresistible

MILAGROS
Aw c'mon now

GABRIEL
Now i think you put a spell on me. C'mon over here. (they move [...] surreptitiously to a corner of the room . Gabriel takes out a small bag of cocaine, prepares it with a straw and offers some)

MILAGROS
My god yr generoso a generous soul if i do say so myself
I WONT TAKE MUCH GABRIEL

GABRIEL
Go ahead i can always get more

MILAGROS
why are you the dope man

GABRIEL
OH NO YOU'VE GOT ME ALL WRONG THERE. I AM IN THE MUSIC INDUSTRY. AS A MATTER of fact I am vice president of YOU GOT IT DAWG records so dont worryabt me

MILAGROS
wow. i don't think i have ever heard of them

GABRIEL
YOU KNOW i almost forgot yr not from here

MILAGROS
i didn't mean that PERSONALLY .

GABRIEL
No it's just that folks don't take hiphop or house music seriously

MILAGROS
i actually listen to old salsa or new jazz

GABRIEL
like sonora matancera, bene more, celia cruz? i like ruben blades and albita

MILAGROS
listen to you how did you find a taino like me

GABRIEL
what is a taino i never heard that word

MILAGROS
we are the original inhabitants of what you call puerto rico and we call boriquen the spanish didn't kill us all

GABRIEL
i see

MILAGROS
What do you see but an episode of genocide

GABRIEL
It's just my great grandfather was a buffalo soldier

MILAGROS
oh so yr forebears killed native americans on purpose as part of Manifest Destiny poor thing a descendant of murderers erasing my people

GABRIEL
how did you know abt them hardly anybody knows abt them

GROS
Africana studies my friend

GABRIEL
Jesus of all the women to run into

MILAGROS
Whats this you wanta woman whoknownothing abt anything?

GABRIEL
oh huh you got mr wrong again i love that you are on top of yr game

MILAGROS
what game?

GABRIEL
not from the business world i see

MILAGROS (LAUGHS)
oh no gracias a dios not from the business world

GABRIEL
well what world are you from

MILAGROS
i make up things for a living i am a writer you know fiction

GABRIEL
yr notthe Milagros Fernandez, Milagros daisy fernandez, who wrote east 174th street, sanjuan, the bronx

MILAGROS
si negro guapo soy yo that's me

GABRIEL
that was on the TIMES best seller list for months i love you I mean yr work

MILAGROS
Oh my goodness thank you very much

GABRIEL
we've gotta go celebrate

MILAGROS
what are we gonna celebrate

GABRIEL
The coming together of two great minds but you don't actually look puerto rican yr a bit dark

MILAGROS
tainos are dark but i must confess a lil african slipped in somewhere

GABRIEL
i thought a sistah lurked in there somewhere
(THEY SHARE SOME MORE COCAINE)

MILAGROS
you cd say that
But before we go anywhere i have to know if you can dance!
la india is singing something very fast salsa gabriel and milagros do a startlingly good dance LOTS OF TURNS AND CHANGING OF HANDS)

MILAGROS
Where did you learn how to dance like that?

GABRIEL
i am a niggah with passport and wanderlust (They start to share the cocaine again) i been to columbia, venezuela, panama, honduras

MILAGROS
& not puerto rico ?

GABRIEL
too close and it's not cuba

MILAGROS
well i can forgive that a lil
i thought we were going some where

GABRIEL
we are . get yr things together. we're going to this after hours place i know that' fabulous

MILAGROS
sounds exciting , , , is it safe?

GABRIEL
yr always safe with me (they move to go BLACKOUT)

The Lizard Series[1]

CHARACTERS[2]

MASSIE ROUGHEN: A dapper older man with vivid memories of King Oliver, Bessie and Mamie Smith, Blind Lemon Jefferson, Robert Johnson, Bennie Moten, Bix Beiderbecke, Sidney Bechet, and Jelly Roll Morton. Massie plays the slide trombone, sings a bit, and can be cajoled to do a mean soft-shoe.

WINONA ROUGHEN-PIERRE: Elegant but streetwise daughter of MASSIE, who sang for a bit with big bands like Duke Ellington[3], Basie, Fletcher Henderson, Louis Prima and will return to work with Cal Tjader, Bill Evans, and Thad Jones. She is the mother of CLIFF, NATE, and BLAISE ROUGHEN-PIERRE.

CLIFF ROUGHEN-PIERRE: Brilliant, restless, saxophonist son of WINONA and TEDDY PIERRE, grandson of MASSIE ROUGHEN, who's showing signs of political and cultural alienation manifest in music of Eric Dolphy, Charles Mingus, Thelonious Monk. In his late teens, like Miles Davis, CLIFF PIERRE will run away to study and play with John Coltrane, Archie Shepp, Albert Ayler and Sun-Ra.

---

1 In Shange's papers, this play is filed under "The Lizard Series," but it is noted that the play was not titled.

2 This list of characters printed as it appears in Shange's papers is incomplete. Several others that are missing: historic figure W. C. Handy and fictional characters such as "Cissie," "Sweet Spady," "Leticia," "J.T.," and characters identified by their roles in the community, such as "Tavernier," "White Guy," and "Black Gambler."

3 Edward Kennedy "Duke" Ellington (1899–1974) was a jazz pianist, composer, and bandleader.

NATE ROUGHEN-PIERRE: Younger brother of CLIFF who is not as intellectual but a gifted electric guitar player who adores Chicago blues and the Dick Clark show. He is hot-tempered, his parents try to dissuade him from music because they're afraid he'll lose his life.

BLAISE ROUGHEN-PIERRE: Spunky, compassionate sister between CLIFF and NATE, who plays piano and sings in various styles, searching for her own. She turns to Billie Holiday, Lambert Hendricks, Ross, Peter, Paul and Mary, Edith Piaf, and Gloria Lynne until she realizes what she's reaching for is somewhere in the midst of Betty Carter, Abbey Lincoln and Odetta.

TEDDY PIERRE: Former trumpet player with emerging be-bop groups post WWII, burned by the fires of segregation and drugs one too many times. He is now an insurance salesman delighted that his times with Charlie Parker, Monk, Stan Getz, Brubeck, and Horace Silver are in the past.

ACT ONE

FADE IN:
EXT. TEDDY AND WINONA PIERRE'S YARD
-- MID-AFTERNOON

We hear conga drums and a field holler which are incongruous with the sight of this tidy suburban cottage. BLAISE is playing the drums. MASSIE ROUGHEN, her grandfather, is belting the holler and adding other rhythmic textures as he dances. Sounds of a tenor horn and electric guitar, pull us up to the porch where CLIFF, tenor, and NATE, electric guitar, are improvising with the others. They are enjoying 'trading eights' with each other. The music takes on a frenzied quality and gets louder as MASSIE'S steps become more intricate.

INT. WINONA'S KITCHEN

WINONA PIERRE, MASSIE'S daughter and mother of BLAISE, CLIFF, and NATE, is at the sink washing exotic lettuce greens against the tempo of the raucous music she's hearing. Finally she tears the bunch of greens in her hands to shred and it flies all over. Exasperated, WINONA storms out of the kitchen to the study where TEDDY PIERRE, her husband, is enjoying the music, smiling and tapping his foot.

TITLES BEGIN OVER:

WINONA
(muttering)
I have never been able to stop this music. All the time this music. Maybe I put it in the food and don't know it. Lord, maybe it's in my genes and I can't help it, but I'm gonna hear myself today. I know that. I'm gonna hear my voice, somehow, somewhere 'round here.

CUT TO

INT.

WINONA walks about the house haphazardly straightening things or picking them up and throwing them down. She is getting more and more frustrated until she suddenly swings the back door open and screams:

QUICK CUT TO

EXT. THE PIERRE'S YARD

WINONA

Awright. That's a take!

The itinerant band winds down. They're all congratulating each other and slapping five.

BLAISE

Wow, Mama, I didn't know you were even listening.

WINONA

Was I listening? I couldn't help but listen!

NATE

(teasingly)

Aw, lookout. Mama's gettin' down.

WINONA

(to Massie)

Papa, this is your doin'. Always talkin' up music; King Oliver,[1] oh, the black folks could sing. Play those horns. Louis Armstrong.[2] Coltrane![3]

The children start to come in under her diatribe, quietly and unobtrusively.

---

1 Joseph Nathan "King" Oliver (1881–1938) was a cornet player and jazz pioneer from Louisiana.

2 Louis Armstrong (1901–1971) was an influential jazz trumpeter.

3 John Coltrane (1926–1967) was a distinguished jazz composer and saxophonist.

WINONA

Do you all believe a song and
a dance put food in your
mouth. All the things you
could do with yourselves. To
make something of yourself.
You don't have to do this.

TEDDY comes from inside the house to the yard, with a concerned look on his face. Stops before WINONA can see him.

WINONA

Papa this is all your fault.
You and whoever invented the
saxophone.

The children are amused. TEDDY walks toward WINONA who is close to tears.

TEDDY

(sweetly)

Baby, you don't mean a damn
thing you're sayin'. You know
that, don't you?

WINONA

I do, too. I mean exactly
what I said.

CLIFF

Well, I don't haveta make
something of myself. I'm a
jazz musician. That's what I
am.

NATE
LIKE 'Hey, Joe get offa my cloud,' right, Mama?

BLAISE slaps the head of the conga: an accent. Everybody laughs.

MASSIE
(trying to make up)
Now, Winona, you didn't turn out half bad yourself, you know.

WINONA
What has this racket they're makin' got to do with me?

The children look at each other askance and giggle or guffaw.

TEDDY
Winona, wasn't anybody makin' a racket. So, if you wanta be mad at somebody, it'll have to be yourself.

WINONA
What are you talking about?

TEDDY
(taking Winona aside)
I'm talkin' about how you decided on your own that you didn't want to sing. You did that and nobody else.

WINONA
(excited)
Teddy Pierre, I had a family
to...

MASSIE
(laughing)
So did I, but I didn't stop
raisin' you to do a soft shoe.
Uh, come to think of it I
didn't stop the soft shoe or
nasty ol' blues to raise you.
Now, so there. Jazz brought
you here.

Everybody starts to laugh. The kids begin their jam session again. Massie dances. Teddy reaches toward Winona to hold her, but she pushes him away.

WINONA
(to kids)
Leave me alone. Just leave me
alone. You're gonna ruin your
lives chasing after some tune
or your name on a marquee. Do
you think I gave up something
I loved so much, for you to
run the hell back for it? I'm
not mad at myself. I'm made
at you, all of you. You give
that music everything you've
got. Then, everythin' you've
got and move. Everything I
tried to give you, turns to

nothin', just gone; poof in
the air.

Teddy starts to move Winona away from the others, very gently. She continues to rant. Teddy softly interacts with her.

WINONA
If all I wanted to do in the
world was sing, don't you
think I'd be singin' Huh?

TEDDY
Winona, I know you could sing.

WINONA
(musing)
Yeah, I can, can't I?

CUT TO

EXT. WINONA'S POV

As Winona and Teddy walk toward the house, the others and their interactions with the instruments and each other are clouded by her tears as she begins to sing. Teddy cradles her head by his neck and they go in the back door.

QUICK CUT TO

EXT.

Massie doing his most fluid fancy step to the children's music. Blaise drops the rhythm, stops playing, looks confusedly at her brothers.

BLAISE
Hey, don't you all feel like
somethin' funny's goin' on?

Nate and Cliff stop playing, try to seem confident.

NATE

Do you remember anything
serious?

BLAISE

I'm serious, my brother.

CLIFF

Aw, cut it out. You know,
Mama. She gets all bent outta
shape, sometimes. There's
nothin' we could do about it.

MASSIE

I'm not so sure of that, son.
I gotta feelin', my child's
hankerin' after some other
times, other days. You know
music usedta make ya happy,
crazy with a kinda joy makes
your body twitch (he
twitches), glide (he glides),
makes yesterday and all that
sorrow simply cease to be,
just cease to be.

CUT TO

EXT. BLAISE'S POV

Massie starts to walk away dejected, hesitates.

QUICK CUT TO

EXT. MASSIE'S POV

All the children are involved with their instruments in some intimate fashion. Massie sees this, straightens himself up.

MASSIE

Listen to me. All you all put that mess down. I'm gonna tell ya, shoot, I'm gonna show ya why my child be talkin' all outta her head. She's got the music in her. She's got the music in her just like you and me. She does.

Massie pulls up the garage door, pushes through a lot of parcels and old furniture until he finds an old trunk that he opens with great difficulty. The children do not follow him. They start playing music in a discordant and arrhythmic manner. Massie finds something special.

CUT TO

EXT. Nate begins to put his instrument away.

QUICK CUT TO

EXT. NATE'S POV

Massie is holding something flat close to his chest and singing a song on the order of "Keep it clean." Nate is troubled by the tone of his Grandpa's voice, motions for the other two to follow him to the garage.

CUT TO

INT. – GARAGE

Massie is holding an aged photograph of himself and TALBOT BOWLES, with the legendary Sam Lucas[1] in the midst of a 'medicine show' performance. Massie is chuckling to himself as he sings. The children come closer to him with an unexpected reverence because Massie is so thoroughly absorbed.

MASSIE

Uhm. Ain't that somethin'?
Look at me. Look at me,
Massie Roughen, standin' right
next to Sam Lucas, himself.
Lord, have Mercy. If I didn't
know it myself, I wouldn't
believe it.

The kids look puzzled.

NATE

Believe what, Grandpa?

CLIFF

Yeah, man. Who's this Sam
Lucas?

MASSIE

Say, Sam Lucas, was just like
us. Takin' whatever the Devil
put in life and makin' it
swing like all get out.

BLAISE

But what were you doin',
Grandpa?

---

1 Sam Lucas (c. 1850–1916) was an entertainer, actor, comedian, singer, and songwriter.

MASSIE

What was I doin'? (He pauses.) I was inventin' myself, like all the other colored folks…just makin' myself up.

QUICK CUT TO

INT. MASSIE'S POV

Massie looks at the assortment of memorabilia, playbills, photos. Odd instruments and costumes he's pulled from the chest; focuses on the photograph of himself with Talbot and Lucas.

DISSOLVE TO

EXT. KING STREET, CHARLESTON, S.C. – DAYTIME

The figure of young Massie tap dancing on King Street on a hot summer afternoon in Charleston is gradually defined. He's singing as well as song of the period, circa late 1890s, "I'm a Ragtime Millionaire." A crowd gathers and tosses pennies. The few black people defer to the whites and try not to tarry, though they notice Massie working so hard. Young Massie gathers his money, is feeling dandy. The crowd drifts away. A seedy white man lingers on the corner. Massie is suspicious, draws his earnings close, gets out of reach of the man, who stares intently.

MASSIE

Why you starin' at me like that, Mister?

ANTON THIBIDEAUX

You forgettin'; I'm white, boy.

MASSIE

No, sir.

ANTON

I was just admiring your
footwork, there. Is actually
a pure delight to see your
limbs just goin'.

MASSIE

(distancing himself)

Thank you, sir.

Massie picks up his earnings.

ANTON

How'd you like to be in a real
show with a stage, and music,
and an audience that comes
just to see you, not these
folks passing by with alla
life's travails on their
minds? Tell me. How would
that suit you?

MASSIE

With costumes? I wanta jacket
with two rows of gold buttons
and a watch on a chain.

ANTON

Hmm. I don't know about all
that but we'll find you
somethin'. By the way, I'm
Monsieur Anton Thibideaux, of

Thibideaux's Louisiana Creole
Medicine Show. Yessirree!

QUICK CUT TO

EXT. COUNTRY ROAD – CAROLINA – AFTERNOON

Massie dancing in front of the Medicine Show performance wagon, accentuating the marvels that Anton announces will be manifest if the members of the audience stop into the tent.

ANTON

Yes, Ladies and Gentlemen, not
only do I have an oil here
prepared from the mystical
land of the Taj Mahal and the
town of Galilee, but we have
proof that no matter what ails
you, Thibideaux's elixir will
relieve you of all misery.
Why I'm goin' to let you see a
li'l pickaninny, was terribly
injured in a sugar refinery
down in Louisiana. C'mon out
here, Talbot.[1]

A slender black boy in a bizarre contortion of his body (like the fellow with Hammer) scampers on stage on his hands. The audience is aghast.

---

1 Historically, the working conditions of the sugar industry were notoriously brutal and injuries were common. In this context, Shange blends that history with that of traveling carnivals in the late nineteenth and early twentieth centuries, which often put disabled people on display for entertainment. Although this was one of the few ways disabled or otherwise physically nonnormative people could earn a decent living, it relied upon a general culture of ableism. Though Talbot is clearly masquerading as a disabled person in order to hawk the elixir, Shange's rendition of the spectacular ableism of carnival culture is accurate.

ANTON

Now, now, my good people. It was Thibideaux's elixir that freed this child from a shape more grotesque than this.

Talbot winks at Massie.

ANTON

(continued)

Talbot, show the people the miracle of modern science that you are.

With great drama, Talbot releases, first, his legs, then, his torso, until he is standing up straight. He runs a bit, jumps, bends over to touch his toes, and then, falls into a dance routine with Massie.

ANTON

(continued)

Yes, Ladies and Gentlemen, young Talbot can even dance. If you want to experience the healing energy of Thibideaux's elixir. Step right this way for a more scientific demonstration.

CUT TO

EXT. TALBOT'S POV

Anton bows, jumps off his podium to collect entrance fees. Talbot and Massie go over to the campfire to eat some stew that's cooking. Every once in a while applause is heard from Anton's presentation. They serve themselves.

TALBOT

This is good, huh?

MASSIE

Not like my Ma's.

TALBOT

What Ma?

MASSIE

Aw, everybody's gotta Ma.

TALBOT

But, where is yours?

MASSIE

Heaven. Nightriders come.
Everybody but me, in Heaven.

TALBOT

Humm. I can't remember no more than Thibideaux, but I know he ain't my Daddy. One time I thought that Sam Lucas was my pa.

MASSIE

Who's Sam Lucas?

TALBOT

(in disbelief)

Why he's the colored fella swore he'd never black-up, and he ain't, not to this day. He got so many songs, folks can't sing 'em all in one day. See,

I wouldn't mind comin' from
that.

MASSIE

Guess not.

TALBOT

Oh, if you're gonna come up
with a new step, I gotta know
cause I can't let you make me
look foolish. I'm a
'miracle,' remember?

They laugh.

MASSIE

I never understand how you do
that.

TALBOT

Don't let your simple li'l
mind imagine you gonna take my
place.

Anton comes from the tent with a wad of dollar bills.

ANTON

Talbot, boy, I assure you
there is no one in this county
can measure up to you.

TALBOT

(indignant)

In this county, why we've been
to fifteen states, and three
territories in just three

years. I'm the best
contortionist east of the
Mississippi.

ANTON

Best colored contortionist, my
boy…

Anton flips through the money. Gives each boy a couple of dollars and keeps the rest of the substantial wad.

TALBOT AND MASSIE

Thank you, Monsieur
Thibideaux.

Anton is walking away from the boys, very content counting his money.

ANTON

G'night, boys.

CUT TO

EXT. MASSIE AND TALBOT ALL BUNDLED UP BY THE FIRE NEAR THE WAGON.

MASSIE

(whispering)

Did you ever meet Sam Lucas?

TALBOT

What?

MASSIE

Did you ever meet Sam Lucas?

Talbot doesn't answer. He's sleeping.

MASSIE
(to himself)
Never blacked up, huh? That's
amazing for a colored man.

Massie falls asleep.

DISSOLVE TO

EXT.

The two large wagons that make up Thibideaux's entourage are slowly making their way down a dirt road early in the day.

ITINERANT BLUESMAN (VO)
'Nigger and a white man playing seven-up
White man played an ace; an' nigger feared
to take it up,
White man played ace an' nigger played
a nine,
White man died and nigger went blind.'

As they go along the road, the wagons come to an abrupt halt. The boys peek out the back of wagon #2, then jump to the ground and run around to the first wagon. One of Thibideaux's roustabouts is throwing up. Thibideaux, himself, is agitated. Hanging from a tree directly in front of them is the body of a black man that had been there awhile.

ANTON
Let's get on our way. This is
none of our affair. (Brings
whip up in the air to prod the
horses.)

TALBOT

But, Mr. Thibideaux, sir. We
need to cut him offa there.
(Thibideaux brings the whip
down on Talbot who is stunned,
but proud.)

ANTON

We'll all end up like that if
we don't get goin'. Now do as
I say, you li'l niggers or
I'll see to it you get as good
as that dead nigger there.
Now, getta move on.

Talbot and Massie solemnly go toward the wagon. A busty carnie girl type mulatta is looking out the back of the wagon at them as they approach. Her name is 'Missy.'

CUT TO

INT. MISSY'S POV - FROM INSIDE WAGON

MISSY

What y'all lookin' so gloomy
about?

The boys look at each other.

MISSY

(continued)

You know, you could tell,
Missy, anythin'. (The wagons
start to move.) C'mon, can't
you see Thibideaux is leavin'?

Mr. Thibideaux, you forgettin'
Talbot an' Massie. Mr.
Thibideaux. (She yells.)

The boys run behind the wagon trying to get in, but they can't keep up. Missy sees the hanged black man, and lets out a terrible holler. The boys keep running after the wagons, screaming for the troupe to stop.

MASSIE
Mr. Thibideaux, don't leave us here.

TALBOT
We won't make no trouble, Mr.
Thibideaux, I swear.

MASSIE
Missy, make 'em stop, please
Missy.

The wagons take off to the horizon. The two little boys walk slowly, lonely and tired, toward the setting sun.

DISSOLVE TO

Early 20th Century skyline of Memphis, Tennessee. Hear bright banjo and mandolin arrangement of 'Alabama Bound.'

MASSIE AND TALBOT (VO)
'Alabama Bound, Alabama Bound,
If the boat don't sink and the
stack don't drown
I'm Alabama Bound.'

CUT TO

EXT. MISSISSIPPI RIVER

CUT TO

INT.

A bawdy music hall with white folks in orchestra seats and blacks in the balcony. Everyone is having a high old time. Talbot and Massie are backed by an entire minstrel band of black and Creole performers. Massie sings, but also plays banjo solo. They both dance.

MASSIE AND TALBOT
(continued)
'Boats up the river, runnin' side by side,
When you get my lovin', kind sweet babe,
You'll be satisfied.'

Talbot and Massie take bows, return for encores.

QUICK CUT TO

INT. DRESSING ROOMS OF MALE PERFORMERS

There's a lot of clatter and chatter. They are changing clothes, washing up, etc. It's very hot.

MASSIE
Damn, that was a good crowd, tonight.

TALBOT
No crowd's good in heat like this. I sure wouldn't leave my porch to sweat with some other people. Just stink and wet, Jesus.

MASSIE
Imagine a night like this with two shows in blackface, too!

MINSTREL#1

Don't shake that tree too
hard. That all I got to say.

TALBOT

Well, what is it that you are
trying to say?

MINSTREL#1

We been sold, is what.

MASSIE

Don't nobody buy and sell
niggers no more.

MINSTREL#1

You ignorant so and so, Lucky
Jim Jones sold the whole show
to them white folks Colonel
Sam's Merry Minstrels. And
you know sho' as I'm livin',
the Colonel sho' gonna make us
black-up. I know what I'm
talkin' 'bout.

MASSIE

I guess that's it for me
then. I'm as black as I'm
gonna get right now.

TALBOT

Oh, it ain't nothin', but a
show, Massie.

MASSIE
But I ain't never showed
myself in 'burnt-cork',
grinnin' and kickin' up my
heels like some fool jigaboo
either…I'm not startin' now,
neither.

MINSTREL #1
I'm stickin' with Lucky Jim's
Colored Cavalcade, I am!

TALBOT
(to Massie)
Well, where'll you go an'
what're you gonna do?

MASSIE
Talbot, you never asked me
that before, in all these
years. And we always ended up
'somewhere.' Brother, I'm
going as far away from 'coon
songs and 'coon' fools as I
get. Won't you come with me,
Talbot?

TALBOT
I can't. I can't live that
life no more, roamin' hither
an' yon. No I'ma stay put,
this time.

QUICK CUT TO

INT. MASSIE'S POV

Massie is looking at Talbot in the mirror on the wall. Massie sees Talbot change into a quintessential blackface minstrel with the broad, vulgar gestures and facial expression. He hears a voice like Al Jolson or Jimmy Rodgers singing "Dem Golden Slippers."

CUT TO

INT. TALBOT'S POV

TALBOT
(continued)
What are you lookin' at,
Massie? You hear me?

MASSIE
(looking away)
Nothin', T., nothin' at all.

Massie goes out of the dressing room. Before he leaves, he turns around to see Talbot once more with tears streaming down his face. Talbot doesn't see him.

DISSOLVE TO

EXT. TAVERN WITH SWINGING DOORS; WHITE ONLY

Massie hears polyphonic smooth blues sounds as he walks down the street, mystifying breaks and rhythm, intrigue. As he walks to the doors, a burly white guy pokes his head out.

WHITE GUY
Whatchu want, boy?

Massie grimaces.

MASSIE
I was wonderin' who was in
there playin' that music?

WHITE GUY
(to folks in bar)
The nigger wants to know who is that playin'... (laughing) Why, I thought all y'all niggers was related... Get on outta my sight, now. Stick yo' head in the back door, see if yo' brothah's in town. (He laughs more) Maybe yo' cousin?

Massie's gaze hardens, but he talks low.

MASSIE
Yes, sir. Thank you, sir.

CUT TO

INT. KITCHEN OF WHITE TAVERN

Massie tries to walk through the kitchen and the black workers, before the end of "Krooked Blues." He's carrying his few worldly goods and his banjo, which makes navigating difficult. He feels some pressure on his bags; freezes.

BLACK GAMBLER
Uh-unh, I'm tryin' to help you, now, young fella.

CUT TO

MASSIE'S POV

A very polished, black-black man is smiling at Massie.

BLACK GAMBLER

I'm Sweet Spady, or, at least,
that's what folks say.
(chuckles) C'mon, I'll sneak
you in or, if we get caught,
tell that ol' fool that I'm
yo' brothah what was lost.

CUT TO

INT. SIDE OF BANDSTAND

Massie and Sweet Spady are chatting and nibbling on rice, beans, ribs or chicken. Their bodies reflect the pulse of the music. Massie is much less inhibited.

SWEET SPADY

See, you have to understand
that once your sound is sweet
enough, not some sweet, or a
bit sweet, but sweet through
and through, the world will
fall to your feet, on the
ground, now.

Massie giggles.

MASSIE

You are talkin' all out ya
head, Sweet. You don't even
know what you sayin'.

SWEET SPADY

Listen, now, this is Sweet
talkin' to you. I know what
the world's gotta offer. Hey,

I've seen colored folks in the movin' picture. I know colored folks live in buildings nigh as high as the sky. Why fellas just like you are playing our music on Broadway in New York City.

MASSIE (thoughtfully)
How you get to know all this?

SWEET SPADY
Survivin' East Texas'll prepare ya for anythin'… (He slips a deck of cards from his sleeve). There is my ticket to freedom. (laughs) Y'all got trumpets, pianos, and banjos, of course, to make y'all's way, but to me, we 'bout equals. I gotta practice. You gotta practice.

MASSIE
Forever and ever?

SWEET SPADY
If you wanta be the best. Now, if you don't wanta be the best, don't matter what in hell ya do. Now, in my business, if I'm not the best, I might be dead, one dead niggah. So, I give it my all, ya understand?

MASSIE
Whoa! Listen at that! (Louis Armstrong is playing a solo.)

Sweet Spady tries to say something to Massie, but Massie keeps trying to make him hush. Finally, when the Armstrong solo is over, Massie turns to Sweet.

MASSIE
What is it?

SWEET SPADY
What I was tellin' ya 'bout bein' the best. See, Louis Armstrong, that's who that was, sounds so sweet, you didn't even wanta hear the real Sweet talk. (Massie looks puzzled) Armstrong is so good, he can make King Oliver's band look like they not so hot.

MASSIE (astonished)
That's King Oliver and The Creole Jazz Band? I've wanted to hear him, I mean, see him, as long as I can remember.

The band starts another tune. A fellow from the kitchen comes over to Massie and Sweet, with agitation in his voice.

KITCHEN FELLOW
All right, y'all. Gimme them vittles and git the hell on

out, 'for the barkeep come an'
throw ya out an' me 'long
witcha. Git a move on, now.
Ain't sposed to be no colored
folks in heah no how.

SWEET SPADY
(Getting up to go)
I know, I heard the man, did
you?

Massie gathers his things hurriedly. The voices of drunk white men float from the bar.

SWEET SPADY
Whatever happens, go a
different direction from where
I'm goin'. We got better odds
that way.

They are moving quickly through the kitchen, knocking into things and looking over their shoulders.

CUT TO

EXT. OUTSIDE KITCHEN ENTRANCE TO WHITE TAVERN

Voices of burly white men get louder. Sweet Spady is fairly nonchalant, but definitely annoyed by this disruption.

SWEET SPADY
Remember what I tol' you:
Practice.

MASSIE
Practice and the world is at
yo' feet.

The voices get louder. Sweet starts to run. Massie watches him a minute and sets off in another direction.

MASSIE (running)
(whispers) Sweet, all I need
right now is to practice
movin' these feet. The
world'll have to come some
other time.

DISSOLVE TO

EXT. NIGHTTIME ON BEALE STREET.

Signs of buoyant street life are apparent, but muted. A few stragglers are on the street. Yet Massie is 'alone.' A phrase of some blues tune might waft through the air, isolated as well. Massie gets to a corner, stops, sits, starts playing his banjo, to himself: a doleful tune.

CUT TO

INT. – MISS MILDRED'S BAWDY HOUSE – MAIN ROOM
CISSIE'S POV

There are rebel yelps and gunfire heard, rolling wagon wheels, and horses galloping. She sees Massie just playing his banjo oblivious to the danger. Cissie runs down the stairs, flings the door open.

QUICK CUT TO

EXT. BEALE STREET – Continuous

Cissie runs to Massie, pulls his arm, tries to gather up his belongings.

MASSIE
Woman, what in God's name are you doin'?

CISSIE
What am I doin'? I'm savin' your fool behind. Don't you hear Johnny Red huntin' tonight?

Massie listens; becomes aware of the approaching caravan of revelers.

MASSIE
Damn. Let's get outta here.

Massie and Cissie gather up everything and run back to the house that Cissie'd left.

CUT TO

INT. BAWDY HOUSE – NIGHTTIME

There are a couple of gambling tables, a bar, a dance floor, and a band area on this level of Miss Mildred's, the proprietor. There are only a few people there right now. Cissie and Massie go up to the bar.

MASSIE
(relieved)
I wanta thank you, Miss, for comin' to my assistance, but I want to assure you, I usually, take care of myself.

CISSIE

I can't see how good the care
you take could be, seein' how
you don't know anybody.

Cissie motions for the bartender to bring them something.

MASSIE

(to the bartender)

Uh, whiskey, please. And
whatever the lady cares for.

CISSIE

(to Massie)

I could see you were in
trouble, didn't know anybody,
'cause you don't know me.

They laugh. Toast. The band starts to come into the bandstand.

MASSIE

Well, everybody seems to know
you here.

CISSIE

That's right.

Massie looks alarmed.

CISSIE

I work here all night long.
Whenever they call my name.

MASSIE

Which is?

CISSIE

Cissie Mack from New Orleans.

MASSIE

Massie Roughen from
Charleston, South Carolina, at
your service, Ma'am.

The band begins to play. Cissie lights up.

CISSIE

You'll haveta excuse me.
That's my cue.

Massie is puzzled.

MASSIE

Of course.

Cissie walks toward that bandstand singing "The Georgia Rag."[1] Massie gets a very content grin on his face; very pleased, he is.

CISSIE

'Down in Atlanta on Harris Street
That's where the boys and girls do meet,
Doin' that rag, that Georgia Rag

Peoples come from miles around
Get into Darktown t' break 'em down,
Doin' that Georgia Rag,
That Georgia Rag.'

---

1 A portion of the song "The Georgia Rag" is included throughout this play, as it appears in Shange's original papers. Shange often used lyrics and music history in her writing to emphasize a setting or invoke an important theme for the characters in her pieces. Shange also used these songs as interludes to transition from one part of the scene to the next, or in characters' performances, as seen here.

The place is filled more now with women of suspicious character and men the same, 'doin' that rag.'

QUICK CUT TO

INT. MASSIE'S POV

Massie is looking at all the steps the folks are doing: The Boombashay; Turkey Trot; Snake Hips; The Rag. He gets excited, takes out his banjo and begins to play. Cissie sees him and gestures for him to stop, but he continues.

CUT TO

INT. CISSIE'S POV

CISSIE

'Come all the way from Paris, France
Come to Atlanta to get a chance,
to do that rag, that Georgia Rag.'

The band finishes their number. People applaud. Guys put their instruments away. Cissie walks toward Massie.

CISSIE

You sound downright good on that thing, but you sure like to take chances: jumpin' in on a number with a bank doesn't know you from a shadow.

MASSIE

Ah, but, now, I know you. And You sing as pretty as you look. (Drawing her to him.)

CISSIE

Uh, I could sing down and dirty, too. I hope you could

talk that way 'cause my
bossman, Mr. W.C. Handy,[1] is
comin' right this way. And
There's not a doubt in my mind
that he's fixin' to speak
direct to you.

W.C. Handy, a stocky black man in a wrinkled white shirt and vest with a pocket watch comes over to the couple in a dignified cordial way.

HANDY
Hey there, Zeke, please bring
me a sherry.

ZEKE (THE BARTENDER)
Yes, Sir, Mr. Handy.

Handy nods to Massie and Cissie.

HANDY
(to Massie)
So, young man, you don't sound
half bad on that ol' banjo.
(Handy looks at it.) But, I
just don't understand where
you been, young fella.

Massie perks up, he hears 'job' in the air.

---

1 Composer and songwriter William Christopher Handy (1873–1958) was widely known as "The Father of the Blues." He also traveled the South as an organic ethnomusicologist, carefully documenting the particular regional variations in African American music.

HANDY
(continues)
Don't you know, you don't just jump in without letting the band leader know that's what you would like to do. And nobody's playing 'jazz' music on banjos and mandolins. That's just country. Sound like a colored medicine show, some black-face.

HANDY
Minstrels tellin' silly jokes. (He relaxes as Massie tenses.) I could understand a steel string guitar, but a banjo. Where are you from, boy?

CISSIE
(mediating)
Why, Massie Roughen, here, is from Natchez, Mississippi. Isn't that right, Mr. Roughen?

MASSIE
(very focused)
What's wrong with a banjo?

HANDY
Nothin's wrong with it, just not as much sound to it as a piano; not rich like a guitar; not strong as a drum, a whole

lotta drums'll give rhythms on
top of rhythms, 'specially
with horns. Your old banjo'd
be lost. Plus it reminds some
folks of slavery times. Folks
want what's new; what's
modern.

There's an awkward silence.

MASSIE
What does any of that have to
do with sittin' in, when some
fellas are playing? I've
always done that, an' never
embarrassed anybody's band.

HANDY
You lucky, is all I could say.

MASSIE
(indignant)
What?

Handy reaches in his pocket, takes out some sheet music, lays it on the bar. Cissie looks uncomfortable.

HANDY
Now. What is this? What are
all these pieces of papers?

MASSIE
Paper with scribbles on them.

Cissie tries not to laugh. Massie gives her a dirty look.

MASSIE

(continued, to Cissie)

You know what it is? Then
tell me.

CISSIE

(to Massie)

I didn't mean nothin', by it.

HANDY

What she means is, how can you
call yourself a professional
musician if you can't read
music? And no, I don't want
you jumpin' in the middle of
one of my arrangements for my
band that I rehearse so nobody
sounds like us, anywhere. I'm
tryin' to help you. Do you
understand anything I'm sayin'
to you, fella?

Massie looks bewildered, shaken.

CISSIE

Ah, Mr. Handy, do we still
have that slide trombone that
Lem won offa one of Black
Patty's touring company?

HANDY

Less Black Patty come to pick
it up and pay the debt, we
sho' nuff still got it.

CISSIE

And we don't have a banjo player or anybody on a trombone, either, do we?

HANDY

No, I don't. But I won't have this fella pickin' on no banjo. I believe (fussing) there is a guitar back up in the attic, too.

CISSIE

Thank you. Thank you. (She hugs Handy.)

MASSIE

(eager)

I want to thank you too…

HANDY

Nothin' to thank me for. I didn't give you anythin'. I'm lettin' you use some things for a spell. Cissie seems to have some interest in you. Only play when I say. Don't play outta turn or behind the downbeat. Learn how to write down what you hear, or you'll never play it the same again, though some things only meant for a 'once'…

Handy keeps muttering to himself, goes to the piano to play a sprightly, very urban tune. Cissie and Massie embrace each other with glee.

MASSIE

I love this music. I love it.
Thank you, Cissie.

Cissie comes out of Massie's grip.

CISSIE

Oh, I thought you might be
angry with me. I didn't mean
to laugh, really. But you
play the banjo so good. And
that trombone's sittin' up
there with no song in it, you
know what I mean?

MASSIE

I got no idea what you mean.
You save me from the
nightriders, then you give me
this 'jazz' music, a horn, a
guitar, W.C. Handy… and
there's always you.

Massie goes to kiss her, but Cissie, coquette-like, bends out of the way.

CISSIE

C'mon, let's go find your
future.

MASSIE

Oh, I thought only medicine
show gals read tea leaves and
palms.

CISSIE

(feigning outrage)

Oh, you. You come with me.

Cissie chases Massie out the main room and up the stairs to the attic.

DISSOLVE TO

INT. MISS MILDRED'S BAWDY HOUSE – NIGHTTIME

The place is filled with folks in high finery and plumes, spats, and sparkles. W.C. Handy's band is playing a nasty 'slow drag.' W.C. takes a solo. Then, Massie on guitar. Then, Cissie sings. The other folks are busy dancing and the bar is busy as are the stairs to the 'other' kind of rooms.

CISSIE

'But chitlins -- we got a few.
Hot chitlins red hot, that's the dish for me
Hot chitlins red hot, oh can't you see?
I got bread in markets from North to South,
Seepin' tastes good right in your mouth
(hey, what)
Hot chitlins, red hot.'[1]

DISSOLVE TO

EXT. MISSISSIPPI RIVERBANKS - DUSK

---

1 A portion of the song "Miss Handy Hanks" is included throughout this play, as it appears in Shange's original papers. Here, Cissie performs the song for a crowd whose economic status surpasses her own, which is suggested by the theme of the song.

Massie and Cissie are walking along. Massie has some sheet music in his hands. Cissie sometimes looks over his shoulder at it. Massie sings what he imagines to be the melody.

CISSIE

No. No. That's not it.
Listen to me. (She sings the
correct melody line.)

MASSIE

Aw. I'm never gonna get this.

CISSIE

(lovingly)

Of course, you will. Don't
worry, 'bout how easy this is
for me, I got perfect pitch
(she smiles).

MASSIE

(serious)

We've got more problems than
me and music. (He pulls her
to the ground. They sit
close.) Cissie, W.C. is
gettin' ready to pull outta
Memphis.

CISSIE

I know.

MASSIE

He says he can't find no more
music 'round here, 'round
Memphis. Hard to believe…

CISSIE
(cutting him off)
Yes, I'll go with you.

MASSIE
But you don't know where I'm goin' and I ain't asked you yet, heifer (laughing), and I still can't read music.

CISSIE
I don't care. I don't care.

Massie picks her up and twirls her round.

DISSOLVE TO

INT. COLORED ONLY CAR OF TRAIN – NIGHTTIME

Massie and Cissie are sleeping entwined. A couple of drunk white men shove, push Massie's shoulders.

WHITE MEN #1
Hey, boy, play somethin'.

WHITE MAN #2
Yeah. Ain't that a whatchamacallit, over there? (Pointing to the guitar case.)

Cissie and Massie are alert and apprehensive, though sleepy.

WHITE MAN #1
What's she do? Coon dance? Or some coon-type hoochie-koochie?

The two white men laugh hard. Massie stands up to defy them, but Cissie grabs his arm that's reaching toward White Man #1.

CISSIE
(whispering)
No, Massie, no. We just want
to play music. No. Please.

MASSIE
(to the white men)
We just carryin' this guitar
to Louisiana, Mister. I don't
play no music, sing neither.
Only church. Just church.

CISSIE
Yes, sir, that's where we do
all our singin'.

WHITE MAN #2
These niggers ain't no fun, no
fun at all…

WHITE MAN #1
Well, let's go find us some
niggers could entertain a li'l
bit. There must be some round
here somewhere.

The two white men continue walking through the car: lifting folks' hats off their heads, turning their heads around, etc.

MASSIE
Cissie, don't you ever do that
again.

CISSIE
You can't let white folks rile you that way.

MASSIE
No. Listen to me. White folks wanta see me dance or grin. They gotta pay me. White folks wanta have a good time. They gotta pay me and keep their distance. I walk like a stood-up-straight man I'm gonna make music stood-up-straight. Take me at my word. There's nothin' about Massie Roughen, funny to sane white folks.

CISSIE
I don't want nothin' to happen to you, is all.

MASSIE
Can't nothin' happen to me. I got you an' all this music.
(They nestle.)

CUT TO

INT. COLORED CAR ON MOVING TRAIN - DAWN

MASSIE'S POV

Massie looks at the countryside: cane fields, magnolia trees, one or two field hands walking along the tracks who wave. Massie takes up his guitar: picks out a minor chord, then, a wistful tune. He pulls Cissie next to him.

MASSIE
(to himself)
This land is so beautiful to be so bloody… but this is what that blues, that jazz, all that music is right out there.

DISSOLVE TO

EXT. NEW ORLEANS – FRENCH QUARTER – STREET – DAYTIME

Massie and Cissie are looking for an address in this historic section. They pass street corners where all sorts of little black bands are playing and young boys dancing.

CISSIE
I am sure this is the right street?

MASSIE
Think so, but Cissie, looks like every colored somebody in this town is doin' a jig or tootin' a horn.

CISSIE
Does seem that way, but when we find Dr. Tavernier, he'll set us on the right path, you'll see… (she looks at paper in her hand.) Wait,

Massie, there it is. That's
Dr. Tavernier's address.

EXT. TAVERNIER HOUSE: PORCH WITH PILLARS AND WICKER LAWN FURNITURE. An older Creole Negro woman opens the doors after Cissie knocks. Massie is beside her.

LETICIA (SUSPICIOUSLY)
May I help you?

MASSIE
We're here to see Dr.
Tavernier.

CISSIE
Yes, Dr. Tavernier.

LETICIA
Is he expecting your visit?

CISSIE
He sure oughtta be. I have
written him a pile of letters.
We did everythin' he said:
bought books, transcribed
solos; played some dreary
concertos…

LETICIA
Yes, I see. Come in, then,
please.

CUT TO

INT. BEAUTIFULLY APPOINTED FOYER WITH LARGE FRENCH DOORS TO ONE SIDE. Leticia knocks on one of the doors. Massie and Cissie are a few steps behind her.

LETICIA (in French)
There's a couple here to see
you, sir.

TAVERNIER (in French)
Who?

MASSIE (loudly)
Massie and Cissie Roughen. (He
puts his arm around Cissie)

CISSIE
That's Mr. and Mrs.

LETICIA
M'sieur & Mme. Roughen, je
pense.

The door lies open. Dr. Tavernier, a very distinguished mulatto, gestures for them to enter the library/music room.

TAVERNIER
Oui. You must be my friends
from Memphis. Bonjour, Massie.
Oui. This must be Ci-Ci, oui?
How lovely you are. Entrez.
Entrez. Leticia, nous
voudrions un peu du café, s'il
vous plaint.

Cissie and Massie are fascinated by the elegance and calm musicality of the Tavernier home. There's a grand piano, a harp, a wall of woodwinds, a marimba, a set of trap drums, and some flutes and percussion instruments of diverse origins. Leticia leaves to get coffee. Dr. Tavernier watches as Cissie and Massie examine the contents of the room.

MASSIE
Yes, sir. Thank you.

TAVERNIER
Oh, please. Just Jacques,
seulement. Jacques.

Cissie is attracted to the harp.

CISSIE
May I?

TAVERNIER
Uhm. Yes. If you have this
perfect pitch you wrote about.
You will play me somethin'
belle, trés belle.

Cissie starts to sound out a tune on the harp, quietly. Dr. Tavernier sits behind a fine wood desk covered with scores and popular sheet music.

TAVERNIER (continued)
So, Massie. You must come and
sit down. You must tell me why
you both must learn so fast,
so much of the language of
music. Come, sit, and talk to
me. (Massie sits down on the
other side of the desk. He can
see Cissie and Dr. Tavernier.)
I have M'sieur Handy's letter
of introduction and of course
a drawer full of queries from
you and Ci-Ci. (He listens a

moment) Oui. There is a melody in that sequence, Ci-Ci. Now look for your harmonies, vary the tempo and you've your first lesson.

MASSIE

(clearing his throat)

Yes, Dr. Tavernier, I want to write down what I hear, pull a piece apart for trombones, trumpets, clarinets, piano, drums. Ever since I heard W.C. Handy, it's as if I been livin' inside a note with waterfalls and riptides…

TAVERNIER

You want to learn to make arrangements and to take these "marvelous" sounds out of your body and put them on paper.

MASSIE

That's right.

TAVERNIER

All right. For you, there will be no sleep. In a while, maybe, no wife. (Massie is alarmed) first, you must hear all the bands in the Quarter. Then, we will write down every sound you remember. That is in

the day. Wait, what is it you
play, now?

MASSIE
Banjo. Guitar. Slide trombone.

TAVERNIER
No piano?

MASSIE
No piano.

TAVERNIER
We need to look for twelve
more hours, then.

MASSIE
Twelve hours? To what?

TAVERNIER
To add to each day, so you
have time to master your
trombone and my piano.

Cissie ends her harp song, smiling. Leticia returns with coffee and pastries. She exits immediately.

TAVERNIER (continued)
And what of the lovely Ci-Ci.
When shall we work together?
Merci, Leticia.

CISSIE
I'm not goin' to work, Doctor.
I'm just goin' to sing.

TAVERNIER
There's no such thing as 'just singin.'

MASSIE
Oh, Cissie knows that, sir. Uh, Jacques. It's just we've got a baby on the way and her studies'd be interrupted.

TAVERNIER
I am so sorry to know this. And with perfect pitch. Aprés le bébé, oui?

Massie and Cissie look each other in the eye, knowing that will never happen.

CUT TO

INT. CISSIE & MASSIE'S FLAT IN NEW ORLEANS

In her parlor, which was already furnished so it doesn't reflect the Roughens' tastes exactly, Cissie is entertaining Mrs. Mahone, the neighbor. Cissie is serving iced tea.

MRS. MAHONE
Well, thank you, Cissie. I didn't know what to expect when the neighbors said theatrical folks were movin' in, but I find y'all most gracious. Most gracious, indeed.

CISSIE
Oh, Mrs. Mahone, you do
flatter me. We're not theatre
folks in the pure sense,
though. No Ethel Waters here.
we are simple singers, dancers
and music-makers.

MRS. MAHONE
That's what you say now, but
I've heard that there are
Negroes making moving pictures
as well as those nasty blues
recordings. Can you imagine
that, when folks are dyin'
every day to improve the race?

CISSIE
Well, what about the blues do
you find so "nasty," Mrs.
Mahone?

MRS. MAHONE
Oh, you know.

CISSIE
No, I don't.

MRS. MAHONE
What do y'all backwater folks
do with the brains the good
Lord gave ya? I'm sorry,
honey, but I can't see how you
can't hear the vulgarity, the
lascivious nature of the

blues. All it is is singin'
'bout lucky money when the
only luck we need for money is
a job. Then, they turn right
around and talk 'bout wifely
duties like some women thought
that was fun. Oh, my dear, the
blues is not for me.

CISSIE (restraining laughter)
Well, Mrs. Mahone, you coulda
fooled me…

MRS. MAHONE
What do you mean by that? Just
what?

CISSIE
Only that you sound like you
know almost as much about the
blues as I do. Money troubles,
love that makes ya dumb and
weak, love that makes ya…

MRS. MAHONE
You stop that right this
minute, Cissie Roughen. You
goin' to mark that chile you
carryin'. That's what you're
goin' to do.

DISSOLVE TO

INT. CROWDED FRENCH QUARTER CLUB, NIGHT TIME.

Sidney Bechet and Louis Armstrong are lead soloists on "Cake Walking Babies," where Bechet takes on the clarinet and the trumpet (cornet). Massie is mesmerized. There's a dapper-looking black man next to Massie at the bar who's equally interested in the band.

MASSIE (to the man)
What a tone, that Bechet's got, huh? Sidney Bechet makes me wanta practice day and night.

CYRIL ÉTIENNE (the man)
Oh, don't tell me. You heard exactly what I heard. (chuckles) I'm Cyril Étienne, Bayou Records.

MASSIE
Musician and all-round entertainer, Massie Roughen. Pleased to meet you.

(Étienne gives Massie his card.)

ÉTIENNE
If you ever have somethin' really hot, make sure you call me first, all right? I imagine I'll be seein' you one place or the other.

CUT TO

EXT. STREETS OF THE QUARTER, LIT UP WITH SIGNS. BEFORE DAWN.

Massie is walking slowly down the streets with his trombone, humming a Louis Armstrong solo.

CUT TO

EXT. BACKYARD OF MASSIE'S BOARDING HOUSE.
EARLY MORNING.

Cissie is hanging laundry. She is very pregnant.

CISSIE

You know what I think? I think
you are jealous. That Bechet
ran all around them trumpets
and you could hear it
happenin'. But you know, you
can't make that trombone even
take a walk. Huh. Bechet got
that li'l bitty horn runnin'
an jumpin'. (laughs)

MASSIE

(helping with laundry)

Yep. I can't match Bechet. I'm
Not there yet, but Cissie,
you're not s'posed to be doin'
laundry, either.

CISSIE

I don't mind.

MASSIE

You're singer, Cissie. Dr.
Tavernier says we're artists,
Not just medicine show coons.

CISSIE

Shhhh, Massie. Don't talk like that. 'Sides, nobody wants to look at somebody as pregnant as me. (laughing)

MASSIE

I'm not joshin', Cissie.

CISSIE

Well, I ain't, neither.

MASSIE

Cissie, put these things away. I know what we could do (pulls laundry away from her).

CISSIE

Leave those clothes alone, Massie. Now put 'em back where you got 'em.

MASSIE

No, no, Cissie, you don't understand. I just figured out what to do. I love you so much. I love to look at you. I love to hear you sing. But big an' beautiful as you look to me, ain't no tellin' how sweet you gonna be to folks who have to imagine you.

CISSIE

What are you talkin' about?

MASSIE

Cyril Étienne of Bayou Records. Always lookin' for somethin', someone new… like you.

CISSIE

Me? A record? Like Bessie Smith. Like Ida Cox. Like Ethel Waters? Like Sidney Bechet and Louis Armstrong? Don't lie to me, Massie. Maybe I should take a nap. That's what I'm gonna do; get a li'l sleep.

MASSIE

(pulling her toward the house)

No time. We got no time to waste.

DISSOLVE TO

INT. BAYOU RECORDS STUDIO

Cissie is singing either "Vampire Woman" by Spark Plug Smith or "The St. Louis Blues" by W.C. Handy. There is an eight-piece band; Massie's on trombone, to Cissie's delight. Cyril Étienne is in the engineering booth with Dr. Tavernier. As Cissie comes to the last refrain, the joint is jumpin'. Cyril Étienne comes out of the booth.

ÉTIENNE

That was cut. You did it, my Mississippi darlin'. Oh, that's how I'll bill you: Cissie Roughen, "Mississippi's

Darlin'." Somebody write that down.

The band is breaking down equipment. Étienne and Tavernier are congratulating and thanking folks. Massie is kissing Cissie's big belly.

MASSIE

(talking to the belly)

You hear your mama singin'? You was born in a song, you understand me? Somebody say music, you best turn around. Oh, Cissie, I'm so proud of you.

CISSIE

And I want to thank you, my fast thinkin' husband. I do, I really wanta thank you. (they kiss)

ÉTIENNE

Aw, "Mississippi Darling'," we don't kiss in here. This is where we make records; lots and lots of records.

TAVERNIER

Massie, this is where I leave you on your own. M'sieur Étienne, he makes records. I make artists. And that, you both are. Oui? (they shake hands)

QUICK CUT TO

EXT. BACK ALLEYS AND SIDE STREETS OF BLACK NEW ORLEANS. DAY

Massie and Cissie are walking close to fences and stoops trying to hear Cissie's record on the radio or someone playing it on the piano.

MASSIE

Cissie, I feel foolish eavesdroppin' on folks.

CISSIE

Well, I feel truly great. Oh, Bessie Smith's got nothin' on me.

MASSIE

That's the first thing you've said that makes sense.

CUT TO

INT. THE ROUGHENS' FLAT IN NEW ORLEANS. EVENING

Cissie is tidying up her kitchen, singing to herself.

CISSIE

(talking to herself)

'First sense you made tonight." (imitating Massie) Shoot. I make sense alla the time. I'm damnded reasonable, you ask me. He's gone most the night, nowhere to be seen, til the sun comes up. And I don't make any… Uh hunh. (she grabs her belly) I know who

that is. (She goes to the
door, pushes the screen open).
Mrs. Mahone! Mrs. Mahone!

CUT TO

INT. ANOTHER CLUB IN THE QUARTER. NIGHT TIME.
Massie is playing with Jelly Roll Morton's band. He's in the middle of his solo.

QUICK CUT TO

EXT. COURTYARD OF MASSIE'S BUILDING. LATE NIGHT
Massie going through the yard singing a Morton ditty. Stops. Checks the money in his pocket.

MASSIE
Oh, yes, Cissie. We're cookin'
with gas, now.

EXT. STAIRWAY. CONTINUOUS
Massie dances up the stairway. Swings open the door.

MASSIE
Cissie! Cissie! You hear me
callin', girl?

CUT TO

INT. CISSIE'S BEDROOM
Cissie is in bed, looking very weak, with a baby next to her. Massie approaches slowly, sits next to her. Mrs. Mahone appears from a corner, as if from nowhere.

MASSIE (to Cissie)
I see you didn't wait for me.
(he tries to joke)

CISSIE
Couldn't stop ... (pauses)

MRS. MAHONE
Don't you try to talk, now. Massie, you got a fine li'l gal there. You take her on outta heah and let Cissie rest. C'mon now. Do what I tell ya.

Mrs. Mahone gives the baby to Massie.

CISSIE
Massie. Massie, I'm callin' her Winona. Winona. (she struggles to sing the name) I know she could sing... (closes her eyes and lies down again)

MRS. MAHONE
NOW, get on outta heah, you Massie. No, don't bring that chile over heah. Can't you see? Cissie's wore out.

Massie leaves with the baby, counting fingers, trying to find the right way to hold the baby. He turns around to see Mrs. Mahone with tears on her face, closing Cissie's eyes. Massie holds the baby tight, lets out an anguished wail that becomes a rhythmic sob. Then, the syncopation of tap dancing.

DISSOLVE TO

INT. BACK STAGE OF GALVESTON, TEXAS, BALLROOM.

A young girl is doing a routine, while other performers mill about. This is Winona Roughen. She does a step that sets herself up to sing.

WINONA (singing)
"Now, baby, the stuff I got is the stuff that makes the fiddler play, make the fiddler play, I've saved it up since the Lord knows when, I ain't gonna save it for any of you men. I've had it so long, I hate to lose it, 'Cause if I get broke, I'll be able to use it."

Massie in tux for the show happens upon Winona's performance. He is amused, doesn't intrude. Winona continues.

WINONA (continued, singing)
"Now this little thing is what the whole wide world is trying to get. This wise baby, she ain't goin' to part from it yet."

Winona starts to dance again. Massie now presents himself. Winona tries to make herself scarce.

MASSIE
Young lady, just what kinda shady talk is that?

WINONA
Now, Papa, I was not talkin'. That was a song. I was singin' a blues song.

MASSIE (ironically)
You don't say.

WINONA
Aw, Pappa. I just wanta do somethin' to help. You know yourself, the Depression's still on. You always say we need every ol' penny.

MASSIE (laughing)
Winona, you talkin' too much and movin' too fast for your age. Focus on your feet.

WINONA
My feet?

MASSIE
Yep. That's what I said.

Massie does a complicated combination

MASSIE (continued)
Now listen, Winona. Then, let your feet make the sounds I make. Hear the rhythms.

Winona tried, but fumbles a bit. Suddenly, the correct interpretation of Massie's choreography is heard.

QUICK CUT TO

INT. MASSIE'S POV
Talbot Bowles is continuing with the choreography, smiling, looks well.

MASSIE (amazed)
Jesus, man. I never thought
I'd see you again. Winona,
This is the fella I tol' you
of; the one from…

Talbot and Massie embrace.

TALBOT & MASSIE (together)
Thibideaux' Louisiana Creole
Medicine Show.

MASSIE
Winona, c'mon over here. Let
Talbot getta look at you. My
daughter, Winona.

Company Manager comes by.

COMPANY MANAGER
Okay, Roughen. It's time to
hit. Benny Moten Band's up
next.

CUT TO

INT. CENTER STAGE OF THE BALLROOM
Benny Moten's Band (early 1930s)
Massie joins the other band members. Talbot is right behind him.

MASSIE
(whispers to Talbot)
I don't dance much anymore
I'ma hornplayer, man.

Talbot doesn't quite believe him. Goes off stage.

QUICK CUT TO

INT. BALLROOM

Benny Moten Band in full swing, playing "Jones Law Blues" or "Blue Room." As Massie goes back to his place after his solo, pauses to whisper something to Moten who nods his head. Then, Massie lays his horn aside and begins a rip-roaring routine like the Nicholas Brothers or The Step Brothers, especially when Talbot and Winona join him in a three-way "challenge." They are a big hit with the crowd and each other.

DISSOLVE TO

EXT. HARLEM STREET. DAY

Massie, Winona and Talbot are strolling together.

WINONA

Mr. Talbot Bowles. I never thought I'd see the day when I'd meet you.

TALBOT

Me, neither.

MASSIE

And just what do you mean by that?

TALBOT

Take no offense, now, but I never figured you for the "family man." (chuckles)

WINONA

My papa is a great papa! We're family enough for ourselves, huh, Papa?

MASSIE (pensively)
You woulda loved Cissie, Tal. She could sing so's the earth shook.

TALBOT
Was the earth shakin', or you?

Winona laughs.

MASSIE
Have some respect, Talbot.

TALBOT
I do, my friend. I've more respect than you know. And I do wish I could have heard your Cissie sing. Matter of fact, I wish I coulda found me a Cissie of my own, 'steada traipsin' all round Europe seein' more than any man's sposedta.

MASSIE
I heard they like colored folks over there?

WINONA
Yeah. I know a whole lotta girls who are dyin' to go with Some Revue like The Chocolate Dandies or just get to Paris, like "La Baker."

MASSIE

Now, that's some woman. Does she really have a leopard?

TALBOT

Now what do you think? Kinda reminds me of one of Thibideaux's tricks. (laughs)

WINONA

In Paris?

TALBOT

Damn straight.

CUT TO

EXT. COLORED ATTRACTION IN CIRCUS IN PARIS. DAY
MASSIE'S POV

A cage with a nude African woman being fondled and investigated by clumsy European hands.

SIDE SHOW BARKER (VO)

That's right, ladies and gentlemen, a true Bantu Negress for your inspection: God's link from the orangutan to modern man.

CUT TO

EXT. PARIS BACK ALLEY. NIGHT

Talbot running from a group of toughs, chasing him with a tail (ox or horse).

TOUGH #1

Hey, you dirty nigger, you forget your tail?

TOUGH #2

I got some bananas for you, monkey!

The young toughs make animal sounds as they corner Talbot and begin beating him.

TOUGH #1

Come on, I want to see the monkey dance!

CUT TO

EXT. HARLEM BROWNSTONE STOOP. DAY.

Massie and Winona hovering over Talbot, who is winded and staring into space.

MASSIE

You awright, man? Talbot?

TALBOT

Yeah. Yeah, I'm okay.

WINONA

Everything's gonna be fine, Talbot. Now you're here with us.

TALBOT

I guess I just listened to too much talk. There ain't no place for colored folks to go and live in peace.

WINONA

Yes, there is, Talbot.

MASSIE

That's right. All we gotta do
is come home; home to Harlem.

The three get off the stoop and continue down the street in a cheerier mood.

DISSOLVE TO

INT. WINONA'S HOTEL BEDROOM.

Massie and Talbot are in the anteroom, where Massie sleeps. Winona, by her dressing table, looks at a photograph of her mother, Cissie.

WINONA

I'm gonna do it, Mama. Just
what you said. I'm gonna sing.
Remember what you said: "Born
in a song, born in a song."
Well, I'm gonna live in me,
Mama.

CUT TO

INT. NEW YORK SUPPER CLUB. NIGHT

Very elegant place with all-white clientele. The Fletcher Henderson Band with Coleman Hawkins and Winona Roughen. The band plays "Honeysuckle Rose." This is a live broadcast on radio. Winona sings. Hawkins takes his 'rhapsodic solo'; Massie and Talbot dance, too. The white people do their 'swing' dances. Set ends. The crowd applauds.

CUT TO

INT. HALLWAY TO DRESSING ROOMS. CONTINUOUS

Massie, Winona and Talbot mixed in jostling fray of the whole band exiting.

ANNOUNCER (VO)
Yes, Ladies and Gentlemen of our listening audience, that was The Fletcher Henderson Orchestra, featuring Winona Roughen and Coleman Hawkins. Tune in again next week for music all through the night.

WINONA
Geez, Hawkins was blowin' tonight!

MASSIE
You know it. Talbot what'sa matter with you?

WINONA
Yeah, what could be the matter after a night like tonight?

TALBOT
You know, sometimes I wish I was somewhere down south doin' a minstrel show.

MASSIE
What?

TALBOT
Yes, that's what I said. In blackface I can hide or get out of their way. I don't like them so close to me, so white, and under those lights. I gotta get outta here. Winona,

put a move on and I'll take
you someplace we could groove,
just let it all go.

CUT TO

EXT. CAB RIDE TO HARLEM

INT. BLACK WAREHOUSE-LIKE DANCE HALL.
The Count Basie Band featuring Lester Young and Billie Holiday is doing the piece "Swing, Brother, Swing." The crowd is dancing up a storm. Winona is taking it all in, especially Holiday and Young. Talbot and Winona push through the crowd to get a table.

TALBOT
Winona, you want a drink? Your
ol' man's not 'round. (smiles)

WINONA
I won't tell if you don't.
Daddy don't 'low much messin'
around. But you know that,
don't you, Talbot?

TALBOT
I know most anythin' there is
to know.

WINONA
Then I'll please have a Brandy
Alexander and stories 'bout my
papa.

TALBOT
Well, in this place you'll be
doin' good to get a scotch an'
water, if I'm not mistaken.

WINONA
Why not? That'll do just fine.

TALBOT
I'm on my way, then.

CUT TO

INT. WINONA'S POV
Talbot walks toward the bar. A couple takes the center of the dance floor as Billie and Pres do their thing on "Swing, Brother, Swing."

WINONA (to herself)
My God, now I see what Papa
means when he says ride the
rhythm. Lester is finishing
that girl's turn and Billie
picks up their aerials, just
like that. So, it's really
four forces pushin' each
other.

Winona pulls some tissue out of her purse, starts to try to draw what she's seen and heard. Very excited, she's whispering loudly. She feels a hand on her shoulder; she starts, turns to say something flip, but stops when she sees the face of J.T. PIERRE. J.T. is wantonly striking, very irresistible.

J.T.
I didn't know pretty young
ladies came out to dance clubs
to talk to themselves…
oh, and write themselves notes
…

WINONA
Why, I'm not…

J.T.
Is any one sitting here? I'm
J.T. Pierre. And you are?

WINONA
Winona Mack Roughen. But you
know I didn't come here by
myself, Mr. Pierre.

Talbot returns, trying to chat up the waitress who puts two drinks on the table.

TALBOT
She's tellin' the truth, young
fella. She's out on the town
with Talbot Bowles, currently
with Fletch Henderson,
formerly with...

WINONA & TALBOT (together)
Thibideaux' Louisiana Creole
Medicine Show. (they laugh)

J.T. PIERRE
Glad to meet you, Sir. My name
is J.T. Pierre, lead tenor
with the Ellington Orchestra
for a spell. (Winona is very
impressed). I didn't realize I
was in the company of fellow
artists. I thought I was
helpin' someone who mistook a
nightclub for the library.

WINONA

I did not, either! I was working out the relationship of the singer, "The Lady, " to "Pres," and then their relationship to the dancers. That's what I was doin'. (J.T. was not prepared for this.)

J.T. waves for the waitress, orders a drink.

TALBOT

That's right. Winona's father is goin' to come out tonight and join us. You know, Winona's mother as a singer, too. Cissie Roughen, "Mississippi's Darlin'." But Winona's got to find her own sound, you know what I mean?

WINONA

Talbot, are you goin' to let me get a word in, 'steada talkin' 'bout me like I'm not here? (She's friendly)

J.T. PIERRE

But you don't <u>need</u> to be here.

WINONA

And what do you mean by that?

J.T. PIERRE
Only a feeling I've got that Billie Holiday and Pres, or anybody and some other body, don't hold the secret for you, or for me.

WINONA
I thought secrets were revealed, like the Gospel…

J.T. PIERRE
They are. (summoning waitress for the bill) Well, let's roll.

TALBOT
Ah, I think we should wait for Massie, don't you, Winona?

WINONA
What? I'm sorry. What'd you say, Talbot?

TALBOT
Lord, Massie don't blame this here on me. (Sees J.T. and Winona heading for the door) Uh, you think you slick, but you not gonna lose me, not at this hour. (trots off)

CUT TO

EXT. LENOX AVENUE WITH FULL SLEW OF CHARACTERS AND NEON. NIGHT

J.T., Winona and Talbot walk down the boulevard. J.T. seems to know every 'fast-living' person they encounter. They come to a smaller 'joint' reminiscent of the Palm Bar. J.T. leads the way.

CUT TO

INT. BANDSTAND IN SMALL BAR OFF AVENUE
The place is so crowded the threesome can't get much beyond the door.

WINONA
I can't see, J.T. Who's
Playin'?

J.T. PIERRE (very serious)
You don't need to see, you
need to listen.

WINONA
But whose group is it?

J.T. PIERRE (impatient)
Did you hear me? I said
listen.

Winona is taken aback. Talbot, too. Massie comes up behind her.

MASSIE
That's Art Tatum on piano. I
can't say I know the other
two.

WINONA
Papa, when did you get here?

TALBOT (to himself)
Not a moment too soon,
neither.

WINONA

Papa, I want you to meet (she hesitates)... Never mind, I'll introduce you when the set's over, I guess.

MASSIE

No need, baby. I know who that is. Mr. Duke Pomade of the Ellington Orchestra.

The set's over. There's applause, some movement of the crowd.

WINONA

Why are you sayin' sucha thing?

J.T. turns around, sees there's some tension. Extends his hand to Massie, who takes it reluctantly.

MASSIE

Yes, J.T. Pierre. Really pleased to meet you. I've been hearing a lot about you from Winona, here.

J.T. PIERRE

You don't say. That's a coincidence. 'Cause I've heard a lot about you from a whole buncha folks.

TALBOT

How about we order some drinks?

J.T. PIERRE

What an excellent idea… (pauses, trying to include Massie). You know, I was sayin' to Winona she should listen for the breath, the space in a piece of music; so she can place her voice in the middle of it, on the edge, or skirtin' it.

MASSIE

Or she could listen for the bass line and scat on that.

J.T. PIERRE

Well, that's a 1i'l old fashioned, to my mind.

TALBOT (teasing)

I think so.

MASSIE

You got somethin' against tradition, boy? On general principle or just when women are concerned?

WINONA (ALARMED)

Papa, please.

MASSIE

You're right, girl. Let's go on home.

TALBOT

Now, that sounds good to me.

WINONA

I'm not ready to go just yet, Papa.

Winona sidles up to J.T., so their bodies are touching. She clutches his arm, pulls him down closer to her.

WINONA (whispering)

Kiss me, J.T.

J.T., loving "winning," grabs Winona in his arms like Massie wasn't there. Massie goes to snatch Winona back, Talbot gives him bear hug, pulls him back. The band starts playing again, loudly.

TALBOT

C'mon, man. She's a grown woman. Leave her alone.

MASSIE

Winona! Winona! I want you to come home with me this very minute. You hear me? Do you hear me?

Talbot pulls Massie out into the street. The music and crowd were so loud Winona never heard Massie say a thing.

CUT TO

EXT. OUTSIDE THE WINDOW OF THE BAR. NIGHT.

Massie glumly watches Winona and J.T. chat intimately, be sensual with each other. For a second, Winona turns into Cissie. Massie shakes his head, takes a deep breath.

CUT TO

INT. THE BAR.

Winona and J.T. are still snuggling and talking. J.T. pulls a newspaper clipping from his pocket.

J.T.

Listen to this, baby. You want to know 'bout the blind leading the blind. I found this article yesterday. This cat, Stravinsky, caused riots in Paris, like discovered somethin' gonna set the world on fire. (quoting) "The players beat all the time merely to keep up and know which side of the beat they are on." Can you believe that? Wait, there's more. (laughs, quotes again) "The ideas are instrumental, or rather, they come after, come from the instruments."

WINONA

What?

J.T.

That's what I said. White folks are crazier than I ever thought. (laughing) The instruments did it. Lord, let the sun turn blue, 'fore they 'low that the Negro created jazz with his intellect and our souls. "The instruments did it, caused it..." Then how come the instruments didn't "make" no white man

play jazz 'till we had the
whole country jumpin'?

WINONA
I know, you're tellin' me
exactly what the man said, but
I can't understand it

J.T.
That's 'cause you know you are
not an "idea." White folks
believe they made us up to
suit whatever needs they have
at any time, but you and I
know better, don't we?

WINONA
Seems like they won't let us
have nothin'. We make music;
we dance; then they say the
horns made us do that. Just
like we're nothin'.

J.T.
Don't talk like that, baby.
You're plenty for me: plenty
rhythm, plenty melody; plenty
everything for me. Can't
nobody take that away.

They kiss.

CUT TO

EXT. DOWN THE STREET. NIGHT
Talbot is standing, faking exasperation

TALBOT (shouting)
You comin', Massie? We old men. We gotta go to bed, now. (teasing)

MASSIE (giving in a bit)
You're right about that. It's been a long, long day. When I get my hands on that girl, I'm gonna...

TALBOT (sternly)
You gonna what?

CUT TO

INT. MASSIE AND WINONA'S BOARDING HOUSE ROOMS. FRONT ROOM. DAY.

MASSIE (angry)
No, cryin' will not help you, young lady. You are goin' away to school in Tennessee where fast li'l heifers like you can learn some manners, some morals...and, and get a husband.

WINONA
I don't want a husband. I want to <u>sing</u>, Papa.

MASSIE
Have you ever in your life seen a bunch of colored folks who wasn't singin'? Oh, I've

done all I knew to do with
you. So you goin'. That's
that.

WINONA
No. No, it's not. This is
about me and J.T., isn't it?
Papa, I can't stay up
underneath you forever. I'm
not your wife.

Winona is shocked by what she's said, retreats.

MASSIE (quietly)
No, you're not Cissie. Not my
Cissie. But a whole lot like
her. (He goes to Winona, holds
her) Your mama was a fine
singer, could hold her own
with anybody. I wish she could
have known you like I know you
... Now Cissie didn't get as
much of an education as she
wanted, and me, well, I got to
say a 'Amen' for Dr.
Tavernier. So, baby, this J.T.
may have stirred me up, but I
never expected you to live on
the road, go from place to
place your whole life long.

WINONA (tentatively)
You know what, Pa?

MASSIE
What, baby?

WINONA
Even though we've been all over the country, most everywhere, Papa, I've never been away from you.

MASSIE (very gently)
I know, but I think you're ready now. This might be your time to strike out on your own.

WINONA (eyes tearing)
I love you, Papa.

MASSIE
You're my heart, Winona. My heart.

DISSOLVE TO

EXT. NEGRO COLLEGE CAMPUS IN THE SOUTH. DAY.
Winona is a solitary figure ambling down a path. She doesn't speak to other students, though she provokes interest in the coeds.

CUT TO

INT. STAIRWAY IN CLASSROOM BUILDING.
Winona is going up the stairs. Voices singing scales are heard. She looks at her watch.

WINONA
Damn, I'm late already.

Winona runs up the stairs, reaches glass double doors, goes through. Her scampering feet are heard. The doors swing.

CUT TO

INT. CLASSROOM. DAY.

Winona walks into the room where the students who were singing scales begin to sing a classical number. The instructor gives Winona a hard look. Winona slips to the back of the group, begins to sing. The instructor raises her head, looks around as if she's lost something. She waves her arms for the group to stop singing, then turns to the pianist, who had continued to play.

INSTRUCTOR (to pianist)

Didn't you hear the students stopped singing? But, if you didn't hear that other peculiar sound, you might not hear anything… All right. Who is slurring their notes? I'm not playing. I want to know who is putting blues phrasing in classical music? (All eyes focus on Winona) I bet I know who is trying to keep every juke joint trick ever known alive in my classroom. Winona Roughen, please sing the phrase beginning with the first retard[1] after the letter G.

Winona is steely. She sings the phrase as if she was trying to win the Apollo Theatre's Amateur Night Competition.

---

1 Musical term referring to a slackening of tempo

INSTRUCTOR (outraged)
Miss Roughen, that was not only brazen disrespect, but an assault on the sensibilities of everyone in this room. I expect a written apology tomorrow, and a proper rendition of the first movement or your time at this college will be brief, indeed. Singing like a colored girl in my room.

WINONA
I was singing like I was raised to sing, M'am. (Winona starts to walk out of the room) Oh, by the way. I can't think of anything that could make me happier than gettin' my colored behind outta here. (She saunters out)

The class is atwitter, the instructor beside herself. The pianist plays a funeral march until the instructor stomps her foot.

INSTRUCTOR
Stop it. Stop it, this second.

CUT TO

EXT. THE CAMPUS OF THE NEGRO COLLEGE. DAY
Winona is running, skipping, turning down the pathway, She even says "Hello" as she goes by the other students.

CUT TO

INT. REAR OF A BUS OUTSIDE WASHINGTON, D.C.
DUSK.

Winona is sitting in the back of the bus, looking at the rolling hills of Virginia, hearing Billie Holiday sing, "Travellin' All Alone."

CUT TO

INT. BACKSTAGE OF MUSIC HALL, CORRIDOR TO DRESSING ROOMS.

The band is breaking down. There's a lot of commotion. J.T. is wiping his brow, his horn still strapped around his neck. Ben Webster approaches J.T.

WEBSTER

That's exactly the kinda
motion you should be makin',
my man. If you ever come in' on
top of me like that, you won't
have no lip to be givin'
nobody lip with…you
hear?

J.T.

I understand what you're
sayin', really I do. It's just
that I was hearin' something
different…

WEBSTER

(cutting him off)

If I didn't hear whatever you
think you was hearin', then
you didn't hear it either. If

I don't hear it first, ain't
nobody gonna hear it. Now, you
got that?

J.T.
I heard you, man. Won't happen
again.

WEBSTER
Better not.

Webster walks on about his business. J.T. sighs, relieved he's not cornered. Then he turns and slaps the wall a few times.

J.T.
I'm tryin' to get these sounds
out of my mind, into this
horn, and that old man's
sayin' I am not hearin' what
I'm hearin'. (recovering)
Winona listens to me. My baby
hears me.

CUT TO

EXT. BUS PULLING INTO D.C. PROPER. NIGHT
The bus goes by a poster advertising the Ellington Orchestra.

CUT TO

INT. REAR OF BUS. NIGHT
Winona anxiously waiting to get off the bus. All the people are taking a very long time.

CUT TO

EXT. OUTSIDE BUS LUGGAGE COMPARTMENT. NIGHT.

WINONA

(pointing to her suitcase)

That's mine. That's the one.

BUS DRIVER

I thought you were going all the way to New York? (He hands her the suitcase and takes her claim ticket.)

WINONA

Not tonight. Not if I can help it. Thanks.

Winona takes her bag, runs to flag a cab.

CUT TO

EXT. STAGE DOOR OF THE UPTOWN THEATRE. NIGHT

The cab drives away. Winona slowly approaches the door. Rings bell. The door opens. Guard stands in front of Winona

GUARD

Can I help you?

WINONA

Yes. Uh, I need to speak with J.T. Pierre. He's with the Ellington Orchestra.

GUARD

Yeah, I know who he is. But I don't know if he's around. (Hedging) Maybe you'd like to leave him a note, a message.

WINONA

Absolutely not. I've gotta see him.

GUARD

I'll see if he's around. Don't believe so.

Winona is beaming and preening, hardly hearing the man.

QUICK CUT TO

INT. BACKSTAGE. HALLWAY LEADING TO DRESSING ROOMS

GUARD

Of course, she could always buy a ticket.

He walks directly to a dressing room, door ajar, where several fellows are laughing. J.T. Pierre is one of them.

GUARD (continued)

Evenin' y'all.

THE GUYS

How're you doin'? Hi., etc.

GUARD

J.T., there's a young lady at the stage door, looking to talk to you. Says she's gotta see you. And she's carryin' a suitcases.

GUY #1

Uh-oh. Another li'l ol' thing's been thrown out her house.

J.T.

Did you catch her name, my man?

GUY #2

J.T.'s the 'Pa,' is that it?

GUY #3

Wasn't that one here last week?

J.T.

You negroes get off my case. I can't help it if the bitches lose they minds.

J.T. and the guard leave, J.T. posturing. The fellas continue to joke and mimic J.T. Their laughter follows J.T. down the hall.

QUICK CUT TO

INT. HALLWAY TO THE BACKSTAGE DOOR. CONTINUOUS

J.T. and the Guard are walking down the hall to the door.

J.T.

Man, I thought I asked you to tell these fools to just leave a note. I can't keep…

GUARD
I did. That's what I did, but
she wouldn't do it.

J.T.
All right. I'll take care of
it. Thanks, boss.

J.T. throws open the door.

CUT TO

EXT. J.T.'S POV. SIDEWALK OUTSIDE THE STAGE DOOR
Winona's legs, torso, and finally her backside and head, which are turned away from him, are visible to J.T.

WINONA (muttering)
I really just saw the sign. I
was on the bus from Tennessee.
I'm comin' from Tennessee.
Well, I left college 'cause I
was goin' to be throw out
anyway. I saw this sign and,
oh, shoot…

J.T. (delighted/smitten)
Winona? aw, darlin', aw,
Winona.

Winona turns. J.T. and Winona almost knock each other down trying to hug and kiss.

WINONA
I had to see you. I saw this.
(points to sign)

J.T.

Kiss me, baby. I know about
the sign.

WINONA

You're not mad at me?

J.T.

(gathering himself together)
Winona, do I look mad to you?
(laughing) I've never met a
girl with b…guts like
you. Plus you talk to
yourself. And I like it.

WINONA

Oh, J.T., this is foolish.
It's cold out here. Let's go
on in.

J.T.

Go backstage?

WINONA

Yes, until you go on.

J.T.

Uh, you can't do that, Winona.
Its's off limits to 'visitors.'
Okay. Women can't come
backstage. Period.

WINONA

Can't come backstage. I'm not
a 'woman,' whatever that
means. I'm a singer.

J.T.
Got it. Don't both your dads dance.

WINONA
I've only got one dad...

J.T.
So, you dance, too?

WINONA
Course I do.

J.T.
Give me that bag, girl! J.T.'s on the money tonight!

WINONA
J.T., what are you talkin' about?

J.T. takes Winona's arm, leads her down the street to the box office of the Uptown.

J.T.
Now, Winona, I know this is goin' to be hard, but when we go in there, you are goin' to be quiet, and do as I say.

CUT TO

INT. UPTOWN THEATRE LOBBY.
There's a crowd in the lobby in prototypical zoot suits and feathers. J.T. leads Winona toward a table that has a poster proclaiming it "Amateur Night with the Duke, Sign-Up."

WINONA
I'm not an amateur, J.T.

J.T.
Shhhh. Hush, now, and sign.

WINONA
Only for you would I…

J.T.
I know, I know. But, see, now we can go backstage.

WINONA
Oh, I can see you from the mezzanine.

J.T.
Naw, darlin', you've gotta be where I can see you.

CUT TO

INT. UPTOWN THEATRE STAGE.

J.T. is in the saxophone section of the Duke Ellington Band. They begin the first phrases of "Three Little Words." Then, the Duke announces the next contestant.

DUKE ELLINGTON
And now, our last contestant in the Uptown Amateur Competition, let's give a round of applause for Miss Winona Roughen.

Winona struts from the volm with great energy, looks up at J.T. on the bandstand and tears up "Three Little Words." Just as she is finishing the last words, J.T.'s horn eclipses what had seemed like the end of the rendition.

CUT TO

INT. J.T.'S POV

J.T. is riffing, watching Winona's delight in him and Duke's confounded fury. When the Duke can hear a break in J.T.'s improvisation, he brings the whole orchestra in to mask anything J.T. might do.

CUT TO

INT. BACKSTAGE

Winona and J.T. are in a corner, talking to Duke.

J.T.

Now, it wasn't like that,
Duke. I wasn't trying to defy
your authority. I heard my
sweet… I heard this young
woman's voice and got carried
away. That's what happened.

DUKE

I'll tell you what happened.
You just about lost any of my
respect and your job. And you
know friends of band members
can't be in any competition.

J.T.

But did you hear that crowd?

DUKE

I'm not concerned with crowds, Mr. Pierre. I'm concerned with my music.

WINONA

Oh, Mr. Ellington, sir, I would never have entered the competition if I'd known all the provisions. I'm very sorry.

J.T.

That's very understandable, Miss. J.T., until tomorrow, then.

Duke Ellington leaves. J.T. wraps his arms around Winona in a very sexy way.

J.T.

C'mon.

WINONA

Why'd we… Now, you see …Duke Ellington himself is goin' to despise me forever. What am I goin' to do?

QUICK CUT TO

INT. DRESSING ROOM.

J.T. is picking up his horns. Winona is looking at him in the mirror.

J.T.

You know what you're goin' to do? You're gonna realize that

Duke Ellington is one man; one
man with one band. There are a
whole lotta other bands, and
there's only one you, Winona.
I don't ever want to say this
to you again. Never apologize
to anybody for your own talent.
I bet even Duke Ellington
wishes he could sing like you.

DISSOLVE TO

INT. AFTER-HOURS CLUB IN ANACOSTIA.

Cave-like club with rounded walls and winding halls that feel like tunnels. Strange types of gangsters, whores (one or two), a drag queen, rough-looking men roam gaily. A bouncer type pats J.T. down, then Winona. She's indignant but J.T. puts his finger to his mouth: hush. Everybody knows J.T. He's very at home.

CUT TO

INT. AFTER-HOURS CLUB.

WINONA'S POV

Winona looks around the room from the table where she and J.T. are sitting. A small group of musicians starts to jam. There's no leader, as such. There are a few tables of just white people. A shady character passes by J.T. and hands him something.

WINONA

What's that? (It's a marijuana
joint)

J.T. (lighting up)

It gets rid of white folks and
niggahs who are too impressed
with their goddamned selves.
That's what it does.

WINONA
J.T., you shouldn't talk like
that. You're scarin' me.

J.T.
Look here, li'l bits. I know
you don't understand now, but
I'm gonna break it down for
you. You and I are just alike.
(Winona's stunned)

CUT TO

INT. AFTER-HOURS CLUB.
J.T.'S POV
Winona's stunned. A new twosome of white guys carrying instruments walks in.

J.T. (continued)
I can't go anywhere without
white boys stealin' from me.
Damn.

WINONA
J.T., who's stealin' from you?
You're not makin' any sense to
me now at all. What's some
white man gonna steal anyhow?

J.T. (confidentially)
My spirit. They are runnin'
off with my spirit. I can feel
'em suckin' my soul right out
my bones.

WINONA
That sounds foolish, J.T.

J.T.
I don't say foolish things.

He kisses Winona tenderly, but his eyes are open. A tiny room becomes visible when a guy opens a door and leaves. Men inside are cooking heroin, fingers searching for veins, silhouetted.

J.T. (continued)
'Scuse, darlin'. I'll be back shortly.

J.T. heads for the little room.

CUT TO

INT. AFTER-HOURS CLUB
Winona jumps into the jam session. She's interacting with the other musicians ell, vibrant, "scatting." She's pleased with herself and the response of the crowd.

QUICK CUT TO

INT. AFTER-HOURS CLUB, THE LITTLE ROOM.
J.T. is leaving the room, high.

CUT TO

INT. AFTER-HOURS CLUB.
Winona is at the table she shared with J.T., looking around nervously. J.T. comes up behind her, puts his hands on her shoulders.

WINONA
Oh, J.T., I was fixin' to leave. I didn't know where you were. I was singin' up a blue streak. Lord, this place is fun.

J.T. (sweetly)
I know, that's why I brought you here. See,
I'm always with…and there's no way
you'd be leaving here or anywhere ever
without me.

DISSOLVE TO

EXT. OUTSIDE THE SAVOY NIGHTCLUB. NIGHT.
Moderate but very Harlemesque crowd in the lobby and sidewalks. Signs for Fletcher Henderson, Cab Calloway and Roughen and Talbot. Winona and J.T. are lingering while in line to go in.

J.T. (a little drunk)
I still think we shoulda gone
on to Well's for some chicken
and waffles, before we got
tied up here.

WINONA
We're here to see my Papa and
Talbot. That's a treat, you
understand. I'm so excited.
I've never been away from Papa
this long.

J.T.
We'll try to break that record
next time.

WINONA
Let's go in, okay? (looking
hurt)

J.T.
Li'l bits. I was playin'.
C'mon, it'll be fine.

CUT TO

INT. THE BALLROOM OF THE SAVOY

There's a mass of bodies on the dance floor. That quiets. Fletcher Henderson' Band begins to play.

ANNOUNCER

Ladies and Gentlemen,
Soldiers, Sailors, Marines and
Airmen, WACS and WAVES, Harlem
salutes you and so do Roughen
and Talbot.

Massie and Roughen do specialty acts: "The Sand Dance" and "The Top Hat." (Variations of tab/soft shoe/percussion)

CUT TO

INT. THE SAVOY.

Winona rooting, from the dance floor, for her dad on stage.

WINONA

That's what it's about, Pa.
That's sweet, Daddy. Go on.

CUT TO

INT. THE SAVOY. THE BAR.

J.T. is drinking heavily. People at the bar look at him with contempt or envy.

J.T. (to bartender)

You see my sweetheart yet,
Larry? One of those hoppin'
Negroes is her daddy. I'ma get
him a rockin' chair for
Christmas, I think. Let him
sit down.

LARRY

J.T., don't be so mean. Those fellas are masters. I mean, ain't too many folks around could put them to shame.

J.T.

Buckwheat couldn't either, by that line of thinkin'. Hey, friend, do me again.

LARRY

If you say so, but you should be feelin' nice right about now.

CUT TO

INT. SAVOY. THE BANDSTAND.

Cab Calloway and his band are performing one of his wild call and response pieces, in which he dances, too.

CUT TO

INT. SAVOY. THE BAR.

Winona gently tugs J.T.'s sleeve.

WINONA

I hope you didn't miss Papa and Talbot. I love to watch them move.

J.T.

Oh, I didn't realize I'd have to get two rockin' chairs.

WINONA

You better not let them hear
you talkin' 'bout no rockin'
chairs. Looks like there's not
a bone in their bodies
smooth, so smooth.

J.T. (loudly)

Larry, wasn't I tellin' you
those two old man up there but
Buckwheat and Jolson to shame.
Jumpin' up and down like caged
monkeys.

WINONA

J.T., I'm tellin' you. Shut up
right this minute. You are
talking' about my father.

CUT TO

INT. THE SAVOY BAR.
J.T.'S POV

MASSIE

Nigger. White folks used to
shoot at our feet to make us
dance. (He picks J.T. off the
floor, throws him against the
bar) Long as a man can walk
with his head up, don't matter
what his feet be doin'.

The dance floor crowd bursts in applause for Cab Calloway.[1] Heads turn from the fight for a minute, distracted. Teddy Pierre walks in J.T.'s direction. Talbot is trying to pull Massie off J.T. J.T. realizes the person he's looking at is his brother, Teddy.

TALBOT

C'mon, Massie. This is a fool.

J.T.

Hey, Teddy, man. Teddy. Help me out.

Teddy sees this is J.T. He rushes over to the site of the spat. Talbot is holding the arm Massie wants to sock J.T. with.

TEDDY

Has J.T. been raisin' a ruckus
over here? He'll listen to me
(Cuts his eyes at J.T.), won't
you, big brother?

MASSIE

Next time my daughter tells
you to shout your damn mouth,
you better do what she says.
(loosening his grip)

TALBOT

I'm with ya on that one. Or
next time, boy, two ol'
monkeys gone jack yo'ass up.

Winona is wiping tears away, staring at Teddy Pierre, mystified.

---

1 Cabell "Cab" Calloway III (1907–1994) was a popular swing bandleader, singer, conductor, dancer, and songwriter.

TEDDY

J.T., why don't you let me
know when you're comin' to
town? I'd keep you out of
trouble, man.

J.T.

Leave me alone, man. 'Sides
how am I supposed to know
where you are? Winona? Winona?
(he sees her) Come over here.
I want you to meet my brother,
Teddy.

Winona blushes, comes over to the brothers. She tries to help straighten J.T. up a bit. He slaps her hand away. Teddy holds his hand out to Winona, but he feels his eyes float into her skin.

TEDDY

I'm glad to meet you, Winona.
Are you in the City for a
while?

J.T.

She'll be wherever I am.

Winona and Teddy look at J.T. in disbelief.

WINONA

Well, Teddy, J.T.'s brother,
I'm delighted to meet a man
whose timin' is so right.

TALBOT
Now, that's the truth. Though all that excitement was more fun than I remembered.

TEDDY
Please tell Massie I enjoyed the hell out of you all tonight.

WINONA
You know my father.

TEDDY
Of course. I work in Fletch Henderson's band, too. Trumpet.

J.T.
I've had enough of this damn place. I told you we shoulda gone to Well's.

MASSIE
You can come home with us, baby.

WINONA
Thanks, Pa, but I'm all right.

CUT TO

INT. HUGE DANCE HALL IN ENGLAND, WITH POSTERS AND STREAMERS CELEBRATING ALLIED TROOPS AND THE USO: FILLED TO CAPACITY.

The Duke Ellington Band is entertaining the troops with solo artists, Dizzy Gillespie,[1] Cootie Williams,[2] Ben Webster[3] and Juan Tizol.[4] Winona and J.T. are featured when Duke announces a tune from home, "Take the A Train," for the 369th Regiment. Winona and J.T. flirt mercilessly.

CUT TO

INT. LONDON UNDERGOUND DURING AIR RAID. DARK, CROWDED.
Winona is sitting with her back against the wall. J.T. is sleeping by her side. Winona is writing a letter.

CUT TO

INT. NEW YORK CITY SUBWAY, A TRAIN MOVING RAPIDLY.

CUT TO

INT. MASSIE'S HARLEM APARTMENT. DAY.
Massie is reading Winona's letter near the window.

WINONA (VO)
Dear Dear Papa, I'm fine.
There's plenty of bombs going
in every direction, but J.T.
and I are safe. We're happy,
too, Papa. Maybe it's
dangerous enough for him over
here. Can't wait to see you.
Give my love to Talbot. Hugs &
kisses, Winona. P.S.: I really
wanna come home.

---

1 John Birks "Dizzy" Gillespie (1917–1993) was a virtuoso jazz trumpeter and bandleader.

2 Charles Melvin "Cootie" Williams (1911–1985) was a distinguished jazz trumpeter.

3 Benjamin Francis Webster (1909–1973) was a jazz tenor saxophonist.

4 Juan Tizol Martínez (1900–1984) was a Puerto Rican jazz trombonist and composer.

QUICK CUT TO

EXT. FAST-MOVING IRT ELEVATED TRAIN AT 125TH STREET. DAY.

Loud train noises, breaking glass, sirens, crowd noises, etc.

CUT TO

INT. MASSIE'S APARTMENT. DAY.

Massie is startled from his calm with the letter by the "riot" noises from outside. He looks out his window.

CUT TO

EXT. HARLEM BOULEVARD. DAY.

MASSIE'S POV

People running about, shouting, looting, breaking windows, etc.

CUT TO

INT. HALLWAY OF MASSIE'S BUILDING.

Talbot is trying to get his woman from clinging to him as he's dressing himself, going toward Massie's door, which is slightly ajar.

CUT TO

INT. MASSIE'S APARTMENT. DAY

Talbot's woman hands him a t-shirt, which he puts on. He pays her no mind. He talks to Massie as he dresses.

TALBOT

We gotta go, now. We gotta see
what is up out there!

MASSIE

Looks like the end of the
world to me, that's what it
looks like!

WOMAN

Naw. It ain't the end of no world. It's our folks sayin' this world ain't all wrapped up in some white world. That's what it is. (She sits)

MASSIE

It damn sure looks like a war to me.

WOMAN

People say two colored soldiers back from the war was beat up and kilt right here in Harlem.

TALBOT

Say what?

MASSIE

Say, crackers went and killed two Negro soldiers, is what.

WOMAN

And I'm tellin' you, these colored folks in Harlem ain't gonna take this no more.

Massie looks out his window at the mayhem on the street.

CUT TO

EXT. HARLEM STREET DURING RIOT. DAY.

Massie and Talbot are in the midst of these crowds creating havoc. Talbot sees somebody shouting "Don't Buy Where You Can't Work" at a far corner. He goes off in that direction. Massie keeps walking.

MASSIE
Oh, my God. Oh, good Lord.

Massie stops, goes into a doorway, pulls out Winona's letter and looks at it. Shakes his head.

MASSIE (cont'd)
Oh, Jesus. Why today? My baby's comin' home today. Oh God.

Massie looks around him at the craziness: People hauling furniture, wearing lampshades, carrying instruments, shouting racial epithets, etc.

MASSIE
Good God! (staccato) Where's Talbot, now?

Massie puts the letter in his pocket, starts to walk slowly a bit disoriented but full of energy.

TEDDY
Massie Roughen? Massie Roughen, is that you?

Teddy Pierre is looking dapper in an Air Force uniform. He stops Massie, hugs him.

MASSIE
Who? Oh, you're that Pierre boy.

TEDDY
No, sir. I'm Teddy Pierre.
(smiling)

MASSIE
Not that other one, huh?

TEDDY
That's right, sir. But I came up as soon as I heard there was trouble.

MASSIE
We're carryin' on awright, I'll say that.

TEDDY
Yes, well. How is Talbot? Is he okay? (hesitates) What about Winona? Is she safe?

MASSIE
That's what I'm tryin' to do in all this hellaciousness! What they gonna do? Burn the roof up off our heads? I don't know where Winona is!

Massie and Teddy begin walking. They are jostled constantly and it's difficult for them to talk through the crowds and the noise.

TEDDY
I thought Winona was in Europe.

MASSIE
She was 'til today.

TEDDY
She's coming back here today?

MASSIE

Look, there's something goin'
on over there.

CUT TO

EXT. HARLEM STREET CORNER.

Outside a pilfered pawn shop, a crowd of agitated Harlemites is gathered. Teddy pushes through the crowd. Laying crumpled and bloody is Talbot. Teddy kneels by him, gently lifts him.

TEDDY

Hey, there, T. We're going to
get you home. Get you all
cleaned up, you hear?

Talbot nods his head, weakly. Teddy lifts Talbot off the sidewalk and through the crowd.

CUT TO

INT. STAIRWAY OF MASSIE'S APARTMENT BUILDING.

Massie and Teddy are carrying Talbot up the stairs. Talbot's woman runs down toward them.

WOMAN

Aw, Jesus. I tol' y'all not to
go out there with those angry
niggahs. I tol' you them
Negroes was mad today.

TEDDY

It looks pretty bad . . .

WOMAN

I don't even wanta know what
happened. Jesus.

MASSIE

He tried to stop some hoodlums
from tearin' up a guitar…
a guitar was all.

TEDDY

Hey, Massie, once we get T.
settled, we can go back out to
look for Winona. What ya say?

MASSIE

Yeah, but I'm gonna go wash up
a little. This ol' boy got me
all covered up with blood.
Ain't that right, Talbot?

Talbot tries to respond, but he cannot. He faints in their arms.

CUT TO

INT. DOORWAY TO MASSIE'S APARTMENT.

Massie pushes open his door, which he'd left locked, with some puzzlement. Teddy is with him. They enter the apartment.

MASSIE

It's just like Winona to come
from one war right to another.

WINONA (gaily)

That's the truth, Papa.

Teddy and Massie are surprised to see Winona and J.T. relaxing "at home." Massie hugs Winona. Teddy and J.T. are civil to one another. Massie shakes J.T.'s hand.

MASSIE
Oh, my darlin', baby girl.
Thank God you're safe.

J.T.
I'm the one that got her here.
(smiles)

TEDDY
Winona, Massie and I've been
looking for you everywhere.

MASSIE
But Talbot's hurt pretty bad.

WINONA
Something happened to T.?

J.T.
C'mon, Winona, somethin'
happened to Harlem. Can't you
smell it?

TEDDY
J.T., Winona doesn't deserve that.

J.T.
I'll tend to my woman's needs,
if you don't mind, brother-
man.

WINONA (to Massie)
Papa, where's Talbot? I want
to see him.

MASSIE
Now's not a good time.
darlin'. Wait a while.

J.T.
That's you all's answer to
everythin'. "Wait a while."
Well, look where it got ya.
Smack dab in the middle of the
fire, that's where. And we're
all gonna burn in Hell, or you
might call it Harlem, while
the white boys steal our
music. Talkin' 'bout we're too
belligerent to tend to beauty.
(laughs) But I tend to you,
don't I, Winona? Don't I?

Before Winona can answer, Teddy goes over to Massie.

TEDDY
Well, sir, you get some rest.
It seems things have worked
out for the best. At least
Winona's safe. I'll check on
T. on my way out. (turns
abruptly to J.T.) I guess I
should say, "Welcome home."
(turns to Winona) Winona, keep
that pretty head high, now.
Good night.

Teddy leaves.

CUT TO

INT. STAIRWAY OF MASSIE'S BUILDING.
Teddy is going down the stairway.

J.T. (VO)
He's gointa tell me how to tend to my woman. Shit (laughs) Ain't noboby could do you like J.T., huh? Ain't that right, baby? Ain't it?

CUT TO

EXT. HARLEM STREET. EARLY EVENING.
The streets are emptied, cluttered with debris. Very lonely. Smoldering remnants of buildings and artifacts strewn at random. Teddy is walking through this. He sees one devastated building with two broken front windows. When he focuses on these windows and the frame of this building, it becomes first Winona's eyes, then her whole face, weeping.

DISSOLVE TO

EXT. WINONA'S WEEPING FACE IN CEMETERY. EARLY AFTERNOON.

CUT TO

EXT. CEMETERY. FUNERAL PARTY. EARLY AFTERNOON.
Massie, Winona, Talbot's woman, the Pierre brothers and a melange of vaudeville and jazz types are present in their full regalia. Winona walks up to the grave, which is still open, and puts in a dozen white roses. Teddy Pierre puts in sheet music. Massie comes with a pair of Talbot's dancing shoes. The minister recites the 23rd Psalm. Then, all of a sudden, the funeral party lights into a New Orleans funeral march. This makes Massie and Winona cry and laugh at the same time. Teddy is watching the two of them hug.

MASSIE

Oh, he'd like this awright.
He'd like a Louisiana bon
voyage, he would.

WINONA

I know, Papa. But who's goin'
to be lookin' after you now?

MASSIE

No offense to Talbot, but it
sure as hell won't be her.
(indicating Talbot's woman,
laughing)

WINONA

I'm serious, Papa. I'm all you
got left.

MASSIE

This is gonna sound strange,
darlin', but I gotta say it.
You save all the good will and
carin' you've got for
yourself, 'cause as long as
you with that fool, J.T., you
gonna need all the comfort you
can find. That bastard'll see
you in yo' grave 'fore he
cares about anybody 'sides
himself.

WINONA

Papa, that's not fair…

TEDDY (cutting her off)
I just wanted to say that I
cared for T. a great deal, and
if there's anything I can do,
for either of you, please let
me know. (looking directly at
Winona) If there's anything,
Winona, anything at all.

MASSIE
(to Talbot's grave)
Talbot, I 'magine some would
say you didn't have nothin'
but the music and it wouldn't
have come to my mind, 'cept by
you, but yes, our music's
worth dyin' for.

CUT TO

EXT. HARLEM SIDEWALK. NIGHT
Massie is walking, muttering to himself.

MASSIE
I did the best I could for
that girl. That bastard's
doin' his best to bring her
down, down, in some slime,
some terrible filth.

DISSOLVE TO

INT. VERY DARK, DILAPIDATED SHOOTING GALLERY
Winona and J.T. are sitting. J.T. is preparing his works. Winona is crying.

J.T.
Okay, Baby. Now tell J.T:
where can you go without me?

WINONA
Nowhere.

J.T.
Now, where can you go with me?

WINONA
Everywhere.

J.T.
Okay, Baby. You relax. J.T.'s
gonna make you feel better. I
don't like it when your father
upsets you. Here, I need to
find a good vein. Darlin',
c'mon.

He shoots her up.

CUT TO

INT. HARLEM SHOOTING GALLERY
WINONA'S POV
Winona has wild auditory hallucinations and visual ones, where she sees J.T. for the demon that he is, but shakes that away. Then she sees Teddy's eyes. She hears crisp trumpet tones versus J.T.'s tenor growl. She hums the melody to "Night in Tunisia" very sensually.

CUT TO

EXT. 52ND STREET, NEW YORK. NIGHT
In front of a club featuring Miles Davis, Teddy Pierre is talking to Charlie Parker, Max Roach.

TEDDY
No, man. I understand the need
to move out of a form that
leaves no room to really
comment, to breathe…

PARKER
It's ordering the
possibilities of any sequence
of notes… How 'bout that?

TEDDY
But you can't dance, man. To
hear Bebop we come to these
little ol' clubs.

ROACH
We don't own these either.

TEDDY
I think I need dancers. They
inspire me.

ROACH
Hey, ease on down to the
corner. You want to dance,
check Dizzy out. He's got this
drummer, Channo Pozo, from
Cuba with him. I might even
see you there.

J.T. is approaching from the corner.

TEDDY

I'd like to know what inspires my brother, J.T.

PARKER

Don't ask if you don't really want to know.

TEDDY

I dig it.

J.T.

Did I hear my name?

THE GROUP

Hey, Man. Evenin', etc.

J.T.

I'm sittin' in tonight.

PARKER

You? You speak to Miles 'bout that?

J.T.

He knows me.

ROACH

He knows who he wants to know, man, when he wants to know 'em. (They laugh)

CUT TO

INT. 52ND STREET CLUB

Miles Davis,[1] with Milt Jackson,[2] and Thelonious Monk[3] on bandstand. Monk is taking his solo on "Bags' Groove," J.T. is fooling around with his mouth piece, though he's quite wasted. He hears chords that should be closing Monk's solo, walks toward the mike. Miles' back is to him, but as soon as J.T. gets within a foot of the mike, Miles turns on his heels.

DAVIS

Don't get on my muthahfuckin' stage.

Miles nods his head. Two nasty-looking bouncers come to escort J.T. out. Teddy is at the back of the club as J.T., making a scene, is led out.

QUICK CUT TO

EXT. 52ND STREET CLUB. MILES DAVIS SET.

Two bouncers leave J.T. on the sidewalk. He gets up, walks quickly, trying to secure his trumpet, his dignity. Teddy starts out after him, but sees a small sign at a club across the street advertising "Winona Roughen."

CUT TO

INT. SMALL CLUB. WINONA ROUGHEN SET.

It's a dingy, vacant sort of place. Teddy looks around.

TEDDY (to bartender)

Hey, man. Is Winona Roughen working here tonight?

---

1 Miles Dewey Davis (1926–1991) was a trumpeter, bandleader, and composer. He is considered one of the most important figures in the history of jazz music.

2 Milton "Bags" Jackson (1923–1999) was a jazz vibraphonist and composer of the song "'Bags' New Groove."

3 Thelonious Sphere Monk (1917–1982) was a jazz pianist and composer.

BARTENDER
I hope so.

TEDDY
What's that mean? I really need to see her.

BARTENDER
Well, that fool boyfriend of hers was raisin' Cain a little earlier and now, I think she's run on down to catch some of Dizzy's set.

TEDDY
Thanks, man. I owe you.

CUT TO

INT. 52ND STREET CLUB, DIZZY GILLESPIE SET WITH CHANNO POZO

Gay, lively crowd, integrated, is caught up in the breakneck guaguanco[1] that Dizzy's band is playing. Teddy is surveying the space, looking for Winona. Channo Pozo[2] takes his solo.

CUT TO

INT. 52ND STREET CLUB, DIZZY GILLESPIE SET

J.T. coming out of the dressing room area of the club, agitated, mumbling to himself.

J.T.
I'm the muthafuckin' genius. Ain't no white folks gonna steal nothin' from me.

---

1 A rumba-based Cuban rhythm

2 Luciano "Chano" Pozo González (1915–1948), was a Cuban percussionist and composer.

CUT TO

INT. 52ND STREET CLUB, DIZZY GILLESPIE SET. CONTINUOUS

Teddy winds precipitously through tables, the crowd, around waiters toward the dressing room area. Teddy goes to the one door he sees ajar.

TEDDY

Winona.

Winona is bruised and bloodied with her works in her hands. When she sees Teddy, she tries to hide them.

TEDDY (continued)

Relax, baby. It's nothing I haven't seen before.

He examines the welts on her. Gets a cloth, wets it, starts to clean her up.

WINONA

I didn't know what to do. J.T. came to the club, said I had to go with him. I had to work. I couldn't go home. But, I known how he is when I don't want to do what he wants to do … So I came over here cause there's people and they're laughin', feelin' the music. I just wanta feel the music. Teddy, that's all I ever wanted.

TEDDY

Winona, how long's he been doin' this to you?

WINONA

(Looks at her body, then at Teddy) Oh… (she looks perplexed) I can't remember …How long, you said?

TEDDY (cradling her head)

Then I know for a fact there's a helluva lot of life you forgot.

CUT TO

INT. DRESSING ROOM OF CLUB. DIZZY'S SET
TEDDY'S POV.
A musician pokes his head in, panting.

MUSICIAN

Hey, Teddy. Thank God you're here. Cops ready to take J.T. on in, man.

TEDDY

Humph. Let 'em take him. Or he'd have to deal with me.

Winona seems worried.

TEDDY (continued)

Uh huh. You got no business worrying about nothin'. Nothin' except whether the

sun's goin' to rise. (Winona
winces and smiles)

DISSOLVE TO

INT. TEDDY'S LOFT. DAY.

Winona's bruises are fading. She's lying naked on the bed. Teddy is cooking.

TEDDY

You know, pretty soon you
gonna be well enough to do
some of the cookin' too.
(chuckles)

WINONA

Don't forget I was raised in
hotels, on the road. We gotta
whole movement goin' cause
Rosa Parks didn't want to sit
on the back of the bus. Hell,
I lived on the back of the bus.

Teddy puts his cooking to rest, comes over to Winona.

TEDDY

You understand why I try to
keep you healthy?

WINONA

Guilt.

TEDDY

Cause I want to share the rest
of my life with you. A long,
long, full life.

WINONA

If you're sayin' what I think you're sayin', we've got to speak to my father.

TEDDY

Isn't that sorta ol' timey, sweetheart?

WINONA

If I were you, I wouldn't be so flip, 'less you wanta tell Massie to carry his shotgun with him to the church.

Winona waits, still. Finally, everything registers with Teddy, who jumps in the air, whoops, runs to Winona and wraps her in his whole body.

TEDDY

A baby! Yes. Our baby. Yes. Yes. And there'll be lots more.

CUT TO

EXT. PARK IN NEW YORK. DAY
Very pregnant Winona is on bench with Massie.

MASSIE

Big as you are, don't you think you should be taking it easy?

WINONA

Papa, I am not my mother. I am not goin' to drop dead, soon as the baby's head sticks out.

MASSIE
No need to be vulgar, no. And you know your mother wanted to be here with you. Don't mock us.

WINONA
Papa, I would never do that. What I was actually thinkin' of was some way to protect the baby.

MASSIE
I must be gettin' old, sometimes I forget that you actually come from Louisiana. (laughs)

WINONA
My idea is to go hear as much jazz as I can during this last month, so the baby comes to this world in music, like Mama did for me. And I want you to go with me.

MASSIE
Oh, why don't you just ask me to babysit?

CUT TO

INT. BRIGHT LOFT SPACE, LOWER MANHATTAN.

Ornette Coleman[1] with Haden,[2] Cherry and Blackwell,[3] playing for small audience. Winona is there with Massie. Massie keeps nodding out.

CUT TO

INT. GREENWICH VILLAGE NIGHT CLUB.
COLTRANE SET.

Coltrane's extended unit is playing a facsimile of "Ascension." Winona is hypnotized by the music. Massie is livid; his lips almost quiver.

QUICK CUT TO

INT. COFFEE HOUSE, LOWER EAST SIDE. DAY.

The New York Art Quarter with LeRoi Jones doing "nihilismus." Winona is grooving with it. Massie is confounded. Then, Ted Joans[4] reads his jazz poem.

DISSOLVE TO

WINONA AND TEDDY'S GARAGE. DAY

Massie and the kids are laughing, as Ted Joans' poem fades out.

MASSIE

And of course, after that all
hell broke loose. Wasn't no
more rhythm, no melodies, a
handful of singers, and just a
lot of noise.

---

1 Randolph Denard Ornette Coleman (1930–2015) was a saxophonist, violinist, trumpeter, composer, and free jazz pioneer.

2 Charles Edward Haden (1937–2014) was a jazz double bassist, composer, and bandleader.

3 Donald "Don" Eugene Cherry (1936–1995) was a free jazz trumpeter, and Edward Joseph Blackwell (1929–1992) was an avant-garde jazz drummer. Cherry and Blackwell frequently collaborated.

4 Theodore "Ted" Joans (1928–2003) was a surrealist jazz poet, trumpeter, and visual artist who was considered a pioneer of spoken word.

The kids try to stop themselves from laughing. The do not believe Massie.

CLIFF

Grandpa, that was before I
went looking for Albert Ayler[1]
in the East River.

MASSIE

Uh-humnn.

BLAISE

And 'fore I thought I was
Abbey Lincoln[2].

MASSIE

Uh-humnn.

NATE

I got nothin' to say.
(He plays a Jimi Hendrix[3] phrase)

CUT TO

INT. WINONA AND TEDDY'S BEDROOM. DAY.

WINONA

Teddy, you know, there's …
some truth, uh, in what you
were sayin' 'bout me bein'
jealous of the kids.

---

1 Albert Ayler (1936–1970), was an avant-garde jazz saxophonist and composer who was found dead in the East River in 1970.

2 Abbey Lincoln (1930–2010) was a jazz vocalist, actor, and political activist.

3 James Marshall "Jimi" Hendrix (1942–1970) was an electric guitarist, composer, and singer. He was among the most influential musical artists of the twentieth century.

TEDDY
I know that.

WINONA
Do you think it's too la …

TEDDY (cutting her off)
No, it's never too late. I'll
do whatever I have to,
whatever you want me to.
Between us we know most
everybody, or somebody.
(laughs) We've done harder
things, baby.

WINONA
Awright. Oh, Teddy, I love
you.

CUT TO

PASTICHE: ARTICLES FROM JAZZ MAGAZINES ANNOUNCING WINONA'S "RETURN": VARIETY, DOWNBEAT, CODA, MUSICIAN, ETC.,

CUT TO

MONTAGE: Winona's group taking bows in Montreaux, Moers Festival, North Sea Festival, Ron Scott's Keystone Korner, Le Chat[1]

CUT TO

INT. MIDTOWN HOTEL. DAY
Winona and Teddy are talking with Massie

1 Noteworthy twentieth-century jazz festivals and venues

WINONA

Papa, I just don't understand it. I can't reach any one of my children and I've been gone for months.

TEDDY

Darlin', we were gone one month and a half. They are probably just cleanin' the house because they know we're closin' in on 'em.

WINONA

Don't joke. This is serious.

MASSIE

Baby, the last thing you need to do is worry yourself about those babies. You gotta show tonight. That's the deal.

Winona picks up a newspaper with an advertisement for her New York premiere, with Andrew Cyrille,[1] Wilbur Ware,[2] and Don Pullen,[3]

WINONA

Oh, Papa. I do want to sing. I'm really doin' it. (She hugs Massie)

---

1 Andrew Charles Cyrille (b. 1939) was an avant-garde jazz drummer.

2 Wilbur Bernard Ware (1923–1979) was a jazz double bassist.

3 Don Gabriel Pullen (1941–1995) was a jazz pianist and organist.

TEDDY

come to bed with me girl, I gotta get you ready for tonight. No, no tears. Cain't bring no tears 'round here. This bed is haunted.

WINONA

Oh, Teddy, it's really tonight.

CUT TO

INT. LITTLE CARNEGIE HALL

The concert hall is jammed with folks of all descriptions and aesthetic beliefs.

TEDDY (VO)

Ladies and Gentlemen, we are pleased to present the Winona Roughen Ensemble.

CUT TO

INT. BACKSTAGE, CARNEGIE HALL

As band goes onto the stage, Winona leans to Teddy.

WINONA

I don't see any of the children.

TEDDY

Don't worry, they'll show. Knock 'em dead, baby.

QUICK CUT TO

INT. STAGE. CARNEGIE HALL

The band is assembled. Winona is downstage center. She takes the mike.

WINONA

I want to thank you for your
warm reception. This moment's
been a long time comin'.

Suddenly, there is a blast of trumpets and drums. From the back of the auditorium. Blaise leads Sun-Ra and his Arkestra down the aisles. Cliff strolls, with his tenor horn wailing. Nate's wa-wa eclipses everything for a second. There's a calm. Talbot and Massie tap their way across the stage. Slowly, Teddy blows his trumpet with warm, mellow tunes. The audience is mocking. J.T. is in the back, scruffy and alone. He leaves and goes out of the concert hall. The music arrangement loses one instrument at a time, 'til there's just a David Murray solo hoverin' over Winona's voice.

CUT TO

EXT. 7TH AVENUE, NEW YORK CITY. NIGHT.

J.T. is walking slowly away from the concert. His shadow is visible. The horn falls out. Last impression is of J.T.'s shadow fading as Winona's voice fades into silence.

THE END

Lavender Lizards & Lilac Landmines:

Layla's Dream

A Theater Piece
by Ntozake Shange

October 2002
University of Florida/ Gainesville, FL

SETTING:

A limbo space between Layla's bed and the inner realms of her mind and imagination.

CHARACTERS:

(all the actors should be able to sing and dance)

Layla La Pierre – the central figure of the piece, is appropriated and revised from *BOOGIE WOOGIE LANDSCAPES.*[1] She is a black woman of about 25-26 years of age. Her spirit is strong but delicate. She is not yet fully developed as a person. An unknown writer, she is a natural beauty and wild in her dreams.

(The other characters are dream people known to Layla from childhood, memories, dreams and her own artistic perceptions. Some of the characters are spirits, some are from Layla's real life.)

THE LOVER:

YVES – a very handsome black and charming ladies man. A poet. Layla's lover. He is manipulative with an evil streak.

FRIENDS:

Boo - a rascal of a black female. She brings strength to Layla.

Kuka - a raucous woman, maybe Latin. She dresses very nicely.

P.T. - an entrepreneurial black man who deals in reality as much as possible.

SPIRITS:

Veronica – a positive spirit who has learned from her experiences. Should be a dancer.

---

1 *Boogie Woogie Landscapes* is a play by Shange originally published in 1978.

Mariposa – a female spirit of color with Chinese-Trinidadian heritage.

Juan Pedro – a magic man and master spirit worker in the Mexican folk tradition.

Frank – an elderly spirit from Charleston s.c. has seen everything and been everywhere.

Xavier – a young male spirit of black or Asian heritage.

POEMS

PART ONE

Layla's Song
reunion: I want to see my people
my man he jump in flowers
Chicago in San Francisco & you/ me/ waait/ love is musik / touch me like sounds/ …
you are sucha fool
Sputnik
wow… yr just like a man
elegance in the extreme
the great northern hotel
Porque No Estas Conmigo[1]: my song for Hector Lavoe[2]
blue horizon

PART TWO

i had 5 nose rings
cooking with jeffrey
some men
with no immediate cause
stand up 'chile'
people of watts

1 "Because you are not with me"
2 Héctor Lavoe (1946–1993) was a highly influential Puerto Rican salsa singer.

LAYLA'S DREAM

(The is Layla's dream. The environment includes Layla's "floating bed" [on wheels or casters] and a background motif composed of a tasteful collage of lizards and faces that fade in and out of focus. The environment should also emphasize a dreamscape world, painted in colors, shades and hues of purples, lavender and blues, with maybe bits of reds and pinks woven in.

Lighting should be magical, fantastical and psychedelic in feeling. The mood and feel is sometimes ritualistic, sometimes fantastical, always mystical and ultimately, angelic.

Costumes may reflect individual aspects of the various characters, but must also distinguish the real world people from the spirit people.

As the lights or curtain rise, LAYLA appears to be sleeping when she is awakened by music. She takes out a journal from under the bed covers and begins writing, which leads to dancing out of the bed, an expressive dance that represents her poetic desires.)

LAYLA

one thing I know for sure/ only
memory & desire are relentless/
& here i am/ & all you see/ is this
brown body w/ hair askew &
barefoot/ my memories actually fill this
room with hundreds of people/ their
spirits linger in faces/ smells & feelins
I'm finding hard to live w/ i'm

crammed w/ others/ & their
realities impinge on my present

do you understand me?

maybe i could be a black anais nin[1]/ &
record every incident/ the wine/ the meals
even a kiss/ or instead a marc chagall[2]
w/ drawin's & words as well to fix/
once/ & for all/ who i am & what i've been
for myself & others/ maybe i could make it all
/ go away/ but then who would i be/ a void
huh?/ 'impossible'

my days on this planet/ in this hemisphere
are too rich to throw away/ i'm goin'
to remember who i am/ who/ who made my
life/ something i can offer as a gift/ a bit worn/ but still
sparkilin'/ i think
sometimes/ if i sleep from now till
eternity/ i'll capture everyone & each
second of my imaginin's/ my past relived in/
fantastical episodes of truth/ but the rising sun
& my insistent desire to live/
make that impossible

(She dances some more.)

maybe you can help me sort/ this
out/

(BOO enters dancing with Layla.)

1 Anaïs Nin (1903–1977) was a French novelist and essayist. Here Shange makes implicit reference to Nin's detailed erotica.

2 Marc Chagall (1887–1985) was a Russian-French modernist painter.

join me in my efforts to know who i am/

(KUKA enters dancing with them both.)

after all you've just met me &

(P.T. enters.)

i'm not real to you/ yet
let me become real to you/ we
can work together/ we can make magic/

(YVES enters.)

together/ bring the spirits down

(SPIRITS start to dance into the room.)

come on/ come on down on me

(A large scale dance including everyone on stage. It is a dance constructed in LAYLA's mind. It includes bits of ritual and ceremony, pomp and elegance, fun and frolic, wild and crazy, and ending in passion for LAYLA and YVES. She grabs hold of him in an embrace.)

i won't let you escape

YVES
who the hell you think is gonna stay with you?

BOO
what the hell are you doing here? how the hell did you get in here?

YVES
she can't stop thinking abt me

KUKA
ain't nobody thinking about you

YVES
ask her! ask her!

P.T.
we don't have to we know what you've done to her.

YVES
yeah? well she still likes it/ don'tcha baby

LAYLA
stop talking about me like i'm not here

YVES
you want me to go? i can go/ i can go any minute. just say the word

LAYLA
Yves, they don't know you like I do/ try to be nice/ okay?

YVES
i don't feel like it.

JUAN PEDRO
ain't nobody interested in what you feel like doin'/ I shoulda left mi chiquita more holy water.

(As the SPIRITS begin to speak, LAYLA is the only human who can hear them, although she can not see them until later. YVES laughs).

LAYLA
my god Yves/ don't antagonize the spirits/ you don't know what they're capable of

YVES
I got you Layla/ just face it

MARIPOSA
no one owns our woman anymore – especially a brujo witch like you. now be quiet/ Layla's called us

VERONICA
and we came

FRANK
we protect you Layla/ you can say anything

LAYLA
but its so awful

YVES
you ain't seen awful/ if you leave me, you'll crumble up like a nasty ole woman

JAVIER
but we are not afraid

LAYLA *(getting excited)*
Yves you must go. you must go right now

YVES
I may or may not be back sweetheart/ linger w/ that
(he exits)

P.T.
what's the matter?

BOO
i can tell you the matter/ that fool she keeps hanging around here

KUKA
time heals all wounds/ she's still wounded/ poor baby/ *pobrecita*

LAYLA
that's not the problem/ i can handle him

BOO
don't look like it to me

P.T.
now now/ some things are harder than we know

VERONICA
she needs a gentleman

JUAN PEDRO
she doesn't need anything/ but some good charms

MARIPOSA
I think its more private than that/ it has something to do with us. maybe we don't spend enough time with her

FRANK
we can't help if she doesn't call on us/ its up to her

LAYLA
oh God!

JUAN PEDRO
well, that's close enough

(Music and movement as SPIRITS move in on LAYLA)

LAYLA
Who are you? and what do you want?

JAVIER
we're your protectors

VERONICA
your dreams

MARIPOSA
your secrets

FRANK
your guides

JUAN PEDRO
your hope and strength

LAYLA
I have all that?

MARIPOSA
of course you do

VERONICA
but you put us to little use

JUAN PEDRO
what do you want us to do?

FRANK
we can do anything/ but you must/ allow us

LAYLA *(ponders for a moment)*
i want to see my people/ the ones who live and the ones living in spirit

FRANK
i've got $5 from the Bank of the Commonwealth of Virginia, $10 from the bank of South Carolina, A Texas treasury warrant worth another $5 and a genuine $100 bill from the Confederate States of America, dated February 17, 1864.

BOO *(looking in an old slave journal she has found in LAYLA'S bed)*
i know what Enoch, John, and Lucy cost.

P.T.
actually, I know what a whole lot of people cost.

BOO
for instance, Louisa and child James, $1,700.

KUKA *(joining BOO at the book)*
Phoebe and child John, $1,600.

P.T *(joining them)*
Carolina, $200

KUKA
Miranda and child, six years, $1,600.

BOO
now I know my papers are in order. As a Fourteenth Amendment person, I've got something akin to freedom.

LAYLA
but I've got no proof. Nothing I can hold in my hand and say, "Hey, I'm a free African with the right to travel, own property, get married, and drink water somewhere." / the first time I slipped past the Mason-Dixon line, I slept with my mamma.

BOO
I guess most little niggers sleep underneath their mothers as long as we can

VERONICA
but without those papers, where you can lay your head, causes tremendous anxiety.

BOO
A grown nigger that's able-bodied and fertile, I lay up in Charleston, round from the slave mart, drinking myself a mint julep, beguiled by the canopy and the evening breeze.

KUKA
when dream time come up on me, some David Niven[1]-looking planter come pullin' me out of my bed talkin' 'bout how I know

1 David Niven (1910–1983) was a British actor and writer.

better than to be layin' in a white lady's bed, with my palm woven mat right at his feet. Well, I slapped this ruffled son of the South with all my might and my hand fell empty.

BOO
Sneers branded red and swollen on my cheek.

KUKA
my nakedness and empty hand, bare feet/ shamed with no papers.

LAYLA
What was I going to do?

MARIPOSA
nothing to let anyone know you are a free soul.

LAYLA
But slavery fell off me like sins run from angels, and I remain empty-handed, broken down in the mystery of what makes me free.

P.T.
Where it goes to/ and who can come takin' my freedom again any old time/ any old body/ like somebody like Strom Thurmond.[1]

BOO
Scribble my words in some plantation ledger, a diary of the day's activities left me lower on the list than the fate of the rice crop

JAVIER
cows

FRANK
horses, and such.

---

1 James Strom Thurmond (1902–2003) was a conservative South Carolina politician and governor who was an avowed segregationist in the Civil Rights Movement.

KUKA
Rosetta, $17, Rena, $1,200, Flora, $800.

LAYLA
I'm further down the account than mares and pigs.

P.T.
Not so accurately observed as the daily silverware.

KUKA
A blemish on my body means less than a scratch on a quarter horse.

BOO
If I walk around without my freedom papers you know I must be a fool.

LAYLA
Now listen carefully, 'cause I might not repeat this again./ I am not out of my mind. Cross-country jaunts are not inexpensive, and I do want to see my people, but I'm not goin' bankrupt trying to buy my freedom back. I've got here in my hand a Criswell note of the Confederate States of America with "the personification of the South striking the union down." This $10 note cost me $1,200 United States currency, today, 2003. I want to walk the Confederacy with my manumission papers up my sleeve or in the bottom of my shoe 'cause slavers, patty rollers, bushwhackers, even the New Orleans police and the Los Angeles police just this year are apt to grab my purse, dump everything, and claim I am an unidentified black female and take me wherever. But I'm convinced this particular personal odyssey can be accomplished. I have no issue about paying for myself in South Carolina, in Texas, in Connecticut, Oklahoma, Virginia, wherever my people are from or were from. Whatever currency my value is recognized in, I am ready and I am determined to have the last bit of myself. I can't pay with my freedom, it cost too much already. Nevertheless, $5 in South Carolinian currency, circa

1832, which was worth nothing in 1865, is now going at $48 United States of America currency, 2003. And I still want to see my people, alive more than those living in spirit. So there's no doubt about it whatsoever, I get to go home free, one way or another, I told you. I want to see my people.

JAVIER
you sounding pretty good already

MARIPOSA
that's the way girl

VERONICA
maybe you don't need us so much after all

JUAN PEDRO
oh no! she still needs us/ don't be fooled

LAYLA
Please meet my friends.
this is Kuka & P.T./ and this is Boo/ we met in grade school / been together ever since

BOO
as long as you keep that Yves out of it. You need a man like mine/ an island man.

(Caribbean music begins)

cause my man/ he jump in flowers
he say/
they smell like me
peonies/ lilies/ lavender & lilac
blossom from my pores/ he say
I a sweet bouquet of golden roses
the petals he kiss/ is me
I try to see me as these flowers

face of violet orchids
arms/ antherium
legs/ proteus/ they so strong
w/ petals of soft feathers
that rub him the right way
he jump in garden/ he say/ is me
we laugh & my petals fly
like rain drops/ of me/ leave he skin
aglow
my man he jump in flowers
believe they smell like me
& he in ecstasy/ he say
the perfumes of the gods
for we/ & always so so sweet

(A bit of dancing to the music, then it subsides into bluesy poetic jazz. YVES has come back on stage during the dance. LAYLA turns to see him, and remembers. Their conversation becomes a kind of dance.)

LAYLA
chicago in san francisco & you/ me/ waait/

YVES
Love is musik /

LAYLA
touch me like sounds/ chicago on my shoulder/

YVES
yr hand/ is now a kiss

LAYLA
i get inspired in the middle of the nite
when you make love to me

YVES
after i've held you & kissed you & felt alla that

LAYLA
i get inspired get cherished/ free of pain/ not knowing anymore what is dream/ but is love/ like they are singin to me

YVES
odawalla/ reese & the smooth ones/

LAYLA
here where you kissed me/

YVES
& I feel you/

LAYLA
I cd make it up again/

YVES
but we're already musik/ joseph / roscoe / lester / don/ & malachi/

LAYLA
I hear em in our sweat

YVES
& nobody is speakin'/ but the rhythms are chicago/ melody on the loose/

LAYLA
when you make love to me/ I shout like the colors on joseph's face/ am bound to air like roscoe's horn/ like the 'cards' are stacked in our favor/

YVES
one slight brown thing bip-bloo-dah-shi-doop-bleeeeeeha-uh/ refusing false romance/

when it waznt what ya wanted/ or who ya thot
waz comin/ but it waz real tenderness/ cant lie

LAYLA
i remember

YVES
you are sucha fool/ i haveta love you
you decide to give me a poem/ intent on it/ actually
you pull/ kiss me from 125th to 72nd street/ on
the east side/ no less
you are sucha fool/ you gonna give me/ the poet/
a poem
insistin' on proletarian images/ we buy okra
3 lbs for $1/ & a pair of 98c shoes
we kiss
we wrestle
you make sure at east 110th street/ we have cognac
no beer all day
you are such fool/ you fall over my day like
a wash of azure

LAYLA
you take my tongue outta my mouth/
make me say foolish things
you take my tongue outta my mouth/ lay it on yr skin
like the dew between my legs
on this the first day of the silver balloons
& lil girl's braids undone
friendly savage skulls on bikes/ wish me good-day
you speak spanish like a german

YVES
oh you are sucha fool/ I cant help but love you

maybe it was something in the air
our memories
our first walk
our first…
yes/ alla that

LAYLA
where you poured wine down my throat in rooms
poets I dreamed abt seduced sound & made history/ you make me
feel like a cheetah
a gazelle/ something fast & beautiful
you make me remember my animal sounds/
so while I am an antelope
ocelot & serpent speaking in tongues
my body loosens for/ you

YVES
you decide to give me the poem

LAYLA
you wet Yr fingers/ lay it to my lips
that I might write some more abt you/ how you come into me
the way the blues jumps outta b. b. king

YVES
how david murray[1] assaults a moon & takes her home/
like dyanne harvey[2] invades the wind

LAYLA
oh you/ you are sucha fool/
you want me to write some more abt you
how you come into me like a roller coaster in a
dip that swings

---

1 David Murray (b. 1955) is a jazz saxophonist.
2 This appears to be a typo referencing jazz vocalist Jane Harvey (1925–2013).

leaving me shattered/ glistening/ rich/ screeching
& fully clothed

YVES
you set up to fall into yr dreams
like the sub-saharan animal I am/ in all this heat
wanting to be still

LAYLA
to be still with you

YVES
in the shadows

LAYLA
all those buildings
all those people

YVES
celebrating/ sunlight & love/ you
you are sucha fool/ you spend all day piling up images
locations/ morsels of daydreams/ to give me a poem

just smile/ I'll get it

(By the end of the poem LAYLA and YVES manage to end up in bed. As they move toward love making, KUKA and BOO move in and turn the bed around, away from the audience's sight. They attempt to change the focus.)

KUKA
cards always gotta have a full deck/ gotta have a woman/ queen of spades/ like malachi slipped in wit the grace of nefertiti or eubie blake/ this aint what we expected

BOO, KUKA & P.T.
THE ART ENSEMBLE OF CHICAGO
(Music changes)

BOO
but it waz colored

P.T.
waz truth

KUKA
waz gotta rhythm/ like you feel to me

BOO
I really wanted to be a waitress to serve em in a negress way/ push
my waist thru a tight black skirt & amble like a alto in bird's mouth/
a secret/ too sweet to
hold tears/ I wanted musik/ & they brought
love in a million tones/ & I am not the same anymore/ not any more

P.T.
you wanted a sigh/ I made like a flute/

YVES *(jumping up from or on the bed)*
I pull/ I ease back &
splee-bah-wah-she-do-the-do-tso/ ring like a new reed/ cant stoppa
cherokee/

BOO
a jackson in yr house/ congliptis/ all around/

KUKA
the art ensemble cd make ya love more/ cd make you love more/
(During the following section the chorus of other voices join LAYLA and create a jazz rife with the words, ending at "like silence.")

LAYLA

Chocolate or miz t. in all her silver/ don't inspire me like I get inspired when you hold me in Chicago harmonies/ & we waltz like vagrants

(CHORUS joins LAYLA in improvised vocal entrances and rhythms, repeating and overlapping, making a jazz symphony of sounds.)

set up/ signal the release of pain/ scream/ sing then sigh/
groan/ sound/ make the sound that kisses me/ one note/ you/ make
me melody/ is/ is musik/ uh true uh/ yes musik is the least love
shd bring you/ most ya'll ever have/ you/ yes/ musik/ you/ let love
musik you/ you kiss me like the sound/ we love/ is the musik
watch us dance/ & let the musik/ you take it all/ get the musik/ let
the musik love you close
like silence

(In the silence that follows, YVES and LAYLA retreat back to the bed for more passion. The lights change as soccer ball is delivered onstage. All the others begin to play soccer. JUAN PEDRO moves forward speaking like a sports announcer over a stadium microphone.)

JUAN PEDRO

Ladies and gentlemen. Welcome to the final match of the World Cup. It's the white/ white Argentineans vs. the blks/ blk magic Nigerians/ the underdog/ as always. Startlin' as Sputnik! Startlin' as the 1st satalite around the earth. LEEETT'S PLAAAAY BAAAAALLLLL!!!!!

(After a few seconds of play, he takes a deep gasp)

uh oh!/ looks like the Nigerians have got the Argentineans by the balls!

like Sputnik/ Sputnik the hottest new item on the earth
earth/ think in any language/ look from any point
folks scratch they heads/ there's somethin' goin on
out there
i'm thinkin'/ but muscles and balls
rhythm & a whole lottta shakin' goin' on
where 'whoops there it is'
don't need no more translation

sputnik hovers
over the skies of
"the gateway to the
west"/ trapped by natural laws of
physics/ arrogance/
pain lack of imagination/

YVES *(appearing from behind the bed adjusting his clothes)*
"oh whaat a nite"
niggahs sing anyway anywhere on
the face of the earth

FRANK
everythin'/ everyone of us
is known
to sputnik's tiny
rovin' eye/ small rigid
pre-reptilian star/

JAVIER
before mir & columbia's
mating ritual/ hand made
star/ laughing/ flying by fires
we call stars/ flames

we know as suns/
linking hopes of us
of whom nothin' is expected/
with facts of what
anglos had forgot/

YVES *(interrupting again with song)*
"yes/ i'm the one love has forgot/ we the ones love has
forgot – we were ones love forgot"

VERONICA
the center of the galaxy is not the
white house/ nor
our most darin' feat/
continuin' to breathe
under the weight of gravity/
bound invisibility/ clingin'
to a beggin' white
boy near south halstead at
3:00 AM / he missed the hodiamont
streetcar by a quarter century/

MARIPOSA
don't know how to negotiate
"the arc of bones"[1] dumas'
cartography reveals
indiscriminately to any
seasoned wayfarer/

VERONICA
becuz the bleedin'
cracker was stopped near lake

1 This is a reference to Henry Dumas (1934–1968), whose short story "Ark of Bones" was published posthumously in 1974. Dumas, a poet and short story writer, was killed by a New York City Transit Police officer.

pontchatrain/ near slidell/ never
ever asked for a streetcar named desire/
blinded as he was/ by rage

MARIPOSA
niggahs go blind & see all the way past
heaven/ blind willie[1]/ blind lemon[2]/ *el ciego arsenio*[3]

ALL THE SPIRITS
so race matters

P.T.
to a blind white boy/ lookin' for sputnik/
humiliated as the petite & tricky
mechanical comrade don't miss a trick/ a flamboyant or
cultured garden west L.A. colored/
the lost style
peripheral to savin' face

BOO
meantime i'm slinkin'
round st. louis
an asp/ a cobra/ a
diamondback outta south
tejas/ whose
power is simply ignored/
everybody's lookin' for sputnik

JUAN PEDRO
how cd it happen/

---

1 "Blind" Willie Johnson (1897–1945) was accidentally blinded by his stepmother at age seven and grew up to became a gospel singer, guitarist, and evangelist.

2 Lemon Henry "Blind Lemon" Jefferson (1893–1929) was a popular blues gospel singer of the 1920s who was born blind.

3 Arsenio Rodríguez (1911–1970) was a groundbreaking Cuban composer and musician who was blind from the age of seven after a horse kicked him in the head.

VERONICA
what got into them/

BOO
god didn't prophecy no bolshevik star/

KUKA
god don't even talk to communists/
so
where'd they get off

LAYLA
upsettin' the balance of the 'Western World'

P.T.
symmetry is paramount
any ex-communicated Italian can attest to that/

LAYLA
the unseen backbone/ the ever re-newing skins/
bodies of us/
we/ that don't get counted in a census of livin' things
or dyin' things for that matter/we of whom
nothing is expected/we did not search the horizon/
desperately seekin' sputnik's shadow & light

BOO
sputnik's gaze
we knew/
we knew she was up there like
our good friend the north star/like we know
to cross the eades bridge wit 38's or low-ridin' chevys/

JAVIER
must be terrible to be surprised by
folks who just don't

count/in the eyes of the god on the penny/
or the dollar
the bank officers/the U.S. navy/ sorta
like
when all them lil niggah chirren disappeared/

MARIPOSA
kinda like slavery/here we are one minute & then
wow/ we somewhere else/

KUKA
like them argentines believed they'd done sold us
all/ alla us/ back to brazil

LAYLA
to pick coffee/

BOO
mine gold/

KUKA
open our legs

LAYLA
anywhere/

KUKA
do anything/

BOO
just go/from the pampas
to buenos aires/ they sold us back to slavery
'way from them/

JUAN PEDRO
& sputnik hovers over us all without permission/
manumission papers/ or the blessin' of el Papa

YVES
Hey
there really are more of us/

FRANK
where we come from/ try & tango
without a colored sense of rhythm/ ha

JUAN PEDRO
& a ball is a ball/
up in the sky or on a soccer field/

VERONICA
sputnik hummed like my grandma
mornin's when our moon
still showed her face unashamed

LAYLA
& argentines protected
who they thought they are/ from what
they thought we were worth/ or worthless/

YVES
but it obviously don't affect
the dynamic of a niggah & a ball/

JAVIER
cd startle you/ cost a bunch a money/
but prices continually rise/ cain't touch him/
huh/

FRANK
remember sputnik

YVES
remember goin' "round & round we go/ got em
goin' in circles... oh oh - oh no - oh no - oh oh"

LAYLA
maybe we'll find more
miracles
if we look to the sky
to the stars
to the fires of our minds

YVES
black & blue/ yes prieto to you
soft as your lover's bosom

LAYLA
every time we shed
ol' ignored skin/ the
galaxy re-adjusts/

JUAN PEDRO
ya see/
balance is a matter
or whether/
we
want
to play ball today/ or not...
(*A silent pause*)

KUKA
hey girls, let's do something female/ this is gettin' to me/ I can almost smell the jock straps in here/ spirits or not

JUAN PEDRO
watch what you say ladies/ watch what you say

KUKA
see/ this is what I mean/ always censoring us/ watchin' us/ telling' us what to do

YVES
you need help/ uppity bitches
single.../ single...

MARIPOSA
you mind your mouth

YVES
why don't you open yours

FRANK
this is layla's house and we won't have that

YVES
whatever you say ole man:

(*LAYLA speaks to YVES*)

LAYLA
you said hangin out with me was just like hangin out witta man/ I cd drink & talk pungently/ even tell a risqué joke or two/ more n that/ I cd talk abt art/ & that musta made me a man/ cuz I sure cdnt scratch my balls/ or pee further n you/ or fuck a tiny fella in the ass/ I didn't have a football letter/ & I cdnt talk abt how many women I'd had/ but then you don't know that either/ all you know is you said I waz just like a fella/ & here I waz thinking I waz as good as any woman/ which to me meant I waz as good as any fella/ but that's an idea without a large following in these parts/ any way the way the relationship evolved/ you & me/ this woman you waz thinking waz like a fella/
well we worked together alla the time/

had poetry readings/ did exercises/ saw shows/ cut-up everybody
else's work on the phone/ & you must know since I hadta be a
fella to understand/ probably you already guessed/ our shared
craft waz poetry/ cuz words/ are all men/ why else wd
you haveta put 'ess on the end of every damn thing/ if it wznt to
signify when/ a woman waz doin something that men do/

so anyway we were poets/ & you, well he liked my
work/ cuz it wasn't 'personal'

YVES
a man can get personal in his work
when he talks politics or bout his dad/ but women start alla
this foolishness bout their bodies & blood & kids what's really goin
on at home/ well & that aint poetry/ that's goo-ey gaw/ female
stuff/ & you waznt like that/ my woman they callt a poet/ wrote
mostly abt 'the music'/ ya know albert ayler/ david murray/ bobo
shaw[1]/ olu dara[2]/ archie shepp[3]/ oliver lake[4]/ you even had a whole
series for the art ensemble of chicago/ now this waz phenomenal/

LAYLA
cuz these men who were poets/ were mostly into coltrane or
bebop/ not havin moved ahead with the times/ & you thot
I musta slept with alla these guyz/ cuz everybody knows/
women don't really know how to listen to music/ or even what's a
gift like billie holiday[5]/ why betty carter[6] & vi redd[7] were never
treated
weird by musicians who were men/ they just didn't get any work/ so

---

1 Charles Wesley "Bobo" Shaw (1947–2017) was a free jazz drummer.
2 Olu Dara Jones (b. 1941) is a guitarist, cornetist, and singer.
3 Archie Shepp (b. 1937) is an avant-garde jazz saxophonist, composer, and playwright.
4 Oliver Lake (b. 1942) is a jazz saxophonist and composer.
5 Billie Holiday (1915–1959) was a jazz vocalist.
6 Betty Carter (1929–1998) was a jazz vocalist.
7 Elvira "Vi" Redd (b. 1928) is a jazz and blues alto saxophonist.

I who am a poet/ musta changed my ways considerably/
& the other poets liked that/ there waznt any reason/ to hold up a
reading cuz some bitch waz late getting up from a good dickin
down/
tho some poetry readings never started cuz some men who were
poets cd never get it up.

but I waz alone a lot of the time with my books fulla
these crazy poems abt this wild music/ so that waz aright/ some-
body asked me one time to tell the truth/ waz I run out on my
husband/ & I laughed/ they tried to make my blood sister/ a lover
I had in the closet/ but when the mother of both me who
was a poet & the sister suspected of bein a lover in the closet
showed up to a reading with the husband of the mother & father
of the poet who waz a women & the lover in the closet/ that rumor
colled out/ still there was a problem/ the poet who waz a woman &
when the poets who were men/ were feelin fiercely good abt bein
men/ they often forgot that this waz a woman whom they all said
was more like a man cuz I cd talk/ & I didn't write none of that
personal stuff/ they forgot they had said this/ & started to make the
wet mouth & heavy arms with me/ & I waz stunned cuz I waz
the one who had no gender to speak of cuz here I waz a woman
who waz really more like one of the fella/ but that waz when the
fellas were bein poets/
when the fellas were bein fellas/ they didn't
care if I cd talk or not/& they sometimes didn't recognize me &
told me they met me in seattle last year at their mother's/

KUKA

she was very nice to the guys & sometimes fed them like their own
mamas wd have

BOO
or lent them some money like a bank wda if banks
weren't apriori scared to death of poets in need of money

KUKA
sometimes when one of their women threw them out/ they stayed at her house/

BOO *(to YVES)*
cuz there waz never a man at her house/ that waz one of the
unspoken rules of her bein considered one of the fella/ or a poet/ cuz if
there waz a man at her house

KUKA
like there waz one time/ when she
forgot that in order to be considered a poet she hadta be one of the
guys/ the poets who were men/ got very indignant & walked out cuz
she waz romancing some fella who wasn't even a poet & wdnt be able
to feed them that night

BOO
not that they had callt or anything

KUKA
see/
among poets who are men & women deigned poets by these men/
there is a strange/ spontaneity/ that says they cd come visit when-
ever they liked & she mustn't call cuz their ol ladies didn't under-
stand that she was one of the fellas/

BOO
& they made it hard on any
fella who wasn't a poet to be a lover of hers/ cuz they wd sho up
all the time with these wounds from the police

KUKA
an irate poet/ attacking the doorbell/
one had his nose broken for stealin an image &
landed up in her kitchen

LAYLA
when I who waz a poet waz just
abt to get down to business in my bed/ & that kinda thing is hard for
a man who is not a poet to take/ plus/ you wd qiz the man who
waz not a poet abt poetry/ & since he waz nota poet & didn't know
the verses of the whole cadre/ you determined to warn their
comrade/ against this sorta man who cdnt recite poems/ & so my
life as a man with the men who were poets waz quite confusing &
very hassled.
so one day I decided that it was probably aright that the men
who were poets thot of me as one of their own kind/ sometimes/ &
sometimes I waz mistaken for their mother/ or a misplaced lover/
but one day when I waz reading to the group/ in a pub some-
where in new york or California/ I said as a women & a poet/
I've decided to wear my ovaries on my sleeve/raise my poems on
my milk/ & count my days by the flow of my mensis

BOO
the men who were poets were aghast/ they fled the scene in fear of becoming unclean

KUKA
they all knew those verses

LAYLA
& I waz left with an arena of
my own/ where words & motions/ imply 'she'/ where havin lovers is
quite common regardless of sex/ or profession/ where music &

mensis/ are considered very personal/ & language a tool for
exploring space/

JUAN PEDRO
the moral of the story:

VERONICA
#1: when words leave you no space for yrself/ make a poem/
very personal/ very clear/ & yr obstructions will join you or
disappear/

JAVIER
#2: if yr obstructions don't disappear/ repeat over & over again/ the
new definitions/ till the ol ones have no more fight in them/ then
cover them with syllables you've gathered from other dying species/

LAYLA
#3: a few soft words have sent many a woman to her back with her
thighs flung over & eager/
a few more/ will find us standing up & speakin in our own tongue
to whomever we god dam
please.

YVES
alright baby/ you just keep talkin'/ I love the way you write/
especially abt me/
you do write about me don't you?

P.T.
not exclusively/ she writes about me sometimes

elegance in the extreme
gives style to the hours
of coaxing warmth outta
no where

elegant hoodlums
elegant intellectuals
elegant ornithologists
elegant botanists

but elegance in the extreme helps most
the strangler who hesitates
to give what there is
for fear of unleashing madness
which is sometimes
uninvolved in contemporary mores

archetypal realities or graciousness

in the absence of extreme elegance
madness can set right in like
a burnin gauloise on Japanese silk
though highly cultured
even the silk must ask
how to burn up discreetly

YVES
don't no niggahs know what no damn gauloise is/ do you really know niggah?

JUAN PEDRO
we know everything we need to know

(P.T. takes a pack of Gauloise cigarettes from his pocket and offers one to YVES.)

YVES
why don't you go burn up some damn silk.

(YVES exits. JUAN PEDRO conjures a magic spell and the stage becomes filled with lush lighting and sound. The music is a Spanish bolero or tango orchestral dance. The atmosphere is that of an old elegant high class ballroom. At least three of the characters pair off and dance duets to the music during JUAN PEDRO's narrative.)

JUAN PEDRO
the great northern hotel/
splendid & washed in roarin' twenties
whirlin' light/ chandeliers
teasin' every sort of sequin
que tipa de[1] rhinestone or
diamonds twirlin' smoother
than a cyclone's vortex
whirlin' con ritmo[2]/ while
cuban chameleons tails in
matanzas[3] at harvest
decide
what color to take on/
what shade de azucar[4] can protect this rough necked
species/ from bein' found
out/ perhaps by the bridge
of a violin/ soarin' with the voices of
orquestra aragon[5]
dismissed as dinosaurs
more trouble than they're worth &
there's always the problem of
rush hour traffic/trippin' over

1 "what type of"
2 "rhythm"
3 A town in Cuba known as the center of Afro-Cuban culture and art
4 "sugar"
5 Orquesta Aragón is a historic Cuban band formed in 1939.

flutes in hot pursuit of pizzacato[1]
con artists who turn sixth avenue
into santiago de cuba[2] &
plain enamoradas[3] consult
la virgen de caridad[4] medusa/
badger graciela for
secrets de amor siempre/amor
in the raised arm of the dominicano/
another holdin' the waist de
una flaca bella[5] almost mad with
the call de las congas de cuba/lizards
& chameleons move differently
on the asphalt outside the dance/
hall/ yet jaguars park near by
drawn by perfumes/ sweat/ the unsuspectin in throes
of self-provoked pleasure/ sensuality
fallin'batum bata bata batum from the
hems of skirts so tight/ prayers
of passion rip bodices shameless
quiverin nipples hard como the
timbalero's[6] last rip & roll/ si
so long ago/waiters in stiff white
jackets/con carne asada[7] & paella[8]

---

1 A technique of plucking strings on a stringed instrument.
2 Second-largest city in Cuba
3 "people in love" or "prone to falling in love"
4 In Cuba "la virgen de caridad del cobre" (which translates to "Our Lady of Charity of Copper") is popularly known as Cachita. Her shrine is in Santiago de Cuba. Cachita is the patron saint of the nation and is syncretized with the Yoruba deity Oshun in Santeria, a New World expression of traditional Yoruba religious practice.
5 "pretty, slender woman"
6 A person who plays the timbales
7 Grilled and sliced beef
8 Popular Spanish rice dish

barely escapin' some camaguey[1] double turn
torso lean on a one/two to turn
then counter-clockwise
cuban chameleons busy themselves
tween piernas[2] leavin' pavlova[3]
in confoundment/labios pout
& turn up to the sounds/
the eyes surprised with the beauty of it all/
viveras en la memoria[4]/ absolutamente
one step leadin' to romance
with strangers invited to intimacy
previously unknown/seductively
hair grazes shoulders/ &
suit jackets of somebody else's
partner/seein' what we can be /
were before the great northern hotel &
orquestra aragon were abandoned
manners & history marked down
like the sale price de un
viejo negro[5] whose
machete left cane
cut sharp / clean
how
the chameleon
still searches for us.

---

1 Camaguey is a city in Cuba.

2 "legs"

3 This is a reference to the much-celebrated principal ballerina of the Imperial Russian Ballet and the Ballets Russes, Anna Pavlova (1899–1931).

4 This is a reference to Orquesta Aragón's song "Vivirás en La Memoria," which translates to "you will live on in memories."

5 "old Black man"

(The music and dance end. The mood changes to the up beat tempos of Hector Lavoe and Jackie Wilson[1] *sound.)*

KUKA

if hector lavoe is not jackie wilson
who sign you to sleep at night?

BOO

in whose arms did you sleep well or not? tell me
cuz i've raced thru streets and dreams kept
undercover
by interpol[2]
and the state police chased me who/
folks swear never existed

KUKA

why i've been held in a
chorus as far as the *archipelago* and all the people knew
el senor hector lavoe
look
you can go with me
as far as *managua*[3] &
the earthquake was no more a surprise
than you
with yr voice
that comes from the gods
and the swivel of the hips of your girl
as you dance or
when she sucks the hearts
out of the eggs of

---

1 Jack Leroy "Jackie" Wilson Jr. (1934–1984) was a popular R&B singer of the 1950s and '60s.

2 The International Criminal Police Organization

3 The capital of Nicaragua

turtles
anglos die to see float
while all the time we dance around them split up
change partners
and fall madly in love/
all this time my love
when they come for you
becuz an inhospitable world/
es incompressible

BOO
don't you know
that jackie wilson took up
the flack that yr girl couldn't handle
listen
criollo
there are people in detroit
on your side & they don't care
how the syllables fall
or the linguistic niche
they create for market identifications
what we are dealing with here is
an inexcusable disruption of a way of life
thousands upon thousands
whose every move
is determined by the sound of your voice

VERONICA
does it matter/ hector/
you seek out women other men wish they'd had the nerve
to want for their own?

MARIPOSA
does it matter you don't
always show up
or you attend and your
voice could not make it?

JAVIER
no, negro, not in my lifetime
cause
nobody put a tec-9 to your head
tied you up like philip wilson[1]
or prostrated themselves
like *machito*
if nothing/ is real
our lives are permanent

if they come with all their arms, it doesn't matter
we are an army of marathon dancers
lovers
seekers

we have never met an enemy we can't outlive/

VERONICA
querido, hector/ i can assure you myself
that nobody's gonna take you away,

JUAN PEDRO
mangle,

LAYLA
deform
the sound of you

---

1 Phillip Sanford Wilson (1941–1992) was a blues and jazz drummer who was stalked and murdered in 1992. His murderer was convicted in 1997.

in our lives
no guns
no napalm
no drugs
no martial law
and U.N. condoned invasions/
of our actualities can take you from me/
oh sparrow/ oh mi ismael,
of the closest I ever got to beni more in my lifetime,
do you really believe
that I would let you cease to be/
carnal/
i asked jackie wilson
and he said "we can't do widout him
he's just like me."

(The music changes to the calypso sounds of "the mighty sparrow"[1] *or softly playing pan/steel drums. MARIPOSA comes forth to LAYLA and offers a lullaby to soothe her soul.)*

MARIPOSA
blue horizon/ trinidad/ she
tilt direct toward
venezuela way/ she not
weak nor set up
on land sinkin' down
in satan's palm/

blue horizon a
dream lived in

1 Slinger "The Mighty Sparrow" Francisco (b. 1935), is a popular Calypso singer, songwriter, and guitarist.

to this day right
now / while I talkin'
these very words out
me mouth / a auntie
me never see & so
all i cd do was dream
bout she / dere on the
cliff in blue horizon

her home chattin'up
the very tides
    how /
she lean so/
        like
she got she eye
on some dashin' buckra[1]
    no-good
but for a night/ this
just the house/ not
me auntie/ who face
i barely trace in
the settin' sun of
blanchisseuse[2]/ cause
de whole village know how
she look better 'n
me/ the chine of the family/ but dey left
outside me grand
activity / dreamin
her up/ ya see/ so

---

1 A colloquial term in African American and Caribbean dialects for a white person

2 A town in Trinidad

i fetch water from the pump cross the
way / like she was a
watchin' / to see what
kind a woman me
mother make a me/

& not a drop/ I tell
ya/ tell ya true
not a sprinkle a
fresh water fall
from me pail/ not even
when de lanky dread
from upper village
call he self 'visitin'/

can ya believe dat
he 'visitin' by de
water pump / but
he locks wan' wrap me'
up / dat de problem
dere / but no a
drop of water spill
cause I catch meself
when I get me heart
tangle up in jah
bounty so close

oh, blue horizon
me auntie built
never re-alizin' / i
gon' live in she dream
fetch water / run

fast fore de fisher
men/ dey set out
wit dey nets a go
catch me dinner / &
alla dem flyin' fish
dem bajan[1] greedy
for / I tell ya/ when
de rain come quick
in the heat/ & this a secret
i tellin ya here/ mind/
now/

when de rain/ she
come down hard in de midst
a de day/ folk busy
everywhere/ doin' who
know what wit shabba
verse playin' tween
dem ears/ in this
rain I run back a
blue horizon/ where
de bathin' stall
    also / tiltin' venezuela way /
in dere / standin' a top
all me clothes/
shelter in de trash of de palm/

i don'do nothin'

i stand dere/ blue
horizon sheildin' me

---

1 Bajan is a common term for people from the island of Barbados. The more formal term is Barbadian.

from all profane
gaze/ rain dancin' hard on me limb/
smellin a thousands
down in maracas beach
jumpin' up/ jumpin' up
in de wave/ one after de
other/ a nakedness
i save for me gods/
to de rear a blue
horizon is loud/
cause de rain heavy like
achin' joy when david
rudder[1] sing he "dust in
dey face" / lord
i cain't tell ya how
fearsome de noise

but i tellin' ya true
i know me luck
    a continuin' phenomenon
cause a very delicate
lookin' lizard appear to
keep me company / each
time i clean me self
up in the rain/ she a
yellow/
calabasa lookin'
lizard/ coral vein
peek from she
in a certain light/ she
stay by me feet

1 David Rudder (b. 1953) is a popular Trinidadian calypso singer.

for a time/ den she
climb me leg & arrive
on me shoulder/

travels like
fog on me skin/
she do/

& i still doin nothin'
not a ting
me/ both lizard and i/
we de same temperature
ya know / she forget abt me cause
we de same heat/ya know
i forget bout she cause only
me shoulder kheloid funny

a calabasa cassava coral
tattoo risin' up
just when de gull
begin chirpin' / like dem
angel/

blue horizon/ trinidad/ quiet now / i
fully expectin'a margarita island breeze
come venezuela way
to answer / alla me prayers

answer alla me prayers

(The lights linger in the music, blue and wavey – while MARIPOSA caresses LAYLA in motherly embrace. The characters on stage softly start to whisper quiet prayers, starting with the words "answer alla me prayers." Their own prayers taken from words they speak elsewhere in the context of the chore poem. The lights slowly fade to black in rhythm with the whispering voices.)

END OF PART ONE

LAYLA'S DREAM: PART TWO

(The lights rise on the stage looking exactly as it did at the end of Part One. The music fades into something Afrocentric and mellow. LAYLA begins speaking from MARIPOSA's lap.)

LAYLA
i had five nose rings

YVES (*entering the stage with the five rings in is hand*)
a gold circle
a silver circle
a star
nefertiti
& a half moon

LAYLA (*rising from MARIPOSA's embrace, moving toward YVES*)
without these I am unarmed
not ready for arbitrary violence

CHORUS OF SPIRITS (*a warning of danger*)
paris winds in winter
    yr face chafed/ seemingly rouged
    a positive response
    to poison

LAYLA
my decorations   emblems   fetishes
gleaming from my cheeks as the sun turns waters to diamond

YVES
these beauties of yours   crawled   poison
to the base of your brain

like cocaine is apt to do
vitamin deficiency
a lack
of fresh air & music

(Music of "Charlie Parker with Stings" begins to play.)

LAYLA
the ring on my face/ like a brand

YVES
or an emerald

CHORUS OF SPIRITS
paris snarls her fog & chill thru your veins
throws you to
the outskirts of yourself

LAYLA
i had five nose rings

KUKA
a gold circle

P.T.
a silver circle

BOO
a star

KUKA
nefertiti

YVES
& a half moon

LAYLA
i am no longer suspected of being/ moslem
i am suspected of scarring myself

YVES
your one claim to shout abt/ yr era of yrself
became a signal of depression

LAYLA
unadorned I march alone these avenues
my head darting forward/ down
no one to see the mark
the absence of the jewel

YVES
yr face betrays you

LAYLA
i frequent corners where men beat each other to death

JUAN PEDRO
in the name of
love

FRANK
i know children who carry knives
to preserve the dignity of their innocence
guns to frighten anyone who comes
too close/

VERONICA
contact
is dangerous here
makes you susceptible to disease

MARIPOSA
the air in paris warped your visions/ gave
distance & psychosis clearance

JAVIER
sometimes there is too much poison
to attend to beauty

LAYLA
i had five nose rings

ALL THE OTHERS (*except YVES*)
a gold circle
a silver circle
a star
nefertiti
& a half moon
they have fallen away

LAYLA
i breathe now
this lack of beauty
& caress the cheek of a child
who imagines no thing
beautiful
no thing
safe

JUAN PEDRO
paris new york
linger in the blood

YVES
like malaria / scarlet fever / typhoid

herpes simplex / herpes complex / syphilis / gonorrhea/ HIV /
AIDS/ chlamydia
linger in the blood/
like disease

KUKA (*to YVES*)
give the girl back her nose rings.

(YVES laughingly hand the rings to LAYLA and walks away.)

P.T.
do you have some kind of fetish man?

JUAN PEDRO
in the old days/ if we ran away they'd cover our heads in iron mask w/ antlers so we'd get caught in the trees trying to escape

P.T.
I like laya's nose rings

BOO
during slavery times/ white folks usedta soak our heads in oil and use em as torch lights to guide guests to their grand parties in the big house.

P.T.
you can compare that to "dahmer[1] man"/ he used to slash a boy with a knife so sharp you could see the pelvic bones/ cook em til the flesh fell off the bones and season to taste

YVES *(picking up on the situation and moving forward)*
how abt 'cookin' with jeffrey?/ we could re-enact the whole thing just like in apt. 213.

---

1 This is a reference to serial killer Jeffrey Dahmer (1960–1994). Many of Dahmer's victims were young Black and Asian men whom he lured to his home with offers of payment for nude photos or demonstrations of sexual interest.

cocks in formaldehyde/ something's boilin on the stove for dinner/ beautiful black dicks lining the spice rack / knives from a prime japanese's kitchen removing' fat/

here we go

(The stage transforms into a TV studio where a cooking show is on the air. We hear applause and theme music start up as YVES continues.)

"welcome to cookin' with jeffrey"/

Ladies and gentlemen thank you for joinin me/ today we're goin' to prepare my famous afro-asian stew with purple potatoes and baby carrots. First we must remove the scalp and all hair/ not good when you're tying this delicacy. The hunt of course was just as exciting as the meal I assure you. Findin' suitable tender meat or mature meat from malnourished wanderin' boys is difficult/ but I've managed to assemble here the adolescent asian meat and more aged black leg to be used in our stew. It's good to just experiment. You may use minced garlic/ rosemary or tarragon to season/ and of course salt and pepper. A bit of cayenne or crushed red pepper will really spice it up, yum yum!

This vat over here is for cuts of meat i've deemed unsuitable for human consumption/just stray calves and arms/ maybe a rib cage or two/ but let's get back to our delicacy of the day. Now, don't imagine that I've randomly gathered this meat. Nononno! I've held many a fine conversation with the ingredients here. Edward smith, ricky lee becks, ernest miller, david thomas,[1] rather common names but tasty just the same/ and then there's the native american who gave me some trouble/ just like konerak the fourteen year old who went

---

1 These are actual names of some of Dahmer's victims.

to the police/but he was so young and pretty, I smoothed that over. Back to cookin'. You'll want to cook this over a medium heat and stir occasionally. I've added some pearl onions, and truffles because I want to have a very special meal for you/ Anthony hughes. Matt turner, oliver lacy/all very precious meats. One day I'd like to perfect a method to age the meat the way the Japanese do beef. Now that would be somethin to wait for. I've prepared scalloped potatoes and a ceasar salad to complement our main dish. Patience. Patience is the key in the hunt as well as the cookin. We've got about forty minutes to wait now, let's say we have a drink?

(Theme music comes up indicating an end to the show.)

Don't forget to tune back in to 'cookin with jeffrey.'

(Music fades or ends.)

Are we off the air yet?

ALL
Yeah!

YVES
well that went well/ don't you think

BOO
yo/ yo/ 'jeffrey man' you lyin son of a bitch/ the "hunt" as you call it was for more than a cozy dinner by the fire place/ he was looking to make some sex slaves/ all colored men with holes drilled in they heads and some crazy concoctions his crazy ass poured in their brains

YVES
well, who cares what happens to a bunch of blk faggots/ nobody missed them/ besides I think it was a good idea/ slaves do whatever you might want & he wanted his dick sucked on command/ & he

wanted to fuck as many colored men in the ass as possible/ he had an insatiable appetite.

BOO
yo "jeffrey"/ you keep talkin like that and some free niggah's gonna bash yr head in

P.T
this aint funny man/

KUKA
ask those boys relatives 'bout that then/ find out from the sisters of jeffrey's "meals" when slavery ended for them

P.T.
yeah/ & why he always comin after us -

BOO
you a sick muthafuckah/ talkin' bout 'cookin with jeffrey'

YVES
so what you want me to say? what is it you want me to say?

(A moment of uncomfortable silence)

JUAN PEDRO
some/ men
don't know anything abt that/
the manliness inherent at birth
is lost as they grow or shrink
to size
some/ men

MARIPOSA
don't know that a well dressed man,
is a good female impersonator

FRANK
that machines replace them & do a better job

VERONICA
some/ men
have no language that doesn't hurt
a language that doesn't reduce what's whole
to some part of nothing

JAVIER
sometimes/ some men think it's funny/ really funny
women have anything to do with them

VERONICA
he was a pretty man who liked pretty things.
surrounded with beat-up luxuries/ old mantillas
from women's heads lay cross his mahogany tables/
bronze nymphs, bulbs in their mouths, lit up
his quarters/ onyx vases steadied scarlet tulips before
French windows he opened when he had espresso
in early morning.
he kept a dressing gown/ mauve dotted with black velvet.
he waxed his floors til they shone & covered them with
near eastern rugs/ the kind little girls spend whole
lives tying.
he walked about grandly.
though he was a little man/ he like to think himself
large.
he had so many pretty things.
he never bent his knees/ that added some inches
& kept him from looking anyone in the eye
there'd be nothing new in his visions. only
old pretty things/ used abused beauties
like the women who decorated his bed from time to time.

he sat them on old sheets & displayed the dusty
manuscripts he collected/ the vintage photographs
he stored/ the women past whose legs he'd pulled
over his hips like a holster
        now this was an honor
to lay naked with a pretty man among his pretty things/
the violated thrown-out pieces of lives he recovered
from rummages scavenging & gutters.
the beauty of it all
was it cost him so little. imagine him
so small a man getting away with all that.
        nothing new. not a new thing.

what's to value in something unblemished?
porcelain must be cracked/ to covet. rugs frayed/
to desire. there must be scratches on the surfaces/
to enjoy what's beautiful

he was really very tiny in the big brass bed.
the beauty of the woman overpowered him. she didn't
even seem afraid in the presence of all his
pretty things
he thought of the most beautiful thing he cd say.
what words wd match his pretty little face
what phrase [to] approach the sunlight mad with joy
on the limbs of this woman next to him
what he could do so perfectly.
he was a little man
& straightening his legs in the bed added nothing to
his stature. he sat up & crushed the frailty of the morning

YVES
"suck my dick & make some coffee"

VERONICA
he squealed

she ran out
with no more than her coat/ her shoes in her hands
keys in her mouth. she thought she must have lost
her mind
but
he was a small man
& cd handle only damaged goods. he sat in his big bed
with his little legs bent/ quite content.
now/ there was something someone else cd collect/
an abused/ used luxury/ a woman
with a memory of daybreak in a near perfect place/
sunlight warm against her face & a man squealing
"suck my dick & make some coffee"

YVES *(emphatic)*
SUCK MY DICK! / & MAKE SOME COFFEE

VERONICA
she always woke before her lovers/ after that.
she never slept near windows/ & the aroma of coffee
left her pale.
& he was a little man/ a pretty man
surrounded with beat-up luxuries/ creating blemishes
scratches fraying edges/ illusions
of filling the bed he slept in

FRANK
it was best to call in the middle of the night.
women living alone are startled by noises at late hours.
it is best to ring twice & hang up.
then ring back/ say nothing.

women living alone are familiar with perversions.

he decided to ring twice/ hang up/ three times.

he felt once she answered/ heard a man breathing/
she'd hang up quickly.
then
he cd call back & she's be so glad
finally a man she knew
a man she cd trust in the middle of the night.

JAVIER
there was nothing he could see in a woman that was
of any use at all. she was forever silly.

YVES
look at that mess you put on yr face/ why don't you
use kohl like Algerian women/ why don't you cover
your face

JAVIER
every time she's try to do what pleased him
he'd find a more indelicate failure.

YVES
what's wrong with your hair? don't you oil your legs?
why do you let your pussy hair grow so long/ cut it off!
get your teeth fixed/ sit over there &
take your pants off.

JAVIER
he liked pornographic still-lifes.
when he cdnt afford the quarter machines/ he invited women
to keep him company/ then he made them ugly.

FRANK

he kept the space empty. so no one wd ever imagine
that a woman lived there/ which is what he wanted
for no one to know.
if she lived empty & angular as he did, she'd become
less a woman & part of the design/ where anything he
wanted to happen/ happened.

the baby gets up every hour & a half. she's a spunky
little baby who cries & smiles a lot. she needs to nurse
& her mama's right there. without sleep or no/ the milk flows.
    he doesn't like that. he said,

YVES

there's no one taking care of me.
her stitches shd heal faster. she shdn't take so
many sitz baths. she takes too long to walk from here to
there/ she doesn't actually haveta walk funny like that
it don't hurt her/ it won hurt.

FRANK

he said/ it wdn't hurt

YVES

don't you remember before that damned baby? it was me.
it was me & you. there's always milk for the baby
none for me/ never too tired for the baby/ never too
tired for the baby

FRANK

he didn't understand
why she sat on the stairway crying all night with the
spunky little baby
he hadn't done nothing but hold her arms back/ & bite

on her titties/ how did he know his teeth wd hurt
how cd he know

YVES
shit/ she always had time for the baby
what was I sposed to do/ the milk flows whether she is tired
or not/ when was I gonna get some

FRANK
he said it wdn't hurt

YVES
it wont hurt/ don't you remember...

JUAN PEDRO
he looked at the flowers on her window sill/
roses, lilacs, lilies & mums. the flowers
on her curtains/ blazing tropical petals
& stamen/
her desk festooned with strange cacti & terrarium.
she had covered her ceilings in arcs of ivy/
made herself a garden full of soft round shapes/
fragrance & manners.
he felt her thighs/ strong and wet.
her body arching like ferns reaching/ she was smiling
& feverish with desire
        strange sounds fell from her mouth
gurgling innocent hot sounds/ crept along his back/
her fingers
sought out the hair long his neck/
the evening fog laced kisses round their bodies/
she thought she heard piano solos/ she thought she heard
trumpets gone marvelously wild in nature's murmurings
        she felt him coming

& let go all her powers
when without warning

YVES
I shot all my semen up her ass

JUAN PEDRO
she kept screaming

VERONICA
WHAT ARE YOU DOING/ WHAT ARE YOU DOING
to me -

JUAN PEDRO
he relaxed/ sighing -

YVES
"I had to put it somewhere. it was
too good to be some pussy."

VERONICA
some men would rather see us dead than imagine
what we think of them/
if we measure our silence by our pain
how could all the words
any word
ever catch us up
what is it
we cd call equal.

(After this, LAYLA's friends begin speaking directly to her.)

KUKA
every 3 minutes a woman is beaten

BOO
every five minutes a
woman is raped/

P.T.
every ten minutes
a lil girl is molested

KUKA
yet I rode the subway today
I sat next to an old man who
may have beaten his old wife
3 minutes ago or 3 days/

BOO
30 years ago
he might have sodomized his
daughter

KUKA
but I sat there
cuz the young men on the train
might beat some young women
later in the day or tomorrow

BOO
i might not shut my door fast enuf/ push hard enuf

P.T.
every 3 minutes it happens
some woman's innocence
rushes to her cheeks/ pours from her mouth

KUKA
like the betsy wetsy dolls have been torn
apart/

BOO
their mouths
mensis red & split/

KUKA
every
three minutes a shoulder
is jammed through plaster & the oven door/

BOO
chairs push thru the rib cage/ hot water or
boiling sperm decorate her body

KUKA
i rode the subway today
& bought a paper from a
man who might
have held his old lady onto
a hot pressing iron/ I don't know
maybe he catches lil girls in the
park & rips open their behinds
with steel rods/ I cdnt decide
what he might have done I only
know every 3 minutes
every 5 minutes every 10 minutes/ so
i bought the paper
looking for the announcement
of the women's bodies found
yesterday/ the missing little girl
i sat in a restaurant with my paper looking for the announcement
a young man served me coffee/
i wondered/ did he pour the boiling
coffee/ on the woman cuz she was stupid/
did he put the infant girl/ in

the coffee pot/ with the boiling coffee/ cuz she cried too much
what exactly did he do with hot coffee
i looked for the announcement/
the discovery/ of the dismembered
woman's body/

P.T.
the victims have not all been
identified/ today they are
naked & dead/ refuse to
testify/

BOO
one girl out of 10's not
coherent/

KUKA
I took the coffee
& spit it up/ I found an
announcement/ not the woman's
bloated body in the river/ floating
not the child bleeding in the
59th street corridor/ not the baby
broken on the floor/
"there is some concern
that alleged battered women
might start to murder their
husbands & lovers with no
immediate cause"

KUKA
i spit up   i vomit   i am screaming
we all have immediate cause
every 3 minutes

every 5 minutes
every 10 minutes
every day

BOO
women's bodies are found
in alleys & bedrooms/ at the top of the stairs

KUKA
before I ride the subway/ buy a paper/ drink
coffee/ I must know/
have you hurt a woman today
did you beat a woman today
throw a child cross a room
        are the lil girl's panties
        in yr pocket
did you hurt a woman today

i have to ask these obscene questions
the authorities require me to
establish
immediate cause/
every three minutes
every five minutes
every ten minutes
every day.

(LAYLA is a bit stunned. But she starts to realize what her friends and spirit guides are trying to illustrate. Her sense of discovery pulls up upright and standing. She turns to look at YVES, who is still somewhere on stage. LAYLA develops a look of determination mixed with just a tiny bit of lingering doubt. The friends and spirits start to become excited by the expectation of LAYLA's growing awareness.)

JUAN PEDRO
you almost got it/

VERONICA
you really do

BOO
'born of the blood of struggle'

P.T.
we all were/

FRANK
even if we don't
know it/

LAYLA
what if poetry isn't enuf?

MARIPOSA
whatcha gonna do then?

JAVIER
paint?

VERONICA
dance?

BOO
put your back field in motion & wait for james brown[1] to fall on his knees like it's too much for him/

P.T.
what?
to much for james?

---

1 James Joseph Brown (1933–2006) was a highly influential and popular funk and soul musician.

JAVIER
yeah/didn't you ever see the sweat from his brow/ a libation of passion
make a semi-circle fronta his body/ a half-moon of exertion
washin' away any hope he had of/ 'standin' it/can't stand it

BOO
& he falls to his knees and three jamesian niggahs in a stroll
so sharp it hurts bring him a cape that shines likes the northern
star/ shinin' i say like you imagined the grease in the parts of yr hair/ or on yr legs/

KUKA
james falls to his knees cuz he 'cain't take it'/ he's pleadin'
'please/ 'please/ please/ don't go

P.T.
we look to see who brought james brown to the floor/
so weak/ we think/ so overwrought/ with the power of love

FRANK
that's why poetry is enuf/ it brings us to our knees

VERONICA
& when we look up from our puddles of sweat/
the world's still right there
there is nothing more sacred than a glimpse of the power of the universe

BOO
it brought james brown to this knees/ lil Anthony[1] too/

---

1 Jerome Anthony Gourdine (b. 1941) was the lead singer of the doo-wop band Little Anthony and the Imperials.

P.T.
even jackie wilson
arrogant pretty muthufuckah he was/ dropped/ no knee pads in
the face
of the might we have to contend with/

JUAN PEDRO
& sometime young colored boys bleed
to death face down on asphalt cuz fallin' to they knees was not cool/
was not the way to go/

KUKA
it still ain't/

BOO
we cain't/
don't wanna escape any feelin'/
any sensation of bein' alive can come right down on us/

VERONICA
& yes
your tears & sweat may decorate the ground like a veve[1] in haiti

MARIPOSA
but in the swooning/

JUAN PEDRO
in the delirium/ of a felt life

VERONICA
lies a poem to be proud of/

LAYLA
does it matter?

---

1 In Haitian Vodun, a veve is a ritual geometric drawing or metalwork object that has spiritual significance.

BOO

can ya stand up, 'chile'?

JUAN PEDRO

the point is not to fall down & get up dustin' our bottoms/
the point/
is you fall on our knees & let the joy of surviving'
bring ya to yr feet/
yr bottom's not dirty/didn't even graze the earth/
no/ it's the stuff of livin' fully that makes the spirit of the poem/
let you show yr face again & again & again

LAYLA

i usedta hide myself in jewelry or huge dark glasses
big hats long billowin' skirts/ 'anything' to protect me/ from the gazes
somebody'd see i'd lived a lil bit/ felt somethin' too terrible for casual conversation
& all this was obvious from looking' in my eyes/ that's why I used to read poem after poem
with my eyes shut/ cept the memory'd take over & leave
my tequila bodyguard in a corner somewhere/ outta the way of the pain
in my eyes that simply came through my body/ they say
my hands sculpt the air with words/ my face becomes the visage of a
character's voice/ i didn't know / - i hid in my craft
& feared someone wd see i care too much
take me for a chump
laugh & go home/

this is not what happened!

(LAYLA is standing now in almost full personal power. She seems confident and aware of herself and her place

in the universe. The others are proud of her. JUAN PEDRO comes forth.)

JUAN PEDRO
can ya stand up, 'chile'?
hands stretched out to touch again
not so you can get up & conquer the world/
you did that when you cdnt raise yr head & yr body trembled so/
that was when the poem took over & gave you back
what you discovered you didn't haveta give up/
all that fullness of breath/ houdini in an emotional maze/ free at last
but nobody can see how you did it/
how'd she get out?
nobody'll know less you tell em

BOO
do you really wanna write/
from twenty thousand leagues under a stranger's wailin?

MARIPOSA
can you move gracefully/ randomly thru the landmines that
are yr own angola?

FRANK
your bosnia!

VERONICA
your own afgani fields!

P.T.
are you shamed sometimes there's no feelin' you
can recognize in yr left leg?

KUKA
does the bleeding you'll do anyway
offend you

or can you make a sacred drawing like ana mendieta
that will heal us all?

LAYLA
do i believe in magic?

JUAN PEDRO
shd you?

LAYLA
i don't know. i still sweat when i write

(All laugh, except YVES, who lingers in the shadow of the stage like a serpent waiting to strike. Soothing, healing, angelic like, joyous music begins to fill the air like perfume. As the next section moves, it grows into a group dance, a celebration of life and LAYLA'S new found awareness.)

FRANK
where we come from, sometimes, beauty
floats around us like clouds
the way leaves rustle in the breeze
and cornbread and barbecue swing out the backdoor
and tease all our senses as the sun goes down

VERONICA
dreams and memories rest by fences

P.T.
Texas accents rev up like car engines/
customized/ sparkling

BOO
powerful as the arms
that hold us tightly black n fragrant

KUKA
reminding us that once we slept and loved
to the scents of magnolia and frangipangi

JAVIER
once when we looked toward the skies
we could see something as lovely as our children's
smiles

JUAN PEDRO
white n glistenin'

LAYLA
clear of fear or shame

MARIPOSA
young girls in braids as precious as gold
find out that sex   is not just bein'   touched

P.T.
but in the swing of their hips and light fallin cross
a softbrown cheek

JUAN PEDRO
or the movement of a mere finger
to a   lip/ many lips/ inviting   kisses southern
and hip as any one lanky brother in the heat
of a laid back sunday rich as a big mama

LAYLA
still in love with the idea of love

BOO
how we play at lovin'
even riskin' all common sense cause we are as fantastical
as any chimera or magical flowers/ where breasts entice

and disguise the racing pounding of our hearts
as the music that we are

FRANK
hard core blues

BOO
low bass voices crooning
straight outta Compton

KUKA
melodies so pretty
they nasty

MARIPOSA
cruising the Harbor Freeway
blowin' kisses to strangers who won't be for long

LAYLA
singing ourselves to ourselves

VERONICA
Mamie

KUKA
Khalid

MARIPOSA
Sharita

BOO
Bessie

JUAN PEDRO
Jock

P.T.
Tookie

JAVIER
MaiMai

FRANK
Cosmic Man

LAYLA
'Mr. Man'

P.T.
Keemah and all the rest/ seriously courtin'

BOO
rappin'   a English we make up as we go along

LAYLA
turning nouns into verbs

KUKA
braids into crowns

JUAN PEDRO
and always fetchin' dreams from a horizon
strewn with bones and flesh of those of us
who didn't make it

FRANK
whose smiles and deep
dark eyes   help us to continue to see
there's so much life here.

ALL *(except YVES)*
there's so much life here! *(repeated like echoes or whispers)*

(As they all dance joyously repeating the phrase, "there's so much life here," YVES crosses to LAYLA. Interrupting the dance, he takes her by the arm.)

YVES
c'mon baby get rid of these freaks.

LAYLA *(breaking free of his grip)*
yr an empty, cruel man. no matter how you mask yr meanness, with wit, good looks, sex, pain.../ I want you to leave me alone/

(There is a pause, then she points toward the exit)

& don't come back.

YVES *(with familiar charm)*
now layla...

LAYLA
go, godammit/go.

(YVES moves a little bit toward the exit. Turns back to LAYLA.)

LAYLA *(with quiet confidence)*
GO!

(The spirits and friends all nod their heads in approval.)

BOO
that's been a long time comin'/ good for you girl.

P.T.
I thought he'd put some kinda spell on you.

LAYLA
I'm not sure he didn't / but it's broken now. I've got the spirits on my side. all I have to do is call on them.

KUKA

I love you, layla.

(KUKA moves to embrace LAYLA, followed by BOO. then P.T. A group hug, while the spirits watch in smiling approval. After the fullness of the hug, the friends slowly begin to back off the stage, as if fading away. LAYLA finds her way back to her poetry journal and her bed. The spirits find comfortable positions on stage, indicating that they will never leave.)

LAYLA

I'm gonna dance again/ I'll join a charanga[1] band and make rhythms with my fingers/ I'll see the stars on a fog strewn night/ let the moon caress my cheek just for daylight. I'll sing old doo-wop songs and meet luther vandross[2] at the end of an oww-wheee/ there's a world out there / I'm gonna hear choruses of the les nubianes/ in late afternoon my heart will be full of kisses and my hands softened by the dew/ there's a world out there i can't wait to see/

I can rest now/ the aroma of lavender soothes my soul/ it's time for sleep & lilac melodies.

(LAYLA puts away her journal under the covers and lays herself down to sleep as the spirits watch over her. The lights fade to blackness as soothing luxurious music swells.)

THE TRANSFORMATION IS COMPLETE!!!

---

1 A traditional Cuban dance music band

2 Luther Ronzoni Vandross Jr. (1951–2005) was a popular R&B vocalist, songwriter, and producer.

SHANGE:

** "Layla's Dream/ Lavender Lizards" sometimes reminds me of my /Earlier work/"Fog"./in her dream state Layla concocted/ her Experiences in order to heal… /yet in "Layla's Dreams" she perseveres while confronting her situation/Some of the male-figures surrounding her/ have moved to support & nurture us she battles that would have her voiceless & invisible/ they come from different cultures/ a myriad Perspectives/ of this world/ we too claim as our own/ & again as in "Spell#7"/ Layla & her coterie free themselves from multiple oppressions…*

Yet what Excites me abt Layla's Dream is the growth i see in my use of language/ where I undercut the meanings of words/& a kind of humor that peeks from circumstances that are truly/ are not comic

I delight in Layla's naivete' & confusions/ I find her efforts honest & hard-won/ Just as in my adaptation of Brecht's/ "Mother Courage and Her children" her colored response to traumas to keep moving on

Yet what excites me abt "Layla's Dream" is the growth is see in my use of language. I've come to place/ where i undercut the meaning of words/a kind of humor that peeks out of circumstances much really are not in any way comic. I've to delight in Layla's naivete & confusions/ I find her Efforts honest hard won. Just as in my adaptation of Brecht's/ 'Mother Courage', Layla response to trauma is to keep moving on/ which we all do/ sometimes with a smile. "The Love Space Demands"/the characters take this world under their own control

Sometimes with a Smile/ Yep anglo audience were furious with the dignity my Mother Courage displays/ while the non-Anglo audiences was on their feet & cheering her own victory/ it meant something else to us/in the Love Space Demands/ characters take this world on own terms/ not unlike our Layla/

"Yes/Yes
hold me
like the night grabs wyoming
& i am more/than i am not
i cd sing sacred lyrics/to songs i don't know/
my cheek/rubs against the nappy black/cacti of yr
chest/
& i am a flood/of super novas/
if you kiss me like that/i'm brown wetlands
yr lips/invite the moon/ to me &/
our mouths open & sing/
our tongues/
the Edge of the Earth"

Now Layla is able to race to her own cliffs of realities that used to make her a cower/ now she can move on & she is fearless.

LATER POEMS AND SHORT FICTION

These works were written between 1996 and Shange's death in 2018. As a leading Black feminist playwright, novelist, poet, essayist, and educator, she was frequently included in college curricula and honored at institutions around the country and world. She continued to experiment and explore with her writing until the very end, incorporating contemporary music styles and language into her work. In this section, the poems are arranged according to Shange's handwritten instructions. Shange readers will notice how she retained her characteristic style, though the work is at times more lyrical than her early writing, which tended to have a starker form that was overtly reflective of vernacular speech. Following the poems, there are two works of short fiction, "Whitewash" and "Fall, Chicago, 1959." Both depict the violence directed at Black children who integrated into white schools in the mid-twentieth century, likely inspired by Shange's own experience with desegregation but also reflective of the continued reality of racist violence directed toward young Black people. Finally, "MBJ" is a hip-hop-inflected choreopoem that traces the genealogy of contemporary Black aesthetics through the transatlantic slave trade, Jim Crow, and colonialism.

grey matters...

either or
in or out
that's the choice they give

what side you play
from night to day
that's the life you live

but wait a minute
i'm not in it

left that box long ago

gave myself permission
to search the middle
found a prism
at the core

blessed to see it
now i free it

found rainbow
through my door

got this feeling
should be dealing
in waters of grey matter....
though unseeming
colors streaming
in waters of grey matter...

who wrote the book
that locked us into
stories of divide

who…what the hook
pulled us tight
to either side

black or white
this not that
that's your way to pray

……….lilac…red…and shards of gold

i'm truth searching…

mirror, mirror
long ago
spoke beyond reflection

told me things
of queens and kings
who reign in 8th dimension

where white is back/ where moon is sun
where wrong births right
creating shades of other

a mysticspace
of brilliant grace
a queendom like no other

got this feeling
should be dealing
in waters of grey matters…
though unseeming
colors streaming
in waters of grey matters…

you live assured

as long as i am me

You are a melody haunting and alluring offering something more
Familiar and memorable like something I've known before
A rhythm pulsating and strong driving me along
Telling sensual stories eclipsing in a song

> You are my music my past and my future
> Where I've come from and where I'm heading
> Where my heart has always been and where it will always be
> You are my music as long as I am me

You're a motif dancing in the air without a care
A flow of feel good ready to take me anywhere
Like a song that everyone wants to sing
That carries you away on the expanse of a wing

> You are my music my past my future
> Where I've come from and where I'm heading
> Where my heart has always been and where it will always be
> You are my music as long as I am me

Without you there would be no singer and there would be no song
Life would be empty w/ me just grace/ Answers shuffling along
No music in the air or hope in the wind
Nothing to look forward to and nothing in the end

> You are my music my past and my future
> Where I've come from and where I'm heading
> Where my heart has always been and where it will always be
> You are my music (as long as I am me) the song that makes us we

You are my song that makes you part of me
The song is you becomes/ the we/ song in we
          is now the song me

the mystery of a black hole is its density / flying in the limbs of eleo pomare

eleo...

when eleo pomare[1] sinewy char-chocolate
columbiano swept thru our world
with a new old dance
la vallenato coursing thru his veins
straight from Cartagena/una caja, an accordian,
& unaa guaracha joining los indios, los negros
y los blancos/ in a step propelled by los africanos/
cartagena the main port of call/ Spain's richesse
of the new world/ eleo saw
the waters of cartagena, emblazened by
the bones of los africanos who didn't become slaves/
eleo's eyes / eleo's muscles raised from his bones
just as his veins punctuated up
from his arms & chest / heels up in a hinge back
from this position he fashions himself
into the movement of la coulera[2]/ panama 30,000 africanos
from the New World died

---

1 Eleo Pomare (1937–2008) was an influential Afro-Colombian dancer who founded a dance company bearing his name. He was known for his politically charged performances.

2 This is a double entendre that translates to the Spanish word for cholera and also a vernacular slur for a gay man (culero).

malaria, pestilence & accidents building the canal/ between
el ritmo de la coulera y los sentimentos de los muertes / eleo
the angry black dance phenomenon/ edged the desperate
haitians of 'the raft' to the peripheral vision of
America/ 'post cards from soweto' sent flames of
resentment & hope, necklacing and random assassination into
the hearts of our people years before Mandela
was saluted in stadiums across the country/ eleo
moved as stark & brilliant as malcolm X/as powerfully
as welfare mothers' protesting/ as fearfully balanced
as a 'junkie' in a nod/ eleo found
whimsical shadows of palm fronds/ skedattlin' lizards
hot dogs with sauerkraut & ketchup/ signs for the
subway/ & a half a head of undone plaits/ a pizzeria
y empanadas spot by a wizened grey head pulling a 3
wheeled shopping cart/ all moving / eleo found movement &
moving/ from the innocence of 'missa luba'[1]/ the
jaunty fling of 'Back to Bach'[2]/ the sorrowful flights
of 'los desamorados' / & the brash impudence of
'narcissus rising'/ eleo moves/ el negro del fuego
regrese to the seen smilin/ a flame we can't
imagine puttin out/ eleo fires up the sky
not unlike our sun/ yet in a parallel universe where we are in perfect
balance

---

1 The Missa Luba is a Congolese version of the traditional Catholic Latin Mass.

2 An album of Bach compositions produced by the French band the Swingle Singers

a silouette en el cielo/ just above santa marta

on releve/ pitchin into a spiral hinge/ on the same leg
a black man flying/ uno negro volante.

tz
11/7/08

man fell out on subway train / slumped down

Once i saw a dope fiend heroin addict
in nod/fall straight down on the platform
and crack his skull right open/his two
friends saw blood gushin' & ran on off fore
the ems cd get there/brothah don't you
know you cd be dead or robbed or awakened
with a nightstick straight cross yr back
i'm tellin ya there's no sympathy for
you a black man in blackout by himself?
on a subway train/ ya bettah get out of there
fore the rush hour come/ & so called
clean livers come and stand far away from
ya cause ya black probably stink &
out yr right mind/ nothin good comin' to ya
a lone blk man out yr right mind on a
train that's carrying a jumble of folks on they
way to work/ if ya wake up/ can ya act like a
man & look em in the eye & act like you got somewhere to go

two evangelical church on top each other

we must have more churches
that liquor stores/ got churches on top of
the other /talkin bout the Healing Missionary
church/c.m.e[1] churches are still around/
c.m.e. churches growin/ big glamorous
baptist churches/ more subdued high episcopal
churches/ got churches for recovering drug addicts/
churches that are historic landmarks of
the underground railroad/ churches on television
twenty four hours a day/ then there was
Daddy Grace[2] whose mission is still
functioning in Philadelphia/ & rev. ike
& his mighty prayer cloths/there was a dance
rehearsal studio/on top of rev. ike's
pulpit/ i was training in ghanain dance/ that's
how come i know/ there always been churches
with some singin & band/ now they got dancers some of
them do/ they even gotta blk catholic church/
but that's newly come along/they got black
folks going to white folks sposed to
work miracles/ i tell ya we must be
close to jesus than the disciples

1 This is a reference to the Amos Healing Missionary Baptist Church in Philadelphia.

2 Charles Manuel "Sweet Daddy" Grace (1881–1960) was a charismatic Cape Verdean–American preacher and founder of the United House of Prayer for All People.

girl with microphone on bottom steps

yes the bar next door is gated up
but you don't wanna rap in there
yes the hip hop "community" is till hard
on yng woman/ but cha don' have to slink
down like that/ interferes with your diaphragm
& that's where' you'll get yr voice from/
there's power there/ remember queen latifah
don' slouch/ neither do salt & pepper/
they strut around with they chests open/ you
gotta do more than have somethin'
to say/ to gotta belive what you sayin'
& stand up like you ready to rumble
with every ounce of sex you got/ well as
yr sense of karma the
rha goddess/ queen godis/ & missy elliot can
attest to that/ remember "Ladies First"
well yr the 2nd generation or maybe the 3rd
generation of yng woman ready to say they
piece/ it's gonna be hard/ but first you gotta
stand up/ strut & let your words dazzle the crowd
ya gotta get off the stairs/ out that corner
take yr microphone & announce to the world
on that you got somethin that's gotta be
heard

boys with hands behind necks

my boys / so fulla gumption &
appetite/ I cd feed em all the day
long/& they'd still/ come back for
somethin/ anythin' at all/ problem is
they growin hand over fist/ they growin'
& that cd mean some trouble
comin/ trouble comin every which way
cd be some beggah boy wit
a knife or a gun/ cd be a drive-by
mistake cd be the police/ tellin
my boys to put they hands right
where they got em/ locked b'hind
they necks/ looks now they practicin'
for what they think is they fate
i'ma pray on that/ Lord don't let
my boys play just thata way
no more/ they got no call to lock
they hands that a way & I surely don't want em to
lord/ let em be children
just a bit longer
til they men.

lady with freckles & cigarettes

she's alluring & sophisticated now
but that masks the call of redbone
when she was young
rebone rhiney maybe even high yellow
shouted at this beauty as she ran
home desperately trying to escape
the taunts / rumors spread about her
that she was uppity & easy/ folks
cdn't make up their minds/ just cause
she had freckles and ran from them
which gave them a sense of great power
their meanness shouted with glee
their name calling laced with lewdness
how cd she survive in a colored world
that laughed at her cause of her skin
that peculiar skin tone laced with freckles
she is beautiful now/ but gaze into
her eyes where she suspects rejection
from anyone who dares to love her
now she's alluring & sophisticated.

pregnant lady reading by window

yes awright / she barefoot & pregnant
but she's reading & world that opens
she's not reading dune or love & rockets
either though i loved them both
she's reading a text in the light of day
with small print / a serious book
she may be pregnant / & shoeless
cause it's comfortable / but she aint
ignorant just cause she's with child
maybe she's listenin' to some jazz
all that culture and information
bout archeology or Beloved[1] or
nkrumah[2] is sinking to the nexus
of the baby's unconscious
they say everything we do while we
pregnant effects the baby
this yng woman maybe barefoot & pregnant
but her baby sure will be well read
& gotta a yen for great blk music

---

1 The 1987 novel by Toni Morrison (1931–2019)

2 Kwame Nkrumah (1909–1972) was the first prime minister and president of postcolonial Ghana.

piano mantle piece

light barely brushes their pictures / but the hope
in the photographs makes light magnificent
the memories flow on their own / or from the glistenin'
trumpet / the smile of the bride / the recruit
before danger & sons a plenty to carry on the family
names / what alarms me & causes heart palpitations
is the tear in "bless this house", how can we
do that with half the music missin' / how can we
celebrate our relatives / our family / if the blessing
from the Lord is carried on with so many notes &
verses missin' / perhaps the Lord will unnerstan' /
we got the piano to sing praises to his name /
we got the piano to get a lil bit closer
to God / gabriel's trumpet is testimony to that / our
children will carry on Lord with just half of yr
praises touchin' their hearts.

flowered wallpaper, straw hat & jesus

don’t he look peaceful / don’t he look
humble in the robes of a simple man/ but
why he ain’t lookin’ at my children / steada
way off in the opposite direction / i’ma have
to do something bout that / the Lord lookin way’
from my brood / maybe what i’ll do is move
things a round some / so long as i don’t have to
move my straw hat

girl on the porch

grand ol' houses that have seen better days
but never anyone like me / why my braid
is stickin' in the air like my grandma's & my
mama's when they were my age
only thing is they didn't think like i do
i think all the time 'bout what's gonna become
of my i gotta mighty fine dress on & it may not
be ironed but i like it jus' the same / i'm
thinkin' out here on the porch too much noise
in the house / a girl needs quiet to get to herself
my made self decorated with my braids / antenna
takin' in the sights & sounds of my today /
lookin' for signs of my tomorrow / but right now
i'm gonna suck my fingers & wait for the
visions / a girl in my position gotta have visions
& what i see right now is a plenty / my dreams
ivies up the walls of the grand ol' house / rushin'
out the corner of my eyes / do you see
somethin' out there for me?

2 babies, 2 young men & girl on porch

jerome, get up out that chair &
let me & yr baby sit down, jo-jo'
whatcha lookin at / yall know bettah
than to let that chile / hang off the
rail like that / sometimes i don't know
what i'm gon'do wit yall / jo-jo what's
goin on down the street aint no
concern of yrs / jerome what got yr eyes
all squinted up like that? / whatever it is
my love will make it go on away / if you
jus' talk to me / don't nobody talk to me
'spect me to read yr minds / i ain't got
that kinda power / all i can do is jus' love
ya / all i know is how to love ya / will
somebody get that baby off the railin / or is
the killin down the street gon' do
us in too?

nana & two toddlers

she be home soon babies
no need to fret / she gotta full-time job
at the hospital / she be tendin' to sick folks /
while i look in after you two / it's good
to set out here on the porch / can see all
the neighbors & the kids / one day
you'll be out there / playin ball or double-dutch
right now you here / & i jus bend yr
ears wit tales that don't even stick with ya /
but a minute / yet when i remember aunt lizzie
to ya / i aint lyin bout her / i jus want
you to hear bout yr family from me
i carry our heritage in my soul / i got to pass
it on to yr soul even if ya caint call it
by name / it's who you are & who ya come from
what matters

playin' no matter what

he's out there / in the rain
with a tire / & half naked /
cdn't wait for the hydrants
to be opened & all the othah
children to come play / oh no
rain peltin his skin is good
enuf / for him & sloshin that tire
thru the streets he's like a commando
makes him smile & the hydrants
aint even on / its jus' him & free time
& the rain
but on sunny days there's always
abandoned cars to explore / to pretend to drive
to climb & choose to climb / explorers
of the city / we äint got much
but our kids do have a yard
it's the city / we locked up there

naked pregnant woman on rooftop

aint this fine / aint this wonderful
my baby and i neath the thunderin sky
strangers all the time wantin to touch my tummy /
for they good luck / but not this time angel /
this is for us / the same waters that cradled noah's
are are cleansin us & leaving us without shame /
i believe em now / my body is beautiful & so
are you / my pum'kin & my chile
look at the puddles that i skip thru / the
gleaming water on our skin / i'm havin such a good time /
naked and wet wit the skies for a cover and the rains for
a night shirt / did you ever think of that / my sugah that
we are clad in the tears in the heavens in the full of the day
& nobodies gonna say we wrong / we jus free the way a woman
aint 'magined to be / i'm sharin this gift with you / oh beloved
chile of
mine / we almos ready for yr birthin / almos ready for you to
...
bathed in the holy waters without no preacher with only
three lil ol' drops / pum'kin we gotta sky full of blessings
rainin / down on us & all we had was the courage
to reveal our naked selves to the horizon & her wonders /
& what's she do / she decorated us / o say our skins dark as night
in the midst of the day she lent us her jewels of gentle defiance

not strangers touchin us for good luck / she protectin us
we the sacred now? / i'm tellin ya / & we aint leavin this roof
where we dancin with the rain / til the sun come out or night falls
lettin us sleep and we don't have to tell our secrets
dancin naked in the rain in the full of the day /
what no respectable lady can

girl in front of cuba sign / hands clasped

she knows that isn't sposed to happen to her /
her nose is flat / her skin sepia / her
hair nappy / it's not sposed to happen here
fidel[1] declared cuba an afro-cuban nation
that's what they taught her / all her life
but she knows better / she's still too
african to work at the tropicana
in feathers and satin / she's never
gonna head a ministry / she might not even
marry / some novio's[2] family furious
with her just 'cause she's too dark
for their son / makes them remember
when in better times / people like that
la negra washed their children & their
toilets / she's never heard pedro's words
"to be called 'negrita' is to be called love"
i wish she cd hear now / baby i'll do her hair
& massage that frown away.

1 Fidel Castro (1926–2016) was a communist revolutionary and leader of Cuba from 1959 to 2008.

2 "boyfriend" or "betrothed"

wake up black man

what are you? deaf? elijah muhammed[1]
shouted that at you every day of his life / even
wallace fard muhammed[2] before him / & there
was garvey[3] with all his black people declarin'
themselves by the thousands in they uniforms
paradin' down the streets of harlem
as africans / but your didn't hear him / rejoicin
when they feds got em / didn't hear til malcolm
and even then you cdn't save him / what about
h. rap brown[4] / he wasn't always a messenger
of allah / he represented you / but no y'all
got pictures of jfk & robert kenny right next
to jesus / do i sound mad / well i am mad / i been
waitin for ya to hear somebody to get
these white folks off my back / and still ya
aint hearin' nothin' bout freedom / aint
heard folks what love ya with all our hearts

---

1 Elijah Muhammad (1897–1975) was the leader of the Nation of Islam from 1934 until his death.

2 Wallace Fard Muhammad (b. 1877; disappeared 1934) was the founder of the Nation of Islam.

3 Marcus Mosiah Garvey (1887–1940) was the founder of the Universal Negro Improvement Association, which advocated a return to Africa for all Black people in the diaspora.

4 H. Rap Brown (b. 1943), now known as Jamil Abdullah al-Amin, was a member of the SNCC who became a prominent Black nationalist in the 1970s.

black man cryin'

say brothah, what happened
somethin' terrible musta happened
so rare to see a black man in such pain
and a tear strewn face
cd it be bout one of yr children?
yr mother? yr girlfriend or yr wife?
i can't stand to see you suffer so
looks like you gonna scream or those
sobbin sounds gonna sneak out yr mouth
like curse words used ta / was it a fire
that trapped all yr love ones? please
tell me so i cd comfort you/some how
yr eyes are so sad / the tears so unavailable
yr face contorted / oh brothah-man
please let me hold you / aint one person
sposed to weep so / all by himself
aint one person to stand in the night sky
feeling worse that muddy waters[1]
wailing

1 McKinley "Muddy Waters" Morganfield (1913–1983) was a famous blues singer known as the father of Chicago-style blues.

the dancin series

folks say we start dancin' / soon as
we can walk / our little backsides
start to bob this way & that / our
arms weave in the air / to rhythms
we now know are holdouts from africa/
we don't know that / but we can dance
anyway / why we improvise from age one
people laugh at us cause our dance is
our own / while the grown-ups & the
teens dance / dances with rules & strict
roles for girls & boys / some times the men &
women seem just to lean on each other /
swaying back & forth / but no matter / we
dance from the time we cd walk &
the music & that beat never ceases to
challenge our little bodies to find
another limb to move right on like
labelle[1] or the jackson five / my mama
likes that music / reminds her of when she
was little like me / just beginning to get
hold of my colored instincts / after all i am
just a tiny african & i got to do what africans do

1 An all-women singing group who were pioneers in funk and Afrofuturism

some musicians tell me "there's no work"

some musicians tell me "there's no work"/
out there" least ways not for the music
they play / joe rasul & david are all in
paris / but i can find some black bands
where we live / play in be-bop blues & r&b/
sure you gotta look / gotta go where folks
aint so wall off / but you can find some
music that's as colored as it is live/
folks dance / the bop the chicago walk & swing /
they revive black big band sounds with a little
old five piece band sound / in texas & louisiana
zydeco music is the rage / some churches
even have zydeco nights / just like bingo
it's ours and we won't let it to / give us
a chance / to make us smile at each other/
hold each other / show what we can do with
all the memories we have of etta james[1]
ellington count basie[2] & the moonglows[3]
maybe even the flamingos[4]/ there's music out there fellas

---

1 Etta James (1938–2012) was a popular multigenre mid-twentieth-century vocalist

2 William James "Count" Basie (1904–1984) was a jazz pianist, composer, and bandleader.

3 1950s R&B group

4 1950s R&B group

aqui me quedo[1]

"hóla, senora" that's what i say
to her every mornin' when i go for
my café con leche / i welcomed her
to the neighborhood / it's good to hear
somebody not speak english & play
merengues all night & day
doesn't matter if the tablecloths are plastic
or a sticky kinda placemat / doesn't matter
if the cook gets my order mixed up /
they listen to my broken spanish / let me
read their "El Diario"[2] tell me / i look
like other dominican women / tell me
what other dominican stores i should
support / where there's good jewelry / good
groceries / & reasonable round-trips
to puerto rico & the dominican republic / all
this comradery / while i sip my second or third
café con leche/si senora "aqui me quedo"
is a wonderful name for the restaurant
i hope the english speakers never run you out.

1 "I'll stay here"
2 This is a reference to the newspaper.

nana in chair / white hair

maybe not nana maybe great great aunt mary
doesn't really matter / she's the family
can call up every generation from her soul
she remembers her husband, greer, getting' called
up for WWII & comin' home limpin' / she's
aware her nephew was called up / korea bound / never
to come home again / her daughters / there were
seven / were more wild than a christian woman
ought to be / but they all went to college or
cosmetology school / some of them widowed now
or divorced / but they doin' well / it's their
children who worried her the most / 2 suicides /
one shot to death by the police in his own
house / two great-grands barren / the others
got too many to care for / one boy in jail for
10 more years / drugs got him / & alcohol almost
all the rest / too many sorrows for one
old lady / but i remember sittin' on her lap
in the rocker / her warm skin & wonderful aroma
that made me safe / i felt love as she rocked
& rocked

dizzy

Spin spin spin spin
the world swims by
faster and faster
green grdn blue white flash
my voice escapes and swirls around me like water
wheeeeee! vibrates behind the eyes
wind between the ears
I can't not stop
and the ground feels so good underneath
my feet float
head throbs
when the sky keep turning / without me

when the wind blows in the ghetto

tick tick tick tick tick
double dutch girls glow gold and
brown behind big buildings
too tall to
let the sky shine here
tick tick tick tick
mama mama the doctor said…
angel voices dance in the breeze
like so many dandelions
where do wishes go
tick tick tick
boom

grandmother's bones

creeeiiiaak
used to be a happy noise
like the old oak groaning underneath her young weight
like sneaking down the steps early Christmas morning
but seventy four years
of spilled milk and sand castles
make abuelita's[1] eyes tired
now her fragile bones
creeeiiiaak inside her
filling the emptiness of too many things lost
but i'm here too and
when she kisses me goodnight
we share a secret smile just after my bedroom door
creeeiiiaaks shut
and for a moment even the dark doesn't scare me
maybe/just for a second
she's not scared either

---

1 A diminutive form of "grandmother" (abuela) that demonstrates affection

others who have not grown accustomed to this place

i cannot stay in one place
i must move all the time from corner to corner
there is nothin to discover i have seen
ladies in violet girdles before who
sway w/ the precision of traffic lights
from side to side their behinds catch
the rhythms of cheap beer signs in
cluttered bodegas & i have gotta have
some one to hold (ups) be gettin in my
way crowds of unemployed men with
rolled up shirt sleeves jumble up the
streets that have been my salvation i
can't get thru to where more slime
ridden souls are hurtin each other
& remain on the fringes much longer
i found out that the chinese man
at the cleaners beats his wife
viciously on thursday at 10:00
she does somethin he thinks is
not happenin so he belts her
across the face with a karate chop
any thurs. mornin you can see this or
visit the drag queens in the 50th st.
station w/ me they smile & wink if

i ever stopped to talk w/ them i
wd know that loneliness is not a
heterosexual domain there are so many
f***** some men must be lone-ly
in one way or another there is
somethin phoney abt bein single in
the streets men only believe you
don' wan' them if you say you're married
so single women must be suspected of
deception or else they are ignorin clues
laid before like meetin a horn player
on nostrand avenue or findin him again
at 23 st walkin mild + deliberate
...
walkin deliberately
searchin for the woman in
braids + gold earrings
who was ridin
the train + never saw
him

Whitewash

Whenever Crystal draws her iguanas, I forget about what's going on around me. Crystal makes the best iguanas, lizards, crocodiles, I've ever seen. She puts them on notes to her friends, so she won't have to sign her name. I've got lots of Crystal's iguana notes. Actually a whole lot of them fell from my notebook right in front of Ms. Steinberg. She's our teacher.

"Helene-Angel,". I felt Ms. Steinberg's voice shoot through me.

"Yes, oh.. Yes, M'am". I am trying very hard to grab up all Crystal's notes to me before anyone
has a chance to really read them. "A lot of things just fell from my notebook."

"That's obvious, Helene-Angel, but these things, those animals or whatever they are, have no relationship to any lessons I've taught here."

I know my face turned two-thousand shades of red and my cheeks got real hot, too. All the other kids were laughing at me, even Crystal.

Ms.Steinberg's body froze, only her eyes and mouth moved: "Every single one of you will be on detention 'infinitely', if this uproar doesn't stop this instant. Do you understand?"

Of course, no one answered. Noone wanted to be on detention 'infinitely'. The silence and the brightly colored iguanas I was trying to quietly put away, must have tickled Ms. Steinberg. She shook her head with her own laughter. She could hardly say, what we wanted to hear, "Okay, you win. That's all for today."

Ms. Steinberg was still chuckling, while all the rest of us hurried for the door. Naomi, who ironed her hair to make it really straight.

Tim, George, and Raphael pushing all the girls out of their way which was really rude, but something my brother, Mauricio, says that boys just do.

I was the only one in my group who had to wait for a 'big brother' to walk me home. I had to wait for Mauricio everyday of I'd be in more trouble than whatever could happen, if I went home my way, you know, on my own. But, I didn't complain too much, even though, my classmates teased me like a pre-schooler. I couldn't say much because Mauricio was not crazy about me tagging along with him either.

Soon as I saw him, I fell in step behind him, so I wouldn't be mistaken for his girl, you understand, right. Mauricio was never satisfied, though. He was still mean to me. He hardly looked at me. Maybe, that's why he didn't see The HAWKS surrounding us.

"Hey, Mud People!" I wanna know how can Mud People wash ? Are You dirty all the time ? WHOOOEEE I Must be the Mud Folks' smell Uhg". Mauricio shouts, "Run, Helene-Angel. Get away from here." Another HAWK laughs, "OH, these lil niggahs speaka de Inglishe, huh "Mauricio is calling me to "Run, Runnnn". But how could I ? I was scared. When I tried to run, another one would block my way, "Do you want to be a good white American or not ?" I turned again, almost slipped. "Let's do the Mud Bunny a favor , huh? What'd ya say, guys? Before I could pull away or hit one of them, I just know for sure I felt this stinging cold n my face, around my

ears and neck. I was dripping white Really itchy, stinging white paint covered me wherever my brown skin used to be, I couldn't understand… Why are these boys doing this to me ? Why are they laughing ?

Walking away from me, laughing, slapping five. One turns around to look at me," You are one Jungle-bunny who never looked better.! Aint ya gonna thank me?"

I didn't move. I think maybe If i sit still this will stop or disappear. I try to rub some of the white off, but then my hands turn white, too. I feel like I've been sitting here forver. All of a sudden, Mauricio
comes to me. "I'm gonna take you home, Helene-Angel,Okay? Don't be frightened, now.
Thay've
all gone." Mauricio seemed sad, but that didn't stop him from lifting my shaking body in his arms.
He tried to hide it, by holding his head away from me. I thought he didn't want the "white" stuff to rub off on him. I got real mad . held my face right against his. He pulled away from me. There was a terrible purple knot on his eye, his cheek was bleeding, lips split. I thought he had left me there. We didn't, couldn't talk to each other. He carried me home, wiping my tears every so often

Grandma didn't say much when we got home. She had that sorrowful look on her face that she used to to get when she told mem about seeing beat-up, bleeding black children, even brown black children, long time ago down South. But, she'd never seen a colored child painted white, That's for sure.
"Life is fulla surprises", she said out loud to me. Yet, she kept muttering under her breah words she swore decent people didn't say. Mauricio was lying down with a chunk of old beef over his eye and ice on his lip. Everytime he tried to get up. Grandma made him lie down. "There was nothing more
you could do, boy. You were outnumbered."

That didn't sit well with Mauricio, but I don't really remember much from there on. I went into, my room and disappeared.

Grandma said all the paint was gone, but I could still see it. I could taste fear in the back
of my throat. But, I was as still as a stone. I could only make those terrible stinging feelings go away by
pretending I was a statue.

I could still hear, though. "BLACK GIRL TERRORIZED!" "SHOE POLISH VICTIM!" "WHITE
FOR A DAY!". I couldn't black the newspaper boys shouting, the neighbors talking, the radio announcing. Mauricio defending me like nothing had happened to him. I would not come out of my room. Grandma left me food by my door. She whispered sweet things to me. That I was still a pretty girl.
I was a hero of the race. A brave girl.

The next morning she said, "Helene-Angel. I don't care who did what to you. Today you are going to
open this door and be strong. See all this mail is just for you."

I knew by the tone of her voice that I was definitely going to have to come out of my room.
But,
I could never go back to school. Anybody with any sense knew that I was an embarrassment to myself, to
my friends, to the whole world, to the universe. I opened the door, but instead of Grandma, it was Crystal , Naomi, Tim, Raphael, and Ms. Steinberg, smiling at me.

"We missed you so much!" Crystal hugged me. She was crying, but she slipped another iguana in my hand and winked at me. Raphael shouted, "If we all stick together, no one w ill dare bother you or
anybody else, right?

Before I could think of an answer, I was swept out on the street surrounded by my classmates. I
turned and saw my big brother way down the block, like a dog with his tail between his legs. I yelled,
C'mon, Mauricio," He looked back at Grandma who waved him on. I waited for him and grabbed his hand.

Crystal's iguana was stuck between our fingers, Mauricio looked at me, "what's this?"

Oh, that's a reminder, I've got a right to be here, and I'm not even an iguana."

ntozake shange
blanchiseusse
trinidad
October 1996

For my daughter, Savannah T hulani-Eloisa
Remember courage & love take care of one another.

Fall, Chicago, 1959

Although there was a nipping chill the Chicago, the Walker children waited for the special bus picking up the Negro children assigned to integrate North Side schools

that prided themselves for being all-white. It was a Chicago fall so the Children were wearing the thick wool sweaters Cinnamon had knit for them all summer long. Larry, Tokyo and James felt the air on their faces and knew it was summer no longer, but thanks their mother they were warm as black and white kittens by the fireplace. Three warm little brown bodies lifted themselves into the bus jostling with other colored children playing hand games and shouting greetings or riddles. They were riding with some enthusiasm and some trepidation. They'd seen other cities in violent crisis because the 'the niggahs' were coming. As the meandering vehicle approached the school building which was looming very large, loud and treacherous to their right. Larry. Tokyo, and James tried to block the sights before them by crouching on the floor and covering their heads with their hands. Bottles broke the windows, followed by eggs, tomatoes and vile curses and screams "Niggahs, go back. Ger back niggahs. No spooks round here. This is for white people. Go , get away from here.' Gerrmans. Italians, some Jews and plain poor white trash furious that come 10 to 13 year old colored children where their children were going to be. It was driving them crazy. Making them rabid. Terrifying the children with the Waalker children and the others, as well as, the newspaper and radio & tv

men. It was an ominous fall morning, like heroin haze kind of day like a lazy Charlie Parker day, taut, delicate and spiraling to God know where. Trash drpm atop the very sewers was thrown at lil mess of colored children. but the Walker family was prideful and Larry the oldest was tending to the safety of his siblings... He saw a darkened doorway and huddled the weeping Tokyo, and a pale James around him, Eventually the police came to carry the colored children to their various neighborhoods. They walked as if Charlie Mingus[1] held them all on his back, a strongunwielding spine could straighten up and face any man. They seemed to wander through Hyde Park with frozen eyes. They'd see burning crosses abd the KKK parades before, but this was this time was different it was their backs that carried the weight of the race and nobody had said a word. Larry's eyes were steady and piercing. He never again would be spat upon no white trash ,ever again . He'd either die first or take every body around him. That he knew for sure and he kept on walking towards home with near hysterical baby sister, Tokyo and the befuddled

James running to the doorman at their doorway. They loaded onto the elevator whispering among themselves,"what are we goinnna tell mommy & daddy""". They had been so proud just this morning. & here they were now ldissheveld and soiled. How can they explain that the white

grown-ups just didn't want them there on the North Side. But they hadn't done anything. Just be colored and trying to learn" what could they possibly say. They were now the ones to be ashamed or beat with cat of nine tails, a bullwhip. That's how fearfull they were of

messing up their parents dreams. When Cinnamon let them in she forgot all about Wagner and the other masters. She only heard Billie Holiday painfully crooning "Strange Fruit". She thought of one of her uncles danglin from a cursed tree with his tongue hanging

1 Charles Mingus (1922–1979) was a highly influential jazz musician, composer, and bandleader.

from his mouth, body twisted and unknown till the sun rose. She saw the small group of coloreds cutting him down with tight jaw and angry eyes. Now she must hold her children close to her bosom, for the blind hate had pelleted her children into 3 centuries of pain and humiliation. She wanted to ask, 'why', buit she knew all ready. Jin Crow follows the and mocked like their very own shadows so dark the KKK's burning crosses could not be seen yet the fires were out of control. Cinnamon gathered her brood saying 'White folks just act like that. There's nothing we can do about it. I simply am determined that you all to have a fine education. 'White folks may tarnish your new clothes, even find pleasure in your pain, but you've got to learn to get used to them and the fact that they can't stand the sight, the very breath of the colored folks, the NeGROS, or any of us. "But Mama Tokyo whined from her special corner in th kiitchen, "they were calli' us niggers" and sh wept. Larry colldy echoed" Somebody should go on ahead and throw rocks at their white trash kids."Cinnamon held her head, exasperated in her trembling hands undone by her very own children's anguish and rage, Not being able to soothe the, she almost ran for Lawrence to quell this mess, to talk some sense to all of theem. She hurried, hearing Larry shouting to the walls all the wretched things he could do to torment white folks.

Cinnamon rushed unto Lawrence's deep brown arms, grabbing onto him, as though he was an armored jeep at little Rock. Lawrence held her head close & let his fingers massage her head through a passel of her thick and curly hair. He could feel her breathing slow as he rocked her in his arms. He wished his wife didn't shutter so by the weight of white folks, though he understood. 'Cinnamon, it's gonna be all right. Sweet heart, believe me, we'll weather this." At that very moment they cold hear Tokyo screaming" I'm never goin' back. Never." and James right behind her saying "they aint gonna hurt me no mo' no sirree" larry was laughing cynically throwing a basketball against the wall, his face im

MBJ

Our ancestors hacked bitterly at sugar cane

LQ#1-YELLOW SPOT

We are the sweet never tasted by their sweat soaked tongues
They begged for us to be here
Never knowing who or what we'd become
We are there echoing elegy perpetually sung
We are their echoing elegy perp---

SOULATI BEATBOX "Night and Day"/ MBJ banter

MBJ
5 months into her pregnancy
she emails me a scanned image of her sonogram
sonic waves fashioned in the shape of our son
what I'm seeing is sound
my senses transformed by this image of a boy
floating
buoyantly drifting
like my hold on immaturity slipping away
a son
IT is now **HE** and I…
Am scared shitless

LQ#2 - YELLOW GENERAL WASH

I am nearly 28
The cosmic age of saturn's return
Karmic retribution awaits like economic reparations my ancestors
have earned
The universe on the verge of payin me back

I feel like everything starts over again
Beginning with this image of blue sound
Heartbeat profound
I've printed the email out and its sitting now, peacefully on my lap
A son…

I've never been a woman
Y'know that's a story unto itself
But THIS being
I've spent my whole life seeing a brown boy's days to come
And before they reach 18 so many brown boy's live already done

Brown boy
Feared
Brown boy
Step aside we don't want you here
Brown boy
Only respect those who respect you
Brown boy
Live your life knowing the mainstream world only respects a few
Brown boys
And this will never be tolerated as an excuse
Brown boy
Guilty until proven innocent
Demonized
You stand accused but you stand firm
Like sacred ground brown…

Boy, am I supposed to teach you these things?

SOULATI TRANSITION to 16ths on the snare, MBJ moves into clock walks

LQ#3 WHITE GENERAL WASH

How many brown boys left to be taught by the wilderness
Destiny hung
Hinged
A doorway to death
Your life is great white fetished hyped and hexed
Do I tell you these things right away brown boy
Only 5 months in the womb we've been hunted for so long my son
My son are you going to be hunted too?

LQ#4 RED GENERAL WASH

Your first enemy is me, the
Nigga mentality
The colonized mind
Live at Dance Place in front of everyone

My lineage unfolds with
Hate
Hate was my great great grand
Had several kids dispersed across several lands
Man co-opted then made manifest
Parties like Division

Greed
Murder
Excess

Greed had incestuous sex with his cousin Neglect from the west
Genetic defect produced an unfortunate deformity
They had a baby named Ignorance, who just couldn't see
Ignorance fell in love with Hate
Who by now had turned in on herself
Burned within self

It would make your heart melt
There was a heartfelt connection between Self-hate and Ignorance
Came thence my racist parent
I mean
My parent Racist…

Traces of the seed originated with Greed
So Racist's primary need was to feed a hunger for eternity
Universal props
So he dropped the "t"
Substituted with an "m"
He said forget the racist individual
I'll be Racism
An institution

God complex delusions started coolin with my dad
Gave him dap
Told him you alla dat
And racism got phat off his own p.r.
Said I'm the star of this show…

Now here he go
He embedded himself in the cornerstone of all the new nations
Made himself chair of the house of appropriations
Nothing was safe…

Until chaste Capitalism slipped in the frame
Hey baby what's your name
Racism spittin game cuz Capitalism was a looker
But she flipped it on him like he was a two bit hooker

He took her
And shook her
(cuz dad's way was violent)
but she looked him dead in the eye

and he fell steady silent
compliant

she said "look Racism…we gonna do it like this…
first of all we're gonna pretend that you don't exist.
then we'll tell the world to serve me,
a much more attractive interest,
but we'll shape everything so we both benefit."
she leaned over slowly
kissed him on the lips
pops nodded his head
its been that way ever since…

shortly thereafter, they had my brother
Slavery

a few years later
along came me…

I'm actually glad I don't possess all these family traits
I don't hate anyone except my carrier and his crew
But i do love my master
And I worship his truth
I must admit
I'm whipped weak by greed's fleet genes running through my core
I got mounds of self-hate behind the closet door of skeletons and
 secrets
Wearing sins and freidrich neitzsche's brilliant theories
But I grow weary drawing defenses against self-constructed attacks
I try to relax
Contemplate my link to ignorance
Which make no sense
Cuz I GOTS knowledge
I know

Timbo
Polo
Nike
Moschino
Nautica
Hilfiger versace vuitton dolce and gabbana prada kani levi's bk ck
dkny anne klein fubu
Guess rolex lex beamers benz
I know them all
And I know the ends don't justify the means
I know god is rectangular and grayish green
I novus ordo seclorum don't include me
I know how to serve my dignity up on a platter
I know how to serve my master
I know how to run in place

Faster and smoother than panthers and cougars and
coons–OH MY…
I know suh..
But I don'ts know why otha minds inclined to design systems which
confine my carrier
And bind them to themselves with political ties for the sole purpose
of promotin their
own economic advantage
I don't understand it
We share the same planet but these walls are like granite and I
cannot escape
All this light got me twisted
Consumed with a fable written in invisible ink that
my master swears in my fate
My master eliminates all fiction
I will deviate never

I'd rather beat my head against the walls of a cell
tryin to remember my name forever
Three rows of 222 bird's eye sized holes
Callin gently
subtly
suggesting in the dark
might be a key which gives my name back to me
But I don't want to be in the dark

LQ #5 fade to no lights/black 25 SECONDS

I don't want to be in the dark
I don't want to be dark
I don't want to be dark
I don't want to be dark
I don't want to be
I don't even want to be…
The almighty
Nigga mentality

LQ 6 Black out
LQ6A Lights up, pose one
LQ6B Black out
LQ6C Lights up, pose two
LQ6D Black out
LQ6E Lights up, pose three
LQ6F Black out
LQ6G Lights up, pose four
LQ6H Black out

LQ #7 WHITE AND YELLOW GENERAL TOGETHER

Faster and smoother than panthers and cougars and coons –
OH MY…

I know suh..
But I don'ts know why otha minds inclined to design systems which confine my carrier
And bind them to themselves with political ties for the sole purpose of promotin their
own economic advantage
I don't understand it
We share the same planet but these walls are like granite and I cannot escape
All this light got me twisted
Consumed with a fable written in invisible ink that
my master swears in my fate
My master eliminates all fiction
I will deviate never
I'd rather beat my head against the walls of a cell
tryin to remember my name forever
Three rows of 222 bird's eye sized holes
Callin gently
subtly
suggesting in the dark
might be a key which gives my name back to me
But I don't want to be in the dark

LQ #5 fade to no lights/black 25 SECONDS

I don't want to be in the dark
I don't want to be dark
I don't want to be dark
I don't want to be dark
I don't want to be
I don't even want to be...
The almighty
Nigga mentality

LQ6 Black out
LQ6A Lights up, pose one
LQ6B Black out
LQ6C Lights up, pose two
LQ6D Black out
LQ6E Lights up, pose three
LQ6F Black out
LQ6G Lights up, pose four
LQ6H Black out

LQ#7 WHITE AND YELLOW GENERAL TOGETHER

In 1984 every young black man in new york city had a pair of
Adidas shell toes or puma suedes
Except me
In 1984 I got my first pair of tap shoes
Black and patent leather like the Nicholas brothers[1] used to rock
My pop wasn't cool with me tap dancing
It reeked of America to him
Coming from Haiti my dad desired American wealth but he
shunned American culture
He didn't understand that the two are really one
Nor did realize that tap dance is African drum
The percussive***
Mirrored sharp pound of sharks shanked against exterior of slave
ships decaying vomit
rocked counter-rhythmic to Atlantic waves
Picture the men entrusted to speak stories through song
Shocked mute by the trauma
For them***

---

1 Harold (1921–2000) and Fayard (1914–2006) Nicholas were a much-celebrated dance duo who were considered the best tap and acrobatic dancers active from the 1930s to the 1950s.

Was born
Rhythm be verse when blood bleeds back to line black like Nile riverbeds
There was no outlet to re-configure communicative way of djembe lullabies
So Africans new to the new world
Devised other means of making the fading gorée island seas shore real

understand the innovation
syncopation constructed to reflect dancing celebration of birth and love and harvest
an entire social order divested of its principal means of announcing its own being
that was the African in the European colonized state
the colonies made it an offense
punishable by death for folks of color to be in possession of any noise making instrument
however they had enough business sense not to devalue their property by chopping off our feet
leaving just enough space
to bring back the beat

tap dance
ad hoc repository of rhythm reflecting the organizing principle of improvisation
the nations built jazz
chitlins
behind the back look aways
we stay transcendent through the transformative art
conjuring conjecture
the extra mile is where we start

in 1984 I would tourjete through the raindrops
imagining the wind was my pops
propelling my flight
pops pride lifting me beyond crack
cocaine
Ronald Reagan around the corner
1984 sauna hot
carl lewis[1] blazin and I'm blazin
pop will you listen to me
its what I wanna ask but I keep tap dancing around the questions
projectin all the security my 9 year old body can muster
wilting in the cool hot of my father's disconnection

fuck it
my dad was in the home
he didn't beat my mom
me and my sister are both healthy and college educated
almost cosby[2] kids
we blow afro bombs through ego-super ego id
cuz freud's paradigms of the mind
didn't have colored folk in mind
so I'd dissect mine for self
for sure

1984 I learned to tap dance
not Clarence Thomas
or bamuthi
song and dance
that is a misnomeric
misappropriation of the art form

---

1 Frederick Carlton "Carl" Lewis (b. 1961) was an Olympic gold medalist sprinter.

2 This is a reference to the family on the television program, *The Cosby Show*, which depicted an upper-middle-class Black household in Brooklyn.

derived from rhythmic regeneration of Gambian *manjani*[1]
reconstructed for Virginia shores

1984 I learned to perform
slide through space
face to face with *ellingtonian* jazz
I learned my movement was jazz
Improvised truths out of false structures
1984 father son relationship ruptured
pop wasn't listening to me
so I'd play call and response between my feet and the floor

pop…

pop…
pop…

I don't feel like tap dancing no more

LQ # 8 PINK SPECIAL

Somewhere between Mother nature and father time
There's a spiraling myth about
A father
Forever chasing the rising son
A modern Sisyphus stuck behind a boulder of sol
The father is mythic and misfit
A mystic
A self-destructing missle
Amiss amidst a monolithic image of what he's supposed to be
A father
Chasing the rising son
Like the horizon rushing to the seam of sky and sea

1 A ritual dance marking special occasions

She would give birth in water if she could
Our conservative insurance and threadbare wallets say she can't
So we compromise
Natural birthing class
Easy to come by in the bay area
Land of hemp granola and all things alternative
It's almost our turn to share how we're
FEELING with the rest of the group
Sitting in a circle
Generation X
Our coach is at the chalkboard
DRUG FREE VAGINAL BIRTH

(personally
knock me the fuck out
but maybe that's why I was born this sex
I don't possess a woman's strength
Her body's all stretched
Our baby's body's growing in length
Arms legs chest head)
You wanna do this drug free go right ahead, be my guest
Now I'm about to be a guest on the hot seat

Bamuthi…
Namaste…
By this time next week
You'll be a FATHER
How are you FEELING

Maybe I should be paying attention to what this white lady's
question
But man I'm reelin back in a daydream of
Mother nature and father time

Crackin riddles about a cat undulating his spine as he strides towards
The son in the east
Thinks he recognizes self in the rising
But he just cannot see
He is blinded by light
His life like time in a dream
The place where relativity ends so long as we sleepo

And somewhere
There are 8 pairs of future parental eyes
Are all on me
Waiting to see if I'm **FEELING**
Anythingbut what I'm feeling is the struggle of the pursuant father in my daydream
I'm **FEELING** the visions of mythic men we see in solar mirrors when we sleep
I'm **feeling** damn good
I'mo be a father next week and then all of a sudden I'm
Feeling like I cant….

You gotta move m'kai

LQ # 9 BLUE GENERAL WASH

You got mountains to climb
Skies to fly seas to seize
Meet new ancestors swinging in the breeze clinging to the thought that trees really be
hangin onto do re mi
The melody of the melancholy mired in mud
Then rises like moons like mau mau[1]
Like maroons must MOVE

---

1 A name for members of the Kenya Land and Freedom Army, a militant African nationalist group active from the late 1940s to the early 1960s

M'kai mountains to climb skies to fly seas to seize
Seeds to roots to branches to leaves

The deepest part of god's imagined possibilities
Billowing like a willowing wind
Are one
Are men must move…

My son m'kai is seven years old
Three months before he was born my grandfather died

Three times in one night
Flatlined and revived
Slipped into a coma twice
The last time he came back bragging about this manchild
he'd just met in the afterdeath
After which his word became flesh
Became sacred text
The next testament
My first breath
My first born
A boy
And man…

He looks just like my granddad
They recently met inside of a revelation while granddad was doing
orbital revolutions around his life
The last time he was confronted at a crossroads by my son m'kai
Of blood and bone and sacrifice
Sanctified
Granddad said I can't wait for you to meet your son

For the first time I really understood where the old man was
coming from

LQ # 10 BLUE CENTER SPECIAL

I believe in him and I must
There's this race to be run and my folks is losin
Past is prologue
Our epicenter is an ancestor's epilogue
An epithet if we ain't eased that ancestor's burden yet
He used his great grandfather's death as a scroll to scribe a scripture
Whisked the man back to life with unborn whisper
Son do you know who you are
An ascendant descendant deciphered from stars
Intone the indescribable like a shadow my son
We are men
Bury nothing but bones
Cry rivers of tears
Deeply we run
A race to be won
Guided like Harriet with visions of sugar plum skinned
Hung thin strange fruit our roots reach deep
We men are men
Amen
Amin
Your din your duty
Your destiny to move
like the way you move me
Your destiny to move like the way
you
move
me…
Your destiny to move like the way
you
move
me…

Your destiny to move like the way
you
move
me…

LQ # 11 FADE DOWN CENTER…TAKE 8 SECONDS TO FADE TO BLACK

After 10 second hold in black

This story begins in the middle
Halfway across the planet
I think…
That I'm awake
Last night at dusk I
Took a red eye across the Atlantic
Landed on the first morning of summer in Europe
For the last 40 sumthin hours it's been day
I think
I might be dreamin
But I'm not sure

I'm in Paris for a festival of
young contemporary choreographers from Africa
By the grace of god, I get to watch
It's one of the perks I've managed to convince the performing arts
machine that I am high art AND hip hop…

FALL
sshh don't tell'em I've gotten stuck I'm in between
Back row of the audience
Falling up
Waking dream
In Paris I
Represent my country in the flesh

The Surrogate for allen Iverson[1] and 50 cent[2]
But What good is a black man in America if stripped of his right to threat?
How hip hop can I be if they let me onto their set?

RETURN

Any way as a guest of the institution
I'm at this dance festival and on the first night
This south African soloist does this joint where she wears a tutu and a big easter bunny costume head-thing and contorts herself into a big plastic bag for like 30 minutes…and then she walks through the audience putting saran wrap over people's mouths and kissing them on their plastic dental dammed lips…and then it ends…that's it.

In my head

DREAM # 2

Music: Dream sig equally touched by kwaito[3]/sarafina[4] and ladysmith mambazo[5]

the image of south Africa is fixed on apartheid, Steven Biko,[6] Robben Island.[7] In my head it is always the late 80's and Mandela is

---

1 Allen Iverson (b. 1975) is a retired professional basketball player who played with the Philadelphia 76ers (1996–2006) and several other teams through 2011. Iverson was an NBA MVP, an all-star, rookie of the year, and a multiple scoring champion who is in the NBA Hall of Fame.

2 Curtis James "50 Cent " Jackson III (b. 1975) is a multi-platinum-selling rapper.

3 An electronic musical genre that developed in the Soweto township of South Africa in the 1990s

4 *Sarafina!* is a 1987 musical by Mbongeni Ngema that was turned into a film in 1992. It depicts the events surrounding the 1976 Soweto uprising in Apartheid South Africa, a key event in the South African liberation struggle.

5 Black South African choral group that became internationally famous in the 1980s

6 Steven Biko (1946–1977) was a Black South African activist and intellectual who was murdered in police detention. Biko is considered the founder of the Black Consciousness Movement in South Africa.

7 Robben Island is the prison island where Nelson Mandela was incarcerated for eighteen of his twenty-seven years in prison.

the first person I ever truly truly wanted to be free. The first major metaphor for liberating me…

The triangle of perspective is crazy….
I'm lookin at this African woman for some sense of root
She's lookin at European performance art trading in amandla for a frayed pink tutu
And Europeans ALWAYS been lookin at me…

KASE with text
Ever since my name was satchmo[1] Langston[2] josephine[3]
Since the days when they bred me
I am the descendant of an experiment (begin gesture phrase) in psyche and body
A fetish taking my place in line
Fractured
wondering when this woman's history stopped being mine
I've been flying for the last forty hours I have no sense of time
I wonder which one of us is sleep, and which one is just tired

and then
Exactly right then
I fall

This story begins in the middle
Halfway across the planet
I think…
That I'm awake
Last night at dusk i

1 Nickname for Louis Armstrong
2 Langston Hughes (1901–1967) was a highly influential Harlem Renaissance poet, novelist, memoirist, and critic.
3 Josephine Baker (1906–1975) was an internationally famous singer, actor, and dancer who expatriated to France in the 1920s.

Took a red eye across the pacific
Landed on the first morning of summer in Japan
For the last 40 sumthin hours it's been day
I might be dreamin
But I'm not sure

I am a Living word lost in translation
Guess this is a near death experience

At the club in japan **(Music: Dream sig with far eastern inflections)**
EVERYBODY in hip hop knows that the culture is HUGE over here
Mostly cuz they heard it on yo mtv rap interviews with the wu tang clan[1]
It is times square times ten
There are so many lights on in Tokyo at midnight the sky looks like 11am plugged into a socket
My hosts are all hip hop kids that INSIST tired as I am that I roll to the spot
I lead with my ego think, why not
I expect, that when I walk in the club the music will STOP
The rivers will part
The reverence will begin

Behold young Japanese motherfuckas that sweat my culture
Authenticity is IN the building
It's me
Born 1975 in Queens,

1 The Wu-Tang Clan is a hip-hop group originating in 1992 in Staten Island, New York.

Nas,[1] A tribe called quest,[2] RUN DMC[3]
The real hip hop is obviously oozing from my pores for all to see and all
Ignore me
The only black guy in the room except for the ones we're all dancing to
I am either so racist, or self-centered, or so oblivious I think that props are due
Head nods
Fists up
Eye contact
None of that

Invisible…race doesn't matter…I'm just another guy who might be a little too old to be at the club…and in the tradition of the wrong guy at the right party, I retire to a corner…music thumpin…haven't been to sleep since yestersumthin…and I fall…

LQ # 12 WHITE AND YELLOW GENERAL TOGETHER

This story begins with the first African American woman I may have ever met
a white chick from Lubbock texas
Molly melching

Big um'n
Came to Senegal 20 years ago to work for unesco
Has never left
Fell in love with a Senegalese man had a baby

---

1 Nasir Bin Oludara "Nas" Jones (b. 1973) is a rapper and the son of the jazz musician Olu Dara mentioned earlier in the text.

2 A hip-hop group founded in 1985 that would become one of the most important acts of the "golden age" of hip-hop

3 Pioneering rap group from Queens, New York, formed in 1983

Was happy
Until He left
She speaks wolof, and twi, and is a BEAST negotiator at the marketplace
Fully integrated into and respected by her community
Among the Senegalese I meet, I am often referred to as a black american
Molly An African american

When I get off the plane in Senegal
I have no plans and no real money
I have molly's phone number in my head, given to me by a friend of a friend
And lots of stories in my head, also given to me by friends of friends…

They say

BOY in Africa, they'll love you
Go meet the dancers
Go find the hip hop
Someone will adopt you
You'll be taken care of don't trip…

3 days in
I've been hustled out of my drawers
and am spending money at a pace that will leave me homeless in 8 days.
I am scheduled to be here for 4 months.

In tears I call molly, she invites me to thies, says I can stay,
Not quite the African I expected to take me in
She runs an NGO here called tostan, she's a champion of women's health

Works to eliminate female circumcision in rural villages
Calls it mutilation

I become her roadie
Sit in the backseat gazing at endless stretches of endless flatland and wide sky as we
drive from one end of the country to the other..

We drive to the middle of NOWHERE yo
NOWHERE, and come to a stop in front of a single stone building with a thatched roof.

3 girls come out all smiles and grace
they greet and I think molly is gonna meet with them and we'll be out
within a minute, a little boy produces a drum and begins playing it, which I think is kind
of annoying to have going during the meeting, but WHO THE FUCK AM I, just KEEP
QUIET, and LISTEN FOR YOUR NAME

I sit on a rock and take it all in

All of the nowhere

Africa

Ok, so the boy playing the drum is this village's version of a mass email,
And pretty soon, I don't know where the hell the people come from, but the little
courtyard with the one building looks like the rose bowl on new year's day, with like
100,000 people come to see the circus in town which is namely, the big white African,
and the short clueless American friend, and

Molly is trying to have this meeting with the like head women of the village council, to
spill her propaganda about stopping this backward indigenous ritual, but nobody can hear
anything cuz of all the commotion and people trying to bust into the building to have a
look at the ONE white woman within a 1000 miles, and finally molly says,

Bamuthi, I need you to distract them, can you figure something out...

So what am I gonna say,

Uh molly I don't speak their language and there's no electricity and i have no
megaphone, microphone radio telephone whatever
How'm I gonna keep them all occupied or whatever
I am wilting I need water I need...

5 minutes later
all the village children
I am surrounded heart pounding
AFRICA

KASE–Montazh movement sequence begins, film sequence begins other me's and
village kids learning the same piece of choreography

don't have to astound em
only distract
no microphone, no turntables, no English

that's my whole act

to survive

I become hip hop empath
I channel the low beginnings
Fires burning all over the Bronx
Post civil rights glass ceilings
No lights
No loot
You just do what you feel to the groove

A dance floor uprising of youth

(I just pray that they buy it)

KASE

The future aesthetic/ the future's not static/it's movin kinetically manic/ you mimic?
You cynic of smith that works with florid words/ the world is THIS
minute/ magnanimous moment/ a future aesthetic/ a mytho-poetic/
cerebral and soulful/ vivid/ kinesthetic/ it's not in your head or your
heart or your feet/ it exists in all three…

they're buying it…

while I make em laugh with my shamrocks
molly speaks to the village council in a language that I have never heard of
she convinces them to abandon a centuries old practice
encourages them to modernize their attitude toward women

I think

I know another Texan who came in to the brown people's country
and tried to get them to adopt a foreign way…

Maybe he should have extended a sign of peace first

Molly extended me…

This is how I became an MC…
Without saying a word…

LQ # 13 RED SPECIAL on TOMMY begins performing 3-4 breaks

In the last gasp of evening somewhere in the Sudanese middle distance
Dogs assail the night with deep throated mean willed bark
Hung in the air like a falling star, exhaust smoke, holding
Cinnamon and cardamom and ash in its folds. In the near dark I am
clutching at jagged memory to grasp my newfound whiteness

My first point of access is the name of a second grader who goes to
school with my son. Sudan. Her parents placed the old Arabic word
meaning 'land of the Blacks' upon her head. Grow into this child.
Oil rich mecca midpoint bush beat. Black. Sudan.

My second clue is the i-tunes ubiquity of the word Darfur which I
know George Clooney and Madonna really care about and I know
lost boys and genocide but I don't know why they're lost and I don't
know who's killing who. A starbucks activist I know what I read
between the door and my dirty soy chai

But I do know that I found clue number three last summer in
the shaking voice of a mother tongue just now loosened in the
still dark shadow of the loss of her son. Inner City schoolkid //life
violently left invalid. Gun blast. Book bag. Blood soaked. Chicago
Mourning.

In the near dark
The sound of
Shouting at an intersection without signal lights

The smell of perfumed oil seeped into wood amid
Burning trash…
arid cleansing
Sharp dust
Stray cats
Loose collections of physics resistant prayer songs

Men touch each other with palm syntax as synapse incensed by the faint scent of danger

6 of us standing on a riverbank at an apex where the blue nile and white nile meet northern sudan
we sharing rolled stems brown leaves and seeds
the darkest among us is the color of solar eclipse
his skin is crisp like the center of my heartbroken iris kissed
living placenta planted in nile papyrus.
Just on the other side of blue Black. Sudan

The men dandelion blow their way through an explanation of Darfur, like first timers at an AA meeting.
Resigned to the reality at odds with the idea.
the government funds militia to displace the least among us, draw borders in blood where bonds of brotherhood might be
difference, they say is skin deep…
Looking around and gesturing the man who looks most like me says we are all considered white here. Now pointing, Except him.

A storm of bashful ivory breaks the seal of the eclipse's lips
Miraculously, at the river there is a nigger among us, and I am closer
to white than I have ever been. I am prescribed to vision American
diversity, I see the chromatic logic of ethnic cleansing with
untrained lens. My paradigm for race is civil rights and apartheid
based.
us and them

Chicago Mourning made the smart play
She moved her family from southern Sudan as a jew would have left 1930's germany while the sound of slaughter was still hushed in the soft horizon. A civil war. Blood for oil. North and south. Brown and black. I meet her in uptown Chicago marching toward Clarendon Park. We are memorializing the lives of 36 youth murdered during the previous school year. Her son is among them. Leaving the continent's worst ever civil war, her son fell victim to another self-perpetuated pandemic assault on black life. She walks at the front of the vigil holding his picture in a simple black frame.
The six of us stand at the nile on higher ground, I am looking at color in the primitive way that we traumatized American Blacks do. If a race war broke out in this room right now, it'd be easier to gauge my odds and figure out the first person I'd have to knock out. We see in binary suppositions here. I know the sides.
We five races, in sudan they see 300 tribes and because I am not among the lowest, here at the nile, in the seed of black civilization I am most near to white

Cultural economies of scale
Class divides
Blood for oil
Genocides
Instinctively I want to assign the role of the bad guy, put him in a black hat
Spy vs. spy

clueless, I wish to claim an enemy…
derive familiar directions from a psychological map always pointing me to this moment when my color works for me
never so basic as a mother's mourning tears…
never so simple as anything you could read while waiting for coffee, in black and white…

LQ # 14 YELLOW LIGHT when MBJ comes back SNAPPING HIS FINGERS

Two brown boys
Too poor to prosper
Two nations too proud to conquer
Two take refuge on makeshift boats
Two prayers ascend
Dear god make her float to
U.S. soil
To Holy land
Too rough the water
Two boys descend to join the sand at the bottom of the sea where
Too many African bodies be…

Too upset

Their spirits are set underneath the water where two boys get a
chance to heave
To cleave to clutch
To hold onto pieces of shattered boat
Like intact dreams they loved so much
They left the countries they loved so much
To escape
To defect
From nothing but the farming of bones and death…

LQ # 15 RED SPECIAL LIGHT GOES OUT // YELLOW SPECIAL STAYS UP

I was in Haiti once
At a vodoun ceremony and I passed out
Personally I think I seen a little bit of blood and I just
Hehh…

Like a little beyonce
But the people I was with
Folks who all honor and respect Haitian culture
Believed I'd been possessed…

They said I fell…

Like this…

A scared puppy or a priest
Either is possible
Who knows where your body goes when your spirit flies away
When you lose your mind what jumps in to take its place

The Haitians called me neg ginen
My grandmere
My oldest living relative once told me that ginen is the tunnel that connects haiti to Africa
So when a Haitian calls you neg ginen[1]
That's the real shit
That's super black
That's a stripe

I wonder what they'd say if they knew my son was half Chinese and my girlfriend was white

LQ # 16 RED AND BLUE GENERAL WASH

TOMMY MAKES MUSIC. MBJ DANCES WHEN MUSIC ENDS

1 Neg ginen is a colloquial term in Haitian Creole meaning "to come from" Guinea West Africa. It expressed solidarity and a common root between people.

LQ # 17 RED AND YELLOW GENERAL WASH

A walk through the park in post war bosnia
It is night and the guy following me is gaining
I cut across the cobblestone street
Make a break for it through the trees

The next day he shows up at my workshop

He looks nothing like the neo nazi I though was trailing me through the shadows
He's probably all of 13
Close cropped hair
Blue eyes
All elbows and knees

He speaks no English
But shows up every day at my workshop to write
Then he starts showing up at my crib at the cock's crow

I still haven't learned the Bosnian words for
Hey you little shit I'm trying to sleep!

Until I do I open the door
He smiles his big goofy grin and starts to beat box
He's 5 and a half feet deep in ethnic warfare's grave
Has found someone to help him dig out
His mouth music make like skipping bullets against the wall of first like dark

Still dreaming, I begin nodding my head to the beat

In the distance the adan calls
It is dawn

The cipher can't wait for the day to break…

LQ # 18 BLUE AND WHITE GENERAL WASH

Cycles to break
No more lying
Much less flying
Call your grandma
Practice faith.

Don't confuse your art with your life
Embody what you write.

Stop contradicting.

Slipped in the groove of institution and reparations

Funk and function equally separating to reveal me in the break

Psychically cycling
I got patterns to shake

Music to make
Culture to love
Guilt to feel
Prayers to say
Cycles to break
Don't instill fear in the boy
Pray with full body
Practice faithfulness
and faith
cycles to break

there's more than one way to live...
more than one way to believe black is beautiful
more than one way to raise kids
more than one way to love
more than one struggle

more than one answer
more than one way to break

It's ethereal
Lyrical miracle
Almost Biblical
The cyclical
Hear it different

It's ethereal Lyrical miracle
Almost Biblical
Hear it different
cyclical
Steerable
Un-nearble hearable
Liminal Spherical
Physical quizzical
Is it
Is it
Is it is it is it real?

When does it end?

The marchin
Margin
2nd line
songs
2009
still playin
the drum
for archin angels
tuba
snare
ax armed and dangerous
tryin to blow the ghost back to life

life is living battling back color
burned like sierra umbra in the armrest of your nawlins funeral
Chicago death best

If you look real close
You can see the infant in his eyes
Advanced in life it does him no good to pretend

Together. Brown people. Mourning sons. A time to heal. Morning comes.

And in the morning is urban oz
Golden aquaponic gardens
Aquaducts where the
Orisha aggregate
And young Boys who in death were buried in earth come back as the word itself
Living color
Remind us of the day's remains
Returns as earth to flirt with life

The truth
I assume
Is the last face you want to see before you die…
Upon Whose face do you wish to set your eyes before leaving…
I grew up in queens
God is my witness
My eyes have cast down at kings
Falling at the precise point of peaking

And the next day
There is a colorful explosion
Like we were all dreaming…Ever closer
Blood red seeds
Strange fruit

Oh my god is it real…
More than one way to break…
Poetry in motion

LQ # 19 FADE OUT TO BLACK

PECHA KUCHA STYLE…b hines photo essay/B's poem

If you look real close
You can see he has about 21
Maybe 27 and a half hairs on his chin
At first you miss the hair
Because the FIRST thing you notice is his skin
If it were soil, his is the earth brown you'd want to sow in.
A Chicago sun
Hard times
He does not blink

So think of this brother brown
Now see this mother black
See how dark the day becomes when you bury the sun
How you set the future back
A mother inters a murdered teen

Look real close as a Chicago spirit
Becomes a canvassed moan
The first frontier of the last element
This color crossing the air clear as the racist undertone
Underlining health care town halls
Don't seem to care about the health of black boys until they come
back as a flash of
orange scrawled against injustices walls

Like the baddest burner scorching obama's blackberry
With viscous viscuous twist of toxic

Fed up
Polychromatic
DEAD UP
Compressed black up
Back up
Against the brick wall
Skull crack shackled scream
The clarion call
Of sisters suckling fatherless sons
recycled meaning in the canvas hung by gallows eve
Dying boys desperate tinted peace

A tree mourns its falling leaves looking at death like a lynched lover in its eye
How you tell the withered winter blossom to go green
In the cloak of its fall
We were all once spells
Of the past like
A fossil turned fuel
Turned mustard seed of bleeding edge
See the warning
It is warming
And that's just the block
Feel the heat like rising ghosts of dead teens levitating among falling stocks

You can smell the slaughter flirting with survival in the paint
Listen to the shouting strain of strangled genius
Can't sleep through the silence
Riddled bullets written in the writhing
Psychotic social norms
Murdered sons
Mothers crying

Corporate cannibals
A country eating its young
Socially relevant
Prescient pasts
Black men hung
Lord they love it when we fail

Look how close we are to defaming the planet
like a black boy rotting in jail
decrepit waste
earth spit respectless dis negative space upon the frail graying gloom of the advancing day in decline

remember the brown boy
look super close and see if you find ONE line about his passing
in the swirling refuse of yesterday's news?
Recycle the evidence…
Burning print and too young bones are active minerals feeding urban ground
Look through lens of color
See pigmented jazz in sound

But if you look real close…
There is hope
Returned all seeing
Dragon textured scale of life
Wind swept black boy
Dreaming violet
Ultra violent ancestral tithe unto the night
Red letter day
Blue letter links
Ecstasy rainbow
Death pulled back from the brink

Life exists in simple exercise
Paint a word
Become flesh
Live in earth
Snakes and trees
Urban eden
Cheat death
Join in community
Color consciousness

Like a fire in Chicago
right outside the window
windpipe
worn from screaming
from the burning of yo kinfolk
how on earth
does life become a sinkhole loco local vocally a writer
I'm a ghost on spinning globe
I shhhh in flaming icy blue you see me I'm a fuckin rider

in a frat of Fatherless men
Watch us toil
Black spine recoils
Like intifada by the border between Brahmins
Look real close
One's a shyster
One's a shaman
Wrapping the body like a blues
Around the throat
Of the broken promise
titanic climactic chaos prophesy the Brahmins
bombin
heated thunder up your bigger Thomas

CRITICAL ESSAYS

This section includes two essays. They display Shange's expansiveness as an artist who worked in various forms and as an intellectual who rigorously pursued understanding Black history and aesthetics in both local and global contexts. The first, "Borders," is a reflection of her own uses of language and in particular how it echoes music and movement through geographies. The second, "Lost in Language & Sound," is what she describes as a "choreoessay," an echo of her classic form, the choreopoem, and has an experimental structure in which she answers questions from an imagined interviewer through actors who are prospectively performing the interview onstage. Shange renders how characters are dimensions of the self for the artist, but also how the artist operates as a conduit for a chorus of voices beyond herself. Her experiences studying under a series of distinguished instructors and analysis of both the traditions upon which they drew and the collaborative nature of dance as an art form are biographically important for Shange as a renaissance artist.

Borders

Like most people of color, black people in The New World, I came by my passion for literature in a circuitous way, a night journey marked by music, movement, improvisation, and smells of perfume, sweat, and humid star-flickering nights. I pay tribute and homage, first, to the wondrous miracle of language on an African's tongue. My house, my neighborhood, my soul, by now, immersed as far as I can recall in the accents of Togo, Liberia, Trinidad, Costa Rica, Chicago, Lagos, New Orleans, Bombay, and Capetown, not to minimize in any way, drawls of Mississippi, clipped consonants from Arkansas, or soprano like chisme (gossip) of Kansas City. So, first, the voices of my people made me want to have them forever. To rid my world of silence, the prohibited, the stiff, and mendacious. A kitchen, a back porch somewhere, or the back of the bus opened rhythmic and lyrical realms to me in the same way that the shuffle of shoes brought music to Miles Davis' ear. Maybe, it's the land we, me & Miles, were raised on, or the river, or what Henry Dumas called the "Arc of Bones" floating in the deep dank Mississippi that lent our spirits to the whispers of our landscapes. I'm not always sure, but I am convinced the constant flow of black folks from all over through St.Louis left an indelible impression on me: my sense of rhythm, melody, irony, and beauty come from that earth, that river.

But, no, that's not all the truth. Some of my sense of language fell from my mother's lips at dusk or Sunday morning, when thanks to her elocution classes, Miss Ellie, recited Dunbar,[1] Cullen,[2]

---

1 Paul Laurence Dunbar (1872–1906) was an important early African American novelist, poet, and short story writer who was widely read and recited in segregated African American schools.

2 Countee Cullen (1903–1946) was a Harlem Renaissance–era poet and novelist.

Hughes, Brown,[1] and Walker[2] as naturally as breaking into song which she also did, sometimes. Remembering that these words from those poets sauntered through the air, remember too that Tito Puente,[3] La Lupe,[4] Jackie Wilson, The Shirelles,[5] Dizzy Gillespie and Charlie Parker entered my world just as freely, only it was when my father, Dr. P.T., came home that bebop, rhumbas and rhythm & Blues became the vernacular of the house, the common dialect of relations with the world and myself. With music came movement because we were colored and southern, dance was something we did/ like other folks walk, or sip coffee, I imagine.

Later, on I sought out language that somehow echoed inarticulate, inchoate impulses I lived with, in the same way I watched Carmen de Lavallade's [6] body make sense of an irrational and vicious place I was supposed to pledge allegiance to everyday. Between, James Baldwin[7] with "The Fire Next Time" and " Amen Corner", I confused Pearl Primus,[8] Katherine Dunham,[9] and Eartha

---

1 Sterling Allen Brown (1901–1989) was a Howard University English professor, poet, and folklorist.

2 Margaret Walker (1915–1998) was a poet, novelist, and historian, as well as longtime professor at Jackson State University.

3 Ernest Anthony "Tito" Puente Jr. (1923–2000) was a percussionist, bandleader, and composer of Puerto Rican descent who was a leader in the development of Latin jazz and mambo.

4 Lupe Victoria "La Lupe" Yolí Raymond (1936–1992) was a popular Afro-Cuban singer of boleros and Latin soul.

5 The Shirelles were a New Jersey–based girl group of the 1950s and '60s.

6 Carmen de Lavallade (b. 1931) is a pioneering African American ballet dancer, choreographer, and actor who was the first African American prima ballerina at the Metropolitan Opera.

7 James Arthur Baldwin (1924–1987) was an essayist, novelist, playwright, and social activist.

8 Pearl Primus (1919–1994) was a dancer, choreographer, and anthropologist known for her preservation and performance of African diasporic traditional dances.

9 Katherine Dunham (1909–2006) was a dancer, choreographer, and anthropologist who created what is known as the "Dunham technique" of dance training and performance.

Kitt[1] defying the limitations of the body and the English language with an art that was rightfully mine, an art I could claim, from which I could spring like Jesse Owens[2] at the starting line.

As a young adult I discovered Beatniks and some black ones like LeRoy Jones (Amiri Baraka), Ted Joans, Walter Delegall,[3] and Percy Johnston.[4] I kept Diane di Prima[5] for myself because she was a woman with fire and myth in her mouth. Then, somebody told me worshipping others leads to mediocrity. So I stopped looking for roots and heroes and heroine I found my peers, Pedro Pietri, Felipe Luciano, Gylan Kain, Etnairis Rivera,[6] Sonia Sanchez,[7] Jessica Hagedorn,[8] Jan Mirikatani,[9] and Thulani Davis, poets I could work with and be inspired by on a daily if not weekly basis. Later, I'd add Susan Griffith,[10] Judy Grahn,[11]

---

1 Eartha Kitt (1927–2008) was a popular singer, actor, and civil rights activist who broke barriers for Black performers in Hollywood.

2 James Cleveland "Jesse" Owens (1913–1980) was a track and field athlete who notably won four gold medals at the 1936 Olympic games in Berlin, enraging Adolph Hitler. When he returned to the United States he experienced Jim Crow discrimination in both the North and South.

3 Walter DeLegall (1936–2004) was one of the founding members of the Howard Poets, a group of student poets at Howard University who built a historic poetry community in the late 1950s.

4 Percy Edward Johnston (1930–1993) was a poet, professor, and playwright. Johnston was also one of the founding members of the Howard Poets.

5 Diane di Prima (1934–2020) was a beat poet, publisher, editor, and educator who would become the poet laureate of San Francisco.

6 Etnairis Rivera (b. 1949) is a Puerto Rican poet and professor.

7 Sonia Sanchez (b. 1934) is a distinguished poet, professor, and Black Arts Movement/Black studies activist.

8 Jessica Tarahata Hagedorn (b. 1949) is an American poet and playwright of Filipina descent.

9 Janice Mirikatani (1941–2021) was a Japanese American poet and activist who was San Francisco's poet laureate (2000–2002).

10 Here Shange intended Susan Griffin (b. 1943), a feminist philosopher, essayist, and playwright who, like Shange, experimented with prose form and punctuation as a way of interrogating politics and power.

11 Judy Grahn (b. 1940) is a lesbian feminist poet recognized as a key figure in the gay and lesbian liberation movement.

Alta,[1] and Leslie Marmon Silko,[2] Joy Harjo,[3] Alurista,[4] and Jimmy Santiago Baca[5] to my list of influences, healers, and friends. Language is for me like the nectar of the living, I find it singing to me everywhere I go. I dance with Dianne McIntyre,[6] Eleo Pomare, Mickey Davidson,[7] Dyane Harvey,[8] and Idris Ackamor,[9] and Cecil Taylor[10] whenever I hear my folks speak. No, I didn't forget Alice Walker,[11] Toni Morrison, and Zora Neale Hurston.[12] I just figured, you could figure that out about me on your own.

---

1 Alta Gerrey (b. 1942) is a feminist poet and publisher, and founder of Shameless Hussy Press. She published the first edition of Shange's *for colored girls*.

2 Leslie Marmon Silko (b. 1948) is a Laguna Pueblo Indian novelist and poet, and leading figure in what has been termed the Native American renaissance of writing in the late twentieth century.

3 Joy Harjo (b. 1951) is a poet, nonfiction writer, musician, and playwright of Muscogee and Cherokee descent who has served as the poet laureate of the United States (2019–2022).

4 Alberto Baltazar Urista Heredia (b. 1947), known as Alurista, is a distinguished Chicano poet and activist known for blending Spanish and English in his works.

5 Jimmy Santiago Baca (b. 1952) is a Chicano and Apache poet, memoirist, and screenwriter.

6 Dianne McIntyre (b. 1946) is a dancer and choreographer who choreographed Shange's *Spell #7* at the Public Theater in 1979.

7 Mickey Davidson is a dancer, choreographer, and founder of her own dance company. Davidson frequently collaborated with Shange.

8 Dyane Harvey is a dancer and choreographer who was a principal dancer in the Eleo Pomare Dance Company for two decades.

9 Idris Ackamoor (b. 1951) is a jazz multi-instrumentalist and composer. In the 1970s, he was a member of Cecil Taylor's Black Music Ensemble.

10 Cecil Taylor (1929–2018) was a pioneer of free jazz, a composer, bandleader, and pianist.

11 Alice Walker (b. 1944) is one of the most important Black women novelists and essayists of the twentieth century.

12 Zora Neale Hurston (1891–1960) was a highly influential anthropologist, folklorist, and novelist of the Harlem Renaissance and beyond. Alice Walker was the principal figure in rescuing Hurston from obscurity with her publication of a Hurston collection, *I Love Myself When I Am Laughing and Then Again When I Am Looking Mean and Impressive* in 1979.

lost in language & sound
a choreoessay

(as lights come up.....three actors are seated center stage writing in journals....stage right, musicians are busy tuning up and making notes....stage left, two dancers stretch and warm up)

VOICEOVER #1

O.K. Ms. Shange...yr level is set..are you ready?

ALL

yes

VOICEOVER #1

great...alright....standby....in 5...4...3...2...1

VOICEOVER #2

good evening, listeners.....thank you for tuning in to lend your ears to WXLR....we have a very special guest in the studio this evening...poet, playwright, novelist, performance artiste & friend, Ms. Ntozake Shange....thank you, Ms. Shange, for stopping by to share with us this evening...

ACTOR #3

thank you for having me...and please, stop with the Ms.Shange.

VOICEOVER #2

(laughs)

O.K....Zake....well that's a great place to start...why don't you share your name...Ntozake Shange...with our listeners. i understand that was not yr birth name...how did you come to be Ntozake Shange?

ACTOR #2

unshackling myself from my slave name, i was blessed to be renamed by two South African exiles in the early 70's...

VOICEOVER #2

wow...O.K....well, so much has been said in describing you...how would Zake introduce Ntozake Shange?

(dancers begin to move, playing with a length of silk...winding themselves/each other up in the cloth...cocooning themselves... unraveling...interacting with actor #2 at intervals during monologue...)

ACTOR #2

I cd say I am the ultimate conclusion of the allure of silk, the shimmer and the breeze of silks. After all, my skin is silken, my grandmother's hands sheer as silk/ my mother's cherry-blond hair hard to picture without the capricious play of light changing her thick mane of a coif moment to moment from golden to cerise, ash blond to emboldened chestnut. These are but a few of the qualities of silk that are my blood. my blood memory, my dreams./ Yet without the extraordinary vision of Ferdinand and Isabela,[1] Cristobal Colon[2] wd not have been charged with the mission to find an alternate route to India, thence China, where silk was born. Colon, Columbus, the adventure wd not have set foot on Santo Domingo in search of the richesse of silks and gold, then synonymous in the Old World, never suspecting sugar, tobacco, rice, and cotton wd be as gold to silk; that Africans, wrapped in a tight ivory cocoon of bondage we call slavery, wd inhabit these 'Indies",/ an indigo damask demographic, fertile, furtive, hybrid,/glistening as silk/ does when the moon changes phase, as we do under a tropical sun./ Silken and foreign to these shores and to the thought, these are the origins of my genealogical essence, my blood trail in the New World, another Silk Road./Though my earliest recollection of all that is

1 Queen Isabella and King Ferdinand of Spain, on whose behalf Christopher Columbus traveled to the Americas

2 The Spanish name for Christopher Columbus

silk, all that swish soft fondling fabric conveys, are perfumed and gliding over my eyebrows in the depths of my mother Ellie's closet. What shrouded my young head, braids and all, was the miracle of the night, of conga drums,/ claves and castanets, formal dinners, chandeliers of translucent swirls of light dancing above the heads of very important guests whose crepe, velvet, chiffon, and silk I'd bask in under the dining table./So like an ocean of unexpected sensation were the skirt hems tickling my shoulders, sometimes I'd forget to gaze at the ankles in silk stockings that lent ordinary brown and bronze calves the magic of rose quartz,/ moonstones,/tourmaline sculpture,/ a secret as as the next brush stroke of Sonia Delauney[1] or Raoul Dufy[2] turning silk painting to a landscape abstractly worn by Parisian women adept at becoming art that cd walk./While we were in the New World far from St. Germain-de-Pres or Tours, ignorant of the aroma and thick layers of medieval Venice, we drew La Habana to us, as if the satin-bodiced and feathered brocatelle of the mulatas at the Tropicana[3] were more than our senses cd bear, enough to sate our sense of beauty and illicit treasures./Were not the seeds of white mulberry trees upon which the silkworm dined contraband, smuggled, hidden dangerous cargo transported by the foolish or foolhardy headstrong bent on wealth and stature? But we needn't concern ourselves with distant and ancient menace. The flickering of home-style black-and-white movies after the flan, after the cigars and cognac, bringing lampas-skinned brown beauties/ swinging from trees, swinging their hips was intimidating enough. Surely, there was no one more beautiful than a woman in silk smiling down at me from a gargantuan Cuban cypress tree,/while I hid at the foot of the stairs waiting for the exception./A velvet cape

1 Sonia Delaunay (1885–1979) was a Jewish Ukrainian and French visual artist, one of the founders of Orphic Cubism, an early twentieth-century art movement that focused on producing images with bright colors and lyrical geometric abstraction.

2 Raoul Dufy (1877–1953) was a French "Fauvist" painter who used layered rich color and bold lines.

3 The Tropicana is a famous nightclub in Havana, that opened in 1939.

with the same pearled pattern was strewn over her left shoulder as she mysteriously moved down the winding staircase. I was speechless, not because I'd been found out, but because I was sure I was not to see my mother in such a state of ethereal sensuality in my lifetime. I almost believed the glow on her face was a reflection of the moon/flirting unabashed in front of my father./My father who was as smooth as silk, though not named "Silk" like so many others of us. His muscular frame interacted with the world as something precious to behold, beyond the possibility of an ordinary anything./ This couple slipping into a black Missouri night to hear the raw silk voice of Tina Turner,/ the velvet intonations of Gloria Lynne or the heightened boucle of Maria Callas were mine. I came from this phenomenon, as Toomer said "rare as November cotton flower."[1]

ACTOR #1.

although i rarely read reviews of my work/ two comments were repeated to me by "friends" for some reason/ & now that i am writing abt my own work/ I am finally finding some use for the appraisals of strangers. One new york critic had accused me of being too self-conscious of being a writer/ the other from the midwest had asserted that I waz so involved with the deconstruction of the english language/ that my writing approached verbal gymnastics like unto a reverse minstrel show. in reality, there is an element of truth in both ideas/ but the lady who thought i waz self-conscious of being a writer/ apparently waz never a blk child who knew that blk children didn't wear tiger skins n chase lions around trees n then eat pancakes/ she waznt a blk child who spoke an english that had evolved naturally/ only to hear a white man's version of blk speech that waz entirely made up & based on no linguistic system besides the language of racism. the man who thought i wrote with intentions of outdoing the white man in the acrobatic distortions

1 This is a quotation from Jean Toomer's 1923 *Cane*, a modernist, hybrid genre Harlem Renaissance masterpiece depicting his life in Georgia.

of english was absolutely correct. i cant count the number of times i have viscerally wanted to attack deform n maim the language that I waz taught to hate myself in/ the language that perpetuates the notions that cause pain to every black child as s/he learns to speak of the world and the "self". yes/ being an African-american writer is something to be self-conscious abt/ & yes/ in order to think n communicate/ i haveta fix my tool to my needs/ i have to take it apart to the bone/ so that the malignancies/ fall away/ leaving us space to literally create our own image.

ALL

(Singing from Spell #7)

"...colored and love it... luv it being colored....colored and lovin'it...luv it bein' colored...color

VOICE#1

i have not ceased to be amazed when i hear members of an audience whispering to one another in the foyers of theaters/ that they had never imagined they cd feel so much for characters/ even though they were black (or colored/ or niggers, if they don't notice me eavesdropping}.

on the other hand/ i heard other members of an audience say that there were so many things in the piece that they had felt/ experienced/ but never had found words to express/ even privately/ to themselves. these two phenomena point to the same dilemma/ the straightjacket that the english language slips over the minds of all americans. there are some thoughts that black people just dont have/ according to popular mythology/ so white people never "imagine" we are having them/in everything i have written & everything i hope to write/ i have made use of what frantz fanon called "combat breath".

ALL

(combat breath mode)

Focused breathing for performance/preparedness for stressful action.

ACTOR#1

although frantz fanon[1] waz referring to francophone colonies, the schema he draws is sadly familiar:

ALL

(continue combat breath mode)

ACTOR #2

there is no occupation of territory, on the one hand, and independence of persons on the other. It is county as a whole, its history, its daily pulsation that are contested, disfigured, in the hope of final destruction. Under this condition, the individual's breathing is an observed, an occupied breathing. It is combat breathing.

(*"Drop.Freeze!"* Song/Spanish version)

ALL

Move in combat-style using diferent Martial Arts including: Capoiera,[2] *Tai Chi,*[3] *etc. Dancers engage/embody* "combat breathing" *throughout monologue. Musicians/M move away from band with martial movements. actor #3 similarly moves to platform-upstage left. actor #3 similarly moves to platform-upside left. actor #2 marches offstage through the audience.*

---

1 Frantz Fanon (1925–1961) was a social theorist, political philosopher, and psychiatrist from Martinique who is considered a leading thinker in postcolonial studies. Here Shange is referring to a concept Fanon described in his books *A Dying Colonialism* (1959) and *The Wretched of the Earth* (1961), in which the colonial condition is so pervasive that even one's breathing is under a condition of occupation. Hence, he went on to argue, revolt is necessary so that the colonized might breathe.

2 A traditional Afro-Brazilian martial art

3 A Chinese martial art and meditation technique

ACTOR #1

fanon goes on to say that "combat breathing" is the living response/ the drive to reconcile the irreconcilable/ the black & white of what we live n where. (unfortunately, this language doesn't allow me to broaden "black" and "white" to figurative terms/ which is criminal since the words are so much larger and richer than our culture allows.) i have lived with this for 31 years/ as my people have lived with cut-off lives n limbs.

in my writing i had to confront/ again & again/ those moments that had left me with little more than fury n homicidal desires. in *spell #7* i included a prologue of a minstrel show/ which made me cry the first times i danced in it/ for the same reasons I had included it. The minstrel may be "banned" as racist/ but the minstrel is more powerful in his deformities than our alleged rejection of him/ for every night we wd be grandly applauded, immediately thereafter/ we began to unveil the "minstrels." who turned out to be as fun-loving as fey:

ACTOR #2

(returning to stage, addressing audience members)

please/ let me join you/ i come all the way from brooklyn/ to have a good time/ ya don't think I'm high do ya/ cd i please join ya. i just wanna have a good time.

ACTOR #1

as contorted as sue-jean:

ACTOR #3

& i lay in the corner laughin/ with my drawers/ twisted round my ankles & my hair standin' every which way/ i waz laughin/ knowin i wd have this child/ myself/ & no one wd ever claim him/ cept me/ cuz i was a low-down thing/ layin in sawdust & whiskey stains/ i laughed & had a good time masturbatin in the shadows.

ACTOR #2

as angry as the actor who confides:

ACTOR #1

(in front of band)

i just want to find out why no one has ever been able to sound a gong & all the reporters recite that the gong is ringin/ while we watch all the white people/ immigrants & invaders/ conquistadors & relatives of london debtors from georgia/ kneel & apologize to us/ just for three or four minutes, now/ this is not impossible.

ACTOR #3

& after all that/ our true visions & rigors laid bare/ down from the ceiling comes the huge minstrel face/ laughing at all of us for having been so game/ we believed we cd escape his powers/ now naïve cd we be/ the magician explains:

ACTOR #1

crackers are born with the right to be alive/
i'm making ours right up here in yr face

(*"Drop. Freeze!"* Song/Spanish version)

ACTOR #2

the most frequently overheard comment abt *spell #7* when it first opened at the public theater/ waz that it waz too intense. the cast & i usedta laugh. if this one hour n 45 waz too much/ how in the world did these same people imagine the rest of our lives were/ & we they ever be able to handle that/ simply being alive & black & feeling in this strange deceitful country. which brings me to *boogie woogie landscapes/* totally devoted to the emotional topology of a young woman/ how she got to be the way she is/ how she sees where she is. here/ again/ in the prologue lies the combat breath/ of layla/ but she's no all-american girl/ or is she?

ACTOR #3

the lil black things/ pulled to her & whimpered lil black whys/ "why did those white men make red of our house/ why did those white men want to blacken even the white doors of our house/ why make fire of our trees & our legs/ why make fire/ why laugh at us/ say go home/ aren't we home/ aren't we home?"

ACTOR #1

she was raised to know nothing but black & white two-dimensional planes/ which is what racism allots every one of us unless we fight. She found solace in jesus & the american way/ though jonestown[1] & *american bandstand*[2] lay no claim to her:

ACTOR #2

shall I go to jonestown or the disco? I cd wear red sequins or a burlap bag, maybe it doesn't matter/ paradise is fulla surprises/ & themselvesfloor of
the disco changes colors like special species of vipers….

ACTOR #1

her lover/ her family/ her friends torment her/ calm her with the little they have left over from their own struggles to remain sane. Everything in *boogie woogie landscapes* is the voice of layla's unconscious/ her unspeakable realities/ for no self-respecting african-american girl wd reveal so much of herself of her own will/ there is too much anger to handle assuredly/ too much pain to keep on truckin/ less ya bury it.

Both *spell #7* & *boogie woogie landscapes* have elements of magic or leaps of faith/ in typical african-american fashion/ not only will the lord find a way/ but there *is* a way outta here. This is the litany from

1 Jonestown refers to the community where members of the People's Temple, who were followers of cult leader Jim Jones, lived in Guyana. On November 19, 1978, 909 people died at Jonestown after being given drinks laced with cyanide.

2 *American Bandstand* (1952–1989) was a music performance and dance television show.

the spirituals to jimi hendrix' "there must be some kinda way outta here"/ acceptance of my combat breath hasnt closed the possibilities of hope to me/ the soothing actualities of music n sorcery/ but that's now why i'm doubly proud of *photograph: lovers in motion*/ which has no cures for our "condition" save those we afford ourselves. The characters michael/ sean/ claire/ nevada/ earl are afflicted with the kinds of insecurities & delusions only available to those who learned themselves thru the traumas of racism. What is fascinating is the multiplicity of individual responses to this kind of oppression. Michael displays her anger to her lovers:

ACTOR #2

I've kept a lover who waznt all-american/ who didnt believe/ wdnt straighten up/ oh I've loved him in my own men/ sometimes hateful sometimes subtle like high for & sun/ but who i loved is yr not believin. i loved yr bitterness *& hankered after that space in you where you are outta control where you cannot touch or you wd kill me/ or somebody else who loved you. i never even saw a picture & I've loved him all my life he is all my insanity & anyone*
who loves
me wd understand

(*"Drop. Freeze!"* Song/Spanish version)

ACTOR #1

while nevada finds a nurtured protection from the same phenomenon:

ACTOR #2

mama/ will he be handsome & strong/ maybe from memphis/ an old family of freedmen/ one of them reconstruction senators for a great grandfather....

ACTOR #1

their particular distortions interfere with them receiving one another as full persons:

ACTOR #3

(as claire:) no no/ i want nevada to understand that i understand that sean's a niggah/ & & that's why he's never gonna be great or whatever you call it/ cuz he's niggah & niggahs cant be nothing.

ACTOR #2

(as nevada:) see/ earl/ she's totally claimed by her station/ she cant imagine anyone growing thru the prison of poverty to become someone like sean.

ACTOR #3

(as claire:) sean aint nothing but a niggah nevada/ i didnt know you liked niggahs.

(*"Drop. Freeze!"* Song/Spanish version)

ACTOR #1

such is the havoc created in the souls of people who arent supposed to exist. The malevolence/ the deceit/ & manipulation exhibited by these five are simply reflections of larger world they inhabit/ but do not participate in:

ACTOR #3

(as sean:) contours of life unnoticed !

(as michael:) unrealized & suspect… our form is one of a bludgeoned thing/ wrapped in rhinestones & gauze/ blood
almost sparkling/ a wildness lurks always…oppression/
makes us love one another badly/ makes our breathing
mangled/ while i am desperately trying to clear the air/ in

the absence of extreme elegance/ madness can set right in like a burnin gauloise on japanese silk. though highly cultured, even the silk must ask how to burn up discreetly.

ACTOR #2

the arbitrary nature of life as an african-american has been heralded, bemoaned, denied, wisht away, and yet we are still here. how cd a people who have been accused of having no history, no culture, no art, no souls, no common sense or rational capacity to survive so long? there is a simple answer that becomes complicated as we undo lies, half-truths, and ignorance. we're here for very specific reasons, as one of my favorite characters in *betsy brown*[1] mr. jeff would say,

ACTOR #1

"I sho' do like to grow things, sho' do like to grow things,"

ACTOR #3

then coyly meander offstage, an al green quiver to to his affirmation of our relationship to the earth, soil, what we can get to come from it.

ACTOR #2

there was very little that was arbitrary in the initial phases of the global trade of african slaves. we were taken to specific places to cultivate specific crops in regions of the new world that mimicked certain african terrain and climate. how do i know this? plantation owners, slave traders, and wives of said personages kept densely exacting diaries or day books of why an african who had been somewhere else was taken outta here to be here to do something he or she could do better than anyone else anybody heard of. take rice for instance.

1 Shange's 1985 novel *Betsey Brown*

ACTOR #1

a bit of manumission
because I have been in Simon Bolivar's library, Dessaline' easy chair, and Jose Marti's bedroom I have no choice. Freedom is not a commodity, nor am I, nor any of my people.

Dancers with Silk, slithering acros the floor…

ACTOR #3

a dogon iguana
one eye openseeing me
seeing my dreams
creep like david
rousseve's feet
from my finely cut
pecs rahway built
niggah's on gleamin'
bridges/ admire so
much they stop
smile snaggle-toothed
gleamin' lust gleanin'
all they know I bettah
not toy wit/ dreams

swimmin' top themselves
rio grande in
rainy season/ so
my calves tease
the border patrol
"jailisco courtin' dance'?"
"no, sornora harves"/ toes
water ritmo/ made it
land/ tattooed like

his arms lizards
slitherin' o top
the wet crossin'
toward acaba
toward me/ like
silk his skin demands
a human touch
can you smell it ?

the pimiento & dust
lettuce & uva now
hard as muscle his lips drawn
permanently
gainst steam
rushin' from
dark patterned family
expresso pots
"papi, esta listo" como
some four legged
underwater creatures
lithe 6 million years
old a conspicuous
cholo agasao

when he quotes
marti[1] nobody notices
but me by the

Malecon[2] hidden in tides
risin with
each morena's[3] wall
etched on our skin
how cd she know
guillen[4] the tricky
cubano light on
his feet/ a black
ox covered with ribbons &
bloody
medals
for his amazin' grace

how el son trips
sacred from his
laughter & la Havana
vieja rolls her
eyes cause once
these words fragiles *
full of coney island
bubbles float from
mouth to nose
to Miami the tortured
negrita in santo domingo
whose mami sewed
polyester hems while
Trujillo[5] imitated
Porfirio's[6] dreams of his
own statue/
loose rice powder round the
bronze
of his brow
my lizard stretches
one limb toward
mahogany branches
worn away by many
poets tired and lonely

1 José Martí (1853–1895) was a Cuban nationalist hero, poet, and foundational figure in Latin American literature.

2 In Cuba specifically, La Malecón refers to the waterfront walkway in Havana, which is an active location for music, dance, and social life.

3 Literally "dark woman"; the term used for Black women in the Hispanophone Caribbean

4 Nicolás Guillén (1902–1989) was an Afro-Cuban poet and journalist and considered the national poet of Cuba.

5 Rafael Trujillo (1891–1961) was a dictator who ruled the Dominican Republic from 1930 until his death. Trujillo's regime was violent and terrorizing and he specifically targeted the Haitian-Dominican population in an effort to purge the nation of Blackness. Shange notes here how Trujillo used makeup to lighten his own brown skin.

6 Porfirio Rubirosa (1909–1965) was a lieutenant for Trujillo and an international jet-setter who socialized with American and European elites.

one water buffalo
yearning for one
chord from yomo toro[1]
the lizard on the
other side of the
border whose breath
blends with hibiscus
sweet tequila &
my hair/lizard closes
his eyes/ skin now
roughened crepe/
limbs cut-buddy
to gallopin apaches
outside Denver/ nestled by
painted trunks
of carved trees/ R.I.P.
(Rest In Peace)/
that leave the Grand
Concourse a great
fiesta or new Orleans
funeral trails/ we
smell each other from
separate territories

my scent confines me
to specific soils

far from the
swamps & rivers
the lizard traps my
ankles without a
sound the pouch
taut round some
one's mouth fallen
open/ "the cafecito
is sweet/si Papi"

when I wiggle slowly
seeking my natural
state of repose
my skin is silk
to touch
tattooed/ a dogon
iguana in her
own soft-boned
splay/ but not
actually/ I'm
over/ there/ no over here/ I
crossed the border
right under yr
eyes

VOICEOVER#1

O.K.....in 5...4..3..2..1.......and we're out....awright everyone
5 minute break

---

1 Victor Guillermo "Yomo" Toro (1933–2012) was a Puerto Rican guitarist and cuatro player.

VOICEOVER#2

O.K., Ms. Shange...we're gonna take a commercial break and change tape....are you O.K.?...can we get you anything?

ACTORS 2 & 3

a Diet Pepsi.....

ACTOR#1

...and a Snickers

VOICEOVER#2

O.K.....guys, get a diet pepsi to Ms, Shange.....Ms. Shange, thank you so much...great stuff...our listeners are blowing up the lines...but, just off the record, Ms. Shange,.... where does this revolutionary spirit that swims through your work...where does it originate?

ACTOR#3

Off the record?.... one of my proudest moment was when Commandante Tomas,[1] Secretary of the Interior of Nicaragua, asked me to join the Sandinista fighters. we were all sunbathing... swimming in the pool of the Managua Hotel where Howard Hughes had spent his last thirty years/ there was much splashing and gadding about as chosen revolutionaries of Latin America awaited the next seminar/ i looked up from the water to find before my eyes 2 military boots/ as i looked further up/ a camoflauge uniform, a sidearm and the shadow of a machine gun/ i shook my head so i cd listen to what he was saying/

---

1 Tomás Borge (1930–2012) was a founder of the Sandinista National Liberation Front, a socialist political party in Nicaragua. "Sandinista" (sometimes spelled "Sandanista" in the following pages) was the common designation for members of the Sandinista National Liberation Front. In the late 1970s and '80s, the United States government opposed the Sandinistas and provided military aid to their opponents known as "Contras." Shange's political identification with the Sandinistas was an indication of her anticolonial and anti-neocolonial leftist politics.

ACTOR#1

"Companera Shange...Commandante Tomas wd like to see you"

ACTOR#3

/ i ducked back under the water/ surely there was a mistake/ i came up for breath to the same military boots/ and the soldier saying

ACTOR#1

"Commandante Tomas wd like to see you now!"

ACTOR#3

/ i felt frozen/ but i managed to get out of the pool/ my whole body blushing as i stood half naked in my bikini/ "yes, yes, i'll be right there".../and i ran to my room to change/ i put on a long skirt/ a blouse that covered my bosom and i decided to leave my earrings on/ as i approached the solider he seemed pleased with my new attire/ we followed the cobblestone path to a heavily armored jeep where a pale man with grey hair sat in the front/ i was directed to the back seat/ the soldier said

ACTOR#1

"Commandante Tomas....Companera Shange"...

ACTOR#3

/the soldier disappeared/ Commandante Tomas turned with kindly eyes and said/ "wd you join us/ will you be a Sandanista?"/ i grazed the machine gun that jutted up from next to Commandante in the front seat/ it was cold/ it was powerful/ it was beautiful/ it was good to feel capable of defending our people/ me, a Sandanista/ I cd hardly believe as I took the machine gun in my arms/ the struggle became more real to me/ and the honor bestowed on me was never to be forgotten.

ACTOR#3 & ACTOR #2

"el amor que tu me das..."[1]

ACTOR#2

dear daddy...

I guess i'm still up by sheer force of habit. Remember how you'd come in from the hospital after ordinary people were long in bed? I can still smell the steak sandwiches from Brunswick St. & the fried shrimp you'd pick up at Five Points. Just when all the night people/ gamblers pimps whores B &E[2] men 3rd shifters/ were satisfying their own wants. The car made a whirring noise that would annoy somebody else. Yet, even in the country, especially in the country in the vacant night absent of music and gleeful conversation that old Cadillac Sounded like sweet Miles, Solo, muted sweet, a classic. Why today we misst Muhal Richard Abrams[3] and the AACM at that places that caught fire during a reading of mine! Guess you should know I never refer to you in the past, even though I know you dead. But you know, you died in the middle of the night, your special time & mine. You were driving lonely Jersey highways on the way from a wrestling match. I loved those roads with you, listening to Louis Armstrong or Tito Puente; distances were always too short. The car, asphalt sliding under our laughter & stories of meeting Dizzy Gillespie or Horace Silver[4] & got Son Seal's[5] autograph on arm. So I brought something to the table, too. But you knew that. Daddy, I hope I didn't embarrass you too much when I had you pick

---

1 "the love that you give me"; this likely refers to the salsa song of that name, although it is not clear which version Shange is citing

2 Colloquial abbreviation for "breaking and entering"

3 Muhal Richard Abrams (1930–2017) was a free jazz cellist, pianist, clarinetist, composer, and arranger.

4 Horace Silver (1928–2014) was a jazz pianist, composer, and arranger who was a hard bop pioneer.

5 Frank "Son" Seals (1942–2004) was a blues guitarist and singer.

me up at Black Jack's[1] in South Trenton, so I could show you my photograph above the bar just when Tookie started to tell you her life story since you brought her into the world & Black Jack came out of his private quarters since it was yr 1st time in his place even though he's been yr patient for years. But, Papa, I knew I cd go to Black Jack's any time I had to dance. Dance hard & fast. Dance how you danced with Mommy with abandon and grace.

You know what else? I don't like the way our family sees yr grave site either. Not that it's not proper. I mean there's an impressive tombstone & some kinda heavy heavy potted perennial. But, Daddy, there should be be an earlier installation, by David Hammonds[2] and a Howardena pindell[3] tapestry should be floating over you to keep evil spirits away & let you feel the evening breeze as she comes to you. Damn, Daddy, I should have gotten Martin Puryear[4] to craft you some sacred cypress wishing web so I cd come in & out of the realms of this world you cherished at will. Then Irma & I, that's Miguel's sister who always thought you were handsome, would get Ricardo the Dominican Santero[5] to come "clean" the whole space. Irma, Miguel, Ricardo & I swam clandestine in the Raritan River & Ricardo washed our heads with fresh coconut milk, right from the shell. That'll do you up just fine & protect you if you go haunting the lil joints in upper Harlem; on the Lower East Side where I paid my dues.

---

1 A historic African American lounge and small music venue in Trenton, New Jersey, where Shange grew up

2 David Hammons (b. 1943) is an African American visual and performance artist who has used a wide range of aesthetic approaches and media in giving artistic expression to Black life and culture.

3 Howardena Pindell (b. 1943) is an African American visual artist, distinguished for exploring social and political themes using abstract forms and multimedia approaches.

4 Martin Puryear (b. 1941) is an African American fine artist known for using traditional craft techniques in his sculptures.

5 Santero is the term for practitioners of Yoruba-derived religions in the Hispanophone Americas. Here Shange makes specific reference to a priest in that tradition.

I really appreciated yr not laughing out loud when Felix de Rooy[1] Showed that achingly long 35 minutes of film as the Caribbean Christ. He's in Amsterdam now, and you were the only poet's daddy who was present & fit right in & Adal's[2] still photographing himself.

ACTOR #1

I wished you stayed here (not that I think you're gone) but I wished you had seen my piece with Ladysmith Black Mambazo, such singing, Daddy. An I've made a personal friend of Archie Shepp, the avant-garde sax man you liked. I know you lifted that left eye-brow and looked somewhere else if I plyed Cecil Taylor or if Cecil started talking metaphysics. Daddy, I danced in the Tropicana in La Habana like you and Mommy before Fidel. The magic is still there but not the terror. I walked the streets of Johannesburg without a pause, swam in the waters outside Durban, jumping waves in a free South Africa, but my last weeks in Manangua were also fulfilling Sandinista dreams. You wda been so proud of me, riding with Commandante Tomas through the mountains, realizing why the power of the automatic machine gun at my side was not yr weapon of choice. You are too gentle for some of what I know.

ACTOR #3

Oh, Papa, I can't forget the night you & Mommy stayed up all night in my very bare apt in Dorchester listening to me and Pedro Pietri, all in black with his portable coffins, reading poetry. Pedro came to your church service in the church where they funeralized you. Papa, I came to love your friends too just because they were your friends & knew you in a way I didn't and can't. Wittico, the elegant; Moose, the passionate; J. Minor, the Cherokee chief; and Pops, your soul

1 Felix de Rooy (b. 1952) is a Curaçaoan poet, artist, and filmmaker.

2 Alberto Maldonado (November 1, 1948–December 9, 2020), styled as ADÁL, was an influential modernist photographer who lived and worked in New York City and Puerto Rico.

mate; and Tom Jones, the dreamer, are precious to me. Even though I rarely see them I don't see them any less than you did.

Daddy, I finally got into that beaded strapless outfit you gave me & I didn't stop lifting weights to do it, either. Somehow I grew into it. I wore it the night the National Black Theatre Festival honored me with Ntozake Shange Day. That was Winston-Salem, North Carolina last summer. Plus, I went to cocktails at Maya Angelou's[1] and spent time with William Marshall[2] and Billy Dee Williams.[3] I wish you had been with us long enough to hear La India,[4] she is an angelic Tina Turner.

ACTOR #2

oh, Daddy, on the more somber side, since you've been gone from this plane, whenever I stay up late, like we used to, old black-&-white movies starring Ronald Reagan come on. He has Alzheimer's now, so he can't feel guilt or remorse for the plight of sick people anymore. If he had his whole brain he still wasn't capable of experiencing compassion. Daddy, the era of politics Reagan ushered in has outlived you and more poor & black people are dying, suffering, homeless, violent, desperate for a vision of a world for us like you had.

ACTOR #3

Daddy, do you think I could help with that? It was only a rumor that CLR James was like a father to me. I know i'm not a boy, but forgive the language, Papa. I'm one fierce muther. You did name me after you. You know what else, Daddy? David Murray, my

1 Maya Angelou (1929–2014) was an internationally renowned writer and civil rights organizer.

2 William Marshall (1924–2003) was a Broadway and film actor, director, and opera singer best known for starring in the *Blacula* Blaxploitation films.

3 William December "Billy Dee" Williams (b. 1937) is an actor who gained popularity in the 1970s as one of the few African American leading men in Hollywood.

4 Linda Viera "La India" Caballero (b. 1969) is a Puerto Rican pop and salsa singer.

ex-husband, my friends Chico Freeman,[1] Fred Hopkins,[2] Jean-Paul Bourelly,[3] Billy Bang,[4] even Spaceman[5] ---every one of them could play a melody that wd make you start swaying yr head so you cd catch every note You were just as much a part of our posse as Max, Milt, Dizzy, Chico H., and both Andy and Jerry Gonzalez.[6] There's no music I hear without sensing you.

ACTOR #1

did I ever really thank you & Mom for bringing gallons of fried chicken, greens and fixins to us when we were sitting in at Hamilton Hall[7] in 1968? Some people's parents stopped speaking to them and cut off tuition. But you fed us. Thank you, Daddy. I know you abhor legions of cops & militant social coups, but we were hungry.

ACTOR #3

getting back to yr alleged grave site. Mi novio, Elmo, who's a black Puerto Rican bluesman from Chicago (I thought you'd like that!), anyway he's promised to help me lay handmade glazed bricks in the typical Zocalo[8] formation to let everyone know wherever you are is

---

1 Earl Lavon "Chico" Freeman (b. 1949) is a jazz tenor saxophonist and trumpeter.

2 Fred Hopkins (1947–1999) was an avant-garde jazz double bassist.

3 Jean-Claude Borelly (b. 1953) is a French jazz trumpeter and composer.

4 William Vincent "Billy Bang" Walker (1947–2011) was a free jazz violinist and composer.

5 William "Spaceman" Patterson (b. 1954) is a guitarist who performed in Miles Davis's band in the 1980s; in 1992 he collaborated with Shange on a musical adaptation of her poetry titled *The Love Space Demands.*

6 Andy (1951–2020) and Jerry Gonzalez (1949–2018) were brothers and jazz musicians who often worked together. Andy was a bassist and Jerry a trumpeter and percussionist. Of Puerto Rican origin, they were both considered important figures in the development of Latin jazz.

7 In April 1968, eighty-six Black students held a sit-in at the Hamilton administration building of Columbia University. Shange was a student at Barnard College at the time and participated in the political action, which lasted a week. The students objected to the university plan to create a gym on what had been public land, which would deprive the largely Black and Latine community of access to green space.

8 Zócalo is a Spanish term for a public square or plaza.

hallowed ground. That you are yr own tradition & yr space is a place for spirits & people to gather when they're in need of solace. Though Victor Cruz[1] & Alejandro cda blessed the place with poems in tongues & some leftover pine spring water we found by the Russian River years ago, the sacred never runs out, Daddy, only the profane is short lived.

ACTOR #1

you almost got it/ you really did
'born of the blood of struggle' we all here/ even if we don't
know it/ what if poetry isn't enuf?
watchu gonna do then?
Paint?
Dance?
Put your backfield in motion & wait for james brown to fall
on his knees
like it's too much for him/ what?
Too much for james?
Yeah/ didn't you ever see the sweat from his brow/ a libation
of passion
make a semi-circle fronta his body/ a half-moon of exertion
washin'away any hope he had of/ 'standin'it/ can't stand it
& he falls to his knees and three jamesian niggahs in a
stroll
so sharp it hurts/

ACTOR #2

to bring him a cape that shines like the
northern
star/ shinin' I say like you imagined the grease in the part of
yr hair

1 Victor Hernández Cruz (b. 1949) is a highly regarded Puerto Rican poet.

or yr legs/ or yr mother's face after rehearsal/ after she had you/
james falls to his knees cuz he cain't take it'/ he's pleadin'

BAND

'please/ please/ please/ don't go'

ACTOR #3

we look to see who brought james brown to the floor/
so weak/ we think/ so overwrought/ with the power of love
that's why poetry is enuf/ eisa/ it brings us to our knees
& when we look up from our puddles of sweat/
the world's still right there & the children still have bruises
tiny white satin caskets & their mothers weep like mary
shda
there is nothing more sacred than a glimpse of the universe
it brought james brown to his knees lil anthony too/ even
jackie wilson
arrogant pretty muthafuckah he was/ dropped/ no knee
pads in the face
of the might we have to contend with/ & sometimes young
boys bleed
to death face down or asphalt cuz fallin' to they knees was
not cool/
was not the way to go/ it ain't/ fallin' to our knees is a public
admission
a great big ol' scarlet letter that we cain't/don't wanna escape any
feelin'/ any sensation of bein' alive can came right down on
us/

ACTOR #1

& yes my tears & sweat
may decorate the ground like a veve in haiti or a sand
drawing in melbourne/ but in the
swooning/ in the delirium/ of a felt life

ACTOR #2

can ya stand up, chile?

ACTOR #1

the point is not to fall down & get up dustin' our bottoms/
I always hated when folks said that to me/ the point
virginia---eisa/ is you fall on your knees & let the joy of survivin'
bring you to yr feet/ yr bottom's not dirty/ didn't even graze the earth/
no it's the stuff of livin' fully that makes the spirit of the poem

let you show yr face again & again & again

ACTOR #3

I usedta hide myself in jewelry or huge dark glasses
big hats long billowin' skirts/'anything to protect me/ from the gazes
somebody see i'd lived a lil bit/ felt somethin' too terrible for casual conversation
& all this was obvious from lookin' in my eyes/ that's why I usedta read poem after poem
with my eyes shut/ quite a treat/ cept the memories take over & leave
my tequila bodyguard in a corner somewhere out the way of the pain
in my eyes that simply came through my body/ they say
my hands sculpt the air with words/ my face becomes the visage of a
character's voice/ I don't know

ACTOR #2

I left my craft to chance & fear someone wd see I care too much
take me for a chump

laugh & go home-style

this is not what happened

is poetry enuf to man a picket line/ to answer phones at the
rape crisis center/ to shield women entering abortion clinics
from demons with
crosses & illiterate signs defiling the horizon at dawn/ to
keep our children
from believing that they can buy hope with a pair of
sneakers or another nasty
filter for a cheap glass pipe/ no/ no/ a million times no

ACTOR #1

but
poetry can bring those bleeding women & children outta
time
up close enuf for us to see/ feel ourselves there/ then the separations
what makes me/ me & you/ drops away & the truth that we
constantly
avoid/ shut our eyes/ hold our breath hopin' we won't be
found out/
surfaces darlin'/ & we are all everyone of those dark &
hurtin' places/
those dry bloodied memories are no less ours than
themselvesmourni'/ yes
the mournin' we may be honorable enuf to endure with our
eyes open/
the coroner cannot simply bring her hand gently down our
eyelids/ leavin'
us to silence.

ACTOR #2

can ya stand up, chile'?

ACTOR #3

Hands stretched out to touch again
not so you can get up & conquer the world/
you did that when you cdn't raise your head & yr body trembled so/
you scared yr mama/ that was when the poem took over & gave you back
what you discovered you didn't have to give up/
all that fullness of breath/ houdini in an emotional maze/ free at last
but nobody can see how you did it/ how'd she get out/
nobody'll know less you tell em/

ACTOR #2

do you really wanna write/
from twenty thousand leagues under a stranger's wailin'?
Can you move gracefully randomly thru the landmines that
are yr own angola/ hey you bosnia/ falujah?!
Are you ashamed sometimes there's no feelin' you
can recognize in yr left leg? Does the bleeding you'll do anyway
offend you or can you make a scared drawing like ana medieta that will
heal us all? Do I believe in magic?

ALL

(in frenzied action....Freeze...look up in thought)

ZAKE

I still/ sweat when I write

ACKNOWLEDGMENTS

On behalf of the Ntozake Shange Revocable Trust, we extend our deepest appreciation to Dr. Imani Perry for her curatorial expertise, editorial insight, and heartfelt commitment to Ntozake and her entire bibliography. Our thanks to Tarana Burke for memorializing her deep friendship and admiration for Ntozake in her foundational commentary enclosed in the book. We thank Krishan Trotman, vice president and publisher of Legacy Lit at Hachette Book Group, for imagining a comprehensive review of the Ntozake Shange Archives at Barnard College that has resulted in this publication and offer our congratulations to Amina Iro and the staff of Legacy Lit on a job very well done in the preparation of this volume. We acknowledge the role of our agent, Jesseca Salky, in the crafting of a complex, multiparty agreement for this project and cannot underestimate the robust contribution of Martha Tenney, director of the Barnard archives and curator of the Ntozake Shange Institute Collection, who, along with a complement of diligent students, made our research into the collection more productive and expeditious.

The Ntozake Shange Revocable Trust

Donald S. Sutton, Literary Trustee
Paul T. Williams, Jr., Managing Trustee

ABOUT THE AUTHOR

Ntozake Shange, author of thirty-six published works, is increasingly recognized as one of America's greatest writers, having, for fifty years, embodied the struggle of women of color for equality and the recognition of their contribution to human culture.

Her choreopoem, *for colored girls who have considered suicide / when the rainbow is enuf*, earned her an Obie Award for its sold-out 1976 off-Broadway run and received a nomination for Best Play for its triumphal two-and-a-half-year run on Broadway. That production retains its title as the longest-running play by an African American writer in Broadway history. In 2022, a revival of *for colored girls,* opened on Broadway to unanimous critical acclaim and seven Tony Award nominations. The play has remained in print since 1974.

Shange won a veritable mountain of awards throughout her career, including a second Obie in 1981, for her adaptation of Bertolt Brecht's *Mother Courage and Her Children* at the Public Theater; an Outer Critics Circle Award; an AUDELCO Award; a Guggenheim fellowship; a National Endowment for the Arts fellowship; the Lila Wallace–Reader's Digest Fund Writer's Award; the *Los Angeles Times* Book Prize for Poetry; the Paul Robeson Award; the National Black Theatre Festival's Living Legend Award; the New Federal Theatre Lifetime Achievement Award; and the University Medal for Excellence from Columbia University. Her work was nominated, in addition, for the Tony, Grammy, and Emmy awards.

Ntozake's literary legacy, preserved at the Shange Institute at Barnard College, comprises thirteen plays, seven novels, six children's books, and nineteen poetry collections, the majority of which are published and in print. She has been posthumously inducted into both the New York State Writer's Institute's and the Off-Broadway Alliance's Halls of Fame. Her poetry collection *Wild Beauties* was received enthusiastically in 2018. A semi-autobiographical work entitled *Dance We Do* was released in 2020 by Beacon Press.

The year 2022 also saw the collaborative establishment, by Barnard College, the New York Shakespeare Festival/Public Theater, and the Ntozake Shange Revocable Trust, of the Ntozake Shange Social Justice Playwright Residency and Shange's induction into the prestigious American Theater Hall of Fame, where her legacy endures as one of the most cherished Black feminist writers of our time.

ABOUT THE EDITOR

Imani Perry is the Hughes-Rogers Professor of African American Studies at Princeton University. She is the author of seven books, including *South to America*, winner of the 2022 National Book Award. She is a recipient of the Lambda Literary Award and the Hurston Wright Award, and was a finalist for an NAACP Image Award, among others. She has written for the *New York Times*; *The Atlantic*; *Harpers*; *O, The Oprah Magazine*; *New York Magazine*; and *The Paris Review*. Perry earned her PhD in American studies from Harvard University, a JD from Harvard Law School, an LLM from Georgetown University Law Center, and a BA from Yale College in literature and American studies.